I0729957

WINGS OF SHADOW

USA TODAY BESTSELLING AUTHOR

SILVANA G. SÁNCHEZ

Copyright © 2025 by Silvana G. Sánchez. All rights reserved.

No part of this book may be reproduced in any form or by any electronic or mechanical means, including information storage and retrieval systems, without written permission from the author, except for the use of brief quotations in a book review.

This is a work of fiction. Names, characters, places, and incidents either are products of the author's imagination or are used fictitiously. Any resemblance to actual persons, living or dead (or undead), events, or locales is entirely coincidental.

Cover design by *SP Designs.*

Edited by A. Knox.

BOOKS BY SILVANA G. SÁNCHEZ

BAD BOY SHIFTERS OF THE UNNATURAL BRETHREN

Branded in Love

Runt of the Pack

Embers of Fate

Branded in Memory

Branded in Wildness

Blood and Mistletoe

Wings of Shadow

THE UNNATURAL BRETHREN

Written in Blood

Call of Blood

Cast in Blood

Blood and Mistletoe

Midnight Kiss

CURSED KINGDOMS

Ash and Snow

Steel and Stone

*Cinders and Blood**

VESELY ACADEMY

Academy of Extraordinary Creatures

The Soul Thief

Curse the Moon

*The Blood of Kings**

Be the first to know when Silvana's next book is available! Follow her on Bookbub to get an alert whenever she has a new release, preorder, or discount!

THE UNNATURAL BRETHREN'S (EXPANDED) READING ORDER

Written in Blood
The Devil's Song*
A Curse of Blood and Diamonds*
Call of Blood
Branded in Love
Runt of the Pack
Cast in Blood
Embers of Fate
Branded in Memory
Blood and Mistletoe
Branded in Wildness
Wings of Shadow
Blood of the Viking*
Blood of the Ancient*
Midnight Kiss

* Release dates to be announced soon.

To those of us whose fate is written in dragon fire.
Burn, baby. Burn.

He who fights too long against dragons becomes a dragon himself;
and if you gaze too long into the abyss, the abyss will gaze into you.

— Friedrich Nietzsche

A NOTE FROM THE AUTHOR

My beloved Darklings,

At last, I'm thrilled to share with you the long-awaited love story of Kaisner Drachenstein and Clarissa Draken. A love forged in the shadows from the very beginning, but a love worth fighting for—the best things in life often are.

The events of *Wings of Shadow* pick up immediately after *Blood and Mistletoe,* so be sure to read that one before diving into this next chapter. I also highly recommend reading *Branded in Wildness* beforehand—a Substack exclusive. (You can download your free copy by subscribing to my Substack, which is also free.)

For those of you new to the Unnatural Brethren or *Bad Boy Shifters* series, welcome. While *Wings of Shadow* can be enjoyed as a standalone, I suggest reading the books in order to fully appreciate the unfolding story. And if you're looking for a more immersive experience, check out the suggested reading order for the Unnatural Brethren's *Expanded* Universe.

For my loyal *Bad Boy Shifters* fans, this one is for you—

especially for those eagerly waiting for Gavriil's destiny to be revealed.

A word of caution, Darklings. This is the darkest installment of the series so far, so please make sure to review the content warnings before you begin.

Without further ado, welcome to *Wings of Shadow*. Prepare to be swept away into a world of fire, magic, and irresistible danger.

Yours in fire and shadow,
   Silvana.

WINGS OF SHADOW

Two dragons. One destiny
A love that could save their world—or destroy it.

A ruthless shadow king with a heart of fire and a will of steel.

Born to a legacy of dark power and trained in forbidden rituals by his tyrannical father, Kaisner Drachentstein has spent decades hunting the one sacrifice that could awaken his dragon and restore his birthright—but what if claiming his destiny means losing the one woman who makes him feel human?

A gifted seer torn between duty and desire.

Raised in hiding after her family's massacre and unaware of her true potential, Clarissa Draken is finally building a life of her own when a dangerous, intoxicating man enters her world with secrets that tie directly to her past—but can she trust her heart to someone who may view her as nothing more than the means to an end?

In a world where power is king and love is the ultimate

gamble, Kaisner and Clarissa must fight for their happily ever after with every ounce of their strength and every beat of their hearts. Will their love conquer all, or will they be consumed by the very forces that brought them together?

CONTENT WARNING

Wings of Shadow contains mature themes and content that may not be suitable for all readers. Please review the following content warnings before reading:

SEXUAL CONTENT

- Explicit sexual scenes between consenting adults
- Detailed intimate encounters with graphic language
- Virgin heroine/experienced hero dynamic
- Possessive and dominant sexual behavior
- Blood play/claiming bites during intimate scenes
- Multiple detailed sex scenes throughout the book

VIOLENCE & COMBAT

- Supernatural battle sequences with detailed violence
- Character death (non-main characters)
- Blood and gore during fight scenes

- Kidnapping and captivity
- Torture implications (not graphic)
- Weapon violence including firearms

DARK THEMES

- Morally gray/anti-hero male love interest
- Obsessive and possessive behavior (romanticized)
- Power imbalances in relationships
- Emotional manipulation
- Themes of revenge and retribution

SUPERNATURAL ELEMENTS

- Detailed transformation sequences (human to dragon)
- Magical rituals and blood magic
- Daemonic summoning
- Prophetic visions that may be disturbing

FAMILY/RELATIONSHIP DYNAMICS

- Sibling conflict and family loyalty tensions
- Arranged/political marriages

SUBSTANCE USE

- Social drinking/alcohol consumption
- Drug use for kidnapping purposes (chloroform-type substance)

MENTAL HEALTH

- Brief mentions of trauma responses

- Anxiety and panic in high-stress situations
- References to PTSD

Reader Discretion Advised:

This book is intended for mature audiences (18+) and contains explicit sexual content, violence, and dark romantic themes. If any of these elements may be triggering or uncomfortable for you, please consider whether this book is right for you at this time.

Note: This is a work of fiction featuring supernatural beings. The behaviors depicted should not be emulated in real-life relationships.

Please read with care.

WINGS OF SHADOW

KAISNER DRACHENSTEIN

Alter Nordfriedhof, Germany.
Five Years Ago

*R*ain falls like bullets from a slate gray sky as I stand at the edge of my father's grave, watching the casket, instants away from gliding into the earth's cold embrace. The weight of my inheritance, the Drachenstein empire, settles heavily on my shoulders, a burden I never wanted but cannot refuse.

As the mourners disperse, their condolences nothing more than a distant buzz in my ears, I step forward, my hand resting on the casket's polished wood. "Father," I whisper, my voice raw with emotion. "I swear to you, on this day, your legacy does not die with you. Whatever it takes, I will restore our family's power. The name Drachenstein will strike fear into the hearts of our enemies once more."

I close my eyes, letting the memories of my father wash over me. His strength, his cunning, his unwavering determination in the face of adversity. He was a force to be reckoned with, a true king in the underworld. And now, it falls to me to fill the void he has left behind.

"I will not fail you," I vow, my fingers digging into the wood, as if I could somehow reach through to him.

As I step back from the grave, I sense a presence at my side. I turn to face Janik, my father's most trusted advisor, his lined features etched with sorrow and tinged with apprehension. "*Mein König,*" he murmurs, cutting through the haze of my grief. "We've found them—your father's killers."

Cold fury settles in my chest, mingling with the ache of loss that threatens to consume me. I look down at the rose in my hand, its crimson petals a stark contrast against the black of my suit. In one swift motion, I crush it, feeling the thorns bite into my skin, relishing the pain that grounds me in this moment.

"Good." The word sails through my clenched teeth. I reach out my hand and open it, allowing the petals to gently fall on the casket as it's slowly lowered.

"Let's get to work," I growl, turning away from the grave site, ready to take on my task as king of our dragon clan.

PRESENT DAY

1

KAISNER

MUNICH, GERMANY.

The last time I gathered my lieutenants like this, half of them didn't survive the meeting.

I sit at the head of the long, ebony table, the smoke from my cigar curling lazily in the air. The room is dimly lit, the only sound the occasional clink of ice in the glasses of the men gathered before me. They are the leaders of the various factions within the Drachenstein empire, each one hand-picked for their loyalty, their cunning, and their ruthlessness.

"Gentlemen," I say, my voice cutting through the silence like a blade through flesh. "It has come to my attention that the Schneider family has been overstepping their bounds. They seem to have forgotten the lessons we taught them years ago, when we crushed their pathetic attempt at a rebellion."

A ripple of laughter echoes around the table, harsh and cold. They all remember that day, the day we painted the streets red with Schneider blood, leaving their broken bodies as a warning to anyone who dared to challenge our power.

"It appears they are in need of a reminder," I continue, tapping the ash from my cigar. "Lukas, I want you and your men to pay them a visit. Make it clear that their territory belongs to us, and that any further attempts to expand will be met with swift and brutal consequences."

Lukas, a hulking brute of a man with cold, dead eyes, nods sharply. "As you command, *Mein König*. We will ensure they never forget who rules this city."

Janik appears at my side, leaning down to whisper, "A message from Viktor Mahindra, *Mein König*. He demands we withdraw from the Mumbai shipping lanes. Thirty days, or face consequences."

I don't react, though my grip tightens on my cigar. "Double security," I murmur back. "Remind Viktor that tigers shouldn't threaten dragons."

Janik nods and withdraws silently.

I lean back in my chair, a faint smile playing at the corners of my mouth. "Good. The rest of you, keep your eyes and ears open. The Schneiders may be the most immediate threat, but they are far from the only ones who would see us fall. We must remain vigilant, always ready to strike at the first sign of disloyalty."

As the men file out of the room, each one bowing their head in deference as they pass, I allow myself a moment of satisfaction. Five years ago, when I first inherited the mantle of leadership from my father, the Drachenstein clan was a shadow of its former self, weakened by internal strife and external threats. But through sheer force of will, through cunning and ruthlessness, and an unwavering commitment to our family's legacy, I have rebuilt us into a force to be reckoned with once more.

And yet, even as I savor the taste of our renewed power, I cannot shake the feeling that something is missing. The dragons that once made our family great. The ancient magic that flows through our veins lies dormant within me, untapped and unused—as it has for all dragon shifters for the last three-hundred years. Restlessly, I have hunted means to awaken that power, to claim my rightful place as the most fearsome dragon shifter the world has ever seen.

Relentless in my pursuit of this goal, I have delved deep into the dark arts of daemonology, immersing myself in the forbidden knowledge of summoning and binding the creatures that dwell in the shadows. Whispers of my newfound proficiency have spread swiftly through the underworld, earning me a reputation as a master of the daemonic arts, a warlock to be feared and respected in equal measure.

But bending daemons to my will and harnessing their unholy strength for my purposes is but a means to an end. The true prize, the ultimate ambition, is the awakening of my draconic heritage, the unleashing of the primal force that slumbers within my blood.

And still, despite my mastery of these dark arts, despite the fear and awe I inspire in those who witness my command over the shadow realms, the key to unlocking my dragon remains frustratingly out of reach. It is a puzzle that consumes my every waking thought, a quest that drives me to the very limits of my sanity.

With each passing day, each failed attempt, my father's legacy presses down on me, a constant reminder of the vow I made to him on the day we laid him to rest. I will have no peace until I have fulfilled that promise, until I have made the Drachenstein name synonymous with fathomless power and true fear once again.

A knock at the door pulls me from my thoughts, and I look up to see my most trusted advisor and enforcer, Janik, stepping into the room. "What is it?" I ask, my voice sharp with impatience.

"Forgive the intrusion, *Mein König*," Janik says, bowing his head. "But I have received word from our contacts in Paris."

"Go on," I utter with a swift nod.

"It seems the Draken clan has done the impossible," he says under his breath. "They have awakened a dragon shifter for the first time in centuries."

My body stiffens as I brace myself on the table's edge. For a moment, I am speechless, my mind reeling with the implications of this news. The Drakens, our most formidable rivals, have achieved the very thing I have been striving toward for years. The thought of them wielding such power, of them claiming the title of the last dragon shifter in the world, fills me with a cold, seething rage.

"How?" I demand, my voice a low growl. "How did they accomplish this?"

Janik shakes his head, his expression grim. "The details are unclear, *Mein Herr*. Our sources are still gathering information. But one thing is certain—this changes everything. The balance of power in the shifter world has been upended, and if we do not act quickly, the Drakens will use this to crush us once and for all."

I clench my fists, my eyes blazing with determined fire. "They will do no such thing," I snarl, rising to my feet. "I will not allow them to claim this victory, to wield a power that should have been ours by right." A pause to steady my quickened breaths. "I will find a way to awaken my dragon, to harness the primal power coursing through my veins, and I will show the world what true power looks like."

Janik nods, a glimmer of anticipation in his eyes. "What are your orders, *Mein Herr*?"

I turn to face the window, looking out over the sprawling expanse of my empire, the city that bows before the might of the Drachenstein name. "Gather our best men," I command, my voice ringing out with unwavering authority. "Reach out to every contact, every informant we have. I want to know everything there is to know about this Draken shifter—their strengths, their weaknesses, their every move."

"Yes, *Mein Herr.*"

As Janik hurries off to carry out my orders, I turn back to the window, my gaze hardening with resolve. I lift my hands, studying the play of warm light on my beringed fingers. Each ring represents a hard-won victory, a step closer to the power that is my birthright.

My hands close into fists, the cool metal pressing into my skin. The path ahead may be fraught with danger, filled with challenges and enemies at every turn, but I am ready to face them all. For my father, for my family, for the legacy that burns in my blood, I will stop at nothing to claim what is rightfully mine.

The Drakens may think they have the upper hand, but they have no idea who they're dealing with. I am Kaisner Drachenstein, the most feared warlock across Europe, and soon, the mightiest dragon shifter to emerge in centuries. And I will reduce to ashes anyone who stands in my way...

The sleek lines of my smartphone light up with an incoming message. With a flick of my finger, I unlock the screen, my eyebrows raising slightly as I recognize the sender.

Cassandra Deveraux.

The Deverauxs. One of the oldest and most influential witch dynasties in Europe, their power rivaled only by the Drakens themselves. What could they possibly want with me now, in the midst of this brewing storm?

I tap on the message, my curiosity piqued. As I scan the contents, a slow smile begins to spread across my face.

Intriguing.

The Deveraux witches are not known for their frivolity, and for them to reach out to me directly... well, it can only mean that the winds of change are blowing more fiercely than I had anticipated.

Returning to my chair, I compose my response with a few quick swipes.

As I hit send, I lean back, my mind already racing with the possibilities that lie ahead. The Drakens may have made the first move, but the game is far from over. And with the Deverauxs as potential allies, the board is set for a power play that will reshape the very fabric of our world.

I am the king in a realm of darkness. And I will not rest until the throne is mine.

2

CLARISSA

PARIS, FRANCE.

The vision comes unbidden—a dark tide rising from the depths of my consciousness, relentless and cold. Behind my eyes, the world slips away, and in its place, an ancient fresco unfurls. Our family tree, delicate and sprawling, stretches across an imagined wall. The painted branches reach skyward, proud and eternal, each name etched in shimmering gold.

But then, the rot begins.

A shadow bleeds from the roots—inky, malevolent, alive. It creeps upward with glacial patience, tainting the pale blue sky above with storm clouds of dread. As the shadow touches each name, each leaf, they wither. Flake. Disintegrate into ash.

I watch in helpless horror as generation after generation of the Draken line crumbles into dust. And still the darkness climbs, unyielding. It reaches the uppermost branches— where my name, Nikolaas's, and Bram's linger, still clinging to life. But it's coming for us. I feel it.

The moment the shadow brushes the edge of my name, I

jolt back into waking life, lungs straining, dragging in air like I've just surfaced from drowning.

Morning light spills through the tall, arched windows of the Deveraux library. Warm, golden. Safe. But its gentle illumination feels at odds with the lingering frost inside me. The chill of that vision clings to my skin, to the marrow of my bones.

This place used to be my sanctuary. A haven of ancient tomes, secret histories, and the soft lull of burning firewood. Now, even surrounded by velvet armchairs and the scent of parchment and leather, I feel suffocated. Haunted.

My fingers tremble as they trail along the spines of the books. Titles blur past—some familiar, some long-forgotten. None of them hold the answer I crave, but I keep looking. I must keep looking.

Ever since my eighteenth birthday, the visions have grown more vivid. More insistent. As if something ancient and powerful is trying to claw its way into my awareness, dragging its warnings with it. But they come in fragments. Fleeting images. They leave me with more questions than clarity.

I've been told they'll strengthen as I approach my twenty-first birthday—the age of ascension for witches. The day I come into my full power. But that promise feels hollow when the darkness draws nearer with each passing night.

One thing is certain.

It's coming.

A darkness not just of vision, but of fate. Something that threatens to unravel everything—the world I know, the lineage I carry, the fragile balance between light and shadow. And I, the youngest Draken and still fumbling through the boundaries of my gift, feel entirely unready to meet it.

"Clarissa, dear, are you all right?"

Juliette's voice pierces the fog of my thoughts like

sunlight through storm clouds. I turn. She stands at the doorway in a gown the color of twilight, her brow furrowed just enough to reveal concern behind her usual poise.

"I'm fine," I lie, painting on a smile as brittle as glass. "Just... tired."

Her amethyst gaze softens with something like recognition. "I'm sure it's quite challenging, dealing with your gift. Especially when it's new."

She glides across the marble floor, the hem of her skirts whispering secrets in her wake. "The visions will make sense eventually, when you come into your full power."

"My twenty-first birthday is still three years away," I murmur, a note of desperation creeping into my voice. "What if whatever's coming can't wait that long?"

Juliette's expression softens with understanding. "The gift doesn't sleep until then, darling. It stirs, it grows, it prepares you." She reaches out to touch my arm gently. "But you mustn't let the visions rule you, Clarissa. You must anchor yourself. Channel what power you do have now. Shape it before it shapes you."

I rake a hand through my hair, frustration prickling at my scalp. "I'm trying. But they're so disjointed. Like pieces from different puzzles jammed together. I can't see the full picture."

Juliette tilts her head, a knowing smile playing on her lips. "And that's precisely why you have us. This library, these books, this legacy—it's all meant to guide you. You're not alone in this, ma chère."

She gestures toward the towering shelves. "There's power in these pages. Answers waiting for the right eyes to read them."

"You're right." I nod, a flicker of hope igniting within me. "I just have to keep digging."

I turn back to the shelves, fingers trailing until they land on a familiar volume. I draw it out gently, the leather worn smooth by generations of hands. *De Occulta Philosophia Libri Tres.* I clutch it to my chest, the weight of it grounding me in a way few things can.

Juliette gathers an antique clock from the mantle as she makes for the adjoining parlor, pausing in the doorway. "You *will* find your answers," she says, without looking back. "You always do."

Only two people know the truth of what I've seen—Nikolaas, my brother and confidant, and Juliette.

Juliette. I wouldn't even begin to try to figure out the exact nature of our connection. Her life goes three centuries back, and the brambles of our family trees are so entangled that it would take a lifetime to unravel them.

But the bond between us feels deeper than mere blood.

She recognized my gift—before I could even understand it myself. She's become my guide ever since, my teacher, my tether to a craft older than memory.

Even then, I've revealed to her the barest threads of my visions.

Nik knows everything about them. He's my anchor when they drag me too deep. But even *he* can't decipher what they mean.

I sigh, the burden of secrecy pressing on my ribs. With one arm wrapped around the tome, I reach for another—then another—until my arms are full, the stack wobbling dangerously.

That's when I hear it.

Footsteps.

Soft, deliberate, echoing in the silence like a promise. But these aren't Juliette's graceful strides or Nik's familiar gait. No —there's something different about them. Heavier. Commanding.

And then the presence hits me.

A force, unseen but potent, brushes against my senses like a cold wind from a forgotten crypt. The air thickens, laced with power and the scent of something primal. My breath stills. My pulse leaps.

Whoever is approaching isn't ordinary. They're not just powerful—they're *sovereign*. They radiate an aura of absolute control, a dominance that demands submission and respect.

Every fiber of my being goes still, instinctively aware that this person walks a path few dare tread.

The footsteps are getting closer now, the sound mingling with the blood rushing in my ears. But suddenly, just as they appeared, they stop.

For a moment, there's nothing but silence, a thick, heavy silence that seems to press down on me from all sides. And then, a voice, low and smooth and full of dark promise, whispers through the stillness.

3

KAISNER

The click of my Italian leather shoes against the polished floor announces my arrival as I stride into the marbled foyer of Deveraux Manor. Cassandra, ever the epitome of Parisian elegance, glides toward me, a warm smile gracing her perfectly painted lips. "Kaisner, darling. The elusive Master of Shadows himself. Welcome to Paris," she purrs, air-kissing my cheeks. "I've been expecting you."

I return her smile with a charming one of my own, my eyes already scanning the opulent surroundings. "Cassandra, a pleasure, as always. Paris seems to agree with you more than America ever did." My words are smooth, practiced, but my mind is elsewhere—two steps ahead in the game we play in our unnatural world.

As Cassandra leads me toward the study, regaling me with tales of the city's latest scandals, a flicker of movement catches my eye. There, on the threshold of the library, stands a vision that steals the breath from my lungs. A beautiful woman, with hair like spun gold and eyes that could shame the brightest sapphires, is carrying a stack of books that seem to dwarf her delicate frame.

I watch, transfixed, as she moves with a grace that seems almost otherworldly. But then, as if the universe itself is conspiring to bring us together, one book slips from her grasp, tumbling to the floor with a soft thud.

Without a second thought, I excuse myself from Cassandra's side and make my way toward the fallen tome. Bending down, I retrieve the book, my fingers brushing against the worn leather cover. As I straighten, I find myself face to face with the beautiful stranger, close enough to catch the faint scent of jasmine that clings to her skin.

"I believe this belongs to you," I murmur, extending the book toward her.

Our fingers brush as she takes it from my hand, and in that moment, a jolt of electricity courses through me, setting my nerves alight. It's as if a circuit has been completed, a connection forged that defies explanation. I feel it rush up my arm, spreading through my body until it reaches my very core, igniting a fire I thought long extinguished.

I search her face, desperate for some sign that she feels it too—this inexplicable pull, this sense of destiny. But she merely offers a shy smile, a delicate blush staining her cheeks. "Thank you, monsieur," she breathes, her voice like a caress.

I open my mouth to respond, to introduce myself, to beg her to tell me her name. But no words come. For the first time in my life, I, Kaisner, the man who prides himself on his silver tongue and quick wit, am struck speechless.

She dips her head, a curtain of golden hair hiding her face as she hurries away, clutching the books to her chest like a shield. I watch her go, my hand still tingling from her touch, my mind reeling from the encounter. As she disappears from the room, I hear her laugh, a sound so pure and enchanting that it pierces through the very core of my being.

Cassandra's voice breaks through my reverie, urging me to join her in the study. But as I follow, my thoughts remain tethered to the beautiful stranger and the inexplicable connection I felt in those brief seconds.

Who is she, this woman who can unravel me with a single touch? And what twist of fate has brought us together under this roof?

As I settle into the plush armchair, Cassandra's voice washes over me, her words laced with genuine warmth. "Kaisner, my dear friend, I can't tell you how much it means to have you here. Paris has been sorely lacking in good company."

I incline my head, a smile playing at the corners of my lips. "Cassandra, you know my friendship is unwavering. We've been through too much together for it to be anything less." I pause, considering my next words carefully. "I hear congratulations are in order."

Cassandra's brow furrows, a flicker of confusion passing over her delicate features. "Congratulations? Whatever for?"

I lean back in my chair, my eyes never leaving hers. "Your engagement to the Ursa King has become quite the topic of gossip, even in the far reaches of Germany. It seems you've managed to secure quite the alliance."

A hint of a flush creeps into Cassandra's cheeks, but she maintains her composure, offering a polite smile. "Ah, yes. The engagement." She purses her lips and swallows hard. "It's a... a *fortunate* match, to be sure."

I don't miss the slight hesitation in her voice, the way her enthusiasm seems forced, almost rehearsed. Interesting. Perhaps there's more to this engagement than meets the eye.

I choose not to press the issue, not yet. There will be time enough to unveil the secrets behind Cassandra's impending nuptials. For now, I have more pressing matters to attend to.

"But I must confess," I continue, steering the conversation back to the purpose of my visit, "there is another reason for my presence here tonight. Rumors of a *dragon shifter* have reached my ears. You know how my curiosity is piqued by such tales."

Cassandra relaxes in her seat, a knowing glint in her eye. "Ah, yes. The Last Dragon Shifter." She pauses, as if stunned herself at the grandeur those words entail. "The rumors are true. His name is Nikolaas Draken." She takes a sip of her tea. "And that beautiful creature you encountered moments ago? That was his younger sister, Clarissa. She's studying the craft under Juliette's tutelage. Visits the manor quite frequently."

I school my features into a mask of polite interest, trying to betray none of the sudden surge of excitement that courses through me at this revelation. "Is that so? How fascinating."

A shadow of movement draws my attention, and I turn to see a woman emerging from an adjacent room, a clipboard clutched in her manicured hands. Our gazes meet, and for a moment, I feel pinned in place by the intensity of her stare. She holds my gaze for a beat longer than strictly necessary before excusing herself, disappearing as quickly as she arrived.

"One of my staff," Cassandra explains, noting my distraction. "An interior designer who specializes in antiques. She's been invaluable in the manor's restoration."

I nod, filing away the information for later.

Cassandra leans forward, her expression turning serious. "But Kaisner, there is another matter I wish to discuss with you. A matter that pertains to your particular talents as a warlock."

I raise an eyebrow, intrigued. My reputation as a master of the Dark Arts is well known in certain circles, but it's rare for Cassandra to bring it up so directly.

"I'm curious about Shadow Beings," she continues, her voice lowering to a conspiratorial whisper. "I've heard rumors, stories that seem too fantastical to be true. But with your expertise, I thought perhaps you could shed some light on the subject."

As Cassandra delves into the specifics of her query, her words washing over me in a steady flow, I find my mind drifting, inexorably drawn back to the encounter in the library. Clarissa. The name rolls through my thoughts like an incantation, conjuring images of golden hair and eyes that sparkle like jewels.

The Last Dragon Shifter's sister.

The realization sends a thrill down my spine, and I have to suppress a shudder of anticipation. Oh, the secrets she must hold, the power that must course through her veins. What I wouldn't give to unravel those mysteries, to taste that power for myself.

But even as my thoughts wander, my keen senses pick up on a subtle detail in the room, a faint scent that tickles at the edge of my awareness. It's a rich, earthy aroma, slightly sweet with hints of amber, vanilla, and spice. *Dragon's blood.* The incense is unmistakable, and its presence here is no accident.

I know the properties of dragon's blood all too well, its ability to ward off evil spirits and create a protective barrier around those who burn it. The fact that Cassandra has chosen to use it now, during our conversation, speaks volumes.

She's being cautious, ensuring that our discussion remains private, shielded from any prying eyes or ears that might seek to use the information against us. It's a smart move, one that speaks to her understanding of the delicate nature of the topics we're about to broach.

I appreciate her foresight. However, I can't help but wonder what other secrets she might be keeping, what other precautions she's taken to ensure the sanctity of this meeting. The Deveraux heiress is a woman of many layers, and I have no doubt that her true intentions run deeper than what she chooses to reveal.

And so I lean forward, my gaze intent, my voice low and measured as I begin to share my knowledge of the Shadow Beings, the secrets I have spent a lifetime uncovering.

As our conversation progresses, I force myself to focus on Cassandra's words, nodding at the appropriate moments, offering insights when prompted. But even as I speak, my mind is elsewhere, drawn back to the golden-haired beauty who has so thoroughly captivated my thoughts.

For I know, with a certainty that borders on prescience, that Clarissa holds the key to something I've been seeking for longer than I care to admit. And I will stop at nothing to possess it.

The game has begun, and the prize is more tantalizing than I ever could have imagined.

4

CLARISSA

Some encounters rewrite destiny in the space between one heartbeat and the next. I step into the library's adjacent parlor, my heart racing, thoughts spinning with confusion and exhilaration. The encounter with this stranger has left me reeling, my skin still tingling from his touch. It was just *a graze of his fingers* against mine, a fleeting contact as he handed me the fallen book, but the effect was electric. Never before had I felt such an incredible rush of energy.

I'm so lost in my thoughts that I barely register Juliette's presence until her voice cuts through the haze.

"Goodness, child. What's the matter?" she asks, concern and amusement blending into her tone.

I blink, startled. Heat rises in my cheeks. I open my mouth to respond, but the words get stuck, tangled with the questions and sensations swirling in my mind.

Juliette's brow furrows, her expression shifting from enjoyment to genuine worry. "Cat caught your tongue, dear?" she prods gently, patting the space beside her on the sofa in a silent invitation.

I shake my head, trying to clear the fog of confusion that seems to have settled over me. "I'm sorry," I stammer, my voice sounding strange and distant to my ears. "I just... Oh, it's nothing."

As I speak, a flicker of hesitation stops me. It's not that I don't trust Juliette—she's been my mentor and confidante since I arrived in Paris, guiding me through the Craft with unwavering dedication. But this feels different. Private. The moment I shared with the stranger seems intimate, a secret I want to keep close to my heart.

And then there's my ability as a seer. For as long as I can remember, I've glimpsed people's pasts and futures, sensed the threads of destiny that bind them. A gift that's only grown stronger under Juliette's patient guidance.

But with that man... there was nothing. No flashes of insight, no whispers of fate. Just a void—an emptiness I've never encountered. It's as if he's shielded from my sight, his path cloaked in shadows that no spell can pierce.

The thought sends a shiver down my spine. Who is he, this man who so easily evades my gift? And what does it mean that our paths have crossed now, in this moment?

Juliette is watching me closely, her keen eyes seeming to see straight through to the heart of my confusion. "Nothing?" she says, her tone light and teasing. "You look like a woman who's just been struck by lightning."

The comment catches me off guard, perfectly timed, and I can't help but burst into laughter. It bubbles up from deep within, a release of the tension and uncertainty that's been building in my chest. Juliette laughs with me, her warmth filling the space, and for a moment, the burden of my concerns lifts, replaced by camaraderie and shared mirth.

"*Lightning* might be an understatement," I manage between giggles.

Juliette's eyes sparkle with mischief, her lips curving into a knowing smile. "Ah, so it's like that, is it?" she asks, her tone suggestive. "Do tell, my dear. Who is this mystery man who's got you all in a tizzy?"

My cheeks flush at her words, embarrassment and excitement rushing through me. "I... I don't know," I admit in a whisper. "I've never seen him before. But when we touched… Juliette, it was unlike anything I've ever felt. A bolt of pure energy, straight to my core." I press a hand to my chest, heart racing under my palm.

Juliette's gaze softens, her thoughts distant. "I know that feeling," she murmurs, voice dreamy. "The first time I felt that pull—that undeniable connection—it was as if the ground moved beneath my feet. My whole world turned upside down."

My lips ease into a gentle smile, assuming she speaks of her late husband. "You're thinking of Willem, aren't you?" I ask softly. The only dragon king in my lineage. His beast was said to be the shade of pure gold, just like my brother's.

The change in Juliette is immediate and stark. Her dreamy expression vanishes, replaced by something cold and guarded. Her fingers tighten around her teacup until her knuckles go white, and when she speaks, her voice is barely controlled.

"Don't." The word cuts through the air like a blade. "Don't speak that name."

I flinch, shocked by the vehemence in her tone. "Juliette, I'm sorry, I didn't mean—"

"That name…" She sets down her cup with trembling hands, her composure cracking like ice under pressure. "It haunts me, child. In ways you cannot imagine."

The pain in her voice makes my chest ache. I reach for her hand, finding it cold despite the fire's warmth. "I don't understand. Willem was your fated mate—the legacy you built together endures to this day."

Juliette is quiet for a long moment, staring into the fire as if seeking answers in the dancing flames. When she finally speaks, her voice carries centuries of pain.

"There were *two* Willems in my life, Clarissa." Her smile is bitter, hollow. "One was my husband—your ancestor, Willem Von Draken. A good man, noble and true, handsome and patient." Her voice softens with genuine tenderness. "He loved me fiercely, with a quiet devotion that should have been enough. More than enough. Yet I was too young, too foolish to treasure what I had, and he was taken from me far too soon."

She pauses, and I see her hands shaking before she clasps them tightly in her lap.

"And the other?" I prompt gently.

"The other..." Her voice drops to barely above a whisper. "The other was the Dragon King, and he was everything he shouldn't have been. Dangerous. Cruel. Utterly compelling." She pauses, her breath catching. "A man who could make you forget your own name with a single glance." She meets my gaze, and I see fear there—real, bone-deep terror. A man whose touch brought only ash and ruin."

My blood turns to ice as tears gather in her eyes. "What happened?"

"He's dead," she says flatly, but there's no relief in her voice. "Has been for centuries. And yet..." she trails off, shaking her head as if dispelling unwelcome thoughts.

"And yet?"

"Nothing." She straightens, rebuilding her composure like armor. "Just an old woman's memories playing tricks on her mind."

But I catch the lie in her eyes, the way her stare darts to the shadows in the corners of the room, as if someone might be watching from the darkness.

"Juliette," I begin, but she cuts me off.

"Enough of such bleak thoughts," she says, though her smile is somewhat strained. "Tell me more about this connection you experienced. When souls recognize each other across impossible odds, it usually means a great deal."

I want to press her about Willem—both Willems—but something in her posture warns me off. Instead, I describe the electric shock, the way time seemed to stop, the void where my visions should have been.

She takes my hand, her grip almost desperate. "Cherish this moment, Clarissa," she says, voice serious. "No matter what happens next, remember this feeling. Hold it close and let it be your guiding light in times of darkness."

I nod, swallowing the lump in my throat. Juliette's words strike a chord deep within me, but now they carry a weight I hadn't expected—a warning wrapped in blessing.

"I will," I promise, determined.

Juliette smiles, though it doesn't quite reach her eyes. "Good," she says, giving my hand a final squeeze before releasing it. "Now, let's examine these visions, shall we? I have a feeling we're closer to unveiling the mysteries in your mind."

We settle into our usual routine—conversations, laughter, shared secrets, and half-forgotten memories. But even as we talk and the hours slip by, my thoughts keep drifting back to two things: the electric touch of the stranger's hand, and the haunted look in Juliette's eyes when I spoke that cursed name.

I don't know who the stranger is, or what role he's meant to play in my life. But I do know one thing with absolute certainty.

Nothing will ever be the same again.

5

KAISNER

Cassandra reclines in her seat as our conversation winds down, a graceful motion that belies the fact that we've just traded secrets capable of toppling empires. "Kaisner, I can't thank you enough for your insight. Your knowledge of the Shadow Beings is truly unparalleled."

I incline my head, accepting the compliment with a slight smile. "It's my pleasure, Cassandra. I'm always at your disposal—especially when it comes to matters of the arcane."

She returns my smile, a glimmer of affection in her eyes. "We are lucky to have you as an ally." She pauses, a thoughtful expression crossing her face. "How long will you be gracing Paris with your presence? I know you've been eager to settle into your estate in Lake Starnberg—a castle, I hear."

I lean back in my chair, considering the question. It's true, I had been looking forward to the solitude and privacy of my new home, a place where I could delve into my studies without interruption. But now, with the tantalizing prospect of unraveling the mysteries surrounding Clarissa and her brother, I discover my priorities shifting.

"Paris has a way of captivating the senses," I muse, my voice low and thoughtful. "I find myself drawn to its charms more than I expected. I believe I shall extend my stay, immerse myself in all the city has to offer."

Cassandra's smile widens, genuine pleasure lighting her features. "Wonderful! You must let me play hostess. There are so many hidden delights I'm eager to share with you."

I chuckle, the sound rich and warm. "I have no doubt. But for now, I'm afraid I must take my leave. I have some business to attend to in town."

She rises, smoothing the folds of her dress. "Of course. I'll walk you to the door."

I hold up a hand, shaking my head. "No need, my dearest. I know the way." I flash her a grin, all charm and confidence. "Besides, I wouldn't want to keep you from your affairs."

Cassandra agrees with a nod, and I take my leave, my strides purposeful as I navigate the manor's luxurious halls. My mind is already racing ahead, anticipating the next move in this enticing game.

As I round the corner, I catch a glimpse of movement, a silhouette disappearing into the darkened parlor. A thrill courses through me, and I quicken my pace, slipping into the room.

I lock the door behind me, ensuring our privacy. Instantly, I am met with an oasis of opulence, every inch adorned with extravagant artwork and antiquities. The dimmed lights cast a sensual glow over the burgundy walls and glossy walnut paneling, setting a sultry mood.

And there, in the center of it all, stands Scarlett, the Deveraux's enigmatic interior designer. An enchanting woman in her late twenties, busy perusing a sample book of fabric swatches on a Louis XVI mahogany table. She's dressed impeccably in a tailored black skirt suit that hugs her curvaceous frame, accentuating her every asset. Her long auburn hair cascades over her shoulders in luscious waves, and her blue eyes sparkle with awareness as she senses my presence.

Her gaze meets mine, a challenge and an invitation all in one. "I've been expecting you," she murmurs, her voice low and seductive. She steps closer, drawn to me like a moth to a flame.

"Have you now?" I keep my tone light, teasing. "And what exactly were you expecting, Fräulein Scarlett?"

She tilts her head, a smirk playing at the corners of her lips. "I think you know what I want, Your Majesty."

The title sends a shiver down my spine, a reminder of the power I wield, the secrets I hold. Oh, this woman is dangerous, a temptress with an agenda of her own.

But then again, so am I.

I close the distance between us, my hand coming up to trace the delicate line of her jaw. "Enlighten me," I breathe, my mouth a hairsbreadth from hers.

And as she leans in, her eyes flashing with a hunger that matches my own, my hands land on her shoulders, eliciting electric thrills coursing through her slender body. "Kneel, sweetheart," I purr. "It suits you." Our stares lock as I guide her down to her knees. Her plump lips part ever so slightly, revealing a glimpse of pearly white teeth and a sensual mischief within.

My heartbeat quickens as she sinks to the oriental rug below me, dropping the sample book in the process. The expensive fabrics fan out across the floor, an ironic display of luxury and decadence at our feet.

I lean against the door, my body stiff with anticipation as I undo my belt. The cool air caresses my growing arousal, making it twitch with desire. Scarlett's sapphire eyes never leave mine as her manicured fingers brush against the length of my trousers, teasing me through the fabric. She knows what I want, what I need, and she's all too eager to oblige.

With a smile that could melt ice, she unzips my pants, freeing me from their confines. Her hot breath hits my sweet spot as she leans in closer, her red-stained lips forming a perfect O. My eyes roll back as her talented mouth engulfs me, her tongue tracing lazy circles around the head of my erection before taking me in deeper. Her delicate hands grip my hips, urging me further as if I needed any more encouragement.

Lost in the moment, my thoughts drift to Clarissa's sapphire eyes and her porcelain skin. I remember the way her dress clung to her curves, accentuating every graceful line of her figure. Her laughter echoes in my mind, a symphony that will surely haunt my dreams. Gods, how I ached for her then. How I long for her now… In my fantasy, it's Clarissa's silky hair in my grasp as I guide her mouth upon me, not Scarlett's.

Moaning inwardly, I feel myself being enveloped in waves of pleasure. Scarlett is skilled in the art of seduction; every flick of her tongue and stroke of her hand, designed to bring about ecstasy. Her practiced fingers dance along the base of my shaft as her mouth continues its relentless assault, her warm, wet licks swirling around me like a proficient dancer. My grip on her hair tightens, urging her on, my breath coming in ragged gasps. I close my eyes, imagining it's Clarissa's soft touch between my thighs, not Scarlett's. The thought of her innocence crumbling before me sends a shiver down my spine.

The room around us disappears as I descend into a haze of pure lust. I can smell the light scent of Scarlett's Versace Crystal Noir mingled with the musky perfume of arousal, but it's the ghostly aroma of Clarissa's Chanel Coco Mademoiselle that fills my senses, teasing my nostrils and height-ening my desire. With each flick of Scarlett's tongue, I envision it's Clarissa's lips on me, her inexperienced touch firing a hunger within me that no amount of experience could ever match.

As I feel myself reaching the edge, I open my eyes to see Scarlett's face etched with an expression of pure concentration. Her sapphire orbs are nowhere near the pale hue of Clarissa's; they don't hold the same depth, the same allure. But for now, they will have to do. Picturing those eyes staring up at me, I release myself into her willing mouth with a primal growl. Her lips tighten around me, milking every last drop of pleasure from my spent body.

As the haze clears, Scarlett looks up at me, her lipstick smudged and hair disheveled, yet she still manages to exude an air of sensuality that would make any man weak at the knees.

But not me. My eyes harden as I return my arousal to its boundaries and fasten my pants.

"Cassandra isn't the only one I have my sights set on," I say casually, adjusting my tie. "I want you to find me everything there is to know about Clarissa Draken."

Scarlett blinks up at me in surprise, but she recovers quickly, wiping the remnants of our encounter from her mouth with the back of her hand. "Of course, sir," she purrs, and rising to her feet, she adjusts her blouse and smooths down her skirt. "Is there anything else you desire?" Her cool indifference, a sharp contrast to the blazing heat she just ignited in me.

I run my fingers through my hair, shoving away the image of Clarissa's angelic face that lingered in my mind's eye. "No, that will do for now," I say coldly.

Without a single word, I unlock the door and step out into the deserted hallway, straightening my suit jacket as if nothing has happened.

The memory of Clarissa's countenance still burns in my mind, an unquenchable fire stoked with this encounter with Scarlett, serving only to fuel the flame. A part of me loathes myself for using her as a stand-in for what I truly crave, but another part doesn't care as long as it sates my desires—however temporarily.

6

CLARISSA

When Cassandra joins us in the library's parlor, sinking into the plush armchair with a heavy sigh, I immediately sense something's wrong. The exhaustion that emanates from her goes beyond ordinary pregnancy fatigue—there's a tension in her shoulders, a wariness in her expression that sets my nerves on edge.

"Seven weeks along, and I already feel like I've been pregnant for an eternity," she admits, her hand resting protectively on her barely there bump.

"I remember the first time I sensed the flutter of life within me," the Grand Witch begins, her eyes sparkling with nostalgia. "It was as if the world had suddenly become more vibrant, more alive."

Juliette launches into cheerful reminiscences about her own pregnancies. But I find myself studying Cassandra's face, noting the way her gaze keeps drifting to the windows, as if she's expecting something—or someone.

"Have you heard from Dristan?" The question slips out before I can stop myself. "Does he know about the baby?"

The room falls silent. Cassandra's countenance pales, her hand tightening on her stomach. Instantly, I regret my words.

"I'm sorry," I stammer, mortified. "I shouldn't have—" I bite my lip, wincing inwardly. Gods, they've only just confided this secret to me, and here I am, blurting it out thoughtlessly. How could I be so careless?

"It's all right," Cassandra whispers, though her voice trembles. "No, he doesn't know. And he can't..." She takes a shaky breath. "As long as I carry Gavriil's brand, Dristan can never come close to me again. The Ursa King's magic is too strong."

The pain in her tone is unmistakable, but beneath it, I detect fear.

Juliette reaches for her hand, voice firm but gentle. "You are never alone, my dear. This family stands with you—always."

Cassie nods, blinking fast, and Juliette, ever the balm, adds with a wink, "Besides, think of all the babysitters you'll have. I, for one, fully intend to spoil this little one rotten."

The mood lightens, laughter bubbling around us. Cassie tilts her head, eyes twinkling. "Speaking of family... *someone* pulled off a rather extravagant birthday party recently."

My cheeks hopelessly burn.

Meanwhile, Juliette settles into her seat, pleased. "Nikolaas transformed that ballroom into a dream. Flowers, music, gowns—it was pure magic."

Cassandra sighs, her gaze distant. "You looked radiant, Clarissa. Like something bloomed in you that night."

"He did work hard," I admit, a smile tugging at my lips. "The staff probably needed a week to recover from his constant adjustments."

Juliette laughs. "Classic Nik. Always perfecting, always giving his best to those he loves."

"It's true," I say, quieter now. "He's been my anchor these past weeks."

The Grand Witch smiles warmly. "And you are his pride, Clarissa. I see it in him. We all do."

"He proved that when he appointed you to lead the Galerie's philanthropic branch," Cassie adds.

The moment returns to me like a cherished spell—his belief in me, the way he made me feel seen. "It still feels surreal," I whisper in silent awe. "That he'd trust me with something so important… What a birthday gift."

"Not a gift, dearest. You've *earned* it," Juliette assures me. "With your mind and your heart."

"And your brilliance," Cassie chimes in. "Starting university courses at fourteen while still in high school, then finishing your bachelor's degree by eighteen. You made it look so easy!"

"It wasn't," I murmur, my smile faltering. Bram's voice echoes in my memory—sharp, demanding. *You're a Draken, Clarissa. Anything less than perfection is unacceptable.*

I blink, chasing the ghosts away.

"You are so blessed," Juliette adds, her tone softer. "The bond between siblings—there's nothing quite like it."

My lips ease into a practiced smile, but even then, I can't ignore the shadow that lurks at the edges of our conversation. Bram, my wayward brother, his absence a solid presence in the room. The silence that falls is heavy with unspoken words, with the burden of questions none of us dare to ask.

I take a deep breath, gathering my courage. "Has he contacted you?" I venture to say, my voice steady despite the flutter of nerves in my stomach. "Bram, I mean."

Juliette looks away, propriety silencing her. But Cassie reaches for me, her touch gentle. "Not yet," she says softly.

I nod, but the pressure on my chest tightens.

"Wherever he is, I believe he's safe," Cassandra adds. "He'll find his way back to us. I'm sure of it."

I want to believe her. I want to believe he still remembers the way home.

Cassie's hand glides over mine, comforting and warm.

My prophetic instincts suddenly flare to life. Images flash through my mind's eye: *Cassandra in an untamed garden, speaking urgently to the shadows. A meeting. A revelation that could shatter alliances…*

When the still pictures disappear, I'm left with a shattering, ominous sensation.

I lean forward, my voice dropping to a whisper. "Cassie, what aren't you telling us?"

Her eyes widen slightly—surprise that I've seen through her facade, followed quickly by resignation. "I was wondering when your gift would kick in," she says with a rueful smile. "Nothing gets past the Draken seer, does it?"

"Not when my family's in danger," I reply firmly. "And you are family. So, please tell me—what's going on?"

Cassandra exchanges a meaningful look with Juliette, some silent communication passing between them. Finally, she sighs. "There's going to be a meeting. With the Ursa clan. And the Drakens, of course." She pauses. "I have something I need to tell you all."

"What kind of *something?*" I press, my seer instincts, screaming that this is bigger than family politics.

Before Cassandra can answer, the door swings open.

Samara appears on the threshold, but instead of her usual casual elegance, there's something almost militant in her posture. She's not here by accident.

"Samara," Cassandra says, relief evident in her voice.

"Here you are. I was wondering where everyone had gone," she utters in a feigned offhand tone.

Her chestnut waves tumble over her shoulders, untouched by the cold. She wears a tailored camel coat over a cream cable-knit sweater and dark jeans, her boots sleek, her gloves fitted.

My emotions tangle. We've grown so close since she began seeing Nikolaas—our shared interests, our late-night conversations—but even now, something guarded lingers between us. A quiet tension, like a thread pulled taut, but never quite snapping.

Some of it stems from Cassie. Samara is nothing but polite in her presence, yet there's a wariness in her gaze—a hesitation she doesn't bother to conceal. Her reservations about Gavriil's engagement are no secret. She believes his heart still belongs to Luciana, the mate he lost. And Cassie, for all her grace and good intentions, isn't her. Not to mention the baby she carries—Dristan Brek's child.

Oh, the layers of this family drama could fill volumes.

"My darling," Juliette says, rising from her chair with open arms. "How wonderful to see you! Come, sit with us."

Cassie straightens. "Actually, I need to speak with Samara—privately."

Samara steps closer to me, resting a hand on my shoulder. "There's no need for secrecy," she says, her voice calm but firm. "I trust both Juliette and Clarissa completely." Her gaze slides toward Juliette, warm with reverence, then back to me.

Cassandra hesitates, then exhales slowly. "Very well."

Sam slips onto the chair beside her. "What is it? What's going on?"

Cassie takes a steadying breath, her hands wringing in her lap. "I wish to extend an invitation to the Ursa clan," she says, the words rushing out. "A meeting with Gavriil, Vladimir, and you. The Drakens will be there as well." She purses her lips. "There's an important announcement I must make—something that could change everything between our families."

My breath catches in my throat, my heart pounding with a sudden, inexplicable sense of dread. A summit of the most prominent lineages in the supernatural world? What could Cassandra possibly have to say that would require such secrecy, such urgency?

Beside me, Juliette is equally tense.

Sam is nodding slowly, her expression thoughtful. "I'll talk to my brothers," she says, resolved. "We'll be there, Cassandra. Whatever you need, we'll be there."

Cassie smiles, a look of relief and gratitude washing over her face. "Dearest Samara," she adds, reaching out to clasp my friend's hand. "You have no idea how much that means to me."

Cassandra takes a brief pause, her demeanor shifting to a more serious and vulnerable state. "We didn't start off on the best foot, you and I," she murmurs, her gaze searching Sam's face for any hint of reaction. "I understand why you might have had your reservations about me, about my relationship with your brother Gavriil."

Samara opens her mouth as if to speak, but Cassandra holds up a hand. "Please, let me finish," she says, and her voice trembles slightly. "I realize my situation is... complicated. My pregnancy and my past have caused difficulties for everyone involved."

Cassie inhales sharply, her shoulders squared as if bracing herself for whatever response might come. "But I want you to know that I am committed to this family, to making things work with Gavriil and with all of you. And I'm hoping that after this meeting, after you hear what I have to say... that maybe you'll be willing to give me a second chance. To start over and build a real friendship between us."

For a moment, Samara is silent, her expression unreadable as she weighs Cassandra's words. My breath hitches as I wait for her response.

Finally, Sam's features soften. "I'd like that," she says quietly, sincerely. "I've not been the most welcoming, and I apologize. But you're right. We're going to be family soon, and that means we need to find a way to work together, to support each other."

She reaches out, clasping Cassie's hand more firmly in her own. "So yes, I'm willing to give this a chance. To give *us* a chance. And I promise that I'll come to the meeting with an open mind and an open heart, ready to hear whatever it is you have to say."

Cassandra's smile widens, joyful tears sparkling in her eyes. "Thank you, Samara," she whispers, her voice choked with emotion. "For giving me this chance, for believing in me."

They embrace then, a fierce, heartfelt hug that seems to go on forever. And as I watch them, as I glimpse the love and acceptance radiating out from them, hope and joy surge through me.

As they part, I catch something shift in Cassandra's expression—a flicker of quiet resolve layered beneath visible relief.

Samara gives her a nod, soft but steady, then glances my way with a wry tilt of her head. "Well, if we're all going to be family now, I should warn you—Clarissa has a habit of reorganizing people's lives. With love. *And* without permission."

"Hey!" I protest, laughing despite myself. "I prefer calling it 'caring intervention.'"

"Is *that* what we're calling it?" Samara grins, the tension in her shoulders easing for the first time since she walked in.

And just like that, the room shifts. The heaviness lifts. For a brief, fragile moment, we're simply three women in a sunlit room, sharing warmth and teasing smiles like something close to ordinary.

These moments—ephemeral, unspectacular—are the ones I've learned to treasure most. In our world, peace is fleeting. But this?

This feels like magic.

7

CLARISSA

The morning air bites at my skin as I descend the grand staircase, my fingers trailing along the cool mahogany banister. Each step creaks softly beneath my feet, echoing through the cavernous stillness of Draken Manor.

I pause at the landing, my gaze drawn to the windows flanking the living room. Outside, the world lies cloaked in a velvet hush—predawn blue stretching across the sky. But there, on the horizon, light begins its slow ascent. Streaks of rose and amber bloom behind the trees, painting the heavens with delicate defiance. No matter how many mornings I witness it, the sight always steals my breath.

And yet, wonder can't lighten the shadows in my mind.

Last night's dream still clings to me—visceral, raw. I stood in a wasteland, the bones of our world buried beneath ash. A greenish light pulsed through storm-churned clouds, casting an eerie glow over the fallen. Deverauxs. Drakens. Alexeevs. All of them, lifeless and broken at my feet.

And from the darkness, a voice rose. Ancient. Malevolent.

"When shadows rise to claim their throne, all shall kneel

before the storm. Light shall perish, hope shall die, and darkness reign beneath starless skies."

I woke breathless, a scream caught in my throat, sweat chilling my skin. Even now, hours later, the words echo inside me. A whisper of the future—or a warning.

I push it down and force a pleasant expression as I reach the bottom of the stairs.

Nikolaas stands by the front door, luggage neatly stacked beside him. He looks up as I approach, a tired smile tugging at his lips. But it doesn't reach his eyes. I can see the weariness in him, the weight of the responsibility that rests on his shoulders. The same unease that coils in my chest.

"Morning, little sister," he greets, voice rough with sleep. "Off to work already?"

I nod, shifting my bag higher on my shoulder. "The gallery doesn't sleep. Not even for the heiress of House Draken."

He huffs a quiet laugh. "I hear *you're* the one who really keeps things running over there."

I smile, but it's thin. Because beneath the teasing lies the ache I can't ignore.

The truth is, I'm worried about him, about the journey he's about to undertake. Amsterdam isn't just another city, another stop on his endless tour of duty. It's the home of our original clan, the birthplace of our family's power and legacy.

"Must you go to Drakenhaven now?" I ask softly. "Can't it wait—just a little longer?"

Nik sighs, fingers raking through his tousled blond hair. "I wish it could. But they've been demanding this meeting for weeks. Ever since my dragon awakened, the old guard's been restless. They want to see for themselves. To remind us of the roots we share."

I lower my gaze, fidgeting with the strap of my bag. "Of course."

He continues, more animated now. "Amsterdam is just the beginning. From there, I'll head to Stockholm. Then Oslo. The Nordic clans are watching us closely. Their support could make all the difference."

A chill runs through me, dread blooming low in my belly. The same dread that's haunted my dreams for weeks. I can't hold it back anymore.

"I'm scared, Nik," I whisper. "These visions... they're getting worse. I see fire and ruin. I see us falling. I don't know what it means, but it feels real. Too real. Darkness is coming for us."

Without hesitation, he steps forward and wraps me in his arms. "I know," he murmurs, holding me tightly. "I feel it too. But I swear, Clarissa—whatever comes, I'll keep you safe. I will protect our clan and those whom we hold dear."

He draws back, his hands on my shoulders, blue eyes burning with purpose. "That's why I must go. We need to be united. We need the strength of *all* dragon clans, the power that flows through our veins. Only together can we face the darkness that lies ahead."

"You're right. We need to be ready." I nod, swallowing the lump in my throat. "I just hate that we finally found each other again... and now you're leaving."

A flicker of sorrow crosses his face. "So do I. But Rissy, you've become something extraordinary. You're strong. You're steady. You're the heart of this family."

He tucks a loose strand of hair behind my ear. "You know what your name means, don't you? *Clarissa*—the one who shines. That's what you are to us. A light in the dark."

Emotion swells in my chest—pride, gratitude, love. "Thank you," I whisper. "For being the brother I always wished for, the leader our family deserves."

Nik's expression darkens at my words. Neither he nor I can control it. I cannot speak of one brother without conjuring the other, speak of Nik's radiance without summoning the memory of Bram's shadows.

He forces a grin. "You're in charge until I get back. Try not to start a war while I'm gone?"

"No promises," I reply, smirking.

He laughs, bending to grab his suitcase. "Honestly? I trust you more than I've ever trusted myself at your age. Just… try to enjoy yourself. Take a night off. Go dancing. Live a little."

"I'll consider it," I say, already knowing how hollow the idea feels.

He opens the door—but pauses. One last glance. One last breath.

Nik steps back, cups my face gently, and presses his forehead to mine. "May the stars light your path, little flame."

And then, he's gone.

8

KAISNER

My fingertips brush against cracked leather spines, leaving trails in the dust. The musty air clings to my skin, heavy with secrets whispered by countless generations of mages. Shadows writhe on rough-hewn walls as guttering candles struggle against the oppressive darkness of my sanctum.

A sudden spark leaps between my fingers, and I inhale sharply. The scent of ozone mingles with aged parchment, a reminder of the volatile energies I court. My heart thunders in my chest, each beat a war drum urging me onwards.

I close my eyes, steadying myself against the nearest shelf. The wood groans, as if sharing the burden of forbidden knowledge. How many hours have I spent here, poring over texts in languages long dead? The answer eludes me, much like the prize I seek.

Slowly, I extend my awareness inward. There—a faint stirring. Deep within my core, something ancient and terrible shifts in its slumber. My breath catches. The dragon. *My dragon.* So close, yet maddeningly out of reach.

I clench my fist, nails biting into my palm. The pain grounds me, a tether to reality as arcane currents threaten to sweep me away. I've come too far to falter now. Whatever the cost, whatever shreds of sanity remain, I will awaken the beast that slumbers in my blood.

But now, as I feel the power surging through my body, the ancient words of summoning falling from my lips like a lover's caress, I know that I'm close. So close that I can almost taste the victory on my tongue, the sweet savor of a destiny finally realized.

The air begins to shimmer and twist, the fabric of reality bending to my will as I channel the dark energy that flows through me. Its form is indistinct, a swirling mass of shadow and smoke that seems to pulse with a life of its own. And then, with a final word of command, a figure emerges, a being of pure darkness and malevolent intent.

Azrakan of the Abyss.

"Why have you summoned me, warlock?" the daemon hisses, its voice like the scrape of claws on glass.

My stare sharpens, locking onto the creature's otherworldly form. The air between us shimmers with unspoken power, and I force myself to hold that unhallowed gaze. Somewhere in the depths of those unfathomable eyes, I glimpse eternity—and my reflection, small and fleeting.

"I seek your counsel," I say, willing my voice not to waver. The words taste of ash and ambition on my tongue.

I swallow hard, steeling myself. "For years, I've scoured tomes and delved into forbidden rites, all to no avail. The dragon within me..." I pause, the admission of failure bitter in my mouth. "It remains stubbornly dormant."

The creature doesn't move, doesn't blink. Its stillness is more unnerving than any sudden movement could be. I press on, desperation lending strength to my words.

"I need your guidance." The plea scrapes my throat raw.

"Your wisdom in the dark arts that have eluded me. There must be a key, a ritual, something I've overlooked."

As I speak, I feel it again—that faint stirring deep in my core. The sleeping dragon, so tantalizingly close. My hands quiver with the effort of restraining myself from grasping at that ephemeral sensation.

I draw a shaky breath, acutely aware of how I must appear to this ageless being: a mortal man, teetering on the edge of power and madness. But I'm beyond caring. I've come too far, sacrificed too much, to turn back now.

"Will you help me?" I ask, my voice barely above a whisper.

The daemon's cackle crashes over me like a wave of ice, extinguishing candles and hope alike. Shadows writhe at the edges of my vision, hungry things drawn by the promise of forbidden power.

"Bold, little mortal," Azrakan purrs, each word dripping with contempt. Its eyes blaze with infernal light, twin pits of hunger that threaten to devour me whole. "You fancy yourself a master of the abyss?"

Something snaps within me—pride, desperation, or madness. I can't tell which. My nails bite deeper into my palms, and I welcome the pain, the trickle of warm blood between my fingers. It anchors me, reminds me of all I've sacrificed to reach this moment.

"I am Kaisner Drachenstein," I snarl, my voice raw and feral. The name echoes in the chamber, carrying with it the legacy of centuries. "Last scion of a bloodline steeped in shadow and flame. My ancestors communed with powers that would shatter your feeble mind, *daemon*."

The words pour out of me, a torrent of rage and determination that surprises even myself. "What is rightfully mine has slumbered too long. I will reclaim it, no matter the cost."

Silence falls, heavy and oppressive. The daemon's gaze

bores into me, peeling away layers of flesh and bone, probing the very essence of my being. I push myself to meet that terrible stare, drawing on reserves of will I didn't know I possessed. My legs tremble beneath me, a betrayal of muscles straining against exhaustion, but I refuse to show weakness. Not now. Not when I'm so close.

An eternity passes before Azrakan lowers his chin, the gesture somehow both acquiescence and challenge. "Very well, *Master of Shadows*." It spits the title like a curse. "I will share what you seek. But know this—the path ahead is paved with agony and sacrifice beyond your mortal comprehension. Are you truly prepared to pay such a price?"

My heart pounds in a frantic rhythm against my ribs. Sweat beads on my brow. Yet beneath the fear, beneath the doubt, something else stirs. The sleeping dragon inside me shifts, as if roused by the proximity of such terrible knowledge.

"I'm ready," I whisper, the words a vow and a death sentence all at once. "Whatever must be done. I will see it through."

The daemon's smile unfurls like a blooming nightshade, beautiful and lethal. My skin prickles, an instinctive warning I force myself to ignore.

"Listen well, Kaisner Drachenstein," it purrs, savoring each syllable of my name. "The key to your awakening lies in blood—not your own, but that of another. One whose veins carry power as ancient as your own."

I lean forward, pulse quickening. "Who?" The word escapes as a guttural growl, feral and hungry. "Name them, and I'll—"

"The Draken girl."

The daemon's whisper cuts through my thoughts like a blade of ice. Each word drips with malicious glee, and I feel them sink into my mind, taking root.

"Her blood is the spark to your tinder," it continues. "Claim it, and you'll rise as dragon reborn—a force to shatter empires and reshape the world in your image."

Exhilaration floods my veins, a heady rush that leaves me dizzy. Clarity hits me with the force of a thunderbolt. Clarissa Draken. The woman who's haunted my dreams, whose mere presence sets my nerves alight. All this time, she's been the key?

Unbidden, a memory surfaces:

The library at Deveraux Manor. Dust motes dancing in shafts of afternoon sunlight. And Clarissa—gods, Clarissa. Her back to me, fingers trailing reverently over ancient tomes. Unaware of the predator in her midst.

I remember the thrill of closing in, of maneuvering her into that secluded alcove. The solid press of oak shelves behind her, the heat of my body before her. A cage of flesh and wood and barely restrained desire.

Her breath catching. A blush staining porcelain cheeks. The air between us charged, crackling with possibility.

This encounter wasn't fate, but vindication. Proof that my relentless drive, my endless scheming, has been leading me toward my true destiny all along. I've been the architect of my own ascension, and Clarissa... Clarissa is the keystone I unwittingly sought.

"How?" I rasp, throat suddenly dry. "How do I take her blood? How do I use it to awaken what sleeps within me?"

Azrakan's laughter assails my senses, a discordant din that shakes the very walls and reverberates in my marrow. "That, little warlock, is your trial to face." Its eyes gleam with cruel mirth. "But heed this warning—the path ahead twists through shadow and flame. It will test your will, your resolve... your humanity."

I clench my fists, sensing the sting of reopened wounds. "I will not fail," I snarl, as much to myself as to the daemon.

The taste of copper fills my mouth—whether from biting my cheek or from the oath itself, I cannot say. "I will claim what is mine. No matter the price."

Azrakan's mirth abruptly ceases, its eyes narrowing to gleaming slits. "Ah, but there's one more thing you should know, young dragon king." Its voice drops to a whisper, forcing me to lean in despite myself. "A caveat, if you will."

Verdammt. My blood runs cold at its tone. "What caveat?" I demand, my voice rough with suppressed fury and fear.

The daemon's mouth stretches into a grotesque parody of a smile, too wide, too many teeth. "The Draken girl's blood," it hisses, "must be offered *willingly.*"

The words hit me like a physical blow. "What?" I breathe, my mind reeling.

"Oh yes," the daemon purrs, clearly relishing my shock. "You can't simply take it, can't trick her or force her hand. She must give it freely, knowing full well what it means. What it will cost her."

I stagger back, my carefully laid plans crumbling around me. "But... but that's impossible. She would never..."

The daemon's laughter starts up again, a grating sound that scrapes against my soul. "And therein lies the true test, little warlock. Not of your strength or your cunning, but of your ability to win her trust, her love. Can you do it, I wonder? Can you make her love you enough to sacrifice everything?"

Its words echo in my mind, a mocking refrain. I think of Clarissa—her fierce spirit, her kind heart, her unwavering loyalty to her family. How could I ever ask her to give that up? How could I twist her feelings for me into a weapon against her nature?

But even as these doubts assail me, another part of me— the part that has schemed and plotted for years—begins to formulate new plans. If I can't take her blood by force, I'll have to win it through other means. I'll have to make her love me so deeply, so completely, that she'll offer it willingly.

"I'll find a way," I growl, meeting the daemon's gleeful gaze with steely determination. "Clarissa Draken will be mine. And her blood will awaken the dragon within me."

Azrakan's laughter echoes through my study, a sound like breaking glass and dying dreams. "Such conviction from one whose heart wavers. I see the doubt festering in your soul, warlock. The... *morality* that still clings to you like a disease. Will you not regret this deal, I wonder?"

I straighten, my lips curling into a cruel smile. "Regret is a useless indulgence. I prefer *certainty*—every move calculated, every consequence accepted before I ever act." I lift my brow. "A moral compass? Yes, I have one. It just doesn't point north. It points to me, to power and inevitability."

As I speak the words, something fundamental shifts within me. The last vestiges of hesitation, of morality, crumble away. In their place, a singular purpose crystallizes— hard and sharp as a diamond's edge.

Clarissa. My key. My catalyst.

My sacrifice.

The daemon inclines its head, a gesture of acknowledgment and respect. "Then go forth, Kaisner Drachenstein. Embrace your destiny, and let the world tremble before the might of your awakened dragon."

With a final, bone-chilling laugh, the creature vanishes, fading back into the shadows whence it came. And I am left alone in the flickering candlelight, my heart hammering with the significance of the knowledge I have gained.

Clarissa Draken, the key to my ultimate power. The one whose blood will unlock the beast that slumbers within me, the dragon that will make me invincible.

I close my eyes, savoring the moment. A smile, sharp as a

blade's edge, tugs at my lips. Dark satisfaction courses through me, intoxicating as the finest wine.

When I open my eyes, the gravity of what comes next settles over me. Not a burden, but armor—the mantle of a conqueror about to seize his prize. My hand doesn't tremble as I reach for my phone. Each movement is deliberate, a predator coiling to strike.

The line connects. "Janik." My voice is low, a stern command. "I need Clarissa Draken's location. Now."

As my enforcer speaks, a map unfolds in my mind. Each detail, a brushstroke, painting the path to my destiny. My smile widens, wolfish and hungry.

"Excellent," I purr, plans crystallizing with every heartbeat. "Have the car ready in an hour. Ensure discretion."

The call ends. I pocket the phone, the thrum of anticipation rushing through my veins. It sings in harmony with the dormant power coiled within me, both yearning for release.

Clarissa Draken. So close now. I can almost savor the iron tang of her blood, feel the surge of primal energy it will unlock.

I move to my private chambers, each step measured and purposeful. There's preparation to be done, rituals to set in motion. As I gather what I need, I allow myself a moment of reflection. How long have I worked toward this? How many nights spent poring over ancient texts, how many deals struck in shadow?

It doesn't matter now. *Der letzte Stein ist gesetzt. Das Spiel gehört mir.* The last stone is placed. The game is mine.

I pause before the mirror, meeting my gaze. The man who stares back is transformed—eyes glittering with barely contained power, the set of his jaw speaking of iron determination. I hardly recognize him, this version of myself on the precipice of divinity.

"Soon," I whisper to my reflection, a vow and a promise. "Very soon."

With one last glance at the mirror, I turn away. It's time to claim what's mine. Time to rewrite the fabric of reality.

And gods help anyone who stands in my way.

9

CLARISSA

The morning sun gilds the Champs-Élysées, painting the Arc de Triomphe in hues of amber and gold. I should be captivated by its beauty, but my mind whirls with the phantom touch of a stranger's hands, the echo of a voice that haunts my waking hours.

I weave through the bustling crowd, my body on autopilot as my thoughts spiral. The man from Deveraux Manor. Nightmares and visions might plague my restless nights, but his face haunts my every waking moment. Those piercing dark eyes and that enigmatic smile linger on my thoughts like a persistent ghost.

I can still feel the thrill of his touch, the electric current that flowed between us when our skin met. It's a sensation I've never experienced before, a connection that both thrills and terrifies me in equal measure—I've yet to decide what to make of it.

Lost in this maelstrom of emotion, I don't notice the tall figure stepping out of a nearby café until it's too late. I collide with a solid wall of muscle; the impact steals my breath.

Strong hands grasp my arms, steadying me before I can stumble backward, and I look up—

Time stops.

It's him. Here, now, real beneath my fingertips. My heart thunders, and I struggle to form words. "We meet again," he murmurs, his voice a velvet caress that sends shivers down my spine.

His touch lingers on my arms, the warmth of his skin seeping through the thin fabric of my blouse, and the same jolt of electricity shoots through my limbs, that same inexplicable pull draws me to him like a raven to a moonlit grave.

I search his face, desperately, my gift straining for any glimpse of his past, his future. But as before, there's nothing —a void where visions should be. It unnerves me, this blankness. Who is he, that he can resist my Sight? What power does he hold?

"Do you believe in fate, baby girl?" he asks, dark eyes boring into mine. "Or is this merely yet another chance encounter?"

The world fades around us, leaving only this moment, this connection.

"A chance encounter can change the course of a lifetime," I hear myself say, the words rising unbidden from some deep, hidden part of me.

A gleam of satisfaction dances in his eyes, the corners of his mouth curling into a smile that is both dangerous and alluring. "Allow me to introduce myself. Kaisner Drachenstein."

The name strikes a chord, stirring half-forgotten memories of whispered legends. "Drachenstein..." Another dragon clan, as ancient and powerful as my own. It explains his presence at the manor, the aura of authority that clings to him like a second skin.

Suddenly, I'm achingly aware of his hand still holding

mine, our fingers intertwined. Heat blooms in my cheeks, embarrassment laced with... something else. Something primal that makes my pulse quicken.

"And you are Clarissa Draken," he continues, his words a silken net drawing me closer. "The enchanting young witch who has captured the attention of more than one powerful family."

I drop my gaze, gently withdrawing my hand. "I don't know about that," I breathe. "I'm just trying to find my way in this world, like everyone else." The words taste hollow, even as I say them. Part of me preens under his attention, while another part screams caution. What does he want from me? And why, despite my better judgment, do I sense this inexorable pull toward him?

His finger tilts my chin up, and I shiver at the contact. "Don't sell yourself short, Liebling," he murmurs, his breath warm against my skin. "You are a rare and precious thing, a true daughter of the Craft. And I have a feeling that our meeting here, in this moment, is no accident."

My mouth goes dry. "What do you mean?" I manage to whisper, barely hearing my voice over the pounding of my heart.

His smile is slow, promising secrets beyond imagining. "I think you know, deep down, that there is a connection between us. Something that draws us together, even in the midst of this bustling city."

His words wrap around me like a spell, and I realize with a start that I'm hopelessly in his thrall. Any thought of escape seems futile, maybe even undesirable.

A flicker of regret crosses his face as he glances at his watch. "But... I'm afraid I must let you go, for now. I wouldn't want to make you late for work."

Reality crashes back. Work. Responsibilities. The

mundane world I inhabit. "Oh, yes. Of course," I stammer, heat rushing to my cheeks. "I should be going."

Before I can step away, he leans close, his breath tickling my ear. "Let me give you a ride. It's the least I can do after keeping you from your duties."

My heart leaps. The thought of being alone with him, confined in a car, sends a thrill of excitement and fear coursing through me. Even as my rational mind screams warnings, I find myself nodding. "Thank you," I manage, slightly breathless. "That would be lovely."

His smile flashes, quicksilver and dangerous. Kaisner offers his arm, and I take it, feeling the firm muscles beneath expensive fabric. A tingle runs through me at the contact as he leads me to a sleek Aston Martin, its obsidian curves gleaming in the morning light.

The ride to the gallery is a blur of stolen glances and charged silence, the air between us heavy with unspoken words and possibilities. I try to focus on the passing scenery, on the familiar streets and landmarks that have become my anchor in this city, but I find my thoughts constantly drawn back to the man beside me, to the heat of his body and the deliciously intoxicating scent of his cologne.

All too soon, we arrive. Kaisner steps out, moving with predatory grace, and opens my door. As he helps me onto the sidewalk, disappointment washes over me. I don't want this to end.

"Until next time, Clarissa," he says, his voice a promise that shoots a thrill through my core. "I look forward to our next chance encounter."

With a final, lingering glance, he slips back into the car and drives away, leaving me standing there on the curb, my heart racing and my mind reeling.

10

CLARISSA

The silhouette of Galerie Lumière rises before me, sunlight dancing across its carved stone and wrought-iron balconies. I pause on the sidewalk, taking in the grandeur of the Haussmann building. It feels like a familiar coat settling over my shoulders, reminding me how much has changed.

Weeks ago, I was buried in Oxford's cloistered stillness, tucked away in dim libraries and brittle silence, my ties to the Draken name reduced to ceremonial holidays and stilted messages from Bram. England had been safe, yes, but stifling. A hiding place. A cage lined with books.

Everything changed when Nik became alpha. His summons arrived—terse, unexpected, impossible to ignore. It cut through the distance like a blade. When I stepped back into our ancestral hall, he didn't blame me for the distance. He didn't mention the fact that I'd been exiled, not by choice but by Bram's decree. He only said, "Welcome home." And just like that, something inside me shifted.

The scent of lemon-scented polish and aged canvas envelops me as I step into the marble-floored foyer. Any other day, this would snap me into work mode. But not today.

Today, the comforting halls of my family's art gallery fail to ground me. Each step seems dreamlike, like I'm floating rather than walking. I cannot deny it. My encounter with Kaisner Drachenstein haunts me; his intoxicating scent, husky voice, and thrilling touch are imprinted on me.

I nod absently to Marie, our receptionist, as I pass her desk. She gives me a quizzical look, no doubt noticing my distracted state, but I can't bring myself to care.

A message from Nik pings on my phone. He's in Brussels now, having secured tentative alliances with the Nordic clans. "Stockholm and Oslo were a success… The Belgian dragons are a tough crowd, though," he writes. "But I'm making headway. Next stop: Madrid."

"Madrid?" A brief smile tugs at my lips. I can't help heaving a sigh. Nik is working hard to lift our clan to its former glory. For that alone, I'll do my part.

But as I reach my office, it's not Nik on my mind—it's Kaisner. The way his gaze pierced through me, as if he'd already mapped out every secret I'd never confessed. I grip the door handle, inhale once, and try to will myself back to normal.

I fail.

Inside, the mundane waits: stacks of files, the soft hum of the air conditioning, an envelope on my desk bearing the crimson seal of the Palais Garnier.

I sink into my chair, fingers absently tracing the smooth mahogany surface. With a sigh, I reach for the letter. *Work*, I tell myself. *Focus on work.*

Carefully breaking the seal, I pull out an embossed invitation.

My eyes widen as I read—a performance of *La Vestale*, in honor of the Draken family's long-standing patronage of the arts. But it's the next line that makes the blood freeze in my veins: In Nikolaas' absence, I'm expected to attend, representing our clan.

Another detail leaps out at me as I continue reading. The invitation proudly announces:

We are honored to feature the world-renowned soprano, Aria Leone, direct descendant of the legendary Letizia Leone, in the lead role.

My pulse quickens. Aria Leone's voice is said to be otherworldly. Her presence adds an extra layer of prestige—and mystery—to the event.

The realization dawns on me, bringing both pride and trepidation. This isn't just any social affair, but a stage where the intricate dance of supernatural politics plays out beneath a veneer of cultural appreciation. What alliances might be forged or broken in the gilded halls of the opera house? What secrets might be whispered behind ornate fans and crystal champagne flutes?

And, unbidden, a thought surfaces. Will Kaisner be there?

I close my eyes and exhale slowly, as if I could expel the distracting thoughts along with my breath. Despite my efforts, Kaisner's enigmatic smile dances behind my eyelids, the phantom pressure of his hand in mine sending a shiver down my spine.

A soft rustle breaks through my reverie. My eyes snap open, heart leaping into my throat.

I'm not alone.

Someone reclines in the plush armchair across from my desk, one eyebrow arched in silent inquiry.

"Earth to Clarissa," Samara says, amused. "You look like

you've seen a ghost... or maybe something far more interesting?"

Heat rises to my cheeks. I stammer, rising fast. "Sam! I didn't realize—sorry, I've just had a... strange morning."

Samara's eyes narrow slightly, her gaze sharp and assessing. I can almost see the gears turning in her head, piecing together my disheveled state, my lateness, my distraction. "Strange, huh?" she says, leaning forward. "Do tell."

I hesitate. But this is Sam. My friend. My brother's mate. The one person I might actually trust with this storm.

I sink into the chair beside her, letting out a long breath. Suddenly, I'm desperate to share this burden.

"There was a man," I begin slowly. "At Deveraux Manor. I didn't tell you before because... I didn't think it would matter. But then I saw him again. This morning."

Her interest sharpens instantly.

"There's something about him, Sam," I whisper. "Something that draws me in and terrifies me at the same time. It's like... like he sees right through me. And I can't see anything about him. My gift, it just... doesn't work on him."

Samara's eyes widen at this. She knows how rare it is for my Sight to falter, even in its unripened stage. "Now you've got my full attention. Who is this mystery man?"

I inhale deeply, steeling myself. "Kaisner Drachenstein. And Sam... I think I'm way over my head."

As soon as the name leaves my lips, the atmosphere in the room shifts. Samara's face drains of color so quickly that for a moment, I fear she might faint.

"Kaisner Drachenstein?" she repeats, her voice low and hesitant. She leans forward, gripping the arms of her chair so tightly her knuckles turn white. "Clarissa, do you have any idea who that is?"

Her phone lights up on the desk between us, the screen

flashing with multiple missed calls from Nik. Six in the last ten minutes.

Sam glances at it nervously. "I should take this," she says, her tone tight. "It might be important."

She answers quickly, stepping toward the window. "Nik? Yes, I'm safe... What?" Her voice drops to barely above a whisper, but I catch fragments: "...the grimoire... her study..."

I pretend to focus on the opera invitation, but my enhanced hearing picks up more than I should. Nik's voice carries through the phone, urgent and commanding.

"Listen, I can't discuss this now," Sam says finally, casting a nervous glance my way. "We'll talk tonight."

She hangs up and returns to her chair, but something has shifted. The easy intimacy between us feels strained, charged with whatever secret just passed between her and my brother.

"Everything okay?" I ask carefully.

"Of course," she says too quickly, then seems to catch herself. "You know how dragons are, possessive by nature—a tad controlling, too. Nik's always been... intense. Especially lately." She draws a breath, clearly trying to refocus. "But enough about that. Kaisner Drachenstein?" Her voice returns to its warning pitch. "Clarissa, do you realize what you're tangled up in?"

I shake my head slowly. "I... I know he's from another dragon clan," I stammer, suddenly realizing I'm missing something crucial.

"Kaisner Drachenstein isn't just *a guy* from another dragon family." She pauses. "He's the king of his clan—the king of *all* the dragon clans in Germany and Eastern Europe. A Master of the Dark Arts, a warlock of formidable power and... questionable morals."

"Questionable morals?" I echo with a frown. "What do you mean?"

"Oh boy," she says under her breath. "Where to begin?" Sam scratches her temple as her gaze drifts away. When her eyes find mine again, she continues. "Kaisner knows no authority but his own. He'll cross lines others wouldn't dare approach—forbidden magic, dangerous alliances, whatever it takes to get what he wants. The magical community whispers about rituals that should have been buried centuries ago, about entities he's summoned that most wouldn't even speak of. He doesn't just break the rules, Clarissa... He *burns* them."

A chill runs down my spine. "But the man I met..." I trail off, confusion knotting in my chest. "He was magnetic, yes, but there was kindness there too. Gentleness, even. How can that be the same person?"

"That's part of what makes him so dangerous," Sam whispers, reaching out to take my hand. "Nik's mentioned him before. He disapproves of everything Kaisner represents. Says he's the worst kind of leader—all raw power and unpredictability. Kaisner Drachenstein rules through fear and force, not the honor and tradition our kin respects."

Her fingers tense slightly around mine.

"Clarissa, listen to me. Kaisner is not someone to be trifled with. If he's taken an interest in you... well, it can't be for anything good."

I swallow hard, my mind racing. The memory of Kaisner's touch, his intense gaze, takes on a sinister edge in light of this new information. "What should I do?" I ask, hating how small my voice sounds.

Sam squeezes my hand. "For now? Keep your distance. Don't engage with him if you can help it. And Clarissa?" She waits until I meet her eyes. "Promise me you'll be careful. There's no telling what someone like Kaisner might be capable of."

I nod, trying to ignore the part of me that still thrills at the memory of our encounter. "I promise," I say, hoping I sound more convinced than I feel.

The sharp edge of her concern softens, and I notice a shift in her expression—a different kind of worry settling in her eyes, one she's striving to hide from me.

"There's something else troubling you, isn't there?" I ask gently, recognizing that look. "Is it the situation with Cassandra? This mysterious meeting is getting to me, too. I can't shake the feeling there's more to it."

"Yes, Cassandra's been acting strangely lately," Sam admits, her fingers intertwining with mine. But a certain guardedness still seems present in her expression.

"It's something else, though. Isn't it?" I press, trusting my gut.

Sam hesitates, choosing her words carefully. "It's just... with Nik away on this tour, I can see how much it's changing him. The responsibility, the pressure to prove himself worthy." Her voice drops, quieter now. "Dragons weren't meant to carry that kind of burden alone."

"He's not alone," I remind her gently, squeezing her hand. "He has *you*. And that makes him stronger than any clan ever could."

Samara's features soften. Her gaze drifts to the photo on my desk—the three of us at my birthday party, Nik's arms around both Sam and me, all of us laughing and carefree.

"Gods, I miss him," she murmurs, the words escaping like breath pressed from a wound. More than longing— mourning. "Not just being apart... I mean, I miss *him*. The way he used to be. Before his dragon's awakening."

Her voice falters. She turns slightly, as if the photo's weight is too much to bear.

"You know," she adds quietly, "it's not easy, being in love with the enemy."

She catches herself then, lips parting as regret flashes

across her face. The slip hangs between us, heavy and unresolved.

I nod reassuringly, my heart aching for them both. Their path is fraught with obstacles, but the love shining in Samara's gaze speaks volumes. "You two are proof that love can conquer all barriers," I say fiercely. "And you have my support, always. When the time comes, it will be an honor to call you not just my sister, but my queen."

Sam's head snaps up, eyes wide. "Queen?" she repeats, confusion etched on her face. "Nik is the Draken alpha... I don't think 'queen' is the term you're looking for." She shrugs with a shy smile.

I freeze, realizing too late my misstep. "Hasn't he told you?" I ask hesitantly, stomach twisting. "Nik intends to gather all the dragon families and unite them under a single banner."

"The... *Draken's* banner," Sam says slowly, understanding dawning.

I nod, swallowing hard. "That's why he left on tour. He will proclaim himself King of the Dragons. So, technically..."

"That would make me..." Samara murmurs, stunned. "At some point..."

"Our queen," I finish softly. "The queen of *all* dragon shifter clans."

We sit quietly, the magnitude of it all sinking in.

I curse myself silently, knowing I've spoken out of turn. "I shouldn't have said anything," I admit, panic rising. "Nik will be furious. He's a planner. I'm sure he had a strategy in place to break the news to you slowly—dammit!"

Samara shakes her head, gripping my hand. "Don't worry. I won't tell," she assures me, her voice steady despite the shock in her eyes. "Nobody must know about this until the time is right—*especially* not my brothers. Things are crazy complicated as it is."

Relief washes over me. "Yes, of course!" I breathe, pulling her into a tight hug.

As we embrace, Samara whispers, "This world we live in can be so cruel at times. We need to stick together, you and I. No secrets between us."

I silently agree, my heart swelling with love and determination. A fierce protectiveness surges through my veins—for Sam, for Nik, for the future we're building. "Always," I whisper, and I mean it with every fiber of my being.

We part briefly. I'm about to say more when a sharp knock echoes through the office. Both of us freeze, the moment shattered as our eyes snap toward the door.

11

CLARISSA

Our eyes fix on the door, and my breath catches. The traitorous part of my mind conjures an image of Kaisner on the other side—those dark eyes, that predatory grace, the dark pull of him that I can't seem to shake, no matter how many warnings Sam gives me.

"Come in," I call, forcing my voice steady. I exchange a brief glance with Sam, silently agreeing to keep our conversation under wraps.

The door swings open, revealing Marie, my personal assistant. Her usually impeccable appearance is slightly disheveled, a few strands of hair escaping her tight bun. "I'm sorry to interrupt, Miss Draken. Your eleven o'clock is here. I forgot to remind you earlier, what with all the chaos from the gala preparations and—"

I hold up a hand. "It's all right, Marie. Thank you." I try to recall the appointment but come up blank, my mind still racing with thoughts of Kaisner, Nikolaas' grand plans, and the looming gala—my first solo event since taking over the gallery board.

Sam rises, smoothing her skirt. "I should go," she murmurs, her eyes meeting mine with understanding. "We'll catch up soon, yeah? Grab dinner this week?"

"Absolutely," I reply, grateful for her discretion.

As Samara makes her way to the door, she pauses, turning back to face me. With a final wink, she's gone, leaving me to tackle this mysterious appointment alone.

I take a deep breath. "Send them in, please," I say, straightening my posture and schooling my features into a mask of calm confidence.

The figure who enters is not what I expected. She is tall and otherworldly, with porcelain skin that seems to shimmer, as if lit from within. Her hair cascades like liquid moonlight —long, straight, and so pale it verges on silver, flowing effortlessly to her waist. But it's her eyes—swirling pools of blue and green, like the northern lights—that captivate me, pulling me into their depths.

Not human.

The air bends around her, shimmering, as if reality itself yields to accommodate her presence. "Clarissa Draken," she whispers, her voice caressing my soul. "I've been looking forward to meeting you."

I stand, extending my hand. "I don't recall scheduling this meeting. Miss…?"

"Niamh Mordain," she says, taking my hand. Her touch is cool, electric. "We have no formal appointment. Some meetings are *written in the stars* before they appear on calendars." She tilts her head, throwing me a knowing look, as if I'm meant to understand the meaning of those words.

Well, I don't.

I blink, momentarily stunned. "Please, take a seat. How can I help you, Miss Mordain?"

Niamh glides into the chair Samara just vacated, her

movements impossibly fluid. "Oh, my dear. I'm not here for help," she says, her kaleidoscope eyes twinkling. "I'm here to *offer* it."

I narrow my eyes, confused. "I'm afraid I do not follow."

She leans forward, her gaze intense. "Clarissa, you stand at a crossroads. The choices before you will ripple through the supernatural world for generations. A guide's counsel might ease the way."

My heart races. "Who are you?"

Niamh laughs, a sound like crystal bells. "I am many things. A keeper of secrets, a weaver of fates, a guardian of forgotten knowledge."

Her fingers sweep a strand of silken hair behind her ear. The movement is casual, almost absentminded, but it reveals a subtle point. It's not pronounced enough to be noticed at first glance, but now that I've seen it, I can't *unsee* it.

"Some call us fae," she continues. "Others, the sidhe. But labels matter little in the grand tapestry of existence."

I lean back, overwhelmed. The fae. Creatures of legend. Proud beings of immense power and inscrutable motives. And one is sitting in my office, offering her help.

"Why now?" I ask. "Why me?"

Her expression darkens. "The balance is shifting. Old powers stir," she says cryptically. "Your brother's ambitions, noble as they may be, have set in motion events that could lead many to greatness... or to ruin."

My throat tightens. "You know about his plans?"

"I know many things," she replies, a sad smile playing at her lips. "The unification of the dragon clans is but one thread. But it is a crucial one, and you... You are the lynchpin upon which much depends."

"Me?" I shake my head in disbelief. "But I'm not... I mean, Nikolaas is the one with the power, the one making the big moves. I'm just—"

"Just the seer whose visions might shape our future?" Niamh interrupts gently. "Just the sister whose love and support give Nikolaas the strength to pursue his dreams? Just the friend whose counsel could sway the course of history?" She inches closer, her gaze boring into mine. "Do not underestimate your importance, Clarissa Draken. *In the game of fate, even the smallest piece can topple kings.*"

I close my eyes, steadying myself. "All right. You said you're here to offer help. What kind?"

Niamh's smile widens. "Knowledge, my dear. For in these times, information is power." She reaches into her dress and produces a small, carved wooden box. "Are you familiar with Shakespeare and Company?"

"The bookstore?" I ask, puzzled.

"Like much in the human world, it's more than it seems." She opens the box, revealing a small gold key. "There's a secret passage hidden within its shelves—a repository of knowledge, both wondrous and terrible."

I freeze, staring at the key. "A secret section? I've never heard of such a thing."

"Few have," Niamh says, her tone conspiratorial. "This knowledge is closely guarded, known only to a select few in each generation. The entrance is concealed by formidable spells, invisible to mortal eyes and undetectable, even to most supernaturals."

She lifts the key from its velvet nest, holding it out to me. In the soft light of my office, it seems to glow with an inner fire, the metal warm to the touch as I take it from her.

"This will grant you access," Niamh explains. "But be warned, Clarissa. The knowledge contained within those hidden shelves is not for the faint of heart. Truths that could shake the foundations of your world, secrets that could topple empires or forge new ones... Are you prepared for such responsibility?"

I take the key, feeling its weight—both literal and metaphorical. "I don't know," I whisper. "But I must try. If what you say is true, if I really am as important as you claim... I can't just ignore this."

Niamh nods. "Wisdom begins with acknowledging what we don't know. You show promise, Clarissa Draken." She stands, graceful as ever. "Choose your moment carefully. Knowledge wields great power, but it can both illuminate and obscure, free or enchain. How you employ that power... that choice rests squarely on your shoulders."

She moves toward the door, and I rise, a thousand questions burning on my tongue. But before I can speak any of them, Niamh turns back, fixing me with one last, penetrating gaze.

"Oh, and Clarissa?" Her voice is soft, but it carries an undercurrent of steel. *"Be wary of the dragon who seeks to awaken."*

With that, she's gone.

I sink into my chair, my mind swirling. A fae, a hidden passage, Niamh's warnings—it's all too fantastical to be true, and yet... the key rests heavy in my hand, solid and undeniable. What secrets does it hold? Could they aid Nikolaas—or stop him entirely?

Nikolaas' plans for unification suddenly seem small compared to the vastness of what I might discover. And yet, I can't help but wonder if there might be anything there that could assist him—or prevent him from unforeseen dangers.

And then there's the dragon Niamh warned me about. Could she have meant Kaisner? The timing seems too coincidental to ignore. But what did she mean by "seeks to awaken"? Awaken what?

I groan and shut my eyes. Somehow, I've been thrust into the center of events far larger than myself, armed with access to knowledge beyond my wildest dreams and burdened with warnings of dangers I don't yet understand.

Part of me wants to stow this key away, to pretend this morning never happened, and go back to my normal life. But I know that's not an option. Not anymore. Whatever is coming, whatever role I'm meant to play in the events unfolding around me, I can't face it unprepared.

12

CLARISSA

The afternoon sun casts long shadows across the cobblestone streets of the Latin Quarter as I approach Shakespeare and Company. My heart races with excitement and apprehension, burdened by the heaviness of Niamh's key in my pocket. The bookstore's weathered façade looks as it always has—quaint, inviting, utterly ordinary. It's hard to believe a secret that could change everything lies behind these walls.

I push open the creaky wooden door, the scent of old books and fresh ink enveloping me like a comforting blanket. For a moment, I'm transported back to countless afternoons spent browsing these very shelves, losing myself in worlds of fiction and poetry. But today, I'm here for something far more extraordinary.

My eyes scan the cramped interior, searching for... what, exactly? A hidden lever? A magical symbol? I realize with a start that I have no idea how to access this secret section. Niamh's instructions were frustratingly vague.

I wander through the maze-like aisles, my fingers trailing

along the spines of books, feeling foolish and out of place. Suddenly, the worn red steps beckon, a crimson invitation up to the store's legendary second floor. Each step creaks beneath my weight, a wooden whisper of countless stories—visitors, readers, dreamers who have climbed this same path before me.

Something tugs at me—a subtle, insistent pull that goes beyond mere curiosity. I'm not climbing these stairs so much as being *guided*, each step feeling less like a choice and more like a predetermined path.

As I reach the top, the space opens into a world both familiar and strange—shelves pressed close, books stacked in precarious towers, soft light filtering through dusty windows.

The fae are mischievous creatures. What if this is all some elaborate prank? What if—?

My thoughts screech to a halt as my hand brushes against something that feels... different. I pause, backtrack a few steps. There, nestled between a worn copy of *The Tempest* and a pristine edition of *A Midsummer Night's Dream*, is a book that seems to shimmer ever so slightly when I look at it from the corner of my eye.

Heart racing, I reach for it. As my fingers make contact, I sense a subtle vibration, like the hum of distant machinery. Instinctively, I know this is it.

I glance around, making sure no one is watching, then pull the book. Instead of coming off the shelf, it tilts backward with a soft click. The entire bookcase swings inward, revealing a hidden door.

For a moment, I stand frozen, awe and disbelief warring within me. Then, with trembling hands, I reach for the key in my pocket. It slides into the lock as if made for it, turning smoothly.

The door swings open, and I step through, half-expecting

to find myself in some fantastical realm. Instead, I'm greeted by what appears to be a simple extension of the bookshop—quiet, cozy, lined with shelves upon shelves of ancient-looking tomes.

At the center of the room stands a large, ornate desk. Behind it sits a man, his head bent low over a stack of books, a quill moving swiftly across parchment as he catalogs. His hair is a mane of chestnut waves, falling past his shoulders. Even from this distance, I can see the sharp angles of his face, the golden tan of his skin. There's something almost... feline about his features.

I approach hesitantly, clearing my throat. "Excuse me," I begin, my voice sounding unnaturally loud in the hushed space. "I was wondering if you could direct me to the, um, *travel* section?"

The man looks up, and I have to stifle a gasp. His eyes are a startling amber, with vertical pupils that contract as they focus on me. But it's his mouth that truly gives me pause—as he parts his lips to speak, I catch a glimpse of keen fangs.

"Travel section?" he echoes, his voice a low growl. "This isn't some mundane tourist trap, girly. What are you *really* here for?"

As he speaks, I notice his ears—pointed like Niamh's, though he lacks her ethereal grace. The sharp tips peek through his hair, marking him as fae despite his gruff demeanor.

I swallow hard, thrown off balance by his curt manner. "I... I'm not sure, exactly. I was given a key, told there was knowledge here that I needed to find."

He snorts, a sound somewhere between amusement and disdain. "Of course you were. Let me guess—divination? Prophecy? That sort of thing?"

My eyes widen in surprise. "How did you know?"

His nostrils flare slightly as he inhales. "You're a witch," he states matter-of-factly. "One of them seers. I can scent your type a mile away." He jerks his thumb toward a section off to the right. "Third aisle, second shelf from the top. Don't touch anything you're not prepared to understand. And anything you read must never cross your lips—*especially* on the other side."

With that, he returns to his work, effectively dismissing me. I stand there for a moment, processing his brusque manner. Then, shaking off my stupor, I go to the indicated section.

As I round the corner of the third aisle, I stop short, my breath catching in my throat. The shelves here seem to melt away, giving way to a small clearing surrounded by towering trees. Their branches intertwine overhead, creating a canopy that filters the light into dappled patterns on the forest floor.

I blink rapidly, trying to make sense of what I'm seeing. This can't be real—we're in the middle of Paris, for heaven's sake! And yet... the scent of loam and wildflowers fills my nostrils, a gentle breeze rustles the leaves overhead, and I can hear the distant trill of birdsong.

In the center of the clearing stands a single pedestal upon which rests an ancient, leather-bound tome. Its cover, a deep midnight blue. As if in a trance, I approach it, my fingers reaching out to trace the embossed golden letters: "Book of Vaelmir: A Volume For Seers Only."

The moment I touch the book, the world appears to shift around me. The symbols beneath the title begin to glow softly, pulsing with a rhythm that matches my heartbeat. The colors of the surrounding forest become more vivid, the sounds sharper. I have the dizzying sensation of standing on the edge of a great precipice, poised between two worlds.

With shaking hands, I lift the Book of Vaelmir from its resting place. It's surprisingly light, yet I can feel the immense power contained within its pages. As I open the cover, a soft whisper of ancient magic caresses my skin, and I know, with absolute certainty, that this book was meant for me to find.

I take a deep breath, steeling myself for what I might discover.

The first page bears an inscription in flowing script: *"To those blessed with the Sight, may this book illuminate the paths of destiny."*

The rest of the pages are filled with intricate diagrams, elegant script in languages I've never seen before, and illustrations that seem to move when I'm not looking directly at them. But as I focus on the text, something extraordinary happens.

The symbols on the page start to shift and dance, coalescing into images that bypass my eyes and form directly in my mind. It's as if the Book of Vaelmir is communicating with me on a level beyond mere sight or language. Scenes play out in my thoughts—visions of past events I couldn't possibly have witnessed, glimpses of potential futures that take my breath away.

I see great gatherings of supernatural beings, their forms shimmering and shifting. I witness battles waged with magic so potent it warps the very fabric of reality. Amidst these scenes, flashes of the Shadow Wars emerge—moments from the ancient conflict that reshaped the supernatural world centuries before my time. The images are fragmented, but I can sense the overwhelming forces at play, the relentless struggle between light and darkness that threatened to tear reality apart.

And through it all, I sense a thread of destiny, a path that seems to lead inexorably to... *me.*

The symbols reform, showing me the intricate web of connections between all supernatural beings. I see how the actions of one can ripple outward, affecting the fates of many. And I begin to understand the unique role of seers in this cosmic dance—we are the watchers, the interpreters, the possible tipping point in the balance of power.

As I delve deeper into the Book of Vaelmir, the scenes grow more vivid, becoming intimately personal. I glimpse days yet to come, the myriad paths I could take, and the consequences that follow. And always, at the center of these visions, is Kaisner.

Our potential relationship unfolds in a whirlwind of possibilities. In one future, our love is a guiding force; in another, it becomes a catalyst for chaos and ruin. What strikes me most is the lack of certainty—each vision a branch on a vast, intricate tree of choices still waiting to be made.

I see how a single decision can send ripples through time, reshaping not only our lives but the fate of the world itself. How can I navigate this tangled web of futures and ensure that I make the right choices for us all?

When I finally lift my head from the pages, the magical clearing has been swallowed by darkness. The gentle afternoon light that warmed my face when I began reading has vanished, replaced by the silver gleam of moonlight through the canopy. An owl hoots somewhere in the distance, answered by the rustling of nocturnal creatures stirring to life. The air carries the cool dampness of evening, and I shiver, realizing that hours have slipped away like water through my fingers.

The visions fade, leaving behind a residue of understanding that I know will take weeks, perhaps months, to fully process. But one thing is clear: the world is far more complex and dangerous than I ever imagined, and my role in the coming events may be more crucial than I ever dared to dream.

With reluctance—and no small amount of relief—I close the book. The burden of what I've learned settles over me like a headstone. I know now that I can never unknow these things, never go back to the person I was before I opened this tome.

I quicken my pace as I return, and when I finally step out of the hidden section, I almost collide with the library keeper. Leaning against a bookshelf, arms crossed, his unsettling amber eyes lock onto me with an intensity that sends a shiver down my spine.

"Found what you were looking for?" he asks, his tone dripping with sarcasm. His gaze sweeps over me, taking in my disheveled appearance.

I swallow hard, trying to compose myself. "Yes. I… I think so."

He snorts, a sound caught between amusement and disdain. "You look like you've seen a ghost, girly… Or perhaps something far worse." He pushes off from the shelf, moving toward me with a predator's grace.

"You have a gift for me," he purrs, hand open and waiting.

I freeze, transfixed by his fiendish smirk.

"A key?" he presses, his patience fraying at the edges.

"Oh!" The sound escapes me like a startled breath. I set the ornate item on his palm, my fingers trembling slightly as our skin briefly touches.

"Remember," he continues as he slips the key into his pocket, his voice a low, dangerous whisper, "the secrets of this place stay within these walls. We don't need another Salem on our hands."

I nod numbly. "I understand."

"Good," he says, his fangs glinting in the low light as he speaks. "Off with you, then."

I hurry past him, my heart thundering against my ribs like a caged bird desperate for escape.

As I step through the hidden door and back into the familiar confines of Shakespeare and Company, the bookstore's musty warmth envelops me. The world around me looks the same, the well-worn shelves and quiet corners unchanged, and yet... everything is fundamentally different now.

How long was I in there? It felt like hours, but the clock on the wall suggests it's been barely twenty minutes.

13

KAISNER

The Parisian evening air bites with January's fierce chill as I make my way down the narrow streets of the Latin Quarter. My breath forms small clouds in front of me, dissipating in the crisp winter breeze. My pace is unhurried, casual to any observer, but my senses are on high alert. The text from my informant burns in my mind: *Clarissa Draken, spotted entering Shakespeare & Company not twenty minutes ago.*

A smirk tugs at the corner of my mouth. Of all the places in Paris, she chooses to wander here? Intriguing. This isn't just any bookshop—whispers in the darker corners of our world speak of hidden aisles, secret sections accessible only to those with... particular talents. Talents that have, frustratingly, eluded even me thus far.

As I approach the bookstore's weathered façade, my mind races with possibilities. Could Clarissa have inadvertently uncovered a buried truth? Or is she, perhaps, more than she appears? The seer gifts of the Draken line are well known, but this... this could be something else entirely.

I pause for an instant, allowing my senses to extend

beyond the physical. Despite the winter's chill, the air surrounding the bookshop shimmers with an energy most humans would never perceive—ley lines converging, ancient magics woven into the very foundations of the building. It's subtle, masterfully concealed, but to one such as myself, it's as clear as a beacon.

My fingers flex involuntarily, power thrumming just beneath my skin. How many times have I tried to breach these mystical defenses, to access the knowledge rumored to be hidden within? And now, Clarissa Draken may have accomplished what I could not.

Admiration and jealousy coil in my chest. She continues to surprise me, this enigmatic woman who has captured my attention so thoroughly. Part of me wants to rush in, to demand answers, to unleash the full force of my considerable charms and powers to uncover her secrets.

But no. Patience has always been my greatest weapon. I've waited too long for the right moment to claim my true power; I can wait a bit more to unravel the mystery that is Clarissa Draken.

With a deep breath, I compose my features into a mask of casual interest. Just another customer, drawn in by the allure of old books and quiet corners. Nothing more.

I slip through the dark green door of Shakespeare & Company, the scent of aging paper and oak immediately enveloping me. My eyes scan the cramped, book-lined rooms, but she's not in the front alcove. Not on the ground floor.

The red stairs call to me, each step deliberate, predatory. I know exactly where she'll be. The second level. That sanctuary of forgotten knowledge, of books that whisper secrets to those who know how to listen. My hand trails along the wooden banister, sensing the accumulated stories of countless visitors.

The upper floor opens before me, a labyrinth of precarious book towers and soft, filtered light. And there—amid the shelves, her silhouette both familiar and alluring—Clarissa stands, lost in the landscape of books.

For a moment, I allow myself to simply observe her. The graceful curve of her neck as she tilts her head to read titles, the way the subdued lighting catches the blonde highlights in her hair. But it's more than her physical beauty that draws me. There's an energy about her, a barely contained power that calls to a primal side within me.

I move through the crowded shop, weaving between oblivious patrons with supernatural grace. As I draw closer to Clarissa, I catch a whiff of her scent—jasmine and sunshine, undercut with something vibrant, almost ozone-like. My nostrils flare, drinking it in.

She's different. *Changed,* somehow, since our last encounter. An electric tension radiates from her, charged with fresh understanding, and... is that a hint of fear?

My curiosity burns even brighter. What has she discovered in this innocuous-seeming bookshop? What secrets now dance behind those captivating eyes?

Only one way to find out.

"Fancy meeting you here, *meine Kleine,*" I purr, allowing my true nature to tinge my voice.

Clarissa startles at the sound, those luminous sapphire orbs going wide as they meet mine. Rosy color blooms in her cheeks—surprise, recognition, something more I can't quite read. My heart thunders at the sight of her softly parted lips.

"You..." she breathes out, and the single whispered word caresses me like a tender touch. "What are you doing here?" A subtle curve of her mouth betrays her quiet delight.

A slow, calculated smile spreads across my features. "The same as you, it would seem. Getting delightfully lost within these literary landscapes."

Her delicate brow furrows ever so slightly. "How did you know I'd be here?"

"A lucky happenstance, I assure you." The lie slips easily from my tongue as I take one deliberate step closer, narrowing the distance between us. Close enough to inhale the soft, floral scent that is uniquely, intoxicatingly, her.

"Although..." I add, tilting near. "I suppose one could also say you seem to have a penchant for appearing wherever I happen to be."

I let the suggestion linger, watching in delight as Clarissa's eyes widen further and that enchanting blush deepens. She looks utterly captivating when flustered.

"I... I don't know what you mean," she stammers, clutching the book in her hands like a lifeline. "This is just my favorite place to browse old tomes."

Her attempt at recovering her composure is as endearing as it is fruitless. I take another step, invading her personal space in a way that's toeing the line of propriety. Near enough to catch the ragged edge of her breath, to witness the pulse fluttering wildly at the base of her elegant throat.

"It seems more than mere coincidence, don't you think? Three times now our paths have... crossed," I murmur, pitching my voice low, so she has no choice but to instinctively lean in.

I allow the implication to hang heavy in the charged air. But I know this is no accident, no twist of fate—rather a grand design of my own careful machinations.

"Perhaps," I continue in that same rumbling tone, "*you're the one* conspiring to cross my path, *Liebste*." I'm quick to amend my boldness with, "And if so, I offer my complete and unreserved approval."

Her lips part on a tremulous inhale, those expressive eyes searching mine. I glimpse the tumult of thoughts and feelings playing out across her features—confusion, intrigue, an unmistakable spark of interest she's struggling to smother.

The thrill of rendering her so exquisitely unsettled causes my heart to pound. I've landed the bait; now to see if she has the courage to bite.

"Forgive me, chère Clarissa." A low, rich laugh rumbles from my chest. "I don't mean to fluster you so. Clearly, the secluded ambiance of this charming bookshop has me feeling... conspiratorial."

I gesture lazily at our surroundings—the towering, vertiginous shelves laden with books, the low slanted ceilings with crisscrossing beams, the lingering smell of aged parchment and secrets.

"Though I must admit, there's something delightfully clandestine about crossing paths with a beautiful woman in a place steeped in so much history and romantic intrigue, *non*?" I lift a brow, the gesture laden with unspoken meaning.

She regains her composure, straightening her shoulders as she tries to appear unaffected by my flirtatious insinuation. But the pretty stain still lingers becomingly in her countenance.

"While I appreciate your... flair for the dramatic, monsieur," she speaks with delicate restraint, "I'm afraid there's no grand conspiracy nor mystery here. Just two literature lovers finding themselves in the same place by chance."

"Is that so?" I counter with silken smoothness, annihilating the remaining space between us. "If that is the case, then allow me to make the most of this spontaneous encounter, mademoiselle."

Plucking the well-worn copy of *Romeo and Juliette* from her hands, I set it back on the shelf behind her in one fluid motion—caging her between the solid oak and the warmth of my body.

"What do you say we continue this discussion over

dinner?" I propose, my voice a low, velvety purr. My eyes lock with hers, dark and intense, a silent promise of intrigue. "I know a quaint little bistro not far from here. Nothing fancy—just good food and... stimulating conversation."

The edge of my mouth lifts in dark amusement as I watch her reaction. I can almost see the wheels turning in her mind, weighing the potential risks against her evident curiosity. The anticipation is delicious.

"Unless, of course, you have more pressing engagements this evening?" I add, a calculated challenge in my tone.

Her chest rises and falls with a subtle shudder. I perceive her resolve wavering, the crackling attraction between us impossible to deny. The momentary catch of her plush lower lip makes my breath hitch as she considers her answer.

A foreign sensation creeps into my core then—unfamiliar, almost laughable in its absurdity. Almost.

The revelation slams into me.

She might actually say no.

For a fleeting instant, I find myself strangely disarmed by her hesitation, by the power she seems to wield over me without even realizing it. It's a strange emotion, this momentary loss of control, this notion of being caught in someone else's thrall. I, who have always prided myself on my ability to manipulate and dominate, am now left reeling by the depth of my response to her.

It's unsettling, this newfound vulnerability, this chink in the armor of my carefully crafted persona. I've never allowed myself to be swayed by emotion, never permitted the weaknesses of the heart to interfere with the cold, hard logic of my ambition. And yet, here I am, my pulse racing and my thoughts scattered—my sanity hanging from a single reaction of a woman I barely know.

When the faintest nod from her comes, I beam victoriously, stepping back to offer my arm in a chivalrous gesture, masking my inner turmoil with a facade of confident charm. "Excellent. Then it's a date, *Liebes*."

As she tentatively loops her arm through mine, I pull her snugly against my side, savoring the delicious shiver that courses through her. The chase is exhilarating, but I have a feeling the prize will be exponentially more so.

This evening is shaping up to be even more delightful than I expected.

14

CLARISSA

*D*ragons, I'm learning, have a talent for making the impossible feel inevitable. My heart hammers as Kaisner's car cuts through rain-slicked streets. I still can't believe I said yes—yes to dinner, yes to him. The man who's haunted my thoughts since the moment we met is taking me somewhere secret, somewhere private. Just the two of us.

A thrill surges through me. So does a flicker of doubt.

What the hell am I doing?

The rational part of me chants *danger*. Kaisner Drachenstein is power and shadows and whispered warnings. But the part that answers him—the part that wakes when he's near—doesn't care.

Outside, city lights blur past the windows, refracted through streaks of rain. I breathe deep, steadying myself. For better or worse, I've already stepped into his world. There's no turning back now.

The car eases to a stop before a nondescript building. Mist drapes the Parisian evening in a ghostly veil, rain soft but steady. Kaisner's out in a blink, umbrella in hand, opening my door before I even reach for it.

"Allow me," he says, offering his hand.

I take it.

The chill of the night vanishes the second he pulls me close under the umbrella. His warmth wraps around me, grounding. Dangerous. Addictive.

We cross slick cobblestones toward a modest entrance. A discreet sign above the door reads *L'Étoile Cachée*—The Hidden Star.

A gust of wind grabs the umbrella just as he opens the door, spraying us both with cold droplets. I laugh. I can't help it.

Kaisner's answering smile is rare and sharp. Real. For just a moment, his carefully constructed mask slips, revealing something genuine beneath the polished exterior. The unguarded expression transforms his face completely—softening the harsh angles, brightening his eyes, making him devastatingly handsome in a way that has nothing to do with his usual calculated charm.

He guides me through the doorway, his hand a whisper of warmth at the small of my back.

I steal a glance at Kaisner's chiseled profile, the memory of Cassandra summoning him to Deveraux Manor flickering through my mind. It steadies me, soothes the edges of my unease. If she trusted him enough to call him into that sacred place, then maybe I can trust him for one evening of... what? Normalcy?

A wry smile tugs at my lips. As if anything involving Kaisner Drachenstein could ever be considered normal.

The door closes behind us, muffling the patter of rain.

Inside, the hush is immediate. No clinking glasses. No murmured conversation. Just golden light and silence.

My steps slow as I take it in—empty tables dressed in white linen and polished silver, crystal glassware untouched. A single rose at each center, soft petals blushing crimson.

"Is it always this quiet?" I murmur.

"I may have asked for privacy," Kaisner says, tone smooth, amused.

My pulse skips.

Of course he did.

He leads me to a corner booth, the velvet seat catching on my dress as I slide in. The space feels intimate, almost secret. Candlelight flickers across wood-paneled walls and casts dancing shadows on the floor.

A grand piano stands in the corner, silent—until it's not. Soft music blooms into the space, as if summoned by thought.

A waiter approaches with reverence, cradling two ancient-looking bottles of wine. "From your private collection, monsieur."

Kaisner barely glances at the labels. "The Château Margaux 1787."

The waiter nods with awe and vanishes.

I blink.

The 1787? My brother once called it *liquid legend*. Only a handful still exist, locked away in vaults or museums. I'd only ever *heard* of it. And Kaisner chooses it like he's ordering a glass of tap water.

As the waiter tilts the bottle, the deep crimson elixir cascades into our glasses with the grace of liquid rubies. The rich, complex aroma wafts up, and I find myself inhaling deeply—blackcurrant, cedar, a faint note of truffle, and something darker, older.

"1787?" I glance at him over the rim of my glass. "Is this even drinkable?"

Kaisner's smile is slow, edged with something ancient. "For most? No. But some things age differently... when guarded by the right blood."

The way he says it—like he's not just talking about wine

—sends a ripple down my spine. He lifts his glass, watching me through the crimson veil. A toast without words.

I clink mine softly against his.

The first sip is velvet and shadow—unreal. As though time itself has been distilled into flavor. The legends don't do it justice.

And neither, I realize, do the warnings about him.

"Quite the vintage," I say, understatement clinging to my voice.

He tilts his glass in acknowledgment. "Some things are worth preserving. Like this moment."

Our eyes meet. Something lingers in the space between us—heat, curiosity, maybe warning.

Hors d'oeuvres arrive—tiny, exquisite bites too beautiful to eat. Truffles. Smoked salmon. Aged cheeses that melt on the tongue.

Kaisner leans back, watching me more than the food. There's a quiet hunger in his gaze—not for the wine or the rare delicacies, but for my reactions, my laughter, the flicker of curiosity in my eyes. It's as if he's memorizing me, moment by moment, the way a collector studies a one-of-a-kind artifact he never plans to part with.

As the evening unfolds, I find myself leaning in, drawn by more than just his presence. His voice, low and deliberate, spins tales of far-off cities cloaked in snow, forgotten catacombs beneath Venetian streets, hidden halls guarded by blood oaths and ancient names. Each story reveals another layer, another mask peeled away—until he no longer feels like a stranger seated across from me, but a man whose soul I've brushed before in a dream.

But it's when he speaks of a recent acquisition—a secluded property on the shores of Lake Starnberg in Germany—that something in him shifts. His voice softens, loses some of its usual sharp edge. He describes the tranquil waters, the thick emerald canopy of the forest, the quiet charm of the nearby village with its old chapel bells and scent of woodsmoke. There's a reverence in his tone when he speaks of the place, like it's more than land. Like it's something close to sacred.

"I've been thinking about spending some time there," he admits, a note of vulnerability in his tone that catches me off guard. "Perhaps... living a quieter life, at least for a while."

The image of Kaisner—this powerful, enigmatic man— seeking solace in such a peaceful setting is both surprising and oddly fitting. It reveals a depth I hadn't glimpsed before, a yearning for simplicity that contrasts sharply with the complexity of his usual world.

Almost without realizing it, I begin to share my own story. The words come unbidden, and I speak of an English childhood tinged with loss, of the sense of displacement that drove me to lose myself in studies and art. I talk about the inexplicable pull that drew me back to Paris, the sense of homecoming when I finally returned, and how the gallery has given me purpose. A sense of place in a world that never quite fit.

Kaisner listens with that same sharp intensity, his gaze never straying from mine. Even when I fall silent, his attention remains fixed on me, as if reading the story written in the shadows of my expression.

For a moment, neither of us speaks. But the silence isn't empty. It's charged—alive with something unspoken yet deeply felt. A tether drawing us closer with every heartbeat.

The wine glass pauses halfway to his lips as Kaisner's gaze suddenly shifts, sharpening with focus. His eyes scan the room with predatory intensity, lingering momentarily on a figure near the entrance. The movement is subtle, almost imperceptible, but I catch it—the slight tensing of his shoulders, the way his free hand moves instinctively toward his jacket.

Then, just as quickly, the moment passes. The mask of charming dinner companion slides back into place, but something has changed. There's an edge to his smile now, a vigilance behind his eyes that wasn't there before.

"Forgive me," he says, noticing my curious expression. "Old habits."

"What kind of habits require that level of awareness?" I ask, unable to contain my curiosity.

He studies me for a long moment, as if weighing how much to reveal. "There are things about me you don't know, Clarissa." His voice drops, pitched for my ears alone. "Things I hope I never have to burden you with."

The cryptic response only fuels my curiosity. "Try me," I challenge softly.

A shadow passes across his features, there and gone so quickly I almost miss it. "Not tonight," he says, reaching across the table to brush his fingers against mine. "Tonight is about us."

The touch sends electricity racing up my arm, and just like that, the spell is recast. Yet even as we return to our conversation, I notice how his gaze periodically sweeps the room, how he's positioned himself to view both me and the entrance.

I wonder what kind of life creates such instincts—and what kind of enemies would follow a man like Kaisner Drachenstein.

"It is a rare occasion whenever two dragons cross paths," he finally says, his voice low and rich with meaning. A sly smile plays at the corners of his mouth, hinting at hidden truths.

A shiver races through me, equal parts thrill and trepidation. I lean in, drawn deeper into the mystery that cloaks him. "Is that what we are?" I whisper, the words heavy on my tongue. "Two dragons circling each other in the midnight sky?"

The moment the metaphor leaves my lips, I feel its truth in my bones. We are more than human. More than what we appear to be. Powerful beings, ancient at our core, wary and watchful—yet drawn together by some force older than fate.

Kaisner's eyes lock onto mine, and in the flickering candlelight, they smolder like embers in a dying fire. The rich maroon of his irises deepens, flecks of gold stirring within them like sparks ready to ignite. For a moment, it's as though the dragon within him rises to the surface, its presence felt, if not seen.

He leans in, his voice a low, resonant rumble that vibrates through the air between us. "Dragons, indeed," he murmurs, dark amusement curling around the words. "But perhaps not merely circling, Clarissa. We're *dancing*—a dangerous, intricate dance. Inescapable, as fate's embrace." He pauses, his gaze sharpening. "The question is, are you prepared for where this dance might lead us?"

His hand reaches across the table, fingers seeking mine with deliberate intent. The moment our skin touches, our fingers interlacing across the white linen, my breath catches, hopelessly ensnared by the gravity of his words—and the terrible beauty of what I witnessed in the Book of Vaelmir just hours ago.

The images flash through my memory: two dragons spiraling through storm-dark skies, locked in an aerial ballet of power and passion. One obsidian black, one pearl white traced with veins of gold—beautiful and terrible in their deadly grace. But the scene had shifted, split, showing me two divergent paths like pages from different books of fate.

In one future, they rule as equals—king and queen of shadows and flame, their love a force that reshapes the world.

Power shared, passion eternal, their bond unbreakable as forged steel.

In the other, only one throne remains. He sits alone among ash and bones, crown heavy on his brow, eyes empty of everything that once made him human. The white dragon is nowhere to be seen...

I blink, and the memory snaps away as quickly as it came.

I swallow the turmoil, forcing my expression to remain calm.

He doesn't notice the shadow that crosses my features, carrying on as if the world hasn't just offered me a glimpse of both our salvation and our doom.

"The Drachenstein lineage," he continues, shifting the conversation with the ease of someone who's learned how to guard and reveal in equal measure, "is one of the oldest and most respected among our kind. For centuries, we've shaped history from the shadows."

He reaches for his wineglass, and the candlelight flashes against the ring on his finger—an intricate design of two dragons intertwined. Somehow, I hadn't noticed it before. Now, it feels significant. Symbolic.

Kaisner's voice lowers, touched with reverent secrecy. "Have you ever heard whispers of the Unnatural Brethren?" His eyes glint with pride—and caution. When I shake my head, he goes on, "Few have, these days. It was meant to be our greatest achievement... and perhaps our greatest folly."

He leans closer, the words soft, conspiratorial. "During the Renaissance, it was my ancestor, Georg Drachenstein, who founded the Brethren. A secret society to unite all super-natural creatures—shifters, vampires, warlocks, witches. One banner. One cause."

His fingers trace the delicate stem of his glass with absent-minded grace, and his expression grows distant. "For a time, it worked. A golden age. We shared knowledge, resolved blood feuds, protected one another from growing human suspicion. It was… glorious."

Then his tone shifts, the shadows deepening behind his eyes. "But the Inquisition came. Witch hunts tore across Europe. Fear spread like wildfire, and unity became our greatest vulnerability."

He takes a measured sip of wine, and when he speaks again, his voice carries the heaviness of centuries. "It was another Drachenstein—my great-great-great-grandmother Eliza—who made the impossible decision to disband the Unnatural Brethren in 1632."

"Thus ending the Shadow Wars," I breathe, stunned. The name stirs echoes from the old lessons of witch lore I'd almost forgotten.

"Mm." He nods, something like awe in his expression. "She was sixteen. Barely more than a child—and yet, she saw what the rest of us could not. If one of us fell, all would."

A muscle in his jaw twitches. His grip on the glass tightens ever so slightly.

"The dissolution of the Unnatural Brethren saved countless supernatural lives," he murmurs, "but it also marked the end of an era. We scattered. Our communities turned inward. Secrets became the walls we lived behind."

He falls quiet, the weight of history settling between us. And in that silence, I glimpse something raw beneath his polished surface. Not just a keeper of legacy, but a man burdened by it.

I take a slow sip of wine, the rich taste grounding me. "You speak of your family's legacy with such reverence," I say gently. "But I sense it's more than just pride. It feels… personal. Heavy."

His carefully constructed facade wavers. Just for a heartbeat—but it's enough. I see it then: the flicker of something raw and unguarded. A hidden vulnerability that strikes deeper than I expect, rattling something inside me.

"The burden of legacy," he says at last, almost to himself. Then he looks at me, eyes dark with something fierce and unrelenting. "It's a double-edged sword, *meine Kleine*. Our family's power... our unique heritage... it's both a gift and a burden."

He draws a slow, steady breath. "And sometimes, I wonder if the price of carrying it is more than even I can pay."

Without thinking, I reach out, covering his hand with mine. The contact sends a jolt through me, but as before, there's no rush of premonition, no glimpse into his past or future. It's both frustrating and oddly freeing.

"I understand," I whisper, aware of my own family's expectations. "The pressure to live up to a name, to be everything that everyone expects you to be. It can be overwhelming."

Kaisner's gaze meets mine, and in that moment, the carefully constructed walls around him seem to crumble. The polished, charismatic figure he presents to the world fades away, revealing a man of startling complexity—vulnerable, conflicted, and achingly human. My breath falters, caught between shock and disbelief at this sudden, intimate revelation.

"Clarissa," he murmurs, his fingers intertwining with mine, his voice rough with emotion. "You see me... *truly* see me, in a way no one else ever has."

The raw honesty in his voice, the depth of emotion in his eyes, makes my heart swell. "And I like what I see," I confess, surprising myself with my boldness.

His answering smile is genuine, lighting up his entire face. It's a transformation so striking that I feel as if I'm falling, tumbling headfirst into something fathomless and utterly terrifying.

The night seems to slip away from us, our conversation flowing as smoothly as the wine. We dance from topic to topic, sharing laughs and moments of understanding that draw us ever closer. The candles burn low, the piano plays on and on, and I find myself wishing this enchanted evening could stretch into eternity.

But reality, as always, must intrude. "I suppose we should be heading out," Kaisner says softly, his eyes never leaving mine. "Surely, you're expected at Draken Manor." There's a note of reluctance in his voice that sends a thrill through me. "Though I must admit, I'm not eager for this evening to end."

I nod, a clash of disappointment and anticipation warring within me. "It has been... quite extraordinary," I breathe.

The Parisian night embraces us as we step outside, the cool air a shock after the bistro's pleasant intimacy. Above us, stars twinkle like scattered diamonds, bearing silent witness to the shift I feel deep in my bones.

Kaisner's hand is warm and steady in mine as we walk to his car. The attraction between us is still there, a kiss of lightning igniting my being. But now there's something more—a connection that transcends the physical, a meeting of minds and souls that leaves me breathless.

As I gaze up at the star-strewn sky, I allow myself to hope, to dream of paths I'd never dared consider before. Yes, the future is uncertain. But here, in this moment, with Kaisner by my side, anything feels within reach.

One thing, however, is beyond doubt. Tonight, I've glimpsed the heart of Kaisner Drachenstein. And in doing so, I fear I may have lost my own.

15

CLARISSA

The sleek car glides to a halt before the manor's imposing gates. Kaisner steps out first, moving with predatory grace to open my door. As I emerge, his phone buzzes with an insistent tone. A shadow crosses his features as he glances at the screen.

"Forgive me, liebling," he says, genuine regret coloring his voice. "Duty calls—an urgent matter that requires my immediate attention."

He gestures toward another figure who stands beside the vehicle—tall, with dark eyes and a scar along his jaw. The man's posture is alert, his gaze constantly scanning our surroundings.

"Marcus handles my security. He'll ensure you reach your door safely." Kaisner's voice softens as his fingers brush my cheek. "Until next time, Clarissa."

Before I can respond, he presses a lingering kiss to my hand, then turns away. I watch as he slides into the backseat with effortless elegance.

The security man—Marcus—steps forward as the car

door closes. "Good evening, Miss Draken," he says. His voice is smooth, measured, unnerving in its calm.

I acknowledge him with the barest tilt of my chin. There's something in his tone—something calculating that doesn't quite match the protective role he's supposedly playing.

The car pulls away, tires crunching on gravel, leaving me with the strange sentinel. As we walk toward the entrance, I can't help but feel I'm being studied, assessed. By the time we reach the door, I'm oddly relieved to bid him goodnight.

A distant rumble of thunder breaks the silence, and I scent the promise of rain in the air. Dark clouds gather on the horizon, obscuring the stars as they creep toward the waning moon.

The massive oak doors swing open, silent on their well-oiled hinges. The entrance hall stretches before me, a cavernous space of marble and mahogany, illuminated by the soft glow of enchanted chandeliers. My footsteps echo as I cross the threshold, each click of my heels on the polished floor a counterpoint to the rapid beating of my heart.

The Book of Vaelmir's revelations tumble through my thoughts, a puzzle I'm only beginning to comprehend. The balance of power among the supernatural bloodlines is shifting, the book had warned. Ancient prophecies are stirring, and the veil between worlds grows thin.

What role do I play in this grand design? I think of Nikolaas, of the unification he seeks to bring about among the dragon clans. How does his vision fit into these cosmic machinations?

And Kaisner... my breath catches as I recall the intensity of his gaze, the warmth of his hand in mine. He's a variable I hadn't accounted for, a wild card in an already complex game. My attraction toward him is undeniable, electric, and terrifying in its intensity. But can I trust it? Can I trust *him*?

Lost in my ruminations, I barely notice where I'm standing, the sudden change in temperature pulling me back to the present. I find myself at the threshold of the manor's conservatory, a cathedral of glass and wrought iron that houses a veritable jungle of rare and magical flora.

Stray beams of moonlight filter through the glass panels of the domed ceiling, casting ethereal patterns across the lush greenery. The air is heavy with the scent of night-blooming flowers and rich, loamy earth.

I step inside, drawn by the soothing promise of solitude. The door closes behind me with a soft click, and I'm instantly enveloped in a cocoon of warmth and verdant life. Massive ferns unfurl their fronds overhead, their leaves glistening with moisture. Vines with iridescent flowers wind their way up ornate trellises, their blooms pulsing with a soft, bioluminescent glow.

As I delve deeper into this indoor wilderness, my fingers trailing along the smooth bark of a moonflower tree, the tension begins to ebb from my shoulders. Here, nestled within the calm vitality of the plants, I can almost believe that the burden of destiny isn't quite so crushing.

I find a small clearing near the heart of the greenhouse, a circular space enveloped by a ring of white stone benches. In the center stands an ancient fountain, its basin filled with crystal-clear water that seems to glow from within. It's here that I finally allow myself to sink onto one of the seats, longing to unwind from the tumultuous day. I close my eyes, inhaling the warm, flower-scented air. And as the soft murmur of thunder rumbles in the distance, I begin to sort through what I learned from the Book of Vaelmir.

The book spoke of a significant shift coming, a realignment of the supernatural forces that govern our world. It hinted at the return of old powers long thought lost, and the awakening of new ones that could tip the frail balance we've maintained for centuries.

But it wasn't all doom and gloom. There was hope, too—a prophecy of a unifier, someone who could bridge the gaps between the supernatural races and usher in a renewed era of cooperation and understanding.

Could that be Nik? My brother is ambitious, driven by a vision of a united dragon society. But could his plans extend even further than I'd imagined?

And where do I fit into all of this?

Then there's Kaisner. My heart quickens at the mere thought of him, and I can't help but recall the way his eyes smoldered in the candlelight of L'Étoile Cachée. He's a mystery wrapped in an enigma, a man of power and secrets who seems to see right through me.

But can I trust these feelings? Is Kaisner truly interested in me, or am I just another piece on his chessboard?

I shake my head. No, the connection I felt with Kaisner was real. The vulnerability I glimpsed in his eyes when he spoke of his family's legacy, the way he opened up to me about his desire for a simpler life—those weren't the actions of a master manipulator. At least, I don't think they were.

As I sit there, surrounded by the quiet rustling of leaves and the soft gurgle of the fountain, a sense of calm settles over me. The enormity of what I've learned, the weight of the decisions that lie ahead—they're still there, but they no longer seem insurmountable.

Resolve surges within me, and I stand, feeling stronger and more centered than I have in days.

"Well, well. What have we here? A little dragon, lost in thought amidst the pretty flowers?"

I whirl around, my heart leaping into my throat. There, emerging from the shadows cast by a massive bird of paradise plant, is a figure I know all too well.

Ivan Lockhart.

The vampire moves with liquid grace, his pale skin seeming to glow in the moonlight that filters through the glass ceiling. His dark hair is swept back from a face of angular perfection, and his eyes—a swirling mix of violet and green—fix on me with predatory intensity.

"Ivan," I breathe, fighting to keep my voice steady. "I didn't realize you were here." Even as I speak, my mind races. What could possibly bring Ivan Lockhart, one of the most powerful vampires in Europe, to Draken Manor? His hatred for our family is legendary, a bitter enmity that stretches back centuries.

His lips curl into a smirk, revealing the barest hint of fang. "Clearly," he drawls, his cultured British accent a reminder of his long existence. "You seemed quite lost in your musings, my dear. Anything you'd care to share?"

As he speaks, a fog seems to lift from my mind. With a jolt of alarm, I realize that my wandering to the conservatory wasn't as aimless as I'd thought. The compulsion that drew me here, the sense of peaceful solitude I'd felt—*it was all Ivan's doing.* Anger and embarrassment wash over me as I remember the warnings I've received about vampire influence on young witches.

I straighten, fighting against the lingering tendrils of his persuasion. My hands clench at my sides, nails digging into my palms. Ivan may be ancient and powerful, and I may be vulnerable to his tricks for another three years, but I am still a Draken. I will not be a puppet in my own home.

"That's enough," I say, my voice steadier than my emotions. "I'd appreciate it if you'd stop trying to manipulate my thoughts." I meet his gaze squarely, pushing back against the allure of his supernatural charisma. "What brings you to Draken Manor at this hour? I wouldn't have thought you'd willingly set foot on our grounds, let alone resort to luring me into a private meeting."

A flicker of surprise—and is that respect?—passes over his face before his usual mask of cool amusement slides back into place. "Impressive, little witch," he murmurs. "Not many of your age can shake off a vampire's influence so quickly. Perhaps Juliette's tutelage is paying off after all."

The mention of the Grand Witch's name sends a jolt through me. But he laughs off my reaction as he adds, "Oh, come now. Don't look so shocked. She's my girlfriend, after all." He shrugs. "We have our chats."

Of course—how could I have forgotten? Juliette is not only the reincarnated Grand Witch, but she was the love of Ivan's life centuries ago, stolen away by a Draken ancestor. Now returned to the world, and to Ivan.

A shadow flickers across Ivan's features, so fast I almost miss it. For a moment, I glimpse the pain and bitterness beneath his carefully designed veneer of indifference. "About my presence here... times change, little dragon," he says, his voice low. "And with them, so must we all."

He moves closer, his movements as fluid as water. "Besides, I've been... curious. You've been spending quite a bit of time at Deveraux Manor lately, haven't you? Juliette's new protégé." A hint of jealousy seeps through the words.

"She has been kind enough to take me under her wing," I say carefully, watching Ivan's reaction. "She's a wonderful teacher."

A soft smile plays at the corners of Ivan's mouth, a genuinely tender expression that transforms his face. "That she is," he murmurs. "Taught by the best." Then his eyes sharpen, focusing on me with renewed intensity. "But I wonder, what does the seer daughter of the Draken clan hope to learn from a reincarnated witch?"

Keeping secrets from her boyfriend, is she? I want to snap back, but I choose my words carefully, aware of the delicate ground we're treading. "The magical world is changing, Ivan. The ancient boundaries between our kinds are blurring. Juliette understands that better than most."

Ivan's eyebrow arches elegantly. "Indeed. And your brother's ascension to alpha has certainly... shifted the landscape, shall we say? Bram's stubborn old guard mentality was becoming tiresome. Nikolaas, at least, seems to have a more... progressive outlook."

I can't hide my surprise at this. Ivan's disdain for my brother, Bram, is well known. But to hear him speak almost approvingly of Nikolaas is unexpected, to say the least. "And you're here to what? Extend an olive branch?"

Ivan's laugh is sharp, almost mocking. "Let's not get carried away," he says, tilting back while showing palms. "But there are changes coming, Clarissa. Big changes. And those of us who have managed to survive this long do so by knowing when to hold on to old grudges and when to... recalibrate our alliances."

His eyes narrow slightly, the depth of ages mirrored in his gaze. "Your family took something precious from me centuries ago. It's a wound that will never fully heal." For a moment, his mask slips, and I see a flash of raw pain that takes my breath away. "But the past is the past. What matters now is the future."

"And what future is that?" I ask, my curiosity overcoming my caution.

Gravity settles over Ivan's face. "One where the old boundaries between our kinds begin to blur, as you say. Where ancient enmities give way to new understandings." He pauses, his gaze intensifying. "Your brother's vision of unification... it's ambitious. Dangerous, even. But it might just be what we need to ride out the coming storm."

A chill runs down my spine. "What storm?"

"Oh, my dear girl," Ivan says, his voice almost gentle. "Surely you must feel it. The shifting of powers, the stirring of old magic. The world is changing, Clarissa—you've said it yourself. And we who wish to survive must change with it."

He begins to circle me slowly, like a shark scenting blood in the water. "Which brings me to you, and your... recent activities. Your apprenticeship with Juliette, your budding relationship with Kaisner Drachenstein... You're positioning yourself at the center of a very delicate web, whether you realize it or not."

My pulse quickens at the mention of Kaisner's name, but I refuse to let it show. "I wasn't aware my choice of mentors or dinner companions was a matter of such interest," I say coolly.

Ivan's laugh is without humor. "Everything is of interest in our world, *especially* when it involves the heirs of two sovereign dragon bloodlines." He stops directly in front of me, close enough that I perceive the unnatural chill that emanates from his body. "Your... dalliance with young Drachenstein has not gone unnoticed."

I turn to keep him in my sight, my muscles tensing instinctively. "It was dinner, Ivan. Nothing more."

"Was it?" he challenges. "Because from where I stand, it looks an awful lot like the opening moves of a very dangerous game."

"What are you implying?" I demand, my patience wearing thin.

Ivan's expression turns serious, all traces of mockery vanishing from his face. "Clarissa, you're playing with fire. The Drachenstein family has a long and complicated history, one that's not always aligned with the best interests of the supernatural community at large."

He reaches out, cold fingers brushing against my cheek in a gesture that's both intimate and threatening. "You have a gift, my dear. A rare and precious ability that many would kill to possess or control. Don't let yourself be blinded by a handsome face and a few pretty words."

I jerk away from his touch, anger flaring in my chest. "You don't know anything about Kaisner, or about me," I snap. "And I'm perfectly capable of taking care of myself."

Ivan's eyes flash with something that might be admiration. "Spirit. I like that. You'll need it in the days to come." He steps back, his demeanor shifting once again to one of casual indifference. "Just remember, little seer, *not everything is as it seems*. The game is changing, the players are taking their positions, and you... you're right in the center of it all."

With that cryptic warning, he turns and begins to walk away, melting into the conservatory's shadows. But before he disappears, he pauses, glancing back over his shoulder.

"Oh, and Clarissa? Do give my regards to your brother when he returns. I have a feeling we'll all be seeing quite a lot of each other very soon."

And then he's gone, leaving me alone in the moonlit jungle of the greenhouse, my mind reeling from the encounter.

The game is changing, he said. *The players are taking their positions.*

16

CLARISSA

low buzz cuts through the stillness, coming from somewhere beyond the conservatory. I cross the space softly, drawn by the sound, and ease open the door to Nik's office.

Samara stands by the mahogany desk, her back to me, one hand holding her phone to her ear while the other carefully places an ancient grimoire into the top drawer. Its leather binding is so dark it seems to swallow light. Even from this distance, the tome radiates malevolent energy—old, twisted, powerful. Mysterious whispers seem to emanate from its pages as she slides it into place, speaking of blood and betrayal, of ancient oaths sworn in shadow.

"Yes, I found it," she says quietly into the phone, her voice strained as she turns a small key in the drawer's lock. "It was exactly where you said it would be... in Juliette's private study." She pockets the key with trembling fingers. "I've locked it away, as you asked. But Nik, this thing—it feels wrong. The moment I touched it..."

A hush falls as she listens to whatever he's saying. Even with the grimoire now sealed away, I can still feel its presence, heavy and suffocating, pressing against my consciousness, its wicked aura seeping through the wood.

"I know it belonged to Willem Draken," Samara continues, her voice barely above a whisper. "But why do you need it? What's so important about a three-hundred-year-old spell book that you'd ask me to steal from Juliette?"

The name hits me like a physical blow. Willem Draken—Juliette's husband from centuries past, before her first death and reincarnation. The man whose love story with the Grand Witch had become legend among our kin. But if Nik is seeking out Willem's grimoire, it means he's delving into magic far darker than anything he's ever attempted before.

I remain frozen in place, my seer's gift recoiling from the drawer's contents. Whatever spells Willem had penned in those pages, they were born of desperation and shadow—the kind of sorcery that exacts a terrible price.

"I understand, my love. But it's dangerous," Samara says, her voice tight with worry as she moves away from the desk. "Nik, you're scaring me. Ever since your awakening, you've been different. More volatile. More..." She searches for the word. "Hungry."

She falls silent, listening, and I watch as her free hand drifts unconsciously to her opposite wrist, brushing against the edge of her sleeve. The soft fabric of her cashmere sweater slips back just slightly, revealing faint bruises, like the delicate smudging of twilight across her skin.

My breath stutters. The grimoire's presence suddenly makes terrible sense. If Nik is losing control of his dragon, if the power is corrupting him from within, he might believe that Willem's ancient magic holds the key to mastering it.

"No, I don't want us to fight," Samara says finally, resignation heavy in her voice. "Just promise me—promise me you'll be careful with whatever's in there. Some knowledge is meant to stay buried."

The chill that climbs my spine is undeniable. I realize, with the conviction of my gift, that this grimoire represents a turning point. A choice that will either save my brother—or damn him.

"Nik, please," she whispers, her voice barely audible over the rain tapping against the glass. "You need to rest. You need to come home. I know you think you're fine, but—"

She falls silent again, listening. Her shoulders sag under an invisible weight, and I can see the toll this conversation—this entire situation—is taking on her.

"Soon?" she says finally, her voice gentler now but edged with an exhaustion that speaks of sleepless nights and constant worry. "Yes... of course I miss you. More than anything." A beat of silence. "I love you."

The call ends with a soft tap. Samara stands motionless for a moment longer, staring at the locked drawer with barely concealed revulsion.

When she turns and sees me, her reaction is immediate —shoulders snapping back, face arranging itself into a practiced, bright expression that doesn't quite reach her eyes.

"Clarissa," she says with a lightness I don't believe for a second. "I didn't hear you come in."

"I was in the conservatory," I answer, stepping into the room. My eyes dart to the desk drawer, the air around it still thrumming with dark energy. "Sorry to startle you."

She waves a hand as if brushing the air itself away. "No, no—it's fine." But she takes a deliberate step away from the desk, clearly eager to distance herself from what she's just locked away.

"Everything okay?" I ask, though I already assume the answer.

"Just... Nik being Nik. You know how he gets when he's worried." Her laugh is tight, sharp at the edges.

I hesitate, gaze dropping briefly to the edge of her sweater where those damning bruises peek out.

She notices. Follows my gaze.

I move closer, unable to keep my sight from drifting to her wrist. "Sam, are those—"

"Oh, these?" she says, tugging the sleeve down in a swift, practiced motion. "Nothing. Just... alpha dragon things." Her smile doesn't reach her eyes. "Sometimes, Nik forgets his strength."

The way she says it—so light, so casual—sends a sharp warning through me. "Sam..." Her name leaves my mouth like a question I'm not brave enough to finish.

She meets my gaze for a beat too long, something wounded and fierce flickering behind her pupils. "Don't look at me like that," she says, her voice low.

She straightens, the Alexeev strength returning to her posture. "Nik is fine. We're fine. He's just... adjusting. His power is overwhelming. You felt it, didn't you? That dinner on Yule. The shift in him."

I nod slowly, unwilling to lie. But now I understand that shift differently. The dragon's awakening was only the beginning. Whatever Willem Draken had written in that sealed grimoire, whatever dark knowledge it contains, Nik believes it's the answer to controlling the beast within him.

She exhales through her nose, folding her arms across her chest. "The Draken Curse," she mutters, almost like an afterthought.

The words hit like a knife to the chest, made all the more ominous by the locked grimoire's oppressive presence.

"What?" I ask. "What curse?"

Her eyes widen for a fraction of a second—too late to hide the truth. "It's nothing. An old tale. A family superstition, really."

I step closer, the air growing thicker with each breath.

From the sealed drawer, the grimoire's whispers seem to grow louder, speaking of blood and madness, of dragons consumed by their own power. "You wouldn't call it that unless you believed in it."

Samara glances away, jaw tightening. She's already said too much. "I have to go," she says abruptly. "Gavriil's waiting for me. He gets anxious when I'm late."

She moves to pass me, but I gently touch her arm. "Sam," I whisper, pulling my hand back. "If something's wrong, you can tell me."

Her body stills, the tension in her spine screaming louder than words. Then she smiles again—serene, unreadable.

"Everything's fine, Clarissa. Really." She squeezes my hand and walks away, her heels tapping lightly on the marble floor.

I stand there long after she's gone, staring at the desk where Willem Draken's cursed spellbook lies sealed away. My mind is buzzing with questions I don't know how to answer. The bruises. The hesitations. Willem Draken's grimoire. And now this—this talk of a curse.

The Draken Curse.

The phrase clings to me, heavy with implication. I can feel it winding through my mind like smoke—elusive, insidious, ancient. What if it's real? What if whatever's unraveling in Nik is only the beginning?

And if it's happening to him…

I glance toward the window, where the rain has begun to fall harder, lashing against the panes like a warning.

What might it do to *me?*

17

KAISNER

The Parisian skyline sprawls before me, a glittering expanse of opportunity and power. From my office overlooking Place Vendôme, the city unfolds like a chessboard—and I'm the king who moves the pieces.

The drone of voices fills the room as my board members debate quarterly projections and market strategies. Their words wash over me like white noise as I take a slow sip of century-old scotch, savoring the burn. Drachenstein Industries might be the face I show the world—all gleaming steel and corporate bullshit—but it's just a mask for the *real* empire. The one that operates in shadows, that makes kings rise and fall, that keeps the supernatural game in check.

"Mr. Drachenstein? Your thoughts on the merger?"

I barely glance up from my ebony desk, where my attention lies fixed on the surveillance photo before me, its glossy surface reflecting the warm glow of my desk lamp. My fingers trace the outline of her face, lingering on the gentle curve of her cheek, the soft line of her jaw. Clarissa—radiant even in this grainy, candid shot—exits the Lumière Gallery, unaware of the camera capturing her every move.

"Proceed as discussed," I murmur, knowing they'll interpret my disinterest as executive authority rather than the distraction it truly is.

I've memorized her routines by now. The way she stops for coffee at precisely 8:47 each morning. How she tucks her hair behind her ear when deep in thought during meetings. The slight hesitation in her step when she passes the Shakespeare and Company bookstore, as if fighting the urge to venture inside.

My collection of photos grows daily. Some might call it obsession. I prefer to think of it as... thorough. Each image reveals something new—a different angle, a fresh expression, another facet of the woman who has consumed my thoughts. My prey. My... mate?

Taking another sip of scotch, I shuffle through more photos from yesterday's surveillance, barely registering the continued discussion around me. The liquid burns pleasantly as I study each one with fierce intensity. My eyes narrow at an image of a young gallery patron standing too close to her, his hand reaching to touch her arm. Without thinking, I crumple the photo in my fist, a low growl rumbling in my chest.

She is mine. Even if she doesn't know it yet.

The shrill ring of my phone pierces through the air, an unwelcome intruder in the midst of the meeting. I glance at the screen, brow furrowing as I recognize the number. It's one of my spies, and for him to breach protocol and contact me now, the information must be of the utmost importance.

With a raised hand, I silence the meeting, my authority tangible in the sudden stillness. "Excuse me, gentlemen. I need to take this." I don't wait for their acknowledgment, already rising and striding from the room, the phone pressed to my ear.

"Speak," I command, my voice low and authoritative.

The spy's report is hurried, his words tripping over each other in his haste to relay the critical intelligence. "Boss, it's the Draken girl. She's being followed."

In an instant, my blood turns to ice, cold fury settling in the pit of my stomach. Clarissa. *My Clarissa, being hunted.* The thought alone sends a red haze descending over my vision.

"Where?" I demand, my tone sharp enough to cut glass.

The details spill forth. "She's heading to the art gallery for work. The tail is skilled, but I've been watching him for the past block."

"I'm on my way," I say through clenched teeth. "Keep her in sight, but do not engage. *Verstanden?*" My instructions are clipped, brooking no argument.

"*Jawohl, Mein König.*" The spy's acknowledgment is a distant thing, my focus already consumed by the need to reach Clarissa, to ensure her safety.

I end the call with a decisive click, my mind racing ahead, calculating routes and contingencies. I reenter the meeting room, my expression a carefully crafted mask of control, betraying none of the turmoil that rages beneath the surface.

"Gentlemen, I'm afraid an urgent matter has come up that requires my immediate attention. We'll have to continue this at a later date." My words are met with murmurs of surprise and concern, but I pay them no heed. They are trivial things, meaningless when measured against the threat to what is mine.

I gather my belongings with swift efficiency, my movements precise and purposeful. Every second counts.

The drive to the art gallery passes in a blur of traffic and tension, my fingers drumming an impatient staccato against the steering wheel. In the rearview mirror, I catch a glimpse of the familiar black sedan that trails in my wake—my ever-present security detail, a necessary precaution in a world fraught with danger.

As I pull up to the café across from the gallery, my eyes are already scanning the surroundings, searching for any sign of Clarissa or her pursuer. My security team maintains a discreet distance. They know better than to draw attention to themselves, but their sole existence is a ceaseless reminder of the dangerous game we play.

And then I spot him, a shadow lurking in the alleyway, a predator lying in wait. Even from a distance, I recognize the telltale signs of a Mahindra Enforcer. The Indian tiger shifters have been thorns in my side for decades, their cunning and mastery of the mystic arts, matched only by their ruthless ambition.

The Mahindra spy is a lean, sinewy man with bronze skin and a shock of dark hair that falls in waves to his shoulders. His eyes, a striking amber hue, are lined with kohl, giving him an almost feline appearance. He moves with the fluid grace of a dancer, his every step imbued with the coiled power of a hunting cat.

But it's the tattoo on his neck that confirms his allegiance —a tiger's head inked in dark gold, its eyes gleaming with ruby-red ink. The sigil of the Mahindra warlocks, a symbol of their ancient power and unyielding pride.

The realization sends a growl rumbling through my chest. The Mahindras have been testing the boundaries of our fragile truce for years now, pushing into territories that are not theirs to claim. But to target Clarissa directly? It's a bold move, even for them.

I slip from the car, my movements silent and predatory as I approach him. He doesn't hear me coming, not until I'm right behind him, my hand clamping down on his shoulder like an iron vise.

He startles, whirling around with a snarl, but the sound

dies in his throat as he takes in my face. Recognition dawns, followed quickly by fear. He knows who I am, knows the power I wield. *Good. Let him tremble. Let him quake in the face of my wrath.*

"I have a message for your master, Vikram Mahindra," I say, my voice a silken purr that belies the steel beneath. "Kaisner Drachenstein sends his regards. It's in your clan's highest interests to stop tracking the Draken heiress. Immediately."

The spy's eyes widen, his face paling beneath the rich hue of his skin. He knows the reputation of the Drachensteins, the power we wield both in the mortal world and the realm of shadows. He nods frantically, his hands coming up in a gesture of supplication. "Y-yes, of course. I will convey your message to him at once."

I release him with a shove, watching with grim satisfaction as he scurries away like the vermin he is. But even as he vanishes into the city's depths, I know this is far from over. The Mahindras are an ancient and proud clan, not easily cowed by threats, even from one as powerful as myself.

I make my way to the café terrace, choosing a seat that affords me a clear view of the gallery. And there she is— Clarissa. She moves through her day, from meeting to meeting, with a poise and grace that takes my breath away, unaware of the danger that lurks in the shadows.

But as I watch her, a troubling thought takes root in my mind. She is unguarded, vulnerable in a way that makes my blood run cold. "Why are you not protected?" I muse with a frown. It makes no sense that her brother, *'the great'* Nikolaas Draken, would leave his own flesh and blood so exposed like this.

Restless, I tap my fingers on the tabletop, the rhythmic sound a counterpoint to the churning of my thoughts. *Verdammt,* it doesn't sit well with me, this apparent oversight on Nikolaas' part. A low growl of frustration escapes my lips, thick with the urgency of my concern for Clarissa's safety.

I pull out my phone, my fingers already dialing the number of my most trusted enforcer. "Janik? *Hier ist Kaisner.* I need a stealth team assembled immediately. Twenty-four seven surveillance on Clarissa Draken. Any concerning activity is to be reported directly to me. *Verstanden?*"

As the call ends, I lean back in my chair, my gaze never wavering from Clarissa's form. She doesn't realize it, but from this moment on, she is under *my* protection.

And gods help any soul foolish enough to threaten what is mine. They will learn, as so many have before them, the true meaning of fear. The true price of crossing Kaisner Drachenstein.

I will burn the world to ash before I let any harm come to her.

18

CLARISSA

The setting sun casts my office in molten hues, turning sleek modern furniture into burnished sculpture. I should find it beautiful. Instead, the warm light sharpens the throb behind my eyes. The screen before me swims, its text unreadable, a haze I've tried and failed to untangle all afternoon.

I blink hard and press my fingertips to my temples. When was the last time I slept through the night? Three days ago? Four? The hours have collapsed into a sleepless blur.

I reach for my coffee mug, find it by muscle memory. One sip confirms it's cold—and bitter. The carafe beside me is empty again. Fourth cup? Fifth? The caffeine only hums uselessly in my bloodstream, a poor substitute for proper relaxation.

A notification pings. Another email. The red bubble in my inbox ticks upward, as if mocking me.

No rest for the weary—not when you're the newly appointed director of Galerie Lumière's philanthropic division.

I grab the mouse, but a flicker in my periphery makes me

freeze. For a breathless instant, I see him—maroon eyes watching, feel phantom hands on my shoulders. My breath catches as I turn. But there's no one there. Only shadows and golden light curling along the edge of the bookshelf.

Kaisner. Always Kaisner.

I close my eyes and press my palms against them, but he's there—burned into my retinas like staring too long at the sun. That secret smile. The molten heat in his gaze. The impossible pull of—

Pain splits my skull like lightning.

My office fractures.

The walls remain, but they're wrong now—too bright, too sharp, humming with otherworldly energy. The air shimmers like heat waves off summer asphalt.

I rise on unsteady legs, skin prickling with warning.

Movement flickers at the edge of sight.

That's when I see it.

A crimson droplet, crawling down the cream wallpaper. Then another. And another. The drops thicken into streams, dark and viscous, pooling at the baseboards. The pungent scent of copper invades my nose.

Darkness spills from the corners like ink. It creeps across the rug, devouring each intricate thread. Shadows climb the desk, the filing cabinet, the bookshelves, leaving a void in their wake. My Monet curls at the edges, its lilies blackening, dying.

The air thickens—and then ignites.

Smoke pours from unseen cracks in the walls. It reeks of scorched flesh. Ash floats through the room like embers, each one hissing with phantom cries. The heat burns my skin.

I try to move. Try to scream. But my muscles lock in place. Whatever power shows me this vision won't let me look away—not until the message is burned into my soul.

The floor beneath me buckles and heaves. Walls crumble

inward with thunderous crashes, revealing not the familiar Parisian streets beyond, but a wasteland of charred earth stretching to the horizon.

Fissures split the blackened ground, glowing orange-red like exposed veins of molten rock. Where the Eiffel Tower once pierced the sky, nothing remains but twisted metal and ash. Bodies carpet the scorched earth—some whole, others torn apart, all frozen in their final moments of agony. Their mouths gape wide, teeth bared in screams that will echo through eternity.

Above this hellscape, the sky pulses with sickly, unnatural light. Smoke coils through violet clouds like serpents, blotting out what remains of the sun. The air tastes of copper and decay, thick with the metallic tang of spilled blood. Somewhere in the distance, inhuman shrieks pierce the silence—sounds no earthly throat could make.

And then, cutting through the cacophony of destruction, a voice whispers with crystal clarity: *"The storm is coming."*

I jolt upright, gasping. My desk is solid beneath trembling hands. The vision fades—but its grip lingers.

Ash coats my tongue. I can still feel the flames.

I all but collapse on the chair, trying hard as hell to steady my breathing. They're getting worse—these visions. More vivid. More violent. Each one a warning. Each one louder than the last.

What am I supposed to do with them? How can I protect my family, my people, when I can't even keep myself grounded?

A chime from my inbox breaks the spell. I force myself to sit upright, ignoring the quivering in my limbs. I have a job to do. Nik is counting on me to lead. And I will not fail him.

I square my shoulders and go through my emails, and the most recent subject line catches my eye: "Urgent: Exhibition Gala Crisis."

My heart sinks as I click on the message, my stare quickly scanning the contents. Our latest project, an exclusive art exhibition that we've been planning for months, is in jeopardy.

I take a deep breath, trying to quell the rising panic in my chest. This event is a huge opportunity for the gallery, a chance to draw the eyes of the art world and cement our reputation as a premier institution. We simply cannot afford to let it fall through.

Quickly, I compose a response, calling for an emergency meeting with the team. Within minutes, my office is filled with a flurry of activity as my colleagues file in, their faces etched with worry and determination. The air is charged with tension, everyone acutely aware of what's at stake.

"What's the latest?" I ask, forcing my voice to remain steady and calm despite the churning in my stomach.

Sophie, my assistant, steps forward. Her usually immaculate appearance is slightly disheveled, reflecting the long hours we've all been putting in. She clutches a folder to her chest, knuckles white with tension.

"We've been trying to reach our target collector for weeks now," she says, her voice tight with frustration. "But it's like he's a ghost. His people keep stonewalling us at every turn."

She opens the folder, revealing a dossier with a blurred photograph paperclipped to the top. "He's known for his incredible collection, perhaps one of the most valuable in Europe. But he's pathologically confidential about it. No one, and I mean no one, has ever seen it in person."

Luc, our head of acquisitions, chimes in, his normally jovial face creased with concern. "We've tried every avenue we can think of. Formal requests, informal connections, even attempted to arrange 'chance' meetings at events he was rumored to attend. But it's like trying to catch smoke with our bare hands."

"His team is a fortress," Sophie adds, shaking her head. "We can't even get past his personal assistant to schedule a simple phone call."

A headache starts building behind my eyes as I absorb this information. This collector, whoever he is, could make or break our exhibition. And right now, it seems like he's determined to break it.

"We can't give up," I say, my voice carrying a quiet intensity that makes everyone lean in. "I want you to redouble your efforts. Leave no stone unturned, no contact unexplored. Reach out to every connection we have, no matter how tenuous. This exhibition is our chance to put the Galerie Lumière on the map, and I'll be damned if we let it slip through our fingers because of one reclusive art aficionado."

"Absolutely!" Luc suddenly exclaims, punching the air with unexpected enthusiasm. The room falls silent, all eyes turning to him in surprise.

Realizing his unusual outburst, Luc clears his throat, a flush creeping up his neck. "Sorry about that," he mumbles, straightening his tie. "I mean, you can count on us, Clarissa."

A ripple of laughter breaks through the tension. A smile tugs at my lips, grateful for Luc's inadvertent lightening of the mood.

Sophie steps forward, her eyes shining with renewed determination. "Luc's right. We're all behind you on this, Clarissa. Whatever it takes."

I look around the room, seeing the same resolve reflected in every face. Despite the enormity of the challenge before us, pride and affection surge for my team. Together, we just might pull this off.

"All right then," I say, clapping my hands. "Let's get to work. We have an impossible collector to impress and a gala to save."

The team nods, their expressions grave but determined. I

can see the fire in their eyes, the shared passion for bringing this project to fruition. It's moments like these that remind me why I love this job, despite the stress and sleepless nights.

"I know we can make this happen," I say, my gaze sweeping over the room. "Keep me updated on any developments, no matter how small."

As the meeting wraps up and my colleagues file out of the office, I slump back in my chair. The leather creaks beneath me, a sound that seems to echo the weariness in my bones. Nik trusts me. He believes in my abilities and my vision for the gallery. I can't let him down.

Just then, my phone buzzes, and I glance down to see my brother's name flashing on the screen. Despite my exhaustion, warmth and affection wash through me as I answer the call, eager to hear Nik's voice.

"Hey, Rissy," he says, his tone warm and familiar. The sound is a balm to my frayed nerves.

"Nik," I breathe, realizing just how much I've missed him. "How's everything going in Spain?"

I listen as he tells me about the city, about the dragon clans' eagerness to know him, to learn more of his abilities. I can hear the excitement in his voice, but also a hint of something else. Longing, perhaps?

"But I miss being home," he admits, his tone softening. "Miss seeing Sam... and uh... the others."

I can't help but giggle, grateful as some of the day's tension melts away. "Oh, I see how it is. You miss Sam and 'the others,' but what about your favorite little sister?"

Nik's warm chuckle fills the line. "Favorite little sister? You're my *only* little sister."

"Details, details," I tease, warming to the task of cheering him up. "I bet you're living it up in Madrid with your green smoothies and... what's that weird Brazilian berry you're obsessed with?"

"Açaí," Nik reluctantly supplies, and I can all but see him rolling his eyes. "And for your information, I'm no longer in Madrid, but in a smaller town—and finding a good açaí bowl here is harder than negotiating with the Ursa clan."

"Oh, the tragedy!" I gasp in mock horror. "Shall I organize a care package? 'Emergency Superfoods for the Traveling Wellness Warrior'? Has a nice ring to it, doesn't it?"

Nik's laughter echoes through the phone, and I'm instantly satisfied. Mission accomplished—big brother cheered up, homesickness temporarily abated.

"Keep it up, sis," he says affectionately. "And I might just extend my stay to avoid your merciless teasing."

"You wouldn't dare," I counter, grinning. "Who else would remind you that normal people *don't* consider protein powder a food group?"

He chuckles.

For a moment, it's only me and Nik, trading quips and laughter, our responsibilities temporarily forgotten. It's a welcome respite from the chaos of the day, and I savor every second of it.

"We miss you too," I say quietly, emotion thick in my throat. In the fading light, I see it—how every choice, even our separation, ties into something larger.

I almost ask about Samara. About the tension in her voice. The bruises. The haunted stare in her eyes. But the words stall on my tongue. It's not the time. Not like this. I'll ask him in person, when there's nowhere to hide—when I can look him in the eye and demand answers he can't sidestep.

Instead, I say gently, "Sam loves you, you know. Fiercely. Even when things are hard." I let the words hang, their meaning clear.

Nik goes quiet. But I don't fill the silence. I let it settle.

Some truths don't need to be spoken aloud to be heard.

"I understand now, why you had to go," I continue. "And don't worry. I'm holding down the fort here, guarding the threshold between what is and what must be."

There's a pause on the other end of the line, a moment of quiet that stretches just long enough to make me wonder if the call has dropped. Then Nik's voice comes through, thoughtful and slightly puzzled.

"You sound different."

My breathing hitches. "Different? What do you mean?"

"I'm not sure exactly," Nik says slowly, as if he's trying to piece together his thoughts. "There's just something in your voice, in the way you're talking. You seem... older, somehow. More assured." There's a note of pride in him as he adds, "Has something happened recently?"

I'm tempted to spill everything—the visions, Kaisner, the fae library. But instead, I force a light laugh. "Oh, you know, just the usual gallery drama. Nothing I can't handle."

"Hmm," Nik muses, and I can picture him nodding thoughtfully. "Well, whatever it is, it suits you. I never doubted you for a second, Clarissa. You're a natural leader. The gallery is lucky to have you... *I* am lucky to have you."

His words warm me, even as guilt gnaws at my insides for the secrets I'm keeping. "When are you coming home?" I manage to ask, unable to keep a hint of longing from my voice.

Silence stretches between us, and I can almost picture Nik's face, the way his brow furrows when he's deep in thought. "Soon," he says finally, warm but vague. "There are still some things I need to take care of here. But I promise, I'll be back the minute this tour is over."

Disappointment flickers through me, but I set it aside. "I understand," I say, my voice steady despite the ache in my chest. "Just... don't stay away too long, okay? Paris isn't the same without you."

We talk for a few more minutes. But all too quickly, Nik has to go, pulled away by another meeting or conference call.

"Take care of yourself, Rissy," he says, gentle and sincere. "And remember, you're stronger than you know. You've got this."

I smirk. "I won't let you down."

As the phone call ends, the smile slowly fades from my face. The unspoken truths lodge in my throat like shards of glass, threatening to draw blood if I dare give them voice.

I couldn't bring myself to speak a word about my visions getting worse, each one more vivid and terrifying than the last. The sudden interest of the fae and vampires in our family's affairs remains locked behind my lips, information too dangerous to share over a phone line. And Kaisner... just thinking his name sends a shiver down my spine. How could I even begin to explain the jumble of emotions he stirs in me?

These secrets press against my chest, begging to be released. But I push them down, swallowing the words that threaten to spill out. It would only cause Nik grief and worry, and I can't do that to him. Not when he's miles away, focused on his journey of self-discovery and the weighty responsibilities of leading our clan.

No, these are my burdens to bear. At least for the time being.

I stare out at the city, now cloaked in velvet dark, lights twinkling like fallen stars. There's still so much to do, so many challenges to overcome—the forthcoming gala, the opera tomorrow, the ominous visions and prophecies...

But for the first time, I feel it. Not peace, exactly. But purpose.

Yes, the storm is coming.

But maybe, just maybe, I'm strong enough to face it.

19

KAISNER

The antique grandfather clock in the corner of my study chimes nine, its deep, resonant tones echoing off the wood-paneled walls. I barely register the sound, my attention fixed on the sea of papers spread before me. The warm glow of the fireplace casts flickering shadows across the room, turning the mountain of reports into an ever-shifting landscape of light and dark.

I lean back in my leather chair, its soft creak a counterpoint to the pop and hiss of burning logs. My fingers drum an impatient rhythm on the polished ebony of my desk as I scan the latest profit margins. The numbers are good—better than good. Our influence is growing, spreading like wildfire across Europe's supernatural underworld.

But it's not enough. It's never enough.

I reach for the crystal decanter at my elbow, pouring two fingers of aged scotch. The amber liquid catches the firelight as I swirl it in the glass, its peaty aroma filling my nostrils. I take a sip, savoring the burn as it slides down my throat. For a moment, I close my eyes, allowing myself this brief respite from the burden of the Drachenstein legacy.

When I open them again, my gaze falls on the portrait hanging above the fireplace. My father stares down at me, his eyes as cold and hard in oil paint as they were in life. The set of his jaw, the arch of his brow—everything about him exudes power and control. The very embodiment of what a Drachenstein should be.

I turn away, unable to bear his scrutiny, even in this painted form. My eyes land instead on the ornate dagger displayed on my desk—a gift from my father on my eighteenth birthday. Its jeweled hilt glints in the firelight, a beautiful and deadly thing. Much like the power I now wield.

"Are you proud, Father?" I murmur to the empty room, my voice barely above a whisper. "Or do you look up from whatever hell you're in and see only the failure you always feared?"

The dragon in me stirs at these words, a low rumble of discontent that I feel more than hear. I clench my fist, power surging just beneath my skin. So close to the surface, yet still out of reach. The slumbering beast that refuses to fully awaken, no matter how I rage against its dormancy.

A sharp knock at the door cuts through my brooding like a knife.

"Enter," I command, my voice steady despite the turmoil within. I don't bother looking up from the papers on my desk, but I'm acutely aware of the door opening, of the familiar footsteps crossing the thick Persian rug.

"*Mein König,*" Janik's voice, as always, is carefully neutral. My loyal enforcer knows better than to betray any emotion without cause. "I have news that may interest you."

I lift my gaze slowly, taking in Janik's rigid posture, the slight tension around his eyes that betrays the importance of whatever he's about to say. "Go on," I say, leaning back in my chair and steepling my fingers. "What's so urgent that it couldn't wait until morning?" My voice comes weary, too exhausted to pretend to care.

Janik approaches my desk with measured steps, each movement precise and controlled. From within his jacket, he withdraws an envelope—cream-colored paper bearing the gilt insignia of the Palais Garnier. The sight stirs something in me, a flicker of intrigue cutting through the fog of fatigue.

"There's to be a performance of *La Vestale* tomorrow night," he begins, his tone carefully modulated as he places the invitation before me. The elegant script seems to dance in the flickering light, each letter a promise of what's to come.

I lean forward, genuine interest kindling in my chest. It's been years since I've witnessed that particular opera—a tale of forbidden love and sacred duty that strikes perhaps too close to home. My fingers trace the embossed edges of the invitation, remembering another time, another life.

"But that's not the most intriguing part," Janik continues, and something in his voice draws my full attention. His next words fall into the room like stones into still water, ripples of consequence spreading outward: "Miss Draken will be in attendance... alone."

The mention of her name shoots a jolt of electricity through my system. I sit up straighter, every nerve suddenly alert. The reports on my desk, the pressure of my father's portrait, even the burn of the scotch—all fade into insignificance. There is only this moment, this news, this opportunity.

"Alone?" I echo, my tone low and intense. I can hear the hunger in my voice and see its effect on Janik as he shifts his weight ever so slightly. "What of her brother?"

Janik's response is prompt, efficient. "Abroad, still, from what our sources say. She'll be representing the Draken family in his stead."

I rise from my chair, moving to the window that overlooks the glittering Paris skyline. A slow, predatory smile spreads across my face as the implications sink in. Clarissa, alone at the opera, without a security detail. It seems *'the great'* Nikolaas Draken isn't as meticulous as his reputation suggests. This oversight is... intriguing. And potentially useful.

I can't help but marvel at the carelessness. For all his grand plans of unification, Nikolaas has left his most valuable asset—his gifted sister—completely exposed. It's a mistake I would never make. One that I will *never* make, where Clarissa is concerned.

"Interesting," I murmur, more to myself than to Janik. "Very interesting indeed."

I whirl around to face my enforcer, noting the barely concealed curiosity in his eyes. He knows me well enough to recognize when something has caught my attention, when the gears of strategy have begun to turn.

"Tell me, Janik," I say, my voice deceptively casual, "what do you make of this... oversight on Nikolaas Draken's part? Sending his sister, unprotected, to such a public event?"

Janik considers for a moment before responding. "It seems... uncharacteristically careless, *Mein König*. Perhaps he trusts in the neutrality of the venue? Or in his sister's abilities?"

I nod, a slow smile spreading across my face. "Perhaps. Or perhaps *'the great unifier'* is not as infallible as he'd have us believe." I move back to my desk, fingers trailing over the jeweled hilt of my dagger. "After all, in our world, even a moment's inattention can have... significant consequences."

A low growl escapes my throat, my fist tightening of its own accord. "I bet every shifter in town will be flocking toward this opportunity," I mutter, the thought of others vying for Clarissa's attention igniting a possessive fury within me.

I take a deep breath, willing my dragon's wrath to calm. When I speak again, my voice is cool and controlled, belying the storm of emotions beneath. "Secure me a private box," I order, my mind already racing with plans. "And make sure my presence isn't widely known. I want the element of surprise."

Janik nods, a glimmer of understanding in his eyes. "Of course, *Mein König*. Anything else?"

I pause, considering. The next move needs to be perfect, a delicate balance of intrigue and allure. "Have flowers sent to her box. White roses, with a note. Sign it with just an initial—K."

My enforcer bows swiftly, but as he turns to leave, a new idea strikes me. "Wait," I command, reaching for a card on my desk. Pen in hand, I hastily scribble further instructions. "This, also."

Janik retrieves the card and exits silently, leaving me alone. I turn to the window, my thoughts consumed by Clarissa Draken. Her sapphire eyes, the soft curve of her smile, the way she tilts her head when she's deep in thought —every detail is etched into my memory.

For too long, I've watched her from afar, biding my time, waiting for the perfect moment to make my move. And now, fate has handed me that chance on a silver platter.

"She has to be mine," I murmur, my voice barely audible even in the silence of my study. My fingers clench into fists at my sides, the need to possess her, to claim her, overwhelming in its intensity. "And soon."

The thought of her in my arms, of claiming her as my own, sends a surge of heat through my body. It's not just desire—though there's plenty of that—but something deeper, less primal. A need that goes beyond the physical, that touches my very soul...

I shake my head, trying to clear these dangerous

thoughts. I can't afford to be distracted by emotion. This is about power, about securing the Draken blood for my own purposes. Nothing more.

But even as I tell myself this, I know it's a lie. Clarissa Draken has awakened something in me, something I thought long dead. And tomorrow night, at the opera, I intend to explore that feeling to its fullest.

As I turn to my desk, my phone buzzes insistently. A text message flashes on the screen from Scarlett—my occasional lover and one of my most skilled spies. Her message is direct, as usual:

Free tonight. Your place or mine?

A month ago, I would have responded immediately, eager for the distraction and release that Scarlett offers. Her skills extend far beyond espionage, and our encounters have always been mutually satisfying. But now...

I find myself hesitating, my thumb hovering over the keyboard. The thought of Scarlett's touch, once so enticing, now leaves me cold. Instead, unbidden, an image of Clarissa Draken rises in my mind.

A surge of longing, so intense it's almost painful, courses through me. I shut my eyes, trying to dislodge these unwelcome feelings. What the hell is happening to me? Since when did I become a man swayed by such sentimentality?

With a frustrated growl, I type out a quick response to Scarlett:

Not tonight. Busy.

I hit send before I can second-guess myself, then toss the phone aside.

The rejection of Scarlett's offer only serves to underscore

the depth of my fixation on Clarissa. Even the prospect of a night of passion with a woman I once found irresistible pales in comparison to the mere thought of her.

My mind is filled with images of the Draken heiress, of the look on her face when she sees me at the opera, of the way her body will feel pressed against mine... Tomorrow can't come soon enough.

The trap is set. Now, all that remains is for my beautiful prey to walk into it.

And when she does, I'll be waiting.

20

CLARISSA

The grand façade of the Palais Garnier rises before me—a temple of art and power etched against the Parisian night. Golden statues flank the entrance, their rapt expressions frozen in eternal devotion beneath the shimmer of crystal chandeliers. The bronze doors gleam with carvings of myth and melody, poised to admit me into a world where reality blurs with spectacle.

The doormen, clad in crimson and gold livery, bow as they open the gilded entryway. "The Lady Clarissa Draken, Heiress to the Ancient House of Draken and Director of the Galerie Lumière."

The announcement rings out, echoing through the marble vestibule where mirrored walls multiply the grandeur.

I suppress a shiver. The title feels distant, ceremonial. We rarely use it—except at events like this, where the vestiges of human nobility mingle with supernatural power. Our family's strength has never rested in names or honors, but in the legacy of dragon blood. Still, tonight, both carry weight.

As I step inside, the noise of the street fades behind me, replaced by the low hum of elegant conversation and the orchestra's faint tuning. The foyer is a sea of silk and sparkle, jewels flashing like stars against the swell of brocade and lace. It could be overwhelming—if I let it.

But I am a Draken. The blood of dragons flows through my veins. I will not be cowed.

My gown, rich golden silk embroidered with intricate patterns that shimmer like dragon scales, whispers over marble as I ascend the grand staircase. The bodice clings to my figure before flaring into a skirt that flows like liquid gold. Every step is deliberate—a statement, a signal. I'm not here to blend in. I'm here to be seen.

As I climb the steps, gazes latch onto me from all directions. That familiar prickling at the nape of my neck confirms it—I'm being watched, assessed, judged. I suppress the urge to glare back at every curious face. Years of training rise to the surface: perfect posture, measured grace, and the serene mask of polite indifference.

Fragments of whispered conversations reach my ears as I pass:

"Is that her? The Draken girl?" "...brother's a dragon shifter, can you imagine?" "...most eligible bachelorette of the century, without a doubt..." "What I wouldn't give for an alliance with that family..."

The words swirl around me like smoke, at once flattering and suffocating. I am not just Clarissa tonight; I am a symbol, a potential chess piece in the great game of supernatural politics. The thought sends a shiver down my spine, but I don't let it show. Instead, I allow a small, enigmatic smile to play at my lips, giving nothing away.

When I reach the top of the stairs, I pause for a moment, ostensibly to adjust the fall of my skirt, but really to gather myself. I can see the Draken family box from here, draped in rich burgundy velvet with our crest embroidered in gold thread. It stands empty, waiting for me to take my place as the sole representative of our lineage.

The absence of Nikolaas is a physical ache, a hollow space beside me that seems to cry out for attention. But I push the emotion aside, steeling myself for the evening ahead. Tonight, I cannot be the little sister, the one who leans on her brother's strength. Tonight, I must be the Draken heiress, poised and powerful in my own right.

A flicker of guilt stirs as I remember my last call with Nik. I didn't tell him about the opera invitation—about stepping in to represent our family in his absence. He already has enough to worry about, and I didn't see the point in adding to the burden he's shouldering. Besides, this is my chance to prove I can handle it—to him, to the others… and maybe most of all, to myself.

"I can do this," I whisper to my reflection, smoothing down the shimmering fabric of my gown. "I *will* do this."

I make my way to the box, acutely aware of the eyes that follow my every move. As I settle into my seat, I allow my gaze to sweep across the opera house, taking in the glittering assemblage of supernatural society. In the box to my left, I recognize the Morozov clan, fierce stares gleaming with wolfish interest. To my right, the Regalis family lounges with innate feline grace.

But my stare doesn't linger on them for long, because there, in a box draped in shadows, I glimpse something that makes my heart stutter. A pair of dark eyes, burning with an intensity that I recognize all too well.

Kaisner Drachenstein.

I force myself to look away, my cheeks flushing with heat. As I turn, my gaze falls on a present I hadn't noticed before. A stunning bouquet of white roses, their petals practically glowing in the subdued light.

With trembling fingers, I reach for the card nestled

among the blooms. As I pluck it from its resting place, an object falls from within, landing on my lap with a soft tinkle. My breath catches as I lift the item—a white-gold necklace with a diamond-encrusted dragon pendant. The craftsman-ship is exquisite, the dragon's scales catching the light and throwing miniature rainbows across my skin.

I open the card, my heart pounding so loudly I'm sure the entire opera house must hear it. The message inside is simple, yet it sends a thrill through my body:

For the most captivating dragon of all.
- K.

My eyes dart back to Kaisner's box, finding his stare still fixed upon me. The intensity in those dark depths makes me feel as though I'm falling, drowning in a sea of hidden longings.

A smile tugs at the corners of my mouth, unbidden and impossible to suppress. My fingers close around the dragon pendant, its cool metal a stark contrast to the heat flooding my body. Every instinct screams at me to maintain decorum, to remember my place and the eyes that are surely upon me.

But in this moment, with Kaisner's gift in my hand and his gaze burning into me from across the theater, I find it increasingly difficult to care about propriety or expectations. My breath comes in short, excited gasps, and I have to consciously remind myself to unclench my other hand, which has balled into a fist in my lap.

I want to run to him. I want to flee. I want to put on the necklace and never take it off. I want to throw it into the Seine's depths… Conflicting desires battle within me, leaving me dizzy and intensely alive.

With a supreme effort of will, I school my features into a

facade of courteous curiosity, as if the bouquet and the gift are nothing more than a pleasant surprise. But inside, I'm a maelstrom of emotion, my heart singing an aria of its own— one of longing, excitement, and the thrill of forbidden attraction.

As the lights begin to dim and the curtain prepares to rise, I chance one last glance at Kaisner. The smile he gives me, small and secret and full of promise, tells me this is only the beginning. And despite the voice of reason screaming in the back of my mind, I can't wait to see what comes next.

I close my eyes, drawing in a deep breath and reaching for the well of strength within me. It's there, a burning coal at my core, the legacy of generations of Draken witches and warlocks. Their power flows through me, a river of fire in my veins.

When I open my eyes again, I am ready. Ready to face the music, the politics, the delicate dance of power and alliances that will play out around me this evening. Ready to be the face of the Draken clan, to make my family proud.

The curtain rises, and with it, the game begins.

The opera unfolds before me, pulling me into Giulia's world—a Vestal Virgin torn between sacred vows and forbidden love. Her torment weaves through the music, each note heavy with anguish, each breath laced with longing. But it's Aria Leone's voice that truly mesmerizes—impossibly pure, impossibly powerful. No mortal throat should be capable of such perfection. Each note she sings seems to bypass the ears entirely, resonating deep within the soul.

As her voice ascends beyond the limits of human ability, something cold settles in my stomach. I've heard whispers about the Leone bloodline—stories passed down through generations of opera patrons. Tales of Letizia Leone, Aria's ancestor, who was said to have struck a bargain centuries ago —her soul traded for a voice that could make angels weep and demons bow. A voice that could entrance kings, topple empires, and seduce the heavens themselves.

Watching Aria now, I wonder if those whispers are more than myth. Her voice breaks on a final, aching refrain, and something inside me tightens. Giulia's pain isn't mine, yet I feel it as if it were—as if Aria's otherworldly gift is drawing out emotions from places I didn't know existed.

What price, I wonder, did Letizia truly pay? And what price does Aria pay now, burdened with that cursed legacy in her throat?

Relief comes with the first intermission.

I resist the impulse to sag into my seat or press a hand to my heart. Instead, I rise with quiet control, posture poised. I long to stretch, to breathe away from the stifling scrutiny of the crowd. Though I don't dare look, I am aware of them— eyes on me, whispers behind fans, speculation humming like static against my skin.

Perhaps I'll linger just out of sight, concealed by the velvet drape of the private box.

I take a breath, willing stillness into my limbs—when a hush falls.

It starts in the neighboring boxes and ripples outward, as if something unseen has shifted the air.

I turn, just slightly, and see him.

A man has risen from the private box adjacent to mine, now stepping through the low velvet partition that separates our spaces. He moves with the smooth, deliberate grace of a predator, each step unhurried, precise. Even in a room filled with supernatural elite, he draws attention like gravity.

His tuxedo fits as if it were sewn onto his frame—black silk over a lean, muscular build. A crimson pocket square blooms against the fabric like a flame in midnight.

He approaches the edge of my box, and the scent that follows him is unmistakable—cedarwood, musk, and something colder, wilder. Not dangerous, exactly. But ancient. Alive.

In his hand, he carries an enchanted rose. The petals shimmer with glamour, subtly shifting hue—deep scarlet, soft blush, golden flame. A silent performance of wealth, magic, and taste.

Then his gaze finds mine—amber eyes threaded with gold, piercing yet unreadable. Like honey struck by lightning.

"Miss Draken," he says, a low growl that resonates in my chest and sends shivers down my spine—though whether from attraction or unease, I'm not entirely sure. "Allow me to introduce myself. Andrei Morozov, Alpha of the Siberian pack."

The Morozovs. One of the most formidable wolf shifter families in the supernatural world. I straighten imperceptibly, mindful of the importance of this interaction.

He inclines his head, voice smooth as dark velvet. "I couldn't help but notice how deeply the music moved you. Perhaps you'd care to explore the… primal undertones over a private supper?"

I accept the rose with a measured smile, careful to let neither warmth nor offense slip through. "Thank you, Mr. Morozov. The performance is indeed stirring," I reply evenly. "But I must decline. My responsibilities to the Draken family require my full attention tonight. I'm sure you understand."

A flicker of disappointment passes across his face, quickly replaced by a knowing smirk. "Of course," he murmurs, the words threaded with amusement and promise. "Another time, perhaps."

He steps back with quiet confidence, retreating to his box like a man who rarely hears no and never minds waiting.

I exhale slowly, turning toward the balustrade in search of

a moment's reprieve. My fingers brush the velvet rail, grounding myself in its cool texture.

Then, movement catches my eye.

Perched on the ledge is a small lion—folded from metallic gold paper, delicate and masterfully crafted. At first, I assume it's a charming trinket left behind by an earlier guest.

But then it stirs.

The origami lion arches its back in an elegant stretch, its golden flanks catching the soft glow of the chandelier. It leaps into motion with feline agility, bounding and twirling in a dance so fluid, so eerily lifelike, I forget to breathe.

With one final pirouette, it stills.

And begins to unravel.

The folds flatten, slow and precise, until only a square of gilded parchment remains. In looping script, a message appears:

> Mlle Draken,
> Your grace reminds me of a lioness guarding her pride. Might I tempt you to a private rendezvous at midnight?
> With anticipation,
> León Regalis.

The Regalis family—lion shifters of impeccable bloodline, stewards of influence beyond the art world. Their interest is never idle. This is not just a flirtation—it's a statement.

I tuck the message away, my mind whirling with the implications of these offerings. Each gift, each carefully worded summons, is more than it appears. They're calculated moves in a grand chess game—bids for power, attempts at forging alliances, subtle grasps at the dragon's legacy that flows within me.

The orchestra stirs, drawing me back to the present as the lights dim and the curtain rises once more.

I sit, spine straight, the rose resting lightly in my lap. And for a while, I let the music carry me away—into Giulia's tragedy, into her defiance, into the storm I can feel building just beyond the stage.

By the time the final, haunting notes of *"Tu che invoco con orrore"* fade into silence, I'm undone. My heart pounds with a tangle of emotions I can scarcely name. Tears gather behind my lashes, and I blink them back, struggling to steady my breath.

Giulia's torment—her wrenching pull between love and sacred duty—has found a mirror in me. Her voice, filled with agony and devotion, lingers like a bruise on the air.

> *"You whom I invoke with horror,*
> *Terrible goddess!*
> *Listen to me at last;*
> *May this miserable heart of mine breathe…"*

The words echo through me, a chilling reflection of my own turmoil.

Like her, I teeter on a precipice—torn between fear and longing. I whisper Kaisner's name in the privacy of my thoughts, even as I recoil from the raw power he holds over me. The *affanno*—that aching, breathless anguish—gathers in my chest whenever he is near. A torment so exquisite it's almost holy.

Somewhere deep within, I find myself pleading. Not to a goddess, but to *him*. To the warlock whose presence both steadies and unravels me. I want him to see me. To hear me. To quiet the storm he's awakened.

And yet… the thought terrifies me.

How did I get here?

What frightens me most is not the intensity of my emotions, but the quiet truth that I don't want to relinquish them.

Thunderous applause erupts around me, but I remain still—adrift in the storm of my thoughts. *La Vestale* has pierced deeper than I ever anticipated, laying bare the conflict I've tried so hard to silence.

Almost without meaning to, my gaze sweeps the opera house, searching for the one face that has come to mean so much to me.

And there he is, in his private box, dark eyes already fixed upon me.

Kaisner.

Our gazes meet, and in that instant, the world falls away. The gold leaf decorations blur into a hazy glow. The plush red velvet of the seats fades to a distant smudge of color. Even the swelling crescendo of the orchestra diminishes to a faint, far-off hum.

All that remains in sharp focus is Kaisner.

His maroon eyes hold mine, and the contact hits me like a live current. My skin prickles. A shiver climbs my spine, sharp and sudden.

I can't look away. I don't *want* to look away.

Every detail of him imprints itself in my mind: the chiseled line of his jaw, his closely trimmed beard, the flicker of hazel hidden in the deep brown of his gaze. The faint crease between his brows betrays the depth of his focus. I see the slow rise and fall of his chest beneath a tailored suit that fits like a second skin—power wrapped in restraint.

He doesn't move. He doesn't need to.

The space between us is nothing. Whether he's across the opera house or standing beside me, I feel him—*in* me. As if my body is attuned to his in some ancient, unspoken way.

Warmth spreads through my chest, down to my fingertips. Not just heat, but something deeper. A recognition. Completion. As if a piece inside me has shifted into place, quiet and irreversible.

The air is charged—alive. An understanding passes between us, silent but unmistakable.

Then, Kaisner rises. He steps back into the shadows of his private suite, moving toward what must be the door.

I don't think. I simply rise from my seat with practiced grace and slip away from our family's box, leaving Giulia's tormented voice echoing behind me.

My heels click softly on the marble floor. Every step seems both reckless and inevitable. What am I doing? The clans will talk. Someone is surely watching. But their eyes are distant, irrelevant—ghosts in the periphery.

The only thing I feel is the pulse of magic, thick in the air.

And the fire that draws me to him.

A tremor runs through me as I move through the opera house's gilded corridors, each step bringing me closer to him. The plush carpet hushes my footsteps, but the blood pounding in my ears is deafening. My hands tremble. I curl them into fists, willing my composure to hold.

Rounding the final corner, I spot Kaisner's men, stationed like statues outside a private balcony. Sharp-eyed. Expressionless. Watchful.

For a breathless second, I brace for resistance. But then, with the smallest nod, they step aside. The gesture is subtle, but the anticipation it sparks inside me is not.

One of them catches my eye. Marcus—tall, with dark

eyes and a scar along his jaw. I've seen him before, always near Kaisner. Always silent. Always armed.

"Enjoy your evening, Miss Draken," he says, his voice cold and precise—smooth on the surface but chilling beneath.

I give a polite nod, but his words linger in my mind. Something in his gaze holds too long, like he's committing details to memory that he shouldn't need to remember.

The ghost of Marcus' stare lingers, sending a shiver down my spine as I approach the tall doors. I stop at the threshold, my breath catching. Beyond waits Kaisner, and with him, a precipice. Power, danger, seduction.

The unknown.

The doors swing open without a sound.

A breeze rushes past, cool and fragrant, carrying the scent of damp stone, night flowers, and something unmistakably him. Aria's voice drifts through the night air, fainter now but still hauntingly beautiful.

I step outside.

Tall marble columns frame the balcony, lit in gold by the city's glow. Below, Paris shimmers—rooftops and bridges spun in light, the Seine a ribbon of dark silk threading it all together. But I hardly notice the view.

Because he's here.

Kaisner stands at the edge of the balcony, facing the night. His silhouette is carved from shadow and starlight, broad shoulders squared, jacket cut to fit him like it was born on his skin.

I stop, breath shallow. Just watching him is like standing too close to a flame.

He speaks into his phone, his voice low, deadly. *"Hast du wirklich geglaubt, du könntest mich hintergehen und damit davonkommen?"*

The German rolls off his tongue like velvet hiding a blade. I don't need a translation. The threat is unmistakable.

He ends the call. Slips the device into his pocket. Then—slowly—he turns.

That single movement stops time.

His eyes meet mine. And everything inside me goes quiet.

Maroon, rimmed with shadow, his gaze cuts straight through me. There's hunger there. And something rawer, darker—grief? Yearning? I don't know. But I feel it. Like it's mine too.

"Clarissa," he says.

My name in his voice is a sin. A vow. A warning.

It ripples through me, turning my spine to ice and my blood to fire. I try to speak, but the words vanish before reaching my lips.

We stand suspended in that charged silence—between choices, between danger and desire, between everything we were and everything we're about to become.

And then I step forward.

One step closer to the fire.

One step deeper into him.

Whatever lies ahead, I know this much: I won't walk away.

Not now. Not from this.

21

KAISNER

The City of Lights sprawls beneath me like a field of scattered diamonds, but not even Paris at her most decadent can rival the brilliance I've found within these walls. The opera hums behind me, gilded and grand—a palace of illusion and spectacle. Fitting. I've orchestrated a performance of my own tonight.

The cufflinks glint at my wrists as I adjust them, not out of vanity but ritual. Every detail, every gesture, is deliberate. *Chance encounters*, after all, require meticulous planning. Especially when the stakes are this high.

She doesn't know the lengths I've gone to. The meetings arranged to seem accidental. The brief glances across crowded halls. The slow, careful draw of her curiosity. Like a wolf circling its prey—not to kill, but to claim.

I've kept my distance. I've watched. Protected. Silently, relentlessly. She's under my guard more often than she realizes, her movements traced by shadows loyal only to me. But even my control has its limits.

Tonight, I breach them.

I pause at the threshold, my hand resting on the door

handle. Clarissa's words echo in my mind, a prophecy waiting to unfold: "A chance encounter can change the course of a lifetime."

Oh, my darling. If you only knew how much truth lay in that.

The night air brushes over my skin as I step onto the balcony I've claimed for this private interlude. Above, the moon drapes everything in pale silver, and below, the city pulses with secrets. The opera fades to a murmur behind thick doors. I breathe in deeply. Her scent lingers in the air already—jasmine and something warmer, more elusive. Like the echo of a dream I can't shake.

Then the phone vibrates in my pocket—an unwelcome intrusion.

I grit my teeth. Some obligations cannot be ignored, no matter how distasteful.

I answer with clipped precision, each syllable laced with quiet fury. The matter is handled swiftly. There's no room for loose ends in my world.

And then, I hear it. The soft rustle of silk, the click of heels on marble.

She's here.

She stands in the doorway like a vision conjured from starlight and willpower. That dress—gods, that dress—clings to her like molten gold, each curve illuminated as though the fabric itself worships her.

"I was beginning to think you wouldn't come," I say, my voice a low murmur shaped by equal parts relief and restraint.

She lingers near the doorway. Her presence is a question, not yet a promise.

"Run if you want," I add, tone velvet and steel. "But we both know you won't."

She steps forward, just one step—but it's enough. The

scent of her surrounds me now, and I'm lost. Her voice trembles as she answers, "I could never stay away... Kaisner, I—"

I close the distance between us, my fingers lifting to brush her cheek. So soft. So real. Her breath catches as I trace the corner of her mouth.

"I know," I whisper. "I feel it too."

The tension between us thrums like a live wire. It's not just desire—it's something older, deeper. Something dangerous.

"We shouldn't be doing this," she says, but she leans into me anyway. Her body, her breath, her heartbeat—they all betray her words. "It's too dangerous. If anyone were to find out..."

My expression hardens, a tempest of possessiveness and desire battling within me. "Do you want me to stop?" I challenge, my voice dark, husky. The words burn, but I must give her the power to choose. "Say the word, Clarissa, and I'll walk away right now."

Every fiber of my being screams to claim her, but I hold back, waiting.

Her eyes flutter closed. When they open again, they burn with a quiet, reckless certainty. "No. Don't stop. Don't ever stop."

With those words, my control finally shatters.

I claim her mouth, my hunger no longer something I can temper. Her kiss answers mine with equal ferocity—heat and hesitation colliding in a storm that threatens to swallow us whole.

When we part, I'm drunk on her taste, her scent, the feel of her body pressed against mine. My hands roam her curves, committing every inch of her to memory. I pull back slightly, needing to see her face, her flushed cheeks, swollen lips. The look in her eyes—desire, wonder, and a flicker of hesitation—sends a fresh wave of heat through me. I've dreamed of this moment, but the reality far exceeds any fantasy.

"There's something about you," she murmurs. "Something... intoxicating. You make me feel so reckless."

The words ignite a primal hunger within me, one I've fought to contain since I first laid eyes on her. "And you, *mein Lamm*," I respond, my voice husky with desire. "You make me feel... alive. Something I haven't felt in a long time."

I brush a stray lock of hair from her face, my fingers lingering on her soft skin, savoring the smoothness. The fire between us is a living, breathing force, threatening to consume us both. But I know I must tread carefully. Clarissa is precious, delicate—a rare flower I ache to possess, but fear crushing with my eagerness.

I inhale deeply, reining in my instincts. Our connection is too significant to rush. Instead, I decide to leave her with a memory, one that will haunt her dreams and call her back to me.

I lock my gaze onto hers, my voice low, rough with heat. "When you're alone tonight, I want you to remember this moment—every breath, every look." I let the pause hang, just long enough to make her ache for more. "Think of me, and how good it'll feel when I finally take you apart."

A shiver courses through her, and I see her nipples harden beneath the silk of her gown. She shudders. "I... I don't think we should talk about this."

"Oh, baby girl... I insist," I murmur, voice dark with intent. "Close your eyes. Let your mind wander. Picture me right here—my body pressed to yours, my breath on your neck." I step in, slow and deliberate, until we're flush. "Take in my scent. Feel what it does to you. That ache? That's mine now."

Her breath catches as she inhales deeply, drawing in my

musky essence—a heady blend of aged leather and exotic spices. "Kaisner... I shouldn't..."

"Mmm... but you want to," I murmur, tracing a fingertip down her collarbone. Her eyelids flutter closed, and a soft moan escapes her lips as she surrenders to the desire growing between us.

"Yes." She exhales, her voice ragged. "And I do... I do think about those... forbidden things."

Her admission is like a flame to tinder, igniting the inferno within me. I growl low in my throat, overcome with longing, I tilt her chin upward, our lips mere inches apart. "Tell me, what do you fantasize about when you're alone in your room? Do you think about me... touching you... worshipping every curve of your exquisite body?"

A blush rises to her cheeks, but she summons the courage to bare her most intimate desires. "I... think about your hands," she whispers, her voice trembling yet resolute. "They're strong... skilled... knowing."

I'm aroused by the vivid scenes that her words conjure.

My hands roam freely, tracing the gentle curves that drive me wild. "Like this?" I whisper, my fingers gliding, tantalizing.

She nods, her breath hitching as my touch grows bolder. "Yes... just like that."

I lean in, with slow intention, until my lips graze the shell of her ear—not a kiss, just a claim waiting to be made.

"Tell me, *Liebes*..." I whisper, voice thick with hunger, smoke and command entwined. "When you imagine my touch—what do you see?"

I pause. Sense the breath catch in her throat.

"No lies," I add, darker now, lips barely brushing her skin. "Because if you won't speak your fantasies... I'll have no choice but to drag them from you. Inch by inch."

She heaves a stuttered breath, her body trembling against mine.

"Your lips... on mine," she confesses, her voice barely a whisper. "Claiming me... possessing me... Trailing hot kisses down my neck... between my breasts... and lower..."

Unable to resist any longer, I capture her lips in a searing kiss, pouring all my desire and longing into it. She responds eagerly, her hands tangling in my hair as she pulls me closer, deepening the kiss.

Our bodies press together, the heat between us intensifying with each passing moment. I trail kisses down her neck, savoring the taste of her skin, the way she arches against me.

"Tell me more," I demand, my voice raw with restraint.

"I—I imagine you parting my thighs... moving between them... Oh gods!" A low cry spills from her lips as I perform her narration to the letter, my hand gliding underneath her skirt.

"Mm... I want to be inside you right now," I groan, the thought unraveling my control. "Helplessly lost in your welcoming warmth. Watching your face twist in pleasure as I devour every part of you... Every moan, every whimper, only for me."

She bites her lower lip, her body a shuddering canvas of longing.

"You are mine," I growl, my hands gripping her hips possessively. "And I will have you, in every way imaginable."

She moans softly, her eyes dark with desire. "Yes... I want that... I want... you."

Her words dissolve into a breathy whimper as I follow her fantasy, brushing my lips along her collarbone, savoring the way she melts beneath me.

"I know what you crave," I whisper into her ear, my breath teasing her heated skin. "You want me to make you feel things no one else can… to unlock a world so forbidden it would leave you trembling for more."

At this, her legs quiver ever so slightly, and she exhales my name—a prayer, a plea. It takes every ounce of my will not to claim her here and now. Instead, I cup her jaw, my thumb grazing her parted lips.

"Touch yourself for me tonight," I growl, the command a velvet chain wrapped in fire. "Slip those delicate fingers beneath the sheets and pretend they're mine—tracing, teasing… driving you to the edge and holding you there until you're breathless with need."

"*Es würde mir so viel bedeuten.*" It would mean so much to me, I purr in my mother tongue. My voice softens, a rasp against her pulse. "Let me own your pleasure… even when I'm not there to taste it."

With agonizing reluctance, I drag my hand away. As much as I ache to fulfill each of her fantasies, not here. Not like this. She deserves more than a fleeting indulgence. *Du schöne, dir gehört nur das Beste…* Only the best for my beautiful treasure.

"Kaisner," she gasps, breathless.

"Go on," I encourage, my voice a low growl. "Think of how those fingertips would dance over your heated flesh, just like mine would, when I claim you with a hunger that knows no limits. Let your thoughts drown in my touch, as I tease and worship your body."

Her breathing quickens, her eyes fluttering shut as she surrenders to my words. I can almost perceive the heat radiating from her, the dampness her desire would leave behind. My entire being aches to be there with her, to savor the proof of her longing.

"Think of me," I growl, my voice thick with need, "as you slip inside your sweet folds. How wet you'd be for me alone. Imagine it's my tongue, lapping at your nectar like the finest ambrosia."

Her chest rises and falls, the rhythm of her breath betraying the fire building inside her. I can envision her hand moving beneath the duvet, pressing her body with mounting urgency. The thought ignites something primal within me, my suit pants straining against my aching length.

She unravels before me—beautiful, uncontainable— more exquisite than any gilded ornament adorning the Opera's grand halls.

"Faster," I command, the words a raw growl that slips past my lips without control. "Picture my fingers plunging deep inside you, stretching you open for what's to come."

She whimpers at the thought, and I can barely hold myself together. The image of her forefinger disappearing into her wetness threatens to undo me.

"That's it," I groan, my voice rough as gravel. "Moan for me, *meine Liebe*... Let me hear how much you crave your Kaisner."

I tighten my grip on the balcony's railing, bracing myself in our precarious reality—both in this moment and the danger that looms. One wrong move, and everything could come crashing down around us, like dominoes toppling in a chaos of our own making.

We stand at the edge of the unimaginable, not just a fleeting encounter, but a spark that could ignite a fire so fierce it would leave our world in ashes if anyone found out.

The union of a Drachenstein and a Draken? It would be unprecedented—an earth-shattering disruption in the fragile power dynamics of our supernatural society. For centuries, our families have been rivals, each vying for supremacy in the shadowed realm we both inhabit.

Her response is a soft, desperate moan, and my knees nearly buckle at the sound. I shut my eyes, my breath ragged as I fight to hold on to the last remnants of restraint. Every inch of me aches to lose myself in her warmth, to claim her under the cold, unyielding gaze of the stars. But I know we cannot risk it—not yet. Not when everything is at stake.

"I can't take much more without you," she finally pants out. The thought of her hand working herself into a frenzy is my undoing. I clutch the balcony railing harder, my fingers pressing into the stone until it seems the only thing grounding me.

"Kaisner!"

I open my eyes, our gazes meeting like two celestial bodies destined for collision. The fire in her stare mirrors the one raging in me, and in that instant, I'm lost—completely undone.

Our lips crash together with an intensity that shatters all our attempts at restraint. We devour each other's mouths, tongues twisting in a fevered, forbidden dance.

Gasping for air, we break apart just long enough to catch our breath before our lips meet again, this time with a desperate hunger. My tongue slides into the slit of her mouth, and as we surrender to the flames of passion, we teeter on the edge of reason itself. Never before have I felt such a ravenous desire for another. This—this is a fire that consumes me from within, one that can only be extinguished by her.

I stand here, trapped in a devastating realization. This devouring blaze sparked by her presence—it's burning through my carefully laid plans, threatening to turn my ambitions to ash. But can I allow myself to fail now, when I'm so close?

For so long, I've walked the path of shadows, my every move calculated, each piece positioned with meticulous care. But now...

My fingers trace the delicate line of her jaw, marveling at how something so gentle could shatter years of resolve.

As we part, my forehead brushes against hers, and my hands glide up her neck, gently cupping her face. "Clarissa," I manage, my voice barely above a rasp. The burden of my dark secrets presses against my chest, demanding release, and the next words spill from my lips without hesitation. "There's something you must know—"

The balcony doors burst open with a sharp crack, the sound jarring us both from our embrace. My heart leaps into my throat, and I sense her body tremble against mine as we turn to face the intruder.

Standing in the doorway, silhouetted by the dim light of the room behind him, is my enforcer, Janik.

"My apologies for the intrusion," he says stiffly, his eyes darting between us before locking onto me. "But my king, it's urgent."

22

KAISNER

I pull myself away from her warmth, and straighten my clothes as I compose my features into the impassive mask of a sovereign.

"What is it?" I ask, forcing my voice to remain even.

Janik takes in our disheveled state, the flushed cheeks, the lingering heat in the air—but doesn't comment. "We've received word from our spies within rival territory," he begins, his voice clipped and professional as always. "They've uncovered plans for an imminent attack on your position—tonight."

Lust burns away in an instant, replaced by the cold rush of adrenaline. My mind shifts gears, already calculating contingencies and counter-strategies.

I turn to Clarissa. My hands frame her face, thumbs brushing her cheekbones like a farewell and a brand. "Go," I tell her, the command a knife to my chest.

Her eyes widen, confusion and hurt flickering across her features. I memorize every detail—the way her lashes cast shadows on her pale cheeks, the tremor in her lower lip, the trust that still shines in her gaze despite everything.

My voice drops, rough and guttural. "I won't let this world drag you into its filth. Not mine. Not theirs... I'd rather tear it apart than let it touch you."

The words echo with finality. I trace her features with shaking fingers, committing her to memory like a prayer I'll carry into whatever darkness awaits.

"You don't look back, Clarissa. Not until I come for you. And I *will* come for you."

She stiffens, her sapphire gaze searching mine. But there's no time for explanations.

"Which faction?" I demand, my voice sharp with urgency.

Janik's usual stoicism cracks, just slightly. It tells me all I need to know. "Intelligence suggests a joint operation, *Mein König*. The Silver Claw Pack is leading the charge, but they've enlisted the Shadowcat Syndicate."

Scheisse. Brute force and dark magic. A dangerous combination. A clever one. I have to admire their strategy, even as I plan their downfall.

Clarissa is still here, her presence both an anchor and a complication. I catch the shadow of worry in her expression as she glances between us.

"Kaisner, what's happening?" Her voice is steady, but fear lingers beneath it, and that hurts like hell. "Who are these people?"

I meet her gaze, torn between the instinct to shield her and the knowledge that ignorance could get her killed. "Remember when I told you there were things about me you didn't know?" My voice softens. "This is one of them. I have... powerful enemies."

"But why? What do they want?" The innocence in her question is almost painful to hear.

"To destroy me," I say simply. "To take what's mine."

The words carry a significance she may not fully grasp,

but I see the realization dawn in her eyes. She is *mine* now, too. The thought of these factions even setting their sights on her ignites a feral rage within me.

I turn back to Janik. There will be time to talk later. Now is the time for war.

"Initiate Protocol Hellfire," I command, my tone leaving no room for hesitation. "And get word to the Reaper—I'm calling in that favor he owes me."

Janik inclines his head and steps away to make the call. I exhale sharply, turning back to Clarissa. The burden of leadership presses down on me, yet in this moment, all I see is her.

"I meant what I said," I murmur. "You need to leave. I can't protect you and fight at the same time." The words taste bitter on my tongue. I, Kaisner Drachenstein, admitting I can't do something? It would be laughable, if it wasn't so damn annoying.

Her sapphire eyes flare with defiance. Fear lingers there, true and tangible, but it's overshadowed by a determination that fills me with a pride I've never known. This is the woman who has captured my heart, who stands tall in the face of danger.

"I won't leave you," she whispers.

Four simple words, and they unravel me. In them, I hear everything unspoken, every promise yet to be made.

I seize her in a desperate kiss, raw and consuming, pouring into it everything I can't bring myself to say. Her lips are a perfect fit, her scent—jasmine and rain—searing itself into my memory. The taste of her, the feel of her, will haunt me long after this night is over.

When we finally part, she surprises me. Her delicate hands cup my face with a tenderness that threatens to undo me completely. Her eyes shine with unshed tears, locking onto mine with an intensity that leaves me breathless.

"Stay safe," she murmurs, tracing the curve of my cheek with her thumb. "Whatever happens, promise me you'll stay safe."

I press a kiss to her palm, knowing I cannot promise what she asks. In my world, promises are sacred, binding. To vow safety would be foolish. So I say nothing.

My stare locks with hers, trying to convey everything I cannot say. The depth of my feelings, the fierce protectiveness that burns within me, the regret at having drawn her into this dangerous world of mine.

I turn to Janik. "Escort Lady Clarissa back to Draken Manor. Take Marcus with you." My voice is harsher than I intend, but I can't afford weakness now. "Double the guard. No one lays a hand on her. *Verstanden?*"

Clarissa flinches, caught off guard by the shift in me. She hasn't yet seen this side—the cold, ruthless king. The man forged by blood and war. Being constantly on high alert would be the life to expect should she choose to accept me as her mate. Oh, but she would have nothing to fear then. Not while I'm around to care for her and make her the happiest woman alive.

Janik bows his head. "Your Majesty."

"Marcus," he calls over his shoulder, gesturing to the man standing near the doorway. "Stay with Miss Draken while I bring the car around. Too many eyes on this street."

Marcus steps forward, his expression unreadable. "My lady." He extends his arm to Clarissa.

For the briefest moment, she hesitates before placing her hand in his.

I watch as she walks away, her midnight-blue gown shimmering under the chandeliers, burning the image into my memory. My jaw tightens as possessiveness surges through me. Another man escorts her from my sight, but it is my name that lingers on her lips.

I force myself to remain still, to resist the urge to rush after her, to take her in my arms one last time. Instead, I linger, my eyes never leaving her.

Only when she's gone do I move, turning to face the storm that's brewing.

CLARISSA

awn bleeds through the curtains like a wound, painting my bedroom in shades of amber and regret. Another sleepless night. Another eight hours spent haunted by the ghost of his touch, the echo of promises whispered against my skin. The city wakes below my window, just another Saturday morning, but I remain trapped in the liminal space between dreams and nightmares.

I drag myself to the mirror, wincing at the shadows under my eyes. Sophie noticed them yesterday, her voice laced with concern as she blamed the upcoming gala. If only she knew. The meetings, the deadlines, the meticulous seating charts—they've been my escape. Structure and schedules are easier to face than the thoughts that keep me awake.

The woman in the mirror looks distant. Pale. Eyes too bright, too tired. My fingers drift to the diamond pendant resting in the hollow of my throat—Kaisner's gift. Its cool weight against my skin sends a shiver through me. A silent echo of that night at the opera.

Three weeks. Three long, tormenting weeks of silence. Of questioning whether that night was real. Whether I meant anything at all. Was I just another conquest, another notch in Kaisner Drachenstein's belt?

A sudden buzz shatters the stillness—my phone.

My body tenses on instinct.

For a single, breathless moment, I think it's him. But no —Nik's name flashes across the screen. Relief and disappointment collide, leaving a hollow ache in their wake.

"Hey," I answer, forcing a brightness I don't feel.

"Clarissa." His voice is tight. Controlled. "Why am I hearing about you attending a gala in our family's name— alone? And leaving the opera early?"

There it is.

My stomach drops. Of course, the rumor mill would churn this out. Truthfully, I'm surprised the call didn't come sooner.

I close my eyes, already picturing his expression. The furrowed brow, the clenched jaw, the impatient pacing in whatever hotel room he's holed up in this time. "It's not what you think," I say, trying to keep my voice steady. "I wasn't feeling well. And I wasn't alone. Some of our people were there."

"Not what I think?" Nik's voice rises. "Clarissa, do you have *any* idea what this looks like? The whispers it's started?"

Anger flares through my veins, hot and sudden. "Our reputation is fine, Nik. I represented us well. The rest is idle gossip, and you know it."

The silence that follows is heavy. I can almost see Nik pinching the bridge of his nose, a habit of his I've only recently learned.

"I'm just worried about you," he whispers. "With every-thing that's going on... Rissy, this isn't like you."

Guilt lances through me. Here I am, keeping secrets from the one person who's always had my back. But how do I explain Kaisner? How do I say I've been unraveling by degrees since the night we kissed—and since he vanished without a trace?

"I'm okay," I say instead. "The gallery's doing well. I've got everything under control. Please, focus on the tour."

We speak for a few more minutes, exchanging the kind of everyday details that mask everything left unsaid. When I hang up, I feel both lighter and heavier. Lighter for having calmed his fears. Heavier because I'm still keeping him in the dark.

I set the phone down and stare at my reflection. Pale skin. Eyes rimmed with exhaustion and grief. Hollow cheeks. A ghost of who I was.

Enough.

I strip off my nightgown and sink into the bathtub, the jasmine-scented water wrapping around me with soothing warmth. I let myself slide beneath the surface, eyes closed, wishing I could wash away the ache, the questions, the hurt of not knowing where I stand with him.

When I emerge, tears mingle with the droplets running down my face. I hate him. Hate him for what he's made me feel, for disappearing without a word. But no amount of fury can cauterize the wound he left behind.

"Damn you, Kaisner," I whisper. My voice echoes off the marble tiles, mocking me with their futility. Because even as I curse his name, my heart aches with longing.

I scrub at my skin almost violently, as if I could somehow erase the memory of his touch, the ghost of his kisses that haunts my dreams. But it's useless. He's carved himself into my very being, marked me as his in ways that go deeper than any claiming bite.

Eventually, the water begins to cool. I step out, wrapping myself in a plush towel, and face my reflection in the fog-streaked mirror. My eyes are red-rimmed, but clearer somehow. Stronger.

I dig through my closet and choose a pale blue sweater dress and cream-colored wool coat. The familiar routine of dressing, of making myself presentable, seems like armor being assembled piece by piece. Each button fastened, each strand of hair smoothed into place, is an act of defiance against the weakness he's conjured in me.

I may love him with every fiber of my being, but I am still Clarissa Draken. And it's time I remembered that.

A swipe of mascara, a touch of color on my lips. Small acts of rebellion against the melancholy that's held me captive. I twist my hair into a neat chignon, refusing to wince at how prominent my cheekbones have become.

My phone buzzes again. This time, it's a text from Samara, asking me to come to Alexeev Manor. The Alexeevs aren't exactly known for their love of Drakens. But if Sam's calling for me, it must be important.

The bustle of Paris greets me as I step outside. The cold air bites at my cheeks, bringing color to my pale skin. It hurts, but it's a good hurt—a reminder that I'm still here, still breathing, still moving forward despite everything.

I may not be okay, not yet. But I'm trying. And for now, that has to be enough.

The taxi ride to l'Île de la Cité resembles a passage between worlds. Outside the window, the city's modern bustle fades, replaced by the quiet elegance of increasingly affluent neighborhoods.

In my lap, my phone vibrates, its cheerful chime unnervingly out of place. I glance down, and my heart clenches.

Time for your daily German lesson!

I stare at the screen, remembering my excitement when I first downloaded the app—how eager I'd been to learn. Now, those once-harmless German phrases cut deep, each one a fresh reminder of him. Of his voice, deep and rich, whispering *meine Liebe* against my skin.

With trembling fingers, I swipe the notification away. I can't bear it—not today. Not when every German word feels like another splinter in my fractured heart.

The phone slips into my purse, face down. One more defeat in a morning already heavy with them.

The manor's iron gates loom before me, intricate and imposing. Before the driver can reach for the intercom, the doors swing open in eerie silence. Ice skitters down my nape.

The driveway stretches endlessly ahead, flanked by perfectly sculpted topiaries and riotous flower beds. The manor itself is a behemoth of stone and glass—stunning in its grandeur, suffocating in its implications. This is the seat of Ursa power in Paris, and I'm walking straight into its maw.

As I approach, the front door opens on its own, revealing a butler who looks as though he stepped out of a period drama. His face remains unreadable as he inclines his head in greeting.

"Miss Draken. This way, please."

I follow him into a foyer vast enough to swallow my entire London flat. The air is thick with history, the weight of generations pressing down on me. Stern-faced Alexeevs stare from gilded portraits lining the walls, their eyes tracking my every move.

A shiver threatens to crawl up my spine. Guest or not, I can't shake the feeling that I don't belong here. That I'm an intruder.

Lost in thought, I don't notice the mountain of a man rounding the corner—until I crash straight into him. It's like colliding with a wall of solid muscle. The impact jolts me backward, but before I can fall, strong hands close around my arms, steadying me with effortless strength.

I look up... and up... and up.

The man before me towers well over six feet, his shoulders broad enough to fill a doorway. His face, framed by a thick, dark beard, is all hard angles and sharp planes—formidable, unreadable, carved from stone.

But it's his eyes that seize me. Maroon orbs, burning with an inner fire. Uncannily familiar. Eerily reminiscent of another pair I can't seem to forget.

"Gavriil Alexeev," he rumbles, his voice so deep it seems to resonate in my very bones. "You must be Clarissa Draken."

I swallow hard, resisting the instinct to step back. "Yes," I manage, willing myself to remain composed. "It's a pleasure to be here, Mr. Alexeev."

To my surprise, his stern expression eases—just slightly.

"Gavriil," he corrects. "Any friend of Samara is welcome… even if they are a Draken." The last part is more of a mutter, accompanied by the faintest curve of his lips—wry, amused, but not unkind.

The unexpected warmth in his otherwise gruff demeanor catches me off guard. I've heard plenty about Gavriil Alexeev, and none of it suggested friendliness—especially not toward a Draken.

"I appreciate your hospitality," I say, offering a brief but genuine smile.

Gavriil nods, then gestures down the hallway. "Samara's in the parlor. I'll take you to her."

As we walk, I can't help but steal glances at my imposing guide. Despite his sheer size and the fearsome reputation that precedes him, there's something almost… gentle about him. It's nothing like the ruthless Ursa King I've heard murmured about in supernatural circles—an enigma I can't quite figure out.

We reach a set of grand double doors. Gavriil pushes them open with ease, revealing a parlor that redefines opulence. Samara is there, engrossed in conversation with a man I recognize immediately.

Alexei Morozov.

Sam looks up as we enter, her face breaking into a wide smile. "Clarissa!" she exclaims, rising to her feet with a warmth that instantly calms me. "I hope my brother didn't scare you," she adds, shooting Gavriil a playful yet reproachful glance. "I'm so glad you could make it."

As I step forward to embrace my friend, an unsettling sensation settles in my chest. I've walked into something more than a casual social call. The air in the room hums with an energy I can't quite place, and the presence of both Gavriil and Alexei only deepens my sense that a much bigger story is unfolding before me.

Whatever reason Samara has for bringing me here, I have a feeling that it's about to shift the ground beneath me. And as I think of Kaisner, of the secrets I'm keeping, and the questions burning inside me, I wonder if I'm ready for any more changes at all.

"Make yourself at home," Gavriil says, a rare warmth lingering under his usual gruffness. Without another word, he turns and leaves the parlor.

Alexei Morozov rises from his seat, his movements fluid and predatory, carrying an air of danger that sends a chill through me. He approaches with a smile that doesn't quite reach his eyes, extending a hand in greeting.

"Lady Clarissa," he says, his voice a rich baritone that fills the room like smoke. "It's a pleasure to see you again."

Before I can respond, he takes my hand with a grip that is firm and lingering. In one smooth motion, he draws me closer, leaning in for the customary air kiss on both cheeks. His cologne, a heady blend of sandalwood and something darker, surrounds me. His beard scratches my skin, and a shiver skitters down my spine. Whether it's discomfort or something else, I can't quite tell.

"Alexei is a dear friend of the family," Sam interjects warmly as he releases me. "Our alliance with the Morozovs goes way back—*to the dawn of the Imperial era.*" She speaks the words playfully, but they're fully intended.

I step back slightly, gathering my composure. Alexei's gaze is cool, calculating, and I can't help but think he's sizing me up, his eyes sharp with determination.

"The pleasure is mine, Mr. Morozov," I manage, my voice betraying the dryness in my throat. I smooth my sweater nervously, a habit I can't seem to shake.

"Call me Alexei," he insists, his tone detached. "May I call you Clarissa?"

"Please do," I reply, offering a warm but cautious smile, still keeping my guard up.

"We were just discussing our shared passion for the arts and the upcoming gala at the Galerie Lumière," he continues. "Samara mentioned her friend runs the place. Imagine my delight when I learned that such a friend was… you." He flashes me a charming smile. "Perhaps you might be able to help us secure invitations?"

A surge of pride swells inside me at the mention of the gallery, but I force myself to remain composed. "Oh, I wouldn't say *I run* the place," I demur, smiling modestly. "But I'd be happy to arrange invitations for you both."

Alexei's smile widens, a calculated glint in his eyes. "That's very kind of you." He glances at his wristwatch with a barely concealed air of impatience. "My dear ladies, I'm afraid I've got to run—I'm expected at the Greniers'."

"Not the Greniers? Oh, I pity you," Sam teases with a playful smile.

Alexei cracks a handsome grin, but as he turns to me, his expression shifts, his lips curling into a smile that lacks any warmth. "I do hope we'll be seeing more of each other, Clarissa. A few of us are planning to check out that new club, Éclipse, tonight. Would you care to join us?"

Something flickers in Alexei's eyes—interest? Calculation? I can't tell.

"We'd be delighted!" Sam says, her voice light with enthusiasm. "It's been ages since I've gotten a taste of the city's nightlife."

With a final nod to us both, Alexei excuses himself. As soon as the door clicks shut behind him, Samara spins toward me, her features packed with barely contained excitement.

"You've made quite an impression on our dear Alexei," she says. "The second he found out about our connection, he practically begged me to call you down here—and he's *not* the begging kind."

Heat rushes to my cheeks. "He seems... nice," I reply, unsure how to respond to the sudden attention.

Samara's expression shifts quickly, her excitement fading into concern. "All right, spill it," she demands. "What happened at the opera? You went by yourself, then bailed in the middle of the second act? What the hell was *that* all about?"

"You've heard, huh?" I murmur with half a shrug.

"*Everyone* did," she replies dryly.

The pressure of the past few weeks crashes down on me all at once. I sink into one of the plush armchairs, suddenly recognizing the exhaustion in my bones. "It's... complicated, Sam."

Samara settles across from me, her gaze unwavering. "Complicated how? Clarissa, you know you can tell me anything. *No secrets between us*, remember?"

I take a deep breath, bracing myself. The diamond

pendant around my neck feels like a stone, heavy against my skin. "I... I wasn't alone at the opera."

Samara's eyebrows shoot up. "Oh?"

"I was with..." I hesitate, knowing that once I say his name, there's no going back. "I was with Kaisner."

A deafening silence falls in the room. The air shifts as shock, concern, and something akin to fear flicker across Sam's face. "So it's true, then?" she whispers, her voice barely a breath. "Someone mentioned it to me last week, but I dismissed it as a rumor."

And just like that, the dam breaks. Weeks of pent-up emotions flood out in a rush. I tell her everything—my electric connection with Kaisner from the very first moment, the intensity that burned between us, the kiss at the opera that had me reeling. My voice cracks as I describe the sudden, painful way he left, the silence that has stretched on since.

"I don't know what to think," I manage, the tears pressing at the back of my eyes. "Was it all a game to him? Did any of it mean anything at all?"

Samara shifts closer, pulling me into her arms. "Oh, my dearest," she murmurs, her voice soft but heavy with sympathy. "I had no idea you were going through all this."

I lean into her, finally letting the tears fall. They streak down my cheeks, hot and unrelenting, each one carrying with it a bit of the pain and confusion I've been holding inside. "Sam, I can't stop thinking about him, but I haven't heard a single word from him. What if... what if I imagined it all? What if I'm just another conquest to him?"

Samara gently strokes my hair, her touch a balm to my frayed nerves. "I've never seen you like this about anyone," she murmurs. "Listen to me, Clarissa. Whatever happened between you and Kaisner, it was real. I'm sure of it."

I sniffle, wiping at my eyes, unable to stop the tears. "But why hasn't he contacted me?"

"I don't know," Sam admits, her demeanor gentle but resolved. "But Kaisner Drachenstein is a powerful man, with a lot on his plate. You mentioned he was being targeted by his enemies the last time you saw him—so maybe that's why he's been radio silent? Maybe... maybe there's more going on than we know."

A soothing stillness embraces us for a moment, the soft ticking of an ornate clock on the mantle the only sound.

"Clarissa," Samara says finally, her tone serious, as if considering each word carefully. "I love you, and I'll support you no matter what. But... Kaisner is dangerous. The Drachensteins have a reputation, and it's not a kind one. Please, promise me you'll be careful."

I nod, gratitude and stubborn defiance swirling inside me. Kaisner may be dangerous, but there's so much more to him than that. I'm certain. I have to be.

"I promise," I say. "And Sam? Please don't say anything to Nik. He'd lose his mind if he knew."

She winces at the sudden realization. "Shit, you're right. Nik is going to hate this. He absolutely loathes that family."

"I know..." I breathe, the tears threatening to spill over again.

Samara mimics zipping her lips. "Your secret is safe with me. Now," she says, a mischievous glint flashing in her eyes, "You need a night out. Let's take Alexei up on his offer and hit Éclipse this weekend. He's a great chaperone, we can trust him. It'll do you good to let loose a little."

Despite my emotional exhaustion, a smile tugs at the corners of my lips. "You know what?" I sniff, wiping away the last of my tears. "That sounds perfect."

As we start making plans, a burden slowly lifts from my shoulders. I may not have answers about Kaisner, but for now, that doesn't matter. What matters is that I'm not alone. With friends like Samara by my side, I can face anything.

24

CLARISSA

The doors of Éclipse glide open, revealing a world suspended between decadence and shadow. The muffled bass from the street erupts into full intensity, wrapping around me like a living thing, pulsing with the heartbeat of the club. The air is thick with perfume, cigars, sweat, and something older, darker—power dressed in velvet.

It takes a moment for my eyes to adjust to the dim illumination. Candles flicker in gilded sconces. Chandeliers drip with crystals, their glow casting fractured light across the crowd. Burgundy velvet drapes frame intimate alcoves, and black Chesterfield sofas sprawl like thrones for the elite. Ivy curls down marble columns, softening the opulence, giving the space a strange, dreamlike quality.

The dance floor pulses—bodies swaying in rhythm, lost in the music. But it's the second tier that draws my eye. The VIP balconies perch above like watchtowers, each one a fortress for powerbrokers cloaked in shadow.

The bar glows at the far end, bottles of top-shelf liquor gleaming like stained glass. Bartenders move like clockwork, pouring more than just drinks—liquid masks, fuel for seduction and sabotage.

Even from here, I can sense them—supernaturals mingled among the horde of humans. Their energy hums beneath the surface, barely contained, a storm waiting to break. Predators in designer suits. Queens masked in silk. Eyes that gleam too brightly. Movements too smooth… This isn't just a nightclub. It's an open arena, and only the strong survive.

As we enter, a ripple cuts through the crowd. Heads turn. Whispers rise. The space parts instinctively, an unspoken acknowledgment of who we are.

Samara squeezes my hand. "Ready?" she says, her voice light, but I catch the sharpness beneath it. She knows exactly what kind of place this is.

I straighten my spine, lifting my chin. Whatever happens tonight, I am the Draken heiress. I belong here as much as anyone.

Our group forms around us as we move further inside. Samara falls into easy conversation with Alexei and his friends. Their laughter rises above the music, sharp and carefree, a contrast to the unease in my gut.

Alexei's gaze finds mine, his smile razor-sharp. "First round's on me," he announces, gesturing grandly to the bar. His friends cheer, already drifting toward it like a pack on the prowl.

I hesitate. For a moment, I feel out of sync, disconnected from their easy revelry. But Samara loops her arm through mine, anchoring me to the moment. "Come on," she urges, her eyes dancing. "Let's have some fun!"

I nod, shoving my uncertainty aside. This is what people do, isn't it? Drink. Dance. Forget.

Alexei orders a round of shots—a vibrant blue liquid that

smells like tropical fruit and recklessness. He hands me one, his fingers lingering a beat too long.

"To new friends and unforgettable nights," he toasts, his grin all charm and calculation.

Glasses clink, drinks disappear. I hesitate for a fraction of a second—then throw the shot back. The burn ignites a fire in my chest, spreading outward in a slow, curling heat.

Alexei's eyes sparkle with mischief as he watches me. "Один—не пушка!" he laughs, his accent thickening. "One is never enough."

Before I can react, he's signaling the bartender, a smile tugging at the corner of his lips. "One more round!"

The glass is refilled almost before I can register his words. This time, I don't pause. I throw it back, feeling the liquid scorch its way down my throat, sharp and raw.

Something shifts inside me—wilder, more vibrant. The alcohol spreads through my veins, dulling the edge of my thoughts, wrapping me in a warm, reckless buzz. I feel lighter. Bolder. Like the world just became a little more manageable.

Alexei leans closer. His voice reaches me again, but it's distant now, like I'm underwater. "Let's make this a night to remember."

I nod, my smile a little too wide, a little too knowing. Countless stares fall on me—but suddenly, I don't care anymore. And as the bass reverberates through my body, I let Samara lead me into the throng of dancers, our bodies moving with the beat, with the pulse of the night.

Gods! This is what it means to be alive, to be young and full of possibility. I'm ready to embrace it all, to let the night and the city sweep me off my feet and into a world of passion and adventure. I'm ready for this. Ready for everything.

Samara's laugh rings out beside me. She pulls me close and we start singing along to the lyrics, our voices lost in the collective energy of the crowd. We sway together, our movements wild and carefree.

The night feels endless, a swirling blur of color and sound, and for the first time in ages, an overwhelming sense of freedom washes through me. I spin with the beat, laughing, the tension in my chest easing with each note. My gaze drifts upward to the second tier of Éclipse.

That's when I see him.

Kaisner.

He stands at the railing of one of the VIP balconies, a silhouette against the warm glow spilling from within. Even from here, his presence is a gravity all its own—an unspoken command that shifts the very air around him. His sharp, cold eyes are fixed on me, burning through the crowd as though I'm the only thing that matters.

Dressed in black, his tailored suit accentuates the broad cut of his shoulders, the power that hums beneath the fabric. The club's golden light casts shadows across his features, sharpening the line of his jaw, the hollow of his cheek.

But it's his eyes that snare me. Even through the dim haze, I sense them. Fiery embers locked onto mine, unwavering.

A sharp pang of emotion crashes over me—excitement, longing, but beneath it all, anger.

Weeks of silence. Weeks of replaying that night at the opera, of questioning what was real and what was illusion. The passion we shared. The abrupt way he left.

And now, here he is. Watching me.

I tear my gaze away, my heart hammering.

As if on cue, a stranger steps into my space. Tall, lean, his amber eyes glowing in the dark—*shifter*.

"May I have this dance?" he asks, his voice smooth, barely audible over the pounding music.

I glance back at Kaisner, who hasn't moved. Still watching.

A reckless idea takes root. What better way to show Kaisner that I won't be taken for granted than to enjoy myself with someone else?

I turn back to the shifter, letting a slow smile curve my lips. "I'd love to."

He takes my hand, guiding me into the rhythm of the crowd. The music swallows us whole. His hands settle on my hips, my arms loop around his neck. The dance is slow, deliberate—a silent performance meant for an audience of one.

I don't glance up. I don't have to. I can *feel* Kaisner's gaze —a smoldering heat searing into my back.

The beat shifts, deep and sensual. The shifter leans in, his breath warm against my ear. I tilt my head slightly, hair spilling down my back, playing into the moment. It's exhilarating, this sense of power that comes from knowing I'm being watched, from knowing that every sway of my hips, every brush of my body against my dance partner's, is a deliberate provocation.

Then—a hand clamps around my arm. Firm. Unyielding.

I turn sharply, meeting Janik's cool, mysterious gaze. His expression is stoic, but there's a glimmer of something— amusement, perhaps—in his eyes.

"Miss Draken," he says, his voice cutting through the music like steel. "Your presence is requested in the VIP area."

The words aren't a suggestion.

I glance up at the balcony where Kaisner stands, his posture tense, his jaw clenched. Even from this distance, I can see the storm brewing in his features, the barely contained rage and possessiveness.

A thrill of satisfaction runs through me. Good. Let him stew in his own jealousy for a bit. Let him suffer a fraction of the frustration and confusion I've been grappling with these past weeks.

My dance partner stiffens beside me. "Hey, man," he snaps, his grip on my waist tightening. "We're in the middle of something."

Janik doesn't move. Doesn't blink. The tension in the air sharpens, coiling tight. A silent conversation passes between them—one that ends with the shifter releasing me, jaw clenched.

"Fine," he mutters. "She's not worth the trouble, anyway."

Janik ignores him, turning back to me with the same professional detachment.

I exhale slowly, forcing my pulse to steady. Then, with a wry smile, I murmur, "Lead the way."

From above, Kaisner remains still. The world sways around us: music, laughter, movement. But none of it reaches us. Not in this moment.

His gaze on me never wavers. And in it, I see everything. The spark of gentle fury. His wounded pride. The challenge.

I lift my chin and follow Janik through the crowd. Each step bringing me closer to the fire.

Janik leads me through the throng, the heat of a hundred bodies brushing against mine as we carve a path toward the VIP stairs. The music still pulses around us, but it appears distant now, muffled by the anticipation coiling in my chest.

I don't look up. I don't need to.

I'm fully aware of Kaisner's presence, his gaze still locked onto me like an anchor pulling me to him. Each step up the stairs is deliberate, measured, but my pulse betrays me— racing, wild, a trapped beast inside my chest.

The VIP section unfolds before me, a stark contrast to the chaos below. Here, power and wealth mingle in the air like expensive perfume. Beautiful women in designer dresses drape themselves across leather couches, while men in tailored suits conduct business over crystal tumblers of aged whiskey. The music thrums through the floor, but it feels distant, muted.

Janik leads me past private booths where deals are struck in shadows, past knowing smirks and calculating stares. We stop before Kaisner's domain, where he stands at the railing overlooking the dance floor below, commanding the space like a king.

And there he is.

I hesitate, the tension pressing down on me. Kaisner doesn't move. Doesn't speak. But the air between us hums, charged with something unspoken, a wire ready to snap.

His hands are still clasped behind his back, his posture rigid, but there's a crack in the composure he wears like armor. Dark rage simmering beneath his calm exterior.

Then, he turns.

His gaze locks onto mine, blazing with barely restrained fury—a slow-burning storm, coiled and waiting to strike.

I stand there, frozen, as he remains still, his presence suffocating. The distance between us feels like an eternity, and yet I know it's only a matter of seconds before he moves.

25

KAISNER

I feast my eyes on Clarissa as she ascends the winding steps to the VIP rooms. She's a vision in that white, skin-tight dress, the fabric clinging to her sinful curves. The sight sends molten heat coursing through me, my fingers itching to trace every dip and swell, to map her with hands and mouth until she trembles with need.

Seeing her here, in one of my nightclubs, is more than a pleasant surprise—*it's a wild card thrown by fate.* As I watch her navigate the crowd, her gaze scanning the space with curiosity and trepidation, a slow, predatory smile curves my lips, anticipation tightening in my gut.

I'm perched in my booth, holding court over the dance floor below, a king surveying his kingdom. The party rages on, my business partners indulging in the finest liquor and the most beautiful women money can buy. The air is thick with alcohol, perfume, and the pulsing beat of music that thrums through my bones.

But when Clarissa stands in the room's threshold, her presence beams through the dull sea of bodies. Everything else fades away. The world narrows to the space between us, crackling with tension.

She moves through the crowd like an avenging angel, her gaze locked on me with an intensity that thrills and terrifies. I've faced enemies beyond mortal comprehension, but nothing prepares me for the storm her presence stirs.

As she draws nearer, I see the change within her. The desire in her eyes deepens, becoming something fiercer. Her posture stiffens, the air around her sizzles with energy, and for a moment, I swear I glimpse the shadow of wings unfurling behind her.

A jolt of astonishment runs through me. I know that shifting is mostly a male trait, yet watching her now, I realize she's as close to a true shifter as I've ever seen in a woman. The dragon inside her is not a faded bloodline—it's a living, breathing thing, as real and powerful as any male shifter I've encountered.

This is no longer just Clarissa Draken. This is a dragon in human form, her ancient power about to burst free. Her energy is so strong that those nearby instinctively step back, widening the space between us.

Her eyes, usually soft blue, now burn with an inner fire that would make lesser men cower. But not me. I am Kaisner Drachenstein, and I hold her gaze unflinchingly, even as a thrill of something alarmingly akin to fear runs down my spine.

At last, she stops inches away. The heat radiating from her is tangible, an expression of barely contained fury. Her scent, usually jasmine and rain, now carries the tang of smoke and brimstone.

Yes, she may be furious. But rage coils just as hot in me —at the memory of that worthless wolf's hands on her, the way she laughed, danced in his arms. It makes my dragon pace beneath my flesh, restless and ready to burn.

"Enjoying yourself down there?" I ask, my voice deliberately controlled, though every instinct screams at me to claim her, to erase any trace of another man's touch from her skin.

She lifts her chin, sapphire eyes flashing with challenge. "Actually, yes. Is that a problem?"

I close the distance between us, unable to resist. My fingers brush against her arm where he touched her, marking my territory. "You know damn well it's a problem." The words come out as a growl. "His hands were all over you."

"You lost the right to care when you disappeared," she snaps. But I sense the shiver that runs through her at my touch. The knowledge that she's still affected by me soothes some of my fury. But not enough. Never enough when it comes to her. The beast in me demands more—demands *everything*. And by all the gods, I intend to take it.

"Where have you been?" she demands, her voice cutting through the music, carrying the force of a roar. "Weeks, Kaisner. Not a word for weeks!"

Her inner dragon is so close to the surface now that I half expect to see scales ripple across her skin. This is Clarissa as I've never seen her—raw, strong, magnificent in her anger. I realize I've underestimated not only her feelings, but the true extent of her power.

In her eyes, I meet the fury of centuries. She's more than a warlock descendant. She's extraordinary—a woman with the heart of a dragon, defying the very laws of our kind. The realization thrills and terrifies me.

Her anger is justified. But how can I explain? How do I tell her every moment of silence was torture, that I stayed away to protect her from the shadows that cling to me?

"Clarissa, I—" I start, but she cuts me off, hurt pouring out of her.

I can't bear it. Swept in despair, I grab her arm, pulling her toward a quieter corner. But she isn't having it. She twists in my grip, her free hand coming up to push against my chest.

"Let go of me," she hisses, her eyes flashing with anger and something deeper, untamed.

I loosen my grip but don't release her entirely. "Clarissa, let me explain!"

"No!" She struggles, her movements fierce. In our tussle, her nails rake across my chest, catching on the fabric of my shirt. There's a ripping sound, and suddenly, cool air hits my skin as the garment partly tears open.

Clarissa freezes, her eyes widening as they fall on the markings visible on my flesh. She catches only a glimpse of the vast dragon tattoo stretching across my chest, back, and shoulders. But it's the section beneath the scales, the daemonic script scrawled in angry red, that truly catches her attention. The symbols burn brightly against my tanned skin, as if they're alive, marking me with something darker than mere ink.

I watch as shock, then concern, and finally fear cross her face. Her hand, still pressed to my sternum, trembles slightly.

"Kaisner," she breathes, anger giving way to worry. "What happened to you?"

The warmth of her palm against my skin sends a jolt through me, soothing the constant burn of the daemonic markings. I fight the urge to lean into her touch, to seek more of that relief.

Instead, I take a deep breath, bracing myself to explain. The truth about the dark magic I've wielded, the price I've paid, and the dangers still lurking in the shadows.

As I meet her gaze, I see not just the woman I've come to care for, but a potential ally in the battles ahead. If only I can find the right words.

My jaw clenches as I remember the ritual—the dark magic I used to eliminate the threat to my clan… and to her.

The daemonic language is more than forbidden lexicon; it's a conduit for power beyond comprehension. Each scripture on my chest represents a life taken, a curse laid, a bargain struck with forces demanding payment in blood and pain.

The backlash of dark magic is brutal and unforgiving. The red lines crisscrossing my skin will soon turn black, yet they'll remain, cruel reminders of the lengths I've gone to protect her.

"These are—" I begin, my voice low and rough, gesturing at the markings.

"Daemonic scriptures," Clarissa interrupts, barely a whisper. Her eyes trace the patterns with fear and fascination. "I know what they are. But... why?"

The shock of her recognition hits me like a physical blow. I hadn't expected her to understand. For a moment, I'm speechless, torn between explaining and hiding this dark part of myself.

"It wasn't just me they were after," I say, voice low and ragged. *"They wanted everything I care about. That means you."* The words taste like ash. "You think I could stand there and watch them circle you like wolves? I've faced monsters since that night at the opera—bargained with devils, bled in shadows. All to stop them from touching you."

I pause, jaw clenched, breath shallow.

"You don't know what I've done, Clarissa. And gods help me, I'd do worse. Just to keep you safe."

Clarissa reaches out, her fingers brushing the script on my chest with hesitant reverence. Her touch burns. "You did this... for me?" she asks, her voice trembling.

I catch her hand in mine, holding it close to my heart. "For you," I confirm, my speech rough. "For *us*. For the future I see with you."

Understanding dawns in her eyes, and it nearly breaks

me. How can she look at me with care when my hands are stained with blood, when my soul is scarred by darkness?

"Oh, Kaisner," she breathes, her voice full of emotion—fear, yes, but also acceptance. Compassion. And beneath it all, a profound connection that makes my heart race and my breath catch.

This moment is a turning point. Clarissa has seen the darkness in me, and yet, she hasn't turned away.

I nod, unable to trust my voice. Yes, I was protecting her. But in doing so, I hurt her in ways I never intended.

"I was waiting for the right time," I explain. "When I could see you without exposing you to more gossip. I never meant to hurt you."

Her anger fades, replaced by a flood of emotion that disarms me. The caress nearly undoes me. "I only care that you're alive and well."

My gaze rakes over her—this woman who means more to me than blood, power, or breath itself. Heat coils low in my gut, hunger, and something bordering on awe darkening my voice. "My sweet baby girl," I murmur, the endearment rasping out like a secret I hadn't planned to confess. "I never thought I'd see you here tonight… and yet, here you are. Like a reckoning."

She swallows hard, her reaction painting a mirror of my own—this charged air between us, this ache that never dulled. "I never thought I'd *be* here," she whispers. "But now I am…" The words dissolve, but the meaning remains—raw, undeniable.

"Now you are," I echo, stepping in until there's nothing but heat between us. My fingers trail up her arm, slow and claiming. "And fate doesn't give second chances, Clarissa. She brought you here for me. For this."

I lean down, my lips brushing her ear.

"Tell me you feel it too—this pull. This fire. Tell me your

body's screaming for mine the way mine's been aching for you since the fucking opera."

She gasps, and it's all I need.

"Good," I growl, backing her into the shadows, a predator cornering his prey. "Because I don't want your fear. I want your surrender. Every moan, every breath, every broken cry that leaves your mouth tonight—mine."

My hand curls around her throat, not to hurt, but to hold. To *own*.

"Kaisner," she breathes, voice shaking like the last leaf before the fall. "I want to be yours."

"You're already mine," I growl, the words ripped from somewhere primal.

And then I'm kissing her—no, *claiming* her. My mouth crashes into hers with fevered intensity, all teeth and tongue and hunger, like I could taste the truth off her lips. It's not soft. It's not sweet. It's a *warning* to the world.

She moans into me, surrendering, melting—and I take. Gods, I take.

My hand slides from her throat to her jaw, angling her head just so I can deepen the kiss, devour her from the inside out. Every flick of my tongue is a promise. Every rough pull of her bottom lip is an apology in blood and heat.

I break the kiss only to drag my mouth down her neck, teeth scraping, breath ragged.

"You feel that?" I murmur against her skin, voice wrecked with restraint. "That's what it's like when a monster falls for something he was never meant to have."

She gasps, and I sense her pulse stutter beneath my lips.

"But you're mine now," I growl, biting down—just enough to make her shiver. "And if anyone tries to take you from me, I'll rip the fucking world in half to get you back."

Her fingers fist in my shirt like she can't bear to let go. Good. She won't have to.

"Say it," I demand, my hand fisting in her hair, tilting her head back. "Say who you belong to."

She's panting, lips parted, eyes glazed with heat and something dangerously close to devotion.

"You," she whispers. "I belong to you, Kaisner."

"Damn right you do."

And this time, when I kiss her, it's not just a kiss.

It's a vow.

The taste of her is intoxicating—sweet, warm, with just a hint of defiance. I deepen the kiss, my touch exploring every curve, every breathless shudder. She gives in, surrendering with a fervor that unravels me. She was made for this—for me.

Clarissa doesn't pull away. She leans into me instead, her body pressing flush against mine, her hands tangling in my hair, nails raking against my scalp with just enough pressure to send a shiver down my spine. My control, already precarious, hangs by a thread.

I break the kiss before I forget myself entirely, before I forget where we are and who might be watching. My forehead rests against hers, both of us breathless, our chests rising and falling in sync.

This is madness. The thought cuts through the haze of desire like a blade. *She's the key to everything I've worked for— the blood that will awaken my dragon, the power that will restore my birthright.* But as I look into her sapphire eyes, all my careful plans crumble to ash. *I can't use her. Not like this. Not when she looks at me as if I'm something more than the monster I've become.*

The daemon's whispers echo in my memory, reminding me of what I came here to accomplish. *Take what you need. Claim your power.* But her trust burns brighter than any dark magic, and I find myself drowning in emotions I swore I'd never feel again.

"I should walk away," I murmur against her lips.

Her fingers tighten in my hair. "Then why don't you?"

I chuckle darkly, the sound low and rough. "You know why."

And now, I understand. Everything has shifted. The darkness within me, the sacrifices I've made, and the ones yet to come—none of it matters.

Because what's between us isn't just heat or desire. It's deeper, rawer. A meeting of souls, a recognition of something true and untamed. As if the universe itself, in all its chaos, conspired to bring us together—two fractured halves of a whole, finally locking into place.

I claim her lips again, the kiss urgent, reckless. My hands explore her, memorizing all her curves, every tremor of delight, worship woven into every touch. And she succumbs, like waves crashing against rocky shores, unstoppable and relentless.

Clarissa is my fate, my greatest temptation, the missing piece I never knew I was searching for. And as I lose myself in her, as the fire between us consumes everything else, I know one thing with certainty.

I will chase this feeling—chase *her*—for the rest of my days.

26

KAISNER

Our lips collide in a fevered dance, tongues tangling, breaths coming in sharp, desperate gasps. Clarissa's hands roam my chest, shoulders, back—each touch branding me, leaving trails of fire. I grip her waist, pulling her flush against me, reveling in the intoxicating blend of silk and softness, the way she fits against me as if made for this.

But as much as I want to lose myself in her, I know I can't. Not yet.

With a groan of restraint, I tear my lips from her, resting my forehead against hers as we struggle to catch our breath. My pulse thunders in my ears, my control hanging by a thread.

"Kaisner," she murmurs, voice husky with need. "Please. I want this. I want you."

Her words slam into me, a lightning strike straight to my core, and for a moment, I falter. My fingers tighten on her hips, possessiveness and hunger warring with restraint. I close my eyes, exhaling sharply.

"*Liebes*," I whisper, my voice raw. "You have no idea how

much I want that. How much I want to claim you, to make you mine."

I trail my fingers along the curve of her face, my touch reverent. "I'll teach you pleasure... and pain," I murmur against her ear, feeling her shudder. "But you're not ready for me. Not yet."

It's the truth, agonizing as it is. Clarissa is light, pure and untainted by the darkness that haunts my world. To give herself to me, fully... it would change her, irrevocably. And though I long to possess her, body and soul, I can't bear to dim her radiance.

She looks up, eyes dark with defiance. "I'm not afraid," she says, steady and sure. "I know what I want, Kaisner. And I want you."

A wry smile tugs at my lips. "I know you do. Believe me, the feeling is more than mutual." I brush a strand of hair from her face, letting my fingers linger. "But there are parts of me, parts of my world, you're not ready to face yet."

I kiss her, slow and deliberate, savoring her taste, the way she melts into me. When I pull back, I let my lips graze her ear. "When the time is right, when you're ready to accept *all of me*—the light and the dark—then, I'll make you mine."

I let the words settle, pressing a kiss to her neck. "Fully." Another to her brow. "Completely." My lips brush her mouth, a vow sealed in fire. "Irrevocably."

She shivers, eyes fluttering closed as she leans into me. "Why wait?" she whispers.

I cup her chin, tilting her face to mine, my expression grave with meaning. "Because, baby girl," I murmur, my thumb brushing over her parted lips. "My desires run deep. Dark." I pause, watching the flicker of intrigue in her gaze. "And once you step into my world, there's no going back."

She doesn't flinch, doesn't waver. "I don't care," she breathes.

A slow, wicked smile spreads across my lips. "Are you sure?"

Her grip tightens on my hand. "I am."

And just like that, my restraint shatters.

I claim her lips in a searing kiss, one hand tangling in her hair, the other branding her waist. The world ceases to exist —no music, no prying eyes, just the undeniable pull between us. But in the distance, I hear the hush of the VIP room. My business partners—the most powerful men in both mortal and supernatural circles—are watching. Assessing. Calculating the shifts in alliances and power dynamics.

But none of it matters. Yes, they're savvy enough to recognize Clarissa as the Draken heiress, to understand the significance of this moment. But they're also wise enough to know that whatever transpires in this room stays here, sealed by unspoken agreements and the fear of retribution.

With a growl, I break the kiss, my breathing ragged. Clarissa stares up at me, lips swollen, pupils blown wide with desire. And I know—she feels it too. The need for more.

Wordlessly, I take her hand, our fingers interlocking. Then, without a backward glance, I lead her away from the booth, away from the flashing lights and deafening bass, toward the hidden staircase leading to the most secret part of the club.

The journey to my office becomes a trail of barely restrained hunger. We stumble through dimly lit corridors, my mouth claiming hers against every wall, every doorframe. Her dress rides higher with each stolen kiss, my hands mapping territory I'm desperate to conquer. Behind us, I hear the distant crash of something falling—a painting knocked askew by her reaching hands, a decorative vase toppled by my elbow. The staff will find chaos in our wake, evidence of desire that couldn't wait for privacy.

By the time we reach my office, we're both breathing

hard, her lipstick smeared, my shirt half-unbuttoned by her eager fingers.

Her body arches under my touch, and I press her harder against the wall, one arm locking around her waist like a vice.

My grip tightens on her hips, dragging her flush against me, and she gasps—a sound so sweet, so desperate, it goes straight to my cock.

"Touch me," I growl, voice low and lethal, each word scraping across the air like claws. "Feel what you do to me."

Her fingers fumble, trembling as they drag down my chest, over the ridges of muscle, down to the brutal truth of my desire. She exhales sharply, pupils blown wide. Heat blooms in her cheeks.

"You feel that?" I whisper darkly, leaning in until my mouth brushes her ear. "That ache—that hunger? It's all yours, Clarissa."

My fingers find the hem of her dress, jerking it up without finesse, without permission. She gasps, and it thrills me. My touch slips beneath the silk and finds heat—wet, wild, waiting for me.

"Fuck…" I snarl, eyes flashing. "You're already soaked. So needy for me you're shaking."

She nods, barely able to breathe.

"Say it," I demand, gaze burning into hers. "Say who you're wet for."

"You," she whimpers. "Only you."

A savage grin splits across my face.

"Good girl."

I lift her with a growl, her thighs wrapping around my waist, and slam her back against the wall. She moans, nails raking down my spine as I drag my mouth over her throat, tasting the pulse that races just for me.

"You said you wanted everything," I murmur darkly. "You're about to find out what that really means."

I carry her to the desk—don't clear it, don't ask. *I take.* Papers scatter. Something shatters. I don't care. She gasps as I lift her onto the edge, spreading her legs with practiced ease, laying her out like a sacrifice. My hands grip her thighs like I own them. Like I own *her.*

"Eyes on me, baby girl," I command, sinking to my knees. "I want to watch the moment you come undone."

Her breath hitches, a soft whimper escaping her lips.

My gaze rises to meet hers, lips brushing the inside of her trembling thigh.

"That's it," I murmur, voice low, reverent, *wicked.* "Tonight isn't about me. Tonight's about *you* falling apart on *my* mouth—again and again—until the only name you remember is mine."

I nudge her thighs wider, pressing heated kisses up the inside, slow and possessive. She moans, hands shaking as they reach for me. I slap one gently away.

"No touching. Not yet. Be good, and I'll give you everything."

Then I bury my face between her legs like a man starved for centuries. When my tongue finally meets her, she cries out—sharp, raw, *perfect.* I lap her up like I've been starved for years. And maybe I have.

I smile against her as I savor her—filthy, reverent, insatiable. "Fuck, you taste like sin," I growl into her heat.

She bucks, fingers tangling in my hair, but I grab her wrists and pin them at her sides, holding her still.

"You don't come," I say, my voice velvet dragged across a blade, "until I fucking say."

She whimpers, begs, pleads. And I devour. Again. And again. And again.

Her taste is sin and surrender, delightful and intoxicating.

"So fucking sweet," I rasp between strokes.

She writhes, pleading now, body strung tight with need

—but I don't let her fall over the edge. Not yet. I draw it out, build her up, tear her down, and build her back again. Over and over.

And when she finally begs—*really* begs—voice broken, form shattered, I let her have it. I pull her to the edge and *keep her there,* tongue relentless, fingers cruel and tender at once, until she shatters on my tongue like a prayer.

Her thighs quake. Her moans echo off the walls of my office. She collapses back onto the desk, dazed and ruined.

I rise slowly, mouth glistening, pupils dark with satisfaction as I watch her chest rise and fall in the aftermath. She's beautiful like this—wrecked, trembling, completely undone by my touch.

"Kaisner," she breathes, voice broken and raw. Her eyes flutter open, finding mine, and what I see there steals my breath. Vulnerability. Need. Something that threatens to destroy us both.

"I need you more than I should," she whispers, the words tumbling out like a confession torn from her very soul. "More than is safe, more than is smart. But… I can't help it."

Her admission scorches through me—no spell, no daemon pact, no blood rite has ever had this kind of power. It cracks through the armor I've spent a lifetime forging, and I welcome the ruin.

I lift her, effortlessly, one hand still tangled in her hair, the other gripping her thigh as I carry her across the room. She clings to me, breathless, her nails scraping my shoulders like she wants to carve her name into me.

Good. Let her.

I set her down on the nearest surface—a marble-topped table, cool against her skin. She gasps at the contact, but I don't give her a second to adjust. I push her thighs apart with my knee and step between them, my hands possessive on her hips.

"Look at you," I rasp, gaze devouring every inch of her. "Spread open for me like you were made for this. Made for *me*."

She moans, low and trembling, and it lights something feral in me.

I dip my head, kissing down her collarbone, biting the delicate skin where her pulse pounds the hardest. I want to mark her there—want the world to see who she belongs to. My tongue soothes the sting before I sink lower, dragging my mouth across her chest, her ribs, the sensitive skin just above her hipbones.

"Kaisner…" she pleads, breath hitching, hips lifting in silent demand.

"No, no, baby girl," I purr against her stomach. "You don't beg for release until I say you can." My tone turns to velvet and steel. "Tonight, *I* decide when you fall apart."

She writhes beneath my mouth as I trail my tongue down her inner thigh, then up again, deliberately avoiding where she aches for me most.

Cruel? Maybe.

Necessary? Absolutely.

I look up at her, eyes locked on mine, voice a wicked promise.

"I'm going to ruin you, *Liebes*… slow enough to ache for it, deep enough to crave it, and hard enough that you'll never belong to anyone else."

She's trembling now—body, breath, soul. Perfect.

And when I finally give her what she craves—when my mouth finds her, hot and relentless—her cry is shattered, sacred, and mine.

She arches off the table as my tongue finally meets the place she needs me most. She cries out, head tipping back, fingers weaving through my hair like she'll lose herself if she doesn't hold on.

Good. Let her lose herself.

My grasp strengthens on her thighs, keeping her pinned open for me as I lap at her with slow, devastating precision. Each stroke is measured, intentional, like I'm learning her by heart—mapping every gasp, every twitch, every broken plea.

"Gods—Kai—"

The sound of my name torn from her lips in that wrecked, reverent tone is better than blood and shadow and power combined. I growl against her, the vibration making her tremble, and I sense the tremor start in her legs.

She's close.

I pull back, lips slick, eyes dark with hunger.

"Not yet, baby girl," I whisper, voice thick with command. "You don't come until I say, remember?"

Her whimper is a desperate, delicious thing. "Kaisner, *please*…"

"I love that sound," I murmur, dragging my knuckles down her trembling body. "But I'm not done tasting you."

And I'm not.

I drop to my knees again, mouth returning to her like worship, like sin, tongue relentless now—merciless. She's crying out, begging, writhing under the weight of sensation, and still I don't let her fall.

Not until I make her break.

Her thighs clamp around my head, a choked sob of my name escaping her, and that's when I finally let her have it.

"Now," I growl. "Let go for me, Clarissa. I've got you."

And she does.

She shatters like glass in my arms—beautiful, fierce, undone. Her cries echo through the room, her body convulsing in wave after wave of pleasure as I hold her through the storm, mouth still tasting, claiming, owning.

When I rise, she's breathless and glowing, her form slack against the marble, her chest heaving.

I lean over her, lips brushing her ear.

"*That*... was just the beginning," I whisper. "I'm not finished until you can't close your legs without thinking of me between them."

Her dazed smile is all the encouragement I need. I claim her mouth in a searing kiss, my tongue sweeping deep, drinking her in like it's the only thing keeping me alive. She's intoxicating—softness and fire, melting against me.

My hand pins firmly her wrists above her head, the other, roams over her, tracing the dips and curves through the delicate silk of her dress, relishing in the way her breath hitches. She's trembling, her body an instrument finely tuned to me, every gasp, every moan, a note in the symphony of her unraveling.

"Please," she begs, tugging at my grip. "I need to touch you."

A slow smile curls my lips against her throat. "That's it, *Liebes*," I murmur. "Feel it. The ache. The longing. Hold on to it. Savor it."

I trail lower, fingers skimming the juncture of her thighs, pressing just enough to make her writhe in sweet agony. "Kaisner!"

I push her to the edge, pull her back again, each touch designed to drive her wild. She thrashes, whimpers, pleads, her body trembling beneath mine. My lips find her ear, my words a sinful whisper against fevered skin.

"When the time is right," I promise, "when you're ready for *all* of me... I'll ruin you *beautifully*. Make you mine in every way that matters."

She shudders, taut as a bowstring, her need a tangible force in the air. I gather her close, holding her in my arms as if I could shield her from everything beyond this moment.

"Soon, baby girl," I murmur. "Soon, you'll be all mine. And nothing—nothing—will stand between us."

But even as I speak, a shadow lingers in the back of my mind. The spite of my enemies is only the beginning. A storm is coming, and I won't let it touch her.

With a slow exhale, I release her. She lies there, lips swollen, breath unsteady, eyes glazed with pleasant exhaustion. I take in every detail, committing it to memory.

Then, I offer my hand. "Come. Let's get you cleaned up."

I lead her through my office to the private washroom beyond—marble and gold reflecting the soft lamplight. The intimacy of the space makes everything more real, more dangerous. I watch her in the mirror as she smooths her hair, fixes her lipstick, each small gesture a reminder of what we've shared and what we're both fighting to resist.

She takes my hand without hesitation as I guide her back through my office, past the scattered papers that bear witness to our passion.

I slide my shirt on over my shoulders, the fabric dragging against flesh marked by her touch. The scent of her clings to me—sweet, wicked temptation—and the ache of holding back still burns like wildfire under my skin. Every second of restraint had been a fucking crucible.

I turn to her, eyes hooded, voice low.

"I don't take trust lightly, Clarissa." My thumb grazes her cheek, lingering where my stubble scraped her flesh. "You gave yourself to me… and I'll never forget it."

I lean in, breath brushing her lips—close enough to kiss, cruel enough not to.

"But let's be clear…" My smile turns dark, reverent. "What we started tonight? That was just a taste. The beginning of your undoing. And when you're ready to fall deeper…" My eyes narrow, voice dropping to a vow. "I'll be waiting to ruin you—completely."

She leans into my touch, mouth curving into a soft smirk. "I'd do anything for you, Kaisner."

My chest tightens at the devotion in her tone, the depth of emotion reflected in her eyes.

"I know, baby," I murmur, brushing my lips against her forehead. "And that's why I have to be careful with you. That's why we take this slow." I tilt her chin up, holding her gaze. "But never doubt this—I want you. Body. Heart. Soul."

And gods help anyone who tries to take you from me, I add inwardly.

I lead her out of the chamber, into the thrumming chaos of the nightclub. The shift is jarring—the flashing lights, the pounding bass, the sea of bodies moving in rhythm. After the intimacy of our private moment, it seems almost obscene.

Clarissa blinks, momentarily dazed as she readjusts. I keep my hand at the small of her back, a touch as much about possession as it is protection. My gaze sweeps the crowd, instinctively searching for threats.

"Your friends," I murmur, nodding toward the group. "They're looking for you."

A flicker of guilt crosses her face. "I should probably go back to them," she admits, though there's no conviction in her voice.

Every fiber of me protests. I want her by my side—not just tonight, but for longer, for something I can't name. But I know I can't cage her. If this is going to work, I have to let her choose me.

"You're right," I say, the words splinters on my tongue. "They'll be worried."

She looks up at me, surprise flickering in her eyes. I didn't demand she stay, and the choice I'm offering her is clearly unexpected. It solidifies my resolve. I want to be the man she deserves.

"I'll call you," I promise. "We have much to discuss. And, Clarissa…" I hesitate. "I need to see you again. Soon."

A soft smile curves her lips. "I'd like that."

I lean in, capturing her mouth in one last kiss—slower, deliberate, a promise. It lacks the fire of our earlier passion, but not the intensity. This kiss is a vow, a silent oath, filled with everything I'm not yet ready to say.

When I pull back, I see the same emotions reflected in her eyes. And before I can stop myself, the words slip free— words I hadn't planned, words that betray me: "In this world of shadows and secrets, you're my only light."

Clarissa stills, breath hitching.

"Go," I say softly, before I change my mind. "Be safe, *Liebes*. And remember—you're mine now. No matter what happens out there, no matter who you're with, you belong to me."

A shiver runs through her. When she speaks, her voice is quiet but unshakable. "And you're mine." The fierceness of her conviction is enough to shoot wildfire through my veins.

She lingers a moment longer, then turns and slips into the crowd.

I don't move. I don't look away. Not until she's gone.

27

CLARISSA

My heart still races as I make my way back to the main area of the club, my skin tingling with the ghost of Kaisner's touch. The encounter in the office left me reeling, my mind spinning with questions and emotions I can barely untangle.

The pulsing beat of the music thrums through me as I step onto the dance floor, the flashing lights casting eerie shadows over the writhing bodies. My gaze sweeps over the crowd until it lands on Sam and Alexei near the bar. Sam's worried expression eases when she sees me, but Alexei's posture is taut, his easy confidence sharpened to a keen edge.

Sam closes the distance in a flash, her voice cutting through the music. "Where the hell were you?" Her relief is edged with irritation.

Heat creeps up my neck. "I just needed some air," I say, the lie thin and weightless. "It was getting a bit stuffy."

Sam arches a skeptical brow. "Uh-huh. And that 'air' wouldn't have anything to do with a certain tall, dark, and dangerous man you disappeared with, would it?"

Before I can answer, Alexei steps in with a smirk and two

drinks in hand. "Clarissa! There you are," he says, his grin rakish. "We were starting to think you'd ditched us for better company."

If only he knew how close he was to the truth.

I take the drink, grateful for the brief distraction. "Never," I say, forcing a bright smile as Sam and Alexei exchange a glance.

The music surges around us, and for a moment, I let the beat carry me, the steady thrum of bass a balm to my restless thoughts. My mind remains half-trapped in that private room, replaying every touch, every word, every charged glance exchanged with Kaisner.

Sam leans in, voice pitched low so only I can hear. "We'll talk about this later," she mouths. I nod, knowing there's no escaping it.

For now, I let the music wash over me as I dance with my friends, laughter spilling from my lips even as Kaisner's parting words echo in my mind: "No matter what happens out there, no matter who you're with, you belong to me."

We lose ourselves in the music, bodies pressed close, moving in time with the relentless beat. For a fleeting instant, I almost feel normal—just another woman in a club, cloaked in flickering lights and fleeting glances.

Then Sam's voice breaks the spell, laced with worry. "Shit. I have to go. Gavriil's in one of his *moods*. Apparently, he'll send the entire Elite team if I don't head back home."

A protest rises to my lips, but her apologetic smile stops me. "It's okay," I say softly. "Go. I'll be fine."

She pulls me into a tight hug. "Call me if you need anything," she murmurs before melting into the crowd.

The club closes in around me, the air thick with heat and sweat and the electric promise of the night. Bodies sway to the music, laughter rings out, and yet, beneath it all, something cold coils at the base of my spine.

A gaze—hungry, intent—lands on me. Not Kaisner's. His is a possessive heat, one that claims and protects. This is different. Colder. Hungrier.

I keep dancing, pretending not to notice, though every nerve in my body is on edge. Human guys watch me with lust, curiosity, admiration—mundane desires with no real danger behind them.

Something darker lurks in the shadows. Predatory. Calculated. Waiting.

The hairs on the back of my neck rise. My skin prickles. I'm not only being watched, I realize.

I'm being *hunted.*

I sharpen my senses, my gaze scanning the edges of the dance floor. And then, I see them.

A bear shifter reclines in a secluded booth, amber eyes gleaming with feral interest. Near the bar, a warlock tracks my every move, the flicker of magic playing at his fingertips. And a vampire—utterly still—watches me with ancient, predatory calm.

They aren't drawn to beauty. They're drawn to influence. To me.

The truth of it crashes over me. I am not just a woman in a club tonight—I am Clarissa Draken, a prize to be claimed. A stepping stone to power.

A hand brushes my elbow, and I flinch.

Alexei's low voice cuts through the music, a smooth invitation. "Shall we dance?"

His expression is easy, but his nostrils flare, catching the faint scent of Kaisner on my skin. He tucks that knowledge away, a card to be played at the perfect moment.

Before I can respond, he guides me back onto the dance floor, his hand firm at my waist. The bourbon on his breath mingles with expensive cologne, his every move a study in controlled dominance. The music thrums through my veins as we dance—a push and pull, a performance for the eyes that watch.

"Buenas noches, bella," a voice purrs, cutting through our dance like a blade through silk. The words roll off his tongue with a lazy sort of charm, though somewhat slurred.

I turn to find León Regalis, the lion shifter alpha, disheveled and reeking of whiskey. His smile is arrogant, but there's a wild edge to it. "Mind if I cut in?" he says, reaching for my hand. And when he speaks, he does it with the entitled ease of a man who's never been denied anything in his life.

Alexei's hold on my waist tightens like a vice. "*I* mind," he growls, his voice a low rumble.

León's smirk widens. "Come on, Clarissa," he says, ignoring Alexei. "Ditch this mutt and dance with a real man."

Tension sparks between them, electrifying the charged air.

"León, don't—" I start, but the crack of a fist cuts me off.

León stumbles back, blood trickling from his split lip, fury burning in his eyes. "You'll pay for that, wolf," he snarls, snapping his fingers.

Suddenly, we're surrounded.

León's men step from the shadows, bodies tensed, eyes hard.

Alexei shoves me behind him. "Stay back," he snarls.

In a flash, chaos erupts around us. Fists fly, glass shatters, screams pierce the air. I'm shoved, jostled, struggling to stay upright. Alexei moves like a force of nature, his strikes precise and devastating, but for every man he drops, another takes his place.

Just when it seems the tide might turn against us, he lands a brutal blow to León's solar plexus, dropping him to his knees. Seizing the moment, he grips my hand and drags me through the roiling crowd.

We're almost at the door when Alexei stiffens, his body going still.

"Alexei?" My voice wavers. "What's wrong?"

He turns, and my breath lodges in my throat. His features have shifted, elongated—feral. His eyes glow yellow in the strobe light, and when he opens his mouth, I see fangs where normal teeth should be.

"Mine," he growls, the word a claim, a threat. "You're mine!"

Sheer black dread washes over me.

"Alexei, don't!" I try to back away, but his hand shoots out, gripping my arm with bruising force. He pulls me close, his hot breath fanning across my face as he leans in, fangs bared and ready to claim me.

A single, deafening crack splits the air, cutting through the pulsing music like a knife. My ears ring, the world around me muffled as if I've been plunged underwater. The crowd freezes—a tableau of shocked faces illuminated by the strobing lights.

Then, pandemonium.

The bass drops out, replaced by screams and the thunder of hundreds of feet as people scramble for the exits. Bodies press against me from all sides, panic a living entity in the air. The acrid smell of gunpowder stings my nostrils, mixing with the sweat and fear emanating from the fleeing crowd.

Another shot rings out, and the concussion echoes in my chest, my heart stuttering in response. Glass shatters to my left, the tinkling of falling shards barely audible over the chaos. Warm liquid splatters across my face.

Alexei's grip on my arm loosens, his eyes wide with shock. He opens his mouth as if to speak, but only a gurgle escapes. Then, like a marionette with snapped strings, he crumples to the floor.

I stand frozen, unable to process what I'm seeing.

Alexei lies motionless at my feet, blood pooling around him, his unseeing eyes staring up at me—I can't breathe. I can't think. The world tilts and spins.

Suddenly, strong hands grip my shoulders, pushing me against the wall. A blurred face swims into focus before me, lips moving, forming words I can barely hear over the high-pitched ringing in my ears. He shakes me gently, repeating himself until his words finally break through the fog in my mind.

"Are you all right?" The voice seems to come from far away. "Clarissa, can you hear me?"

I stare down in horror to see my pristine white dress now stained bright crimson. My gaze drifts to Alexei's body, drawn by shock and disbelief. A hand grips my chin, forcefully turning my head away from the gruesome sight.

"Don't look at him! Look at *me*, Clarissa. Look at me!"

I blink, focusing on the face before me. Kaisner. His eyes are wild with concern, his jaw clenched tight. When I see the gun holstered under his jacket, realization dawns, cold and horrifying.

"Y-you... you shot him..." I mumble, my body shaking uncontrollably. "You..." I try to take a deep breath, but my lungs refuse me. Black spots dance at the edges of my vision. Panic sets in.

"Clarissa!" Kaisner's face blurs before me, his voice distant and distorted. "Clarissa, *breathe!*"

But it's too late. The world tilts sideways, darkness rushing in to claim me. The last thing I'm aware of is Kaisner's strong arms catching me as I fall.

Then, blissful nothingness.

28

CLARISSA

onsciousness returns slowly, wading through a thick fog. The first thing I'm aware of is a low murmur that ebbs and flows like distant waves. My eyelids are too heavy to open, so I lie still, letting the sound wash over me.

As my senses gradually sharpen, I begin to distinguish words.

"He was their fucking alpha…" A man's voice, taut with anger. "Yes, it's a problem. Make it go away. Fast."

The voice is familiar, but my groggy mind can't quite place it. I force my focus, willing the fog to lift.

Other sensations seep in. The bed beneath me is soft, not a hospital cot. Smooth, cool satin glides against my skin—sheets? My brain struggles to catch up.

With monumental effort, I manage to crack open my eyes. Light floods in, momentarily blinding. I blink rapidly, trying to adjust.

I'm in a room I don't recognize—richly furnished, golden sunlight muted by gauzy curtains. Not home. Not safe. My heart stutters.

How long was I unconscious?

A shiver shakes my form. The cool satin sheets are the only thing covering my naked body.

The realization jolts me fully awake, a gasp escaping my lips before I can stifle it.

The voice cuts off. I turn my head to see Kaisner pacing at the foot of the bed, phone pressed to his ear. His gaze snaps to mine—relief, concern, and something darker flicker in his maroon eyes.

"I'll call you back," he says into the speaker, never taking his gaze off me. He ends the call and moves to the bed, his presence enveloping me.

"Hey, baby girl," he murmurs, a low rumble that resonates through my being, setting my nerves alight. "How are you feeling?"

I open my mouth, but no words come out. How am I feeling? Confused. Terrified. The events of last night—Alexei's inhuman form, the violence, the blood—flash through my mind.

"Kaisner," I rasp, my voice hoarse. "What... what happened?"

He hesitates, then reaches out, brushing a strand of hair from my face. The tenderness in his touch is at odds with the tension in his jaw. "You're safe," he says, his tone fiercely protective. "That's what matters."

But as the mental fog continues to clear, I know that's not enough. "Alexei," I whisper, my chest tightening. "Is he...?"

"Dead," he says flatly. The word lands heavy in the silence.

The terror of what he's saying crashes over me like a tidal wave. I flinch. "You killed him," I whisper, each word rising. "You killed Alexei!" Horror and fury boil over. I clutch the sheet to my chest and slap Kaisner, hard.

For a moment, he looks stunned—then his eyes narrow dangerously.

We struggle, my hands clawing at him as he tries to restrain me. But he's stronger, much stronger. In a matter of seconds, I'm pinned to the mattress, my wrists held firmly at my sides.

"That was *not* Alexei Morozov!" he growls, his face inches from mine, breath hot against my cheek. "He was long gone, and that beast would've killed you."

Kaisner's chest heaves as he regains his composure, his body a solid weight above me. I'm acutely aware of my nakedness, of the heat radiating from his skin.

"What do you mean?" I ask, voice trembling, warm tears brimming in my eyes. "I saw you shoot him. I saw him die!"

Kaisner loosens his grip, but doesn't let go. "What you saw," he murmurs, his tone intense, "was a shifter gone feral. The Alexei you knew was no more. If I hadn't acted, you'd be dead."

I want to argue, to scream, but a flash of Alexei's glowing eyes, his distorted voice, the inhuman claws reaching for me... it all comes flooding back. The fight drains out of me as the truth settles in.

"I had no choice, Clarissa," he says, calmer now, releasing me as understanding washes over my expression.

The memory of Alexei's features, his fangs bared and ready to claim me, races through my mind. I shudder, pulling the sheets tighter around me.

"My clothes," I manage to say. "Where are they?"

A flicker of something—embarrassment?—crosses Kaisner's face. "They were... ruined," he says carefully. "Blood. I had them disposed of."

I nod, my confidence slipping away as the reality sinks in. I'm naked in a strange bed, with a man who killed to protect me.

"Where am I?" The question slips out, the silk sheets tightening around me, reminding me of my vulnerability.

The hardness in his gaze fades, a hint of pride in his voice. "My penthouse. I own the building, actually."

The casual mention of owning an entire building in Paris is a stark reminder of how little I know about him. Kaisner Drachenstein, dangerous and wealthy beyond measure, is still an enigma.

He must sense my unease because his expression softens. He shifts on the edge of the bed, his weight causing the mattress to dip. His hand hovers for a moment before resting gently on my sheet-covered leg.

His touch grounds me, bringing the night's events rushing back. "Alexei..." I begin, a whisper escaping my lips, "he tried to claim me."

"*Kill you*," Kaisner corrects, voice hard as steel. His hold tightens imperceptibly on my leg. "The beast had devoured whatever humanity remained in him. He would've destroyed you."

A shudder runs through me at his words. Alexei's transformed face flashes before my eyes. Kaisner's right—there had been no humanity left in Alexei in those final moments.

"I... I didn't realize," I stammer, the horror of what I narrowly escaped crashing down on me. "I didn't think he... would ever..."

Kaisner's expression softens further. He shifts closer. His hand moves from my leg to cradle my face, his thumb gently stroking my cheek. "This world... *our* world... it's more dangerous than you know. Monsters hide behind human faces, predators waiting for any sign of weakness."

His eyes, usually so guarded, are open now, filled with something deeper, more intense. "But I promise you this—as long as I'm around, nothing will harm you. *I will burn this city to the ground before I let anyone touch you.*"

The fervor in his voice should frighten me. Instead, I find myself leaning into his touch, safety washing over me despite the dark promise in his words. In this moment, with Kaisner's hand on my cheek and his vow suspended between us, I feel protected like never before.

But as I look into his eyes, I can't help but wonder—in a world of monsters and predators, what kind of creature is Kaisner Drachenstein? And what does it mean that, despite everything, I'm drawn to him like a moth to a flame?

"I understand this is a lot to process," he says, his voice low and intimate. He lowers his hand again, resting it on my leg. His thumb traces slow circles on my thigh, sending shivers through me. "You're safe here, Clarissa. With me."

I meet his gaze, struck by the sincerity there. "I know," I whisper, surprised to find that I mean it. Despite everything, I do feel sheltered with him.

His touch slides up, resting on my hip. The heat of his palm burns through the sheet, igniting a fire within me. "There's so much I want to tell you," he murmurs, leaning in closer. "So much I want to share."

My pulse quickens as he draws near. For an instant, I think he's going to kiss me. Instead, he presses his forehead to mine, our breaths mingling in the space between us.

A soft rap at the door breaks the silence, so faint I almost miss it. Kaisner's head whips around, his body tensing for a fraction of a second before relaxing. He walks to the entrance, opening it just enough to exchange hushed words with someone outside.

When he turns back, a long, sleek garment bag drapes over his arm. The black fabric gleams under the soft light, the zipper catching a glint as he moves. His footsteps are silent on the plush carpet as he approaches the bed.

"I hope you don't mind," Kaisner says, his voice a deep,

velvety timbre that sends a shiver down my spine. "I took the liberty of arranging an outfit for you."

He lays the bag on the bed with careful precision, his movements deliberate. The mattress dips slightly under the weight, and I catch a whiff of a fresh floral fragrance emanating from its wrapping.

Kaisner's fingers trail along the zipper, a teasing gesture that sends a jolt through my body. My pulse quickens, heat rushing to my cheeks. "Why don't you get dressed?" he suggests, his eyes meeting mine with an intensity that makes the room warmer. "Dinner's waiting when you're ready."

The promise in his voice—of food, yes, but of so much more—hangs in the air. I nod, curiosity building as I wonder what he's chosen, what the evening holds.

As Kaisner leaves, I unzip the bag, gasping softly at what I find inside. The gown is a masterpiece of midnight blue silk, simple yet undeniably elegant. It fits like a dream, as if it were made for me. Knowing Kaisner, it probably was.

When I emerge from the bedroom, Kaisner's gaze darkens as he takes me in, his look a blend of appreciation— and something more primal. "Beautiful," he murmurs, offering his arm. "Shall we?"

He leads me to a dining room that takes my breath away. Floor-to-ceiling windows offer a panoramic view of Paris, the Seine snaking through the city, Notre-Dame rising majestically in the distance. The table is set for two, gleaming china in soft lighting, a bottle of wine already breathing.

As we sit, I stare at the elegant food before me, my stomach twisting at the thought of eating. The events at the club replay in my mind—Alexei's blood on my hands, the dullness in his eyes as life faded from them. How can I eat?

The scrape of chair legs pulls me from my thoughts. Kaisner shifts his seat closer, his presence overwhelming— comfort and quiet authority that make my pulse race.

"You need to eat," he says, his voice gentle but firm. When I shake my head, he leans closer, his gaze darkening with concern and something more possessive. "Clarissa, you haven't eaten all day. I won't watch you waste away."

"I'm not hungry," I protest weakly, but Kaisner is already reaching for my fork. He spears a piece of perfectly cooked fish, bringing it to my lips.

"Just a few bites," he murmurs, his tone brooking no argument. "For me."

The intimacy of the gesture makes my cheeks flush. Part of me wants to resist, assert my independence, but there's something oddly comforting about his insistence. About being cared for so thoroughly, even if his methods are a bit… forceful.

When I finally open my mouth and accept the morsel, his eyes flash with satisfaction. "Good girl," he says softly, already preparing another bite. "Now, some water."

He reaches for my glass, cupping the back of my neck as he brings it to my lips. The gesture is tender yet controlling, and I find myself yielding to his care despite my frazzled state. With each bite he coaxes into me, each sip of liquid, the numbness recedes, replaced by a growing awareness of his presence, his touch, his unwavering attention.

I'm struck by the surreal nature of this situation. Less than twenty-four hours ago, I watched a man die. Now I'm having dinner with his killer, dressed like I'm attending a gala.

Grief, guilt, and worry gnaw at my insides.

"Clarissa," Kaisner's voice pulls me from my thoughts. He's watching me intently, concern etched in his face. "Talk to me. What's going through your mind?"

The floodgates open. "It's my fault," I whisper, the remorse I've held back spilling over. "If I hadn't been there, if I hadn't danced with Alexei—"

"Stop." Kaisner's tone is firm but gentle. He reaches across the table, taking my hand in his. The comfort of his touch anchors me. "Alexei lost control of his beast. It's a risk all shifters face, especially those who don't train rigorously to govern their animal side."

I look up, meeting his gaze. "But you've never… I mean, your blood carries the dragon lineage, yet you're always self-possessed."

A shadow passes over Kaisner's features. "You're a constant challenge," he says softly, darkly teasing. "What you saw with Alexei… it could happen to any shifter who lets their guard down."

The gravity of his words sinks in. I think of Nikolaas, of all the shifters in my acquaintance. Have they all been fighting this internal war without me knowing?

"What happens now?" I ask, fear creeping in as I recall the chaos at the club, the body on the floor.

Kaisner's expression hardens. "It's been handled," he says, his tone leaving no room for argument. "The media's been silenced, and any news of this incident will be buried. You have nothing to worry about."

I'm tempted to demand more details. But part of me is relieved. The thought of being at the center of a supernatural scandal is too much to bear.

As we eat, the conversation drifts to lighter topics. Kaisner tells me about the building, about his business ventures in Paris. Despite the bleak emotions that threaten to overwhelm me, I find myself relaxing, drawn in by his charm and wit.

It's only as we finish dessert that I realize something: throughout the entire evening, I haven't had a single vision. No flashes of the future, no cryptic images dancing on the fringes of my consciousness. In fact, I can't remember the last time I had one—especially when I'm with Kaisner.

The realization sends a shiver through me. Is it the stress of recent events blocking my gift? Or is there something more at play?

I look up to find Kaisner watching me, a question in his eyes. For a moment, I consider telling him about my absent visions. But something holds me back.

Instead, I offer him a small smile.

Kaisner's expression softens, and he takes my hand again. As our fingers intertwine, I sense that familiar spark of connection. Whatever's happening with my visions, whatever dangers may be lurking, in this moment, I feel safe. Protected.

The warmth of his breath ghosts across my skin, igniting a fire that spreads from my core to my fingertips. For a moment, I'm tempted to bridge the minuscule distance between us, to lose myself in his embrace. His lips are so close to mine that I can almost taste him, the promise of his kiss an intoxicating lure.

But the rational part of my mind reasserts itself. "I should go home," I whisper. The words pain me even as I speak them, but they're necessary. "I need... some time to process this."

Kaisner pulls back slightly, his maroon eyes searching my face. I see a flicker of disappointment quickly masked by understanding. "Very well," he murmurs. He takes my hand, bringing it to his lips for a soft kiss that makes my heart flutter. "I'll have a car sent for you when you're ready."

I nod, not trusting my voice. As I rise, about to return to the bedroom and gather myself, Kaisner's words stop me.

"Clarissa," he says.

His usual mask of cool indifference has slipped away. In its place is an expression of such raw passion that I'm stunned.

"I... I need you to know," he begins, his voice rough with

emotion, "how much it means to me that you're alive. That you're here, safe."

His words shatter me to the core, bringing tears to my eyes. "When I saw you in danger at the club, I realized..." he pauses, swallowing hard. "I realized that I can't lose you. You've become... essential to me. In a way I never expected, never even thought possible."

A tear escapes, rolling down my cheek. I've never seen Kaisner like this—vulnerable, open, his carefully constructed walls crumbling before my eyes. It's both beautiful... and terrifying.

"Kaisner," I breathe, at a loss for words. How can I express the storm of emotions he has stirred in me?

He stands, closing the distance between us in two long strides. His hand comes up to cup my face, thumb gently wiping away my tear. "You don't have to say anything," he murmurs. "I just... I needed you to know."

For a while, we stand there, lost in each other's eyes. A charged atmosphere hangs in the air, vibrant with unspoken words and possibilities. I'm tempted to stay in this moment forever, safe in the cocoon of Kaisner's presence.

But I need time—time to think, to understand my feelings. With Herculean effort, I step back, breaking the spell.

"Thank you," I breathe, pouring my confused emotions into those two simple words. "For everything."

Kaisner nods, understanding passing between us silently. As I turn to leave, I sense his stare like a brand against my spine, following me as I walk away.

Still, I cannot deny it. Kaisner Drachenstein, with all his complexity and darkness, has become my anchor in this storm. And somehow, that thought is my sole comfort.

29

CLARISSA

Three weeks since I watched a man die, and I'm expected to smile at a board meeting.

The past few days have blurred into silence and uncertainty. After Éclipse, I locked myself away, the world fading from color to gray. The nightmare of Alexei's transformation haunted me—his glowing eyes, bared fangs, and the memory of his death weighed on me. Each moment seemed like I was drowning in gunshots, blood, and fear.

I compelled myself through the routine—showering, dressing, eating—but all was amiss. The world moved on without me, indifferent to my grief. I couldn't face Samara or anyone, not yet. Two missed calls from Kaisner sat on my phone like accusations I wasn't ready to answer.

No word of Alexis' death has reached the Ursa or Morozov families. The story circulating is that he went into hiding after a fall-out with the Regalis clan, a convenient lie that keeps everyone in the dark. The result of Kaisner's careful machinations. I've done my best to distance myself from him ever since that night, but the memories linger, unwelcome and unresolved.

Even so, here I am, back at work, trying to move forward. The fear still clings, but I can't stay locked away forever.

The familiar scent of oil paint and polished wood wraps around me as I step into the Lumière Art Gallery. It's been too long since I last set foot here. I told everyone I'd been under the weather—a story that concealed the sleepless nights, the lingering fear that clawed at my thoughts.

As I move toward my office, warm smiles and murmurs of relief greet me. "Welcome back, Miss Draken," my colleagues say, their voices carrying both concern and excitement. "We have good news to share."

Their enthusiasm is infectious, stirring a sensation inside me—a flicker of the person I used to be. Maybe this is exactly what I need. To immerse myself in art and creation, to build something meaningful amidst the wreckage of my personal life. With a smile that feels only slightly forced, I follow them into the meeting room, bracing myself for whatever developments have unfolded in my absence.

As I settle at the head of the long, polished table, my gaze sweeps over the familiar faces before me. A swell of pride rises in my chest. We've poured everything into the upcoming exhibition—securing funding, curating the perfect collection, designing an experience worthy of the Lumière name. And now, with the final details falling into place, I allow myself a rare moment of satisfaction.

I sink into my chair, but my thoughts drift elsewhere. To Nik.

He's been gone for over a month. His last message mentioned his tour through Western Europe and the Mediterranean, securing support where he could. But Germany and Eastern Europe—especially with Kaisner at their helm—remains a question mark. Those clans have the power to make or break Nik's bid for Dragon King.

I'm proud of him, of course, but worry gnaws at me. The supernatural world is treacherous, its politics a tangled web of power and deception. And Nik stands at the center of it.

The meeting progresses, and I notice a shift in the room. The standard business professionalism is laced with something else—excitement, barely contained. Amélie keeps sneaking glances at Luc, her eyes bright with a secret. Sophie fidgets with her pen, a knowing smile pulling at her lips. Even Jean-Pierre, always the picture of restraint, drums his fingers on the mahogany table, his usual stoicism fading.

I lean back in my chair, arching an eyebrow at their behavior. "All right," I say, amusement slipping into my voice. "What are you all hiding?"

Luc clears his throat, adjusting the lapels of his impeccably tailored suit. With deliberate precision, he moves to the front of the room. A large screen dominates the wall. With a click of a remote, it flickers to life.

"Miss Draken," he begins, his voice laced with anticipation, "while you were away, we had a... development. One that's going to change everything for our upcoming gala."

The screen floods with images—priceless artworks, rare sculptures, masterpieces I've only ever glimpsed in the most exclusive catalogs. My breath catches. It's the private collection we've been chasing for months. The one we thought was out of reach.

Amélie springs from her seat, her hands clapping together in excitement. "We did it, Clarissa! The reclusive collector finally agreed!"

I lean forward, fingers curling around the edge of the table. "How?" My voice is steady, but my mind races. "How did you manage that?"

Luc's grin widens as he clicks to the next slide, revealing a series of email exchanges. "That's the most incredible part.

We were ready to walk away, admit defeat. But then..." He lets the suspense linger, his gaze sweeping the room. "He reached out to us. Personally."

A collective gasp ripples through the team. Sophie leans in, her voice hushed. "It's like he knew exactly what we needed. He set his terms, made his offer. It's... unprecedented."

A rush of conflicting emotions floods me—exhilaration, suspicion, something undefinable. "This is remarkable," I manage, schooling my voice into excitement. "And unexpected." I hesitate, then ask the only question that matters. "And *who* is this mysterious benefactor? Do we finally have a name?"

The room stills. Luc clicks to the final slide. A name flashes across the screen, bold and unmistakable. My stomach clenches.

"*Freiherr* Kaisner Drachenstein," Luc announces, his voice ringing through the silence.

I grip the arms of my chair, steadying myself against the sudden shock. Kaisner Drachenstein. The man who's haunted my thoughts, my dreams. The one whose touch set my skin ablaze, whose kiss stole my breath.

Heat prickles in my nape, but I force my expression into one of polite curiosity. Conversation erupts—speculation, theories, whispers of intrigue. My colleagues are enthralled, swept up in the mystery of the enigmatic benefactor.

But I know better. Kaisner never does anything without purpose. And if he's involved, it means my carefully reconstructed world is about to be upended once again.

I'm only half-listening, my mind consumed by memories. The way his eyes locked onto mine across the crowded dance floor, the crackling electricity between us, the heat of his hands on my skin. The taste of his lips.

"I still can't believe he agreed," Amélie gushes, snapping me back to the present. "Some of those pieces haven't been seen in public for decades!"

A drawer slams shut. I flinch, pulse spiking. The sound ricochets through me like an echo of that night at Éclipse. Weeks have passed, yet the memories cling to me—sharp, unrelenting.

"We've been asking for ages, and his offices always refused. I wonder what changed," Luc muses. Then, grinning, "And he's donating a never-before-seen Kandinsky sketch to the Lumière Foundation. That alone will have donors scrambling to get in."

Their voices rise in a chorus of praise and speculation, but I only catch fragments.

"A *Freiherr*, no less," Sophie adds with reverence. "German nobility. That explains the old-world elegance and the vast collections."

"I hear he's single," someone whispers. "Can you imagine capturing his heart?"

"Single or not, he's a mystery," Amèlie chimes in conspiratorially. "No one really knows much about him. It's like he materialized out of thin air."

"Well, I hear he's gorgeous," Camille giggles, fanning herself with a stack of notes. "Tall, dark, and dangerous."

Heat flares at the back of my neck. Kaisner's piercing gaze flashes through my mind, the ghost of his touch reigniting a spark I thought I'd extinguished. I shift in my seat, willing the memory away. But it lingers, a whisper against my skin.

"We should focus on the exhibition," I say, my voice steadier than I feel. "Not idle gossip."

But even as the words leave my lips, they ring hollow. Because deep down, I know the truth. I'm just as fixated on Kaisner Drachenstein as they are. Perhaps even more.

"Of course, Miss Draken," Amélie says, subdued. "We're just excited. It's not every day we work with someone of his caliber."

I force a smile. "I understand. But let's keep things professional. We have a lot to prepare."

The conversation shifts back to logistics, but my thoughts remain tangled. Kaisner Drachenstein. After weeks of silence, he's shattered my fragile detachment with one grand gesture.

When the meeting concludes, I retreat to my office. I exhale slowly, willing my pulse to steady. But the sense of unease lingers—an instinct whispering that something is off, that I'm missing a vital piece of the puzzle.

Drawn by impulse, I move toward the filing cabinet, my fingers deftly flipping through the folders until I find what I'm looking for—the contract for the Drachenstein exhibition, signed with a flourish by Kaisner himself.

I trace the bold slant of his signature, a slow sweep of my fingertip. "Who are you really, Kaisner Drachenstein?" I murmur.

Before I can second-guess myself, I settle into the plush leather chair behind my desk, my fingers flying over the keyboard. I pull up every scrap of information I can find—articles, press releases, financial reports. But the more I search, the more I realize: I'm only scratching the surface. There are layers to him, depths concealed beneath carefully curated façades.

My mind drifts back to that night at Éclipse, to the words Kaisner whispered in my ear, his breath warm against my skin.

"When you're ready to accept all of me—the light and the dark—then I will make you mine. Fully. Completely. Irrevocably."

A shiver dances down my spine, anticipation curling in my stomach.

What does it mean to accept *all* of him? To embrace not only the polished exterior he presents to the world but also the shadows lurking beneath? Can I truly give myself over to a man I barely know, whose motives remain a mystery?

The questions swirl in my mind, a dizzying storm of doubt and desire. But even as I wrestle with uncertainty, I can't deny the truth. The enigma that is Kaisner Drachenstein calls to me, an unsolved mystery I can't resist unraveling.

With a sudden burst of determination, I reach for the phone. My fingers dial the number for our offices in Germany almost on sheer instinct.

As the phone rings, I settle into my chair, gaze drifting toward the large window overlooking the Rue du Faubourg Saint-Honoré. The city moves below in elegant chaos, but my focus narrows.

On the opposite sidewalk, a figure lingers.

Recognition jolts through me. I saw him last night, a shadow at the edges of my world. And now, here he is again. Watching. Waiting.

A chill coils around my spine.

The line clicks, and a crisp voice cuts through my thoughts. "Lumière Foundation, German branch. How may I assist you?"

I take a steadying breath. "This is Clarissa Draken," I say, determined. "I need you to pull up everything you can on Kaisner Drachenstein. Business dealings, personal history—everything. Leave no stone unturned."

A pause. Then, the voice returns, tinged with something unreadable. "Understood, Miss Draken. We'll begin immediately. Expect a report by the end of the day."

I murmur my thanks and hang up.

The hours slip by in a blur of meetings and phone calls, juggling contracts, logistics, and endless emails. Yet, no matter how much I try to focus, my thoughts keep circling back to Kaisner—the elusive art collector whose sudden generosity has upended my carefully structured world.

Just as I'm about to call it a day, my phone buzzes. A notification flashes across the screen, making my breath hitch.

DOSSIER: FREIHERR KAISNER DRACHENSTEIN

My fingers tremble as I open the file, scanning the pages of information the German team has compiled. Business dealings. Holdings. Philanthropic efforts. And beneath the surface—whispers of something darker. His rumored connections to the shadowy underworld of art and antiquities. Traces of power plays that never made the headlines. And...

I blink, snapping my gaze away from the screen.

Everything there is to know about this man is right here.

Everything.

A slow, unsteady breath leaves my lips as I recline in my chair, eyes drifting toward the window. Outside, the city hums with life, a familiar rhythm of dusk settling over Paris. But beyond the blur of pedestrians and evening lights, a figure stands motionless on the opposite sidewalk.

A jolt of recognition courses through me.

He's still there.

The same man I spotted last night—half-hidden in the shadows, watching. Now, under the golden haze of the setting sun, his presence is clearer, yet no less unnerving. His posture is casual, almost nonchalant, but there's a sharpness to him. A readiness.

A silent shadow, always a step behind me.

With a slow inhale, I power down my computer, the screen going dark. My reflection stares back at me—composed, unreadable. But inside, something restless stirs.

"I don't know *who* you are," I murmur under my breath, slipping my phone into my bag. "But I'm going to find out."

Jaw set, I gather my belongings, straighten my shoulders, and prepare to step into the night—into whatever awaits me beyond these doors.

30

KAISNER

The room is silent, the air thick with unspoken tension as I sit at the head of the long table, fingers steepled before me. My most trusted advisors surround me, their expressions grim, mirroring the weight pressing against my chest. This meeting is not about business. Not about alliances, territories, or wealth.

It is about betrayal.

A betrayal so deep it threatens the very foundation of our clan.

As I scan the faces around me, a more personal burden settles in my gut—Clarissa's absence. It has been weeks since I last heard from her, weeks of forced restraint as I honored the space she asked for, even as the ache of her silence gnawed at me. My informants keep me updated—she's withdrawn, avoiding the world, but safe.

Safe. The word should bring me solace, but instead, it taunts me. Because safety is a fragile thing.

That night at Éclipse… it was too much. Too savage. Too raw.

I can still see the fear in her eyes, the way her hands

trembled in mine after gunfire rang out and blood tainted the air. She stepped too far into my world that night, straight into the darkness of shifter brutality and clan violence. And I let it happen.

I should have protected her. Should have known she wasn't ready for the reality of my life—the cruelty, the power struggles, the unspoken laws. She wasn't raised in this world. She doesn't bear its scars like I do.

Now, I may lose her because of it.

The irony isn't lost on me. For years, my greatest fear was failing to awaken my dragon self. Now, that fear pales in comparison to the thought of losing her. The shift in my priorities unsettles me more than I care to admit.

I think back to the moment I first saw the request from the Lumière Foundation. My staff and lawyers had been blocking their inquiries for months, following my standard protocols. But the instant I learned it was Clarissa's organization? Everything changed. I reached out personally, bypassing all the usual channels, reckless in my need for any connection to her—even if only through her work.

But she hasn't responded. Not a word.

I told myself I wouldn't pressure her. That I'd give her the space she needs. After Éclipse, after everything she witnessed, she deserves that much.

But waiting is its own kind of torture. Every day without her voice, every unanswered message, every moment of silence stretches the distance between us. I don't know if she's avoiding me out of fear, or if I've already lost her to the violence of what happened that night.

And yet, I can't force her hand. Not when I'm the one who led her into the dark.

So I wait. And the waiting kills me.

I glance down at the file before me. The damning evidence it contains cuts deeper than any blade.

Photographs spill across the polished ebony table—grainy surveillance images, clandestine meetings in dimly lit alleyways. In one, Marcus is passing a manila envelope to a tall, bronze-skinned figure I recognize instantly.

Vikram Mahindra's right-hand enforcer.

Transcripts of intercepted phone calls reveal Marcus's treachery in his own words.

"The Draken girl," his voice murmurs over the recording. *"Drachenstein's obsessed with her. She's his weakness."*

The paper crumples in my tightening fist.

Printouts of emails detail the classified information he leaked—Clarissa's daily routines, her favorite cafés, the security measures I had put in place to protect her.

But the final blow is the handwritten note, Marcus's familiar scrawl outlining a plan so vile it makes my blood run cold.

"Kidnap the girl, and Drachenstein will fold. We can end this war in one swift move."

Rage surges through me, molten and unforgiving. My vision blurs at the edges, my hands flexing as I struggle to contain the violent urge clawing its way to the surface.

Clarissa—an innocent in all of this, a woman with no ties to our world beyond me—was to be used as a pawn.

Because of him.

Because of *this.*

The law of our clan is clear. The punishment for treason is swift and absolute. And yet, even now, some foolish part of me hesitates. Marcus was more than a soldier in my ranks. He was a brother. A man who fought at my side.

But that man is dead.

All that remains is a traitor.

I exhale slowly, steadying myself. "Bring him in."

The heavy doors swing open, and Marcus is dragged

inside. His hands are bound, his face drawn with fear. He stumbles as my guards force him to his knees before me.

He keeps his head bowed, but the tremor in his shoulders does not escape me.

"Marcus." My voice is cold, devoid of emotion. "You stand accused of treason against the Drachenstein clan. Of conspiring with our enemies. Of betraying the trust I placed in you."

I pause, letting the words sink in. Letting him feel the gravity of his sins.

"But your greatest crime," I continue, my tone sharpening, "was against Clarissa Draken."

At that, he lifts his head, his eyes wide with something like regret. It means nothing to me.

"You leaked information about her movements. You compromised her safety." I lean forward, my fury barely leashed. "You planned to have her taken. Used. Bargained away like some pawn in your pathetic attempt at diplomacy."

His mouth opens—whether to plead or to lie, I do not know. I do not care.

"You knew what she meant to me." My voice is barely above a whisper now, but it cuts sharper than any blade. "And still, you sold her out."

His breath hitches. "Kaisner, please." The words come raw, desperate. "I never meant for her to be harmed. I was only trying to end this war."

I exhale slowly, measured, staring down at the man I once trusted. Rage settles over me like a storm rolling in, dark and inevitable.

"By betraying me?" the question is hushed, lethal. "By offering up the life of the only person I cannot afford to lose?"

Marcus flinches as if struck. His shoulders sag, the fault of his choices pressing down on him like a man drowning under the tide. "I was wrong," he whispers. "I see that now. But please, Kaisner, for the sake of our history—"

"There is no history," I cut him off, my tone edged with finality. "Not anymore."

A bitter silence stretches between us. For a fleeting moment, I consider mercy. I think of the battles we fought together, the blood spilled, the victories we toasted with fire and steel. Once, he was my brother-in-arms. Once, I might have forgiven him.

But Marcus made his choice. And now, he will answer for it.

"Betrayal is an art, Marcus," I murmur, the sound smooth as glass. "But so is retribution. And I? I am an artist of the highest order."

I take a step closer, watching as realization dawns in his eyes—the cold, sick understanding that there is no escape from what comes next.

"Did you truly think I wouldn't find out?" My tone turns almost amused, though there's no humor in the air between us.

I crouch before him, my gaze locking onto his, unflinching. "Your greatest sin wasn't betraying me." My voice drops to a whisper. "It was believing I'd let you survive it."

I rise, then give a slow nod to my guards. One steps forward, a blade gleaming in the dim light.

Marcus's breath comes in short, panicked gasps. He struggles against his bindings, his pleas turning into incoherent cries of desperation.

I do not look away. Because this is the burden of leadership. These are the choices that define a king.

The blade falls.

His screams are brief.

Silence follows.

I straighten, my expression unreadable. Around me, my

men shift, uneasy in the wake of what they have witnessed. I let them sit with it. Let them understand the lesson woven into Marcus's demise.

When I finally speak, my tone is quiet, but it carries through the chamber with the force of a decree.

"Let this be a warning." I meet the gaze of each man in the room. "Treason will not be tolerated. And any threat against Clarissa Draken will be met with the full might of the Drachenstein clan."

I pause, allowing the words to settle, allowing the air to hum with their finality.

"*Treue ist nicht verhandelbar,*" I state coolly. Loyalty is not negotiable.

With that, I turn, striding from the chamber without a backward glance.

My heart is heavy. My hands are stained.

But Clarissa is safe.

And I will stop at nothing to keep her that way.

31

KAISNER

Blood has a way of lingering—on your hands, in your memory, in the spaces between what you've done and what you'll do next.

The crack of colliding billiard balls slices the silence as I brace over the table, linen taut beneath my palms. Sleeves shoved up past corded forearms, I sight down the cue—not at the ivory spheres, but at Marcus' ghost still hanging in the smoke. His final plea. The flash of silver. Blood pooling black in the low, flickering light.

I straighten with a growl, knuckles whitening around the whiskey tumbler. Neat. No ice. No mercy.

The burn down my throat does nothing to scorch away the memory.

Marcus was a brother. A friend. But in this world, betrayal is a death sentence. Especially when it threatens Clarissa. Especially when it threatens everything I've built.

The burden of leadership presses down on me, a constant, unrelenting force. I am the axis upon which this empire turns, and weakness is a luxury I cannot afford.

A knock rasps against the doors. Sharp. Intrusive. I set

the glass down with controlled precision that belies the irritation simmering beneath the surface.

"Enter," I snap, voice diamond-hard.

When no immediate response comes, my inner dragon bristles. Whoever's out there better have a damn good reason for this interruption.

I don't move. Let them come to me. I watch as the handle turns slowly, the door opening with a measured creak that seems to stretch time itself—

Her.

Clarissa stands haloed in hallway light, sapphire eyes blazing through me. My pulse roars.

For a moment, I'm thrown off balance. But I recover quickly, my gaze narrowing as I take her in. A deceptively simple couture dress skims her curves, hinting at the shape beneath. A masterpiece of restraint and temptation. The fabric drapes like liquid midnight, whispering against her skin with every breath she takes.

Her chin is lifted, her posture defiant, and I can't help but admire the sheer audacity of her standing here, in my domain, uninvited.

"You found out where I live," I murmur, a touch of dark delight in my cool tone as I lean back against the billiard table. I take a slow sip of my drink, my eyes never leaving hers. "I'm impressed."

"Don't be," she replies, voice sharp, cutting through the air like a blade. "Your *men* led me here." Accusation laces the words, anger simmering beneath the surface.

Another shock, another revelation that leaves me reeling. This woman, this beautiful, enigmatic creature, is not at all what I imagined. She's full of surprises, each one more intriguing than the last.

I set my drink down on the table. "Clarissa," I begin, a hint of a smile tugging at my lips.

She steps into my sanctum, all defiance in stiletto heels. "You're *stalking* me?" she snaps at me with a frown.

Pride and something far darker coil in my chest. She's playing a dangerous game, confronting me like this. But then again, I've always enjoyed a bit of danger.

In three strides, I'm mere inches away. The door slams behind her, my palm flat against oak as I cage her in. Bergamot and fury radiate from her heated skin.

"Not stalking," I purr, leaning closer, inhaling her rebellion. "Protecting."

"I don't need your protection," she breathes, clipped, gaze unwavering. "I don't want a security detail. I want an ordinary life."

Her bold resistance is intoxicating, awakening something primal within me. She's standing there, challenging me in a way no one else would dare, and all I can think about is how badly I've underestimated her, how little I truly know of the depths of her strength.

"Baby girl, but that's impossible," I explain, my darkened stare roving her face with untamed hunger. "You are *far* from ordinary. There are dangers in this world, ones you don't even realize."

"Call off your dogs, Kaisner," she demands, unwavering. And in her eyes, I see a fierceness, a determination that only fuels the flames of my desire, my need to possess her, to make her mine.

I tilt my head, studying her, a predatory smirk curling my lips. "Or what?" I challenge, voice low. "What will you do if I refuse?"

For a moment, she hesitates. A flicker of uncertainty. Then it's gone, replaced by the same fiery resolve. "You don't want to find out."

A chuckle rumbles in my chest, dark and humorless. I reach out, tucking a strand of hair behind her ear. My fingers linger, brushing against her skin, and I sense the faintest shiver run through her.

"Lovely place you've got here," she says, gaze straying from mine to sweep the room. "It's a pity it's so heavily guarded."

I inch closer, my lips barely grazing the shell of her ear. "A necessity for a man in my line of work."

She stiffens, her breath catching. I hear the sudden racing of her heart, and it takes every ounce of control not to pull her into my arms, to claim her mouth and show her just how much I want her.

She swallows hard, eyes locked on mine. "Selling guns?"

A thrill of satisfaction runs through me. So she's been doing her research. Digging into my past. The thought of her taking an interest in me, in what I do, is a heady one, a rush of power and desire that leaves me momentarily breathless.

"It's perfectly legal," I lie, fingers grazing her jaw, reveling in the way her breath hitches.

"As *legal* as your business with narcotics?" she inquires, tone lethal.

I can't help the smirk that tugs at my lips, the surge of admiration I have for her boldness, her willingness to confront me even in the face of her uncertainty and fear.

But amusement fades as I glimpse determination in her gaze. "Ever since I inherited this clan's leadership, I've strived to diversify our assets. Nightclubs. Restaurants. Even the occasional arms deal… It takes time to shift an empire."

My hand glides along her waist, and when she stumbles back, I press her gently against the door, my body a solid wall of heat and muscle against her own.

"Now that you know all that I am… tell me, *Liebes*," I purr, my lips trailing along the column of her neck, tasting the sweetness of her skin, "why have you come?"

Her pupils dilate, breath shallow.

"Are you here to fight me?" I pause, my mouth hovering a breath away from hers. "Or have you come to fuck me?"

For a heartbeat, neither of us moves. The air between us tightens, charged with something neither of us can name.

Then, in a rush of heat and fury, her lips crash against mine.

The kiss is electric, violent in its intensity. Fingers tangle in my hair, nails scrape against my scalp, and I welcome it— welcome the fire, the collision of our worlds. She tastes of defiance and desperation, of something I never dared to crave, but now cannot live without.

Never breaking contact, I lift her onto the billiard table, her smooth legs wrapping around my waist. My hands roam, memorizing every curve, every gasp, every trembling sigh.

This woman will be the ruin of me…

And gods help me, I won't stop her.

Her hands slide between us, unfastening the button of my pants with a deft urgency that sets my blood aflame. I suck in a sharp breath as her fingers brush against my length —an unspoken promise of what's to come. I kick off my shoes, my clothes following in a careless heap. I'm left in my boxers, the fabric straining against my arousal, aching for her.

She's a goddess, this woman. Alabaster skin glowing in the dim light, sapphire eyes heavy with desire. Her dress slips from her shoulders in a whisper of silk, pooling at her waist before I ease it past her hips, revealing a lace-trimmed set designed to entice and destroy. I trail a single finger over the delicate fabric, teasing the hardened peaks beneath before tugging them just enough to draw a gasp from her lips. She arches, offering herself, and I take my time, savoring every shiver, every breathy moan.

The contrast is intoxicating—the rawness of her need against the elegance of our surroundings. The flickering glow of the hearth, the glint of cut crystal decanters, the silent, ever-watchful eyes of the surveillance cameras that I switch off with a flick of my wrist. For the first time in years, this room is truly private.

It's like fucking in a cathedral, this mingling of lust and opulence. The billiard table looms behind us, an altar to our depravity. With careful precision, I ease her onto the green baize, the soft cloth cool beneath her bare skin. I grip her wrists, pinning them above her head as I press myself against her core.

"*Baby girl*," I growl, my free hand curling around her hip, fingers digging possessively into her skin. "Am I your first?"

Her lashes flutter open just enough for me to glimpse the hunger simmering in her gaze. She bites her lower lip, pearl-white teeth sinking into the plush flesh. "Y-yes," she gasps, voice trembling but resolute.

I lean in, my breath ghosting over her ear, savoring how she shivers beneath me. "I won't be gentle," I warn, my tone a dark promise.

Her response is immediate—her body arches into mine, seeking more, craving the delicious edge of pain tangled with pleasure. "Gods, I hope not," she moans, the sound reverberating between us, seeping into my skin.

Something in her tone gives me pause. My grip tightens instinctively, my brow knitting as an unspoken question forms on my lips. But before I can voice it, she speaks again.

"I'm a virgin, Kaisner," she pants, her breath warm against my jaw. "Not a saint."

The words snap the last frayed thread of my restraint. A savage hunger surges through me, burning away any lingering hesitation. My fingers press into her hips as I drag her to the very edge of the table, positioning her exactly where I want her. Her body molds to mine, soft and yielding, yet defiant—made for me.

And I have every intention of making her mine.

"Are you sure about this?" I growl against her ear, my voice rough with restraint. "Once we start, there's no going back."

"Yes," she gasps, breathless, her fingers fisting the baize beneath her. "I want you… more than… anything…"

She bites her bottom lip, and then, in a whisper that detonates inside me— *"Fuck me senseless, Kaisner."*

Lightning ignites in my veins, raw and electric, surging straight to my core. Any last thread of patience snaps. I seize her mouth in a ravenous kiss, my tongue claiming hers as our bodies fuse together, heat against heat. My hardness strains against my boxers, aching to sink inside her, to brand her as mine. But I'm not in a hurry. Not yet.

This is her first time. *Our* first time.

And I'll make damn sure she remembers every second.

I kiss a path down her frame—her breasts, the hollow between them, lower still—my lips mapping her skin with slow, deliberate reverence. She arches beneath me, a symphony of gasps and shivers, her body pleading for more. I savor her response, how she blooms under my touch, trembling on the precipice of pleasure she's never known.

And I intend to ruin her for anyone else.

Sliding a hand down the arch of her spine, I slip her panties off, the lace whispering against her skin before falling away like a discarded secret. My mouth follows in its wake, trailing fire along her neck, across her collarbone, to her cleavage. Clarissa writhes beneath my touch, her soft moans threading through the air like a melody meant only for my ears.

I reach behind her and unhook her bra, the delicate scrap of lace slipping from her shoulders and joining the rest of her clothing in forgotten abandon. Her breasts spill free— perfect, aching for my attention. I take my time, teasing the taut peaks with slow, deliberate strokes of my tongue, savoring the way her breath catches, the way her fingers curl into the baize.

I pause, drinking her in.

She is a vision of temptation against the emerald green, her skin luminous in the dim light, every curve and hollow sculpted by the shadows.

Mine.

Lifting her legs over my shoulders, I spread her open and descend, claiming her with my mouth.

A sharp gasp leaves her lips, her fingers fisting the felt as my tongue explores every secret inch of her. She tastes like sin and surrender, like something I'll never get enough of. I drag my tongue over that sweet bundle of nerves, and her body arches in offering, a strangled moan tearing from her throat.

"More," she begs, a low cry. "I need more."

I chuckle mischievously, my fingers tracing patterns on her skin. "I want to hear you beg. Say it—say you need me to ruin you," I say, my voice firm but gentle.

The quiet whimper of her obedience, the breathless anticipation in her eyes—it carves through me like a blade made of fire and pleasure.

Her scent—arousal tinged with the faintest trace of her expensive perfume—floods my senses, fueling my hunger. I grip her thighs tighter, holding her still as I push her closer to the edge, my tongue flicking and stroking in a rhythm that has her breath coming in desperate, uneven gasps.

She writhes against me, her hips undulating, searching for more, chasing that final push into oblivion.

And I am determined to take her there.

I slide two fingers inside her, slow at first, stretching her, letting her feel every deliberate inch. She breathes sharply, her body arching into me, her hands desperately seeking a hold on the baize. I find that perfect spot within her, curling my fingers just so, and a choked cry spills from her lips, raw and unrestrained.

I smirk against her inner thigh, reveling in the way she unravels for me. My other hand roams freely, trailing fire across her skin—cupping the curve of her breast, rolling her nipple between my thumb and forefinger, teasing until she's writhing, desperate for more.

My focus is singular, my hunger absolute. Her pleasure is mine to command.

She moans again, the sound low and breathless, and I know she's close. Her thighs quiver beneath my grip, her body tightening around my fingers, her breath coming in ragged little gasps.

I increase the pace, my tongue flicking over that swollen, sensitive nub with relentless precision, driving her toward the edge with every stroke, every calculated movement.

And then, she shatters.

A cry tears from her throat, her back bowing in offering, her body seizing around my fingers as pleasure consumes her. The sight of her—flushed, undone, trembling in my arms— is nearly enough to wreck me.

I draw it out, coaxing her through the aftershocks, pressing open-mouthed kisses along her thighs as the tension in her muscles slowly eases. She exhales a shuddering breath, the sound half a purr, her hands threading lazily through my hair.

"That was…" she whispers, her voice thick with pleasure. "Divine."

A slow, satisfied grin spreads across my lips.

But I'm far from done with her.

Withdrawing my fingers from her slick heat, I bring them to my mouth, tasting her, savoring her essence. Sweet and decadent, warm and intoxicating. My blood sings with the primal need to claim her, to bury myself deep and make her mine in every way.

I position myself between her parted thighs, and drag the tip of my aching length through her slick folds, teasing her, tormenting us both.

She gasps, her body jerking in response, her hips tilting ever so slightly, inviting me in.

I hover at her entrance, my restraint hanging by a thread.

"Are you ready for me, baby?" I murmur, my voice thick with need.

Her eyes meet mine, pupils blown wide.

"Yes," she breathes, and that single word is my undoing.

I push inside her, slow and deliberate, savoring the exquisite stretch as her body yields to me. A sharp gasp parts her lips, her fingers tightening against my shoulders. She's fire incarnate—hotter than sin, tighter than restraint. I sink deeper, her heat clenching around me, the sensation so raw, so consuming, it borders on agony.

"Hold still," I pant out, rough as my grip on her hips tightens. "I'm going to make you feel every inch of me."

Her nails rake down my back, drawing a guttural sound from my throat. She rises into me, wild and untamed, chasing more, urging me past restraint.

"Faster," she breathes, a demand, not a plea. I answer with action, driving into her with a primal rhythm that speaks of possession, of dominance.

Clarissa is everywhere—her scent, her heat, how she moans my name like a benediction. I give her what she craves, our bodies moving together in a violent, perfect synchrony, the push and pull of our pleasure an unrelenting force.

A frustrated whimper escapes her as I withdraw, but I silence her with a firm grip on her waist. Before she can protest, I flip her onto her stomach, dragging her hips up until she's aligned with me, her spine arching in invitation.

I sheath myself inside her once more, this time deeper, harder. A strangled cry tears from her lips as she braces against the table, her knuckles whitening against the green baize.

Her moans melt into the crackling warmth of the hearth, the scent of sex mingling with woodsmoke and something else—dark and unyielding.

She pushes back against me, seeking, demanding. I grip her hips with bruising force, holding her exactly where I want her.

"Look at you," I rasp, leaning over her, my lips tracing the curve of her shoulder, my breath scorching her ear. "Taking me so damn well."

She keens, her back bowing as I drag my hand up her spine, relishing the delicious tremor beneath my touch. She hisses through gritted teeth as I thrust into her, deep and merciless. Her body tightens around me, her voice breaking on a gasp.

"Oh yes… Right there!" she pants, guiding my rhythm with desperate need.

"You're mine," I snarl, punctuating each punishing thrust. "Every breath, every moan—mine."

"Kaisner—!"

A growl rumbles through me, low and primal. I fist her hair, tilting her head back until her neck is bared to me, a silent offering.

"Say it," I demand, my lips grazing her pulse, sensing the wild flutter beneath my tongue.

Tears jewel her lashes, her breath catching in a fractured sob of pleasure.

"Yours."

The single word nearly shatters me. My control frays,

unraveling at the seams. With a predator's grin, I drive into her relentlessly, each thrust branding her, staking my claim.

Our bodies collide, the slick heat between us igniting like a struck match. The air thickens, humid with our ragged gasps, our moans blending into the warm hush of the room.

Her nails scrape along the green baize, a sharp contrast to the velvet friction between us. She cries my name like a plea, like a prayer.

"I'm... so... close..." she whimpers, her voice breaking at the brink of ecstasy.

"You'll only come when I say so." My tone is harsher now, unwavering. "Do you understand?"

"Uh-huh," she moans.

A low, rumbling growl of approval rolls through my chest as she obeys without question—there's no feeling in the world like the sight of her surrendering to my will.

"You'll take every command I give you—because you're my good girl, aren't you?" I slow, dragging my hands over her sweat-slicked skin, teasing. The very tips of my fingers brush her trembling thighs, so close yet just out of reach.

"Tell me what you want, *Liebes*," I murmur in her ear, my voice a deep, gravelly promise.

She writhes against me, desperate. "More," she whimpers. "I want... more."

A growl vibrates in my chest, thick with hunger.

I slip out of her and haul her against me, her slick skin molding to mine. Her legs wrap around my waist on instinct, her breath hot against my throat.

The electricity between us crackles, charging the air as I lift her, her slender frame weightless in my grasp.

She moves first—her body sinking onto mine, taking me in one smooth, greedy motion. A strangled sound rips from my throat.

I carry her to the couch, lowering her slowly, savoring

every pulse and clench around me before settling down, her thighs straddling my hips. Her fingers drag down my chest, nails scoring, marking. She rocks against me, her pace torturous, teasing.

"Oh, Kaisner..." she moans, my name unraveling on her tongue, "harder... faster..."

A muscle twitches in my jaw. I grip her hips, take control.

Her gasp turns into a cry as I drive into her, our rhythm a feral, frantic collision of bodies and breath.

She shudders, her moans laced with delirium as I lift her higher, changing the angle, forcing her to take me even deeper.

With a snarl, I shift, pressing her against the leather, hoisting her legs over my shoulders. Her breath hitches—half surprise, half surrender.

A dark, primal urge overtakes me, obliterating restraint.

"Keep your eyes on me," I murmur, dragging the words over her skin like silk.

I thrust into her, harder, deeper, wrenching a strangled cry from her lips, her hands scrambling for purchase against the couch.

"Moan for me, *Liebes*," I growl, voice husky, full of dark satisfaction. "Don't you dare hold back. I want to hear every filthy sound you make."

Clarissa's cries of pleasure shatter the silence, echoing off the high ceilings like a hymn to the divine. I increase my pace, pistoning my hips into hers with wild abandon, our bodies connecting with an untamed intensity that defies reason.

Her walls tighten around me, a perfect vice, her back arching as her head falls against the cushions. She's close—so close. I can feel it as she trembles, as her breath stutters and her fingers clutch desperately at my skin.

"Come for me," I rasp, my voice rough, commanding. "Let go. Let me see how pretty you look when you break."

A fractured moan breaks from her lips, a sound torn between surrender and ecstasy. And then it happens—her release washes over her like a tidal wave, taking us both under its powerful current.

Her body seizes around me, muscles pulsing, waves of pleasure rolling through her in a breathtaking display of abandon. Her nails dig into my back, hard enough to mark, to claim. I welcome the sting. I want it. Her imprint on me.

Her climax triggers mine, the intensity of her unraveling dragging me over the edge with her. I bury my face in the crook of her neck, a groan ripping from my chest as I empty into her, my entire body throbbing with the force of it. The world tilts, reality narrowing to the exquisite pressure of her, the way we fit together, the way we fall apart and come undone as one.

Gasping for air, I press my forehead against hers. Sweat-slicked skin, tangled limbs, breath mingling in the quiet aftermath. We ride out the aftershocks together, our bodies molded so perfectly against each other that the thought of separating seems impossible.

I don't want to move.

When our senses begin to return, I shift just enough to take in her face. Her sapphire eyes, still heavy-lidded with pleasure, meet mine. But there's more to it—a depth, a knowing. An understanding I wasn't ready for.

It sends a shiver skittering down my spine. Not of fear, but of something far more dangerous.

Connection.

I have never felt so close to another person as I do now.

I tuck a damp lock of hair behind her ear, fingers lingering on her flushed skin, unwilling to break the moment. She's luminous, the glow of satisfaction softening every edge, and I experience it then—the ache, deep in my chest. A foreign thing. A thing with claws.

I clear my throat, reluctant to examine it. Resistant to name it.

"Kaisner," she whispers, her voice hoarse from her cries. "That was... beyond anything I could have imagined."

I smirk, the corner of my mouth tugging upward, but even that seems unsteady.

Clarissa's eyes flutter closed, a lazy smile curving her kiss-swollen lips. "I never knew it could be like this," she breathes, tracing idle patterns on my chest with her fingertips. "Never knew I could feel so... complete."

Possessive pride unfurls inside me, dark and fierce.

She's mine.

The thought pulses through me, an absolute, an inevitability. I was her first.

Her only.

I take her hand to my mouth. "No one else will ever touch you like this," I purr, pressing my lips to her wrist. "Remember that."

But beneath that dominance, beneath the satisfaction of staking my claim, something else stirs—a tenderness I wasn't prepared for. A quiet, aching wonder that this woman, this impossible woman, has let me in. Has let me see her, truly see her, in all the ways that matter.

And now that I have?

I don't think I can ever let her go.

I brush my knuckles along the delicate line of her jaw, tilting her face up to meet my gaze. "Clarissa," I murmur, my voice rough with emotion, my thumb tracing the soft curve of her cheek. "You are everything I never dared to dream of."

Her lips part on a breath, sapphire eyes shimmering with unshed tears, mirroring the storm inside my chest. "Kaisner," she whispers, my name reverent, fragile. "I... I don't know what this is, what we are. But I don't want it to end. Not now, not ever."

Something tightens inside me, a sensation I can't name. I lean down, capturing her mouth in a kiss that is slow, sweet —a promise wrapped in silk and fire.

"It won't." The words are a vow, low and unyielding as I rest my forehead against hers. "This is just the beginning, my love."

She nods, her fingers finding mine, twining together in a silent affirmation. A pact sealed in touch, in breath, in the unspoken certainty that neither of us dares to put into words.

I hold her close, reveling in the steady rhythm of her heart against mine, and for the first time in my life... I am whole.

For so long, I have been a man divided—torn between duty and desire, between the burden of my lineage and the hunger of my own damnation. Between the darkness that has always been my birthright... and the light I never thought I deserved.

But with Clarissa by my side, the war inside me stills.

She is my peace. My salvation. The gentle touch that soothes the jagged edges of my soul.

And I know, with a certainty that goes beyond mere words, beyond reason, beyond logic—I will do whatever it takes to keep her safe. To protect the fragile, precious gift of her love.

Even if it means going to war with those who seek to tear us apart.

Even if it means confronting the ghosts of my past, the sins I've buried deep in the shadows.

Even if it means exposing the secrets I have long since locked away.

I will do it all. And more. For the chance to build a future with this woman.

As I run my fingers through the silk of her hair, as I commit every breath, every sigh, every moment to memory, I make a vow—one that is as eternal as the night sky above us.

I will be her strength. Her shelter.

I will love her with every breath in my body, with every beat of my blackened, brutal heart. And nothing in this world—or any other—will ever take her from me.

Nothing.

Falling in love with a dangerous man is like learning to breathe underwater—exhilarating, until you realize you're drowning. The days pass in a haze of stolen glances and secret smiles. Each clandestine meeting with Kaisner is a delicious risk that leaves me craving more. It's not all grand gestures—some moments are quieter, like the late-night coffees he sends when I'm working, or the texts that make me laugh out loud in bed. In these simple, thoughtful acts, my affection grows stronger.

Our first real date is unexpectedly perfect. I'm sketching at the Jardin des Plantes, lost in the quiet hum of spring, when his shadow falls across my sketchbook. Kaisner stands there, a vision in light linen and tailored trousers, his playful gaze softening the sharpness of his presence. "Fancy meeting you here, Miss Draken," he murmurs, his voice low and intimate, stirring something dangerous beneath my skin.

We wander the gardens, our conversation rich with arcane knowledge only beings like us would understand.

"Beautiful," Kaisner purrs as we stop by a patch of wolfsbane.

I glance at him, arching a brow. "But deadly."

His gaze lingers on the plant before flicking back to me, the corner of his mouth lifting with a mischievous smile. "Like you."

Heat flares low in my belly, and I hate how easily he affects me with just three syllables.

I hold his stare. "And like you."

His slow, wolfish smile sets me alight. Danger, it seems, is a language we both speak fluently. The tension between us coils tighter with every glance, every brush of skin.

By the time we reach the labyrinth, it's almost unbearable. Hidden by high hedges, he pulls me close, and when his lips find mine, it's reckless, raw—inevitable.

From there, our secret rendezvous grow bolder. Secluded corners of the Jardin des Tuileries become our sanctuaries— whispered conversations and stolen kisses behind sculpted bushes. Late-night drives through Paris serve as our refuge, the glow of the city our silent witness as we explore each other with fevered touches in the shadowed back seat of his sleek car.

Days turn into weeks, and I find myself falling deeper. It's not just physical attraction—though that's certainly part of it. It's the way Kaisner listens when I speak, his attention sharp and undivided. How he challenges me with questions that force me to think harder, to see beyond the mundane. It's the vulnerability I glimpse in his eyes when he thinks I'm not looking, the tenderness in his touch that belies his tough exterior.

Yet, even as we revel in our private world, reality is never far away. Our responsibilities, the threat of discovery, always linger at the edges of our stolen moments. The upcoming gala looms—a reminder that our lives are public, political, dangerous—and any misstep could destroy everything.

And Kaisner? As the event draws near, he becomes a

constant, exquisite torture. He's at the gallery daily, dressed to perfection, flanked by his lawyers and efficient assistants, reviewing contracts, discussing logistics, negotiating every fine detail of the exhibition.

I sit across from him in meeting after meeting, knees brushing beneath the table. Every accidental touch is a shock to my system. His cologne haunts me, warm and dark, making it difficult to focus. Every glance he casts my way is heavy with unspoken desire. Every look, a silent promise of *later*.

It's maddening, working so closely with him, pretending to be nothing more than cordial acquaintances. My entire being wants to stand up and shout to the world that I love him, that he's mine and I'm his. But I can't. We can't. If Nik —or anyone—discovers our secret, it won't just destroy us. It will fracture alliances, destabilize power, unravel the delicate balance of our supernatural community.

So we play our parts. We maintain the facade. We speak through glances, coded words, the barest brush of fingertips as we pass documents. Subtle touches that say *I love you*, that promise *soon*, that remind us we are not alone.

At night, alone in my bed, I replay each interaction. Every near-touch. Every almost-kiss. The anticipation builds, a steady crescendo of desire and frustration that threatens to overwhelm me. I see the strain in Kaisner too—in the way his jaw clenches, his hands fisting at his sides when we're forced to maintain our distance. It's a quiet, torturous longing that burns through every moment we have to pretend.

As the gala draws ever closer, the pressure intensifies. The success of this event is crucial for the gallery, for my family's reputation, for the frail alliances in our world. And at the center of it all is Kaisner—our benefactor, our star attraction, my secret love.

I long for the night of the event, dread it too. It will be the ultimate test of our restraint. A night where we must perform our roles perfectly, flawlessly, while denying the fire smoldering between us.

But for now, we cling to what we can. Stolen glances. Brushed fingertips. A hidden world of subtle, defiant victories against the forces that would keep us apart.

The soft ping of an incoming email breaks the stillness of my office. I glance at my screen, expecting another dull update, but the subject line stills my breath:

OPEN WHEN ALONE – K.

I close the door, heart thrumming. Fingers trembling, I open the message. A single image appears—a rose petal, red and lush, with elegant script overlaid:

Noon. The usual place. Bring only yourself.

A thrill shivers through me, sweet and sharp. Our clandestine meetings are growing more reckless, more dangerous. And I know, even as desire blooms hot in my chest, that I'll go. I'll always go. The risks be damned.

The hours crawl by. At 11:55, I make an excuse and slip from the gallery. A sleek black car waits at the curb. The driver steps out and opens the door.

"Where are we going?" I ask, sliding into the cool leather seat.

He smiles, polite but tight. "I'm sorry, mademoiselle. Mr. Drachenstein's instructions were very clear."

I don't press. I already know better.

The drive takes us to the edge of the city, where we pull up beside a private airfield. My pulse quickens as I spot Kaisner's jet gleaming on the tarmac, its engines humming low and expectant.

And there he is.

Kaisner stands at the base of the stairs, dressed in tailored linen trousers and a crisp white shirt, the sleeves rolled up to expose tanned, tattooed forearms. He holds a bouquet of deep red roses, and as his eyes meet mine, the world narrows to him. To this.

"You look ravishing, as always," he murmurs, pressing a kiss to my cheek. His lips linger longer than propriety allows. "But I thought you might prefer a change of attire."

He gestures to a garment bag draped over his arm. "Shall we?"

Once aboard, I change into the dress he's chosen—a wrap of pale pink and blue seafoam silk that ripples with every breath. When I emerge, Kaisner is waiting with a glass of champagne.

"To stolen moments," he says, eyes never leaving mine as we clink glasses.

As the jet takes off, Kaisner pulls me close, his lips finding that sensitive spot just below my ear. "Do you have any idea how maddening it is," he murmurs, "to see you *every —single—day* and not be able to touch you like this?"

I gasp as his teeth graze my skin. "Kaisner... we shouldn't..."

But my body betrays me, arching into his touch, needing it. Needing him.

"Tell me to stop," he says softly, voice low and dark.

I don't. I can't.

Instead, I pull him in, claiming his mouth with mine. We lose ourselves to the heat, to the desperate, dangerous need that burns between us. Hands roaming, lips searching. Reality vanishes beneath us.

All too soon, the pilot announces our descent. I glance out the window, and my breath catches.

Rugged cliffs plunge into sapphire water, the Amalfi Coast stretching beneath the sunlight like a secret paradise.

A sleek yacht waits for us at the marina, its white hull gleaming in the Mediterranean sun. As we set sail, the coastline unfolds—a dream of pastel villages, sun-dappled terraces, and lemon groves spilling down cliffs, hidden coves beckoning with crystal-clear waters.

Kaisner stands behind me, his arms a steel band gripping my waist.

"Beautiful, isn't it?" he murmurs. His voice curls around me like smoke. "But not half as beautiful as you."

I turn in his embrace, overcome by the sheer romance of it all. "Kaisner, this is… It's too much. We can't keep doing this. The risk of—"

He hushes me with a kiss, soft but insistent. His lips linger, pressing a vow into my skin before he pulls back enough to murmur, "Let tomorrow worry about itself. Today is ours, baby girl… Just ours."

And in that moment, I want to believe him.

We dock in Positano, the town rising above us in a riot of color and charm. Kaisner leads me through winding cobbled streets and up endless stone stairs until we reach a restaurant perched high on the cliffs. The view steals my breath—a stretch of limitless blue sea, blurring into the horizon.

We dine beneath the glow of hanging lanterns, the sea breeze carrying the scent of salt and lemon. Over plates of fresh seafood and crisp local wine, we talk and laugh, shedding the weight of politics and legacies. Here, we are not leaders or heirs or enemies. We are just two people savoring the moment.

Kaisner's hand finds mine across the table, his thumb drawing slow, lazy circles over my palm. The simplest touch, yet it sparks something deep inside me.

"I wish we could stay here forever," I sigh, my gaze tracing the gold-tipped waves beyond.

His gaze finds mine, shadowed and intense. Hungry. "Say the word, Clarissa, and I'll make it happen. We could disappear, just you and me. Leave the expectations. Leave the politics behind." His voice drops, low and firm, each word a promise carved from stone.

The sincerity in his words knocks the air from me. There's no hesitation, no flowery sentiment, no illusion. Just Kaisner, stripped bare. Raw. Vulnerable. And just then, I believe him. With every part of me, I believe.

But reality crashes down too soon.

"You know we can't," I whisper, pain lacing my voice. "Creatures like us… We can never truly escape our lineage."

A shadow crosses his features—regret, maybe, or resignation. He doesn't argue. "I know," he adds quietly. "But a man can dream."

He rises, hand steady as it closes around mine. His thumb brushes my knuckles, and the touch is an apology. "Come," he says, voice low and rough. "There's somewhere else I want to show you."

We descend to a hidden cove, cloaked in shadows and kissed by the amber hues of the setting sun. The cliffs guard us, the sea whispers to the shore, and the air is thick with salt and desire.

Kaisner's arm snakes around my waist, pulling me flush against him. His eyes catch the last light of the day, smoldering. "You're more dangerous than any fire," he murmurs, just before our lips meet.

The kiss is soft at first, a question, a plea. But when I answer—when my mouth opens beneath his—it becomes something deeper, wilder. Like lightning striking dry earth. His tongue sweeps into me, tasting, claiming, and I can only cling tighter.

My fingers tangle in his hair as I pull him closer, craving more. Needing more. His hand slides up my spine, trailing heat in its wake. Every nerve ignites beneath his touch. I arch into him, molding myself to his body as if I were made for him. Maybe I was.

The world tilts, and suddenly I'm on my back, the cool sand a stark contrast to the fever of my skin. Kaisner's weight presses me down, grounding me even as his kisses lift me toward the stars.

My hands roam his chest, feeling the shift of muscle beneath linen. Desperate, I tug at his shirt until he breaks the kiss long enough to pull it over his head, casting it aside. He's pure strength and heat beneath my hands, all corded muscle and raw power.

And then his mouth is on me again, devouring, tasting, worshiping.

For a second, I catch a glint of something around his neck—an amulet, intricate and ancient, pulsing with an energy I don't understand. But the thought is fleeting. His mouth finds that sensitive spot just beneath my jaw, and reason dissolves.

The crash of waves becomes our soundtrack, their rhythm matching the ragged rise and fall of our breaths. His fingers skim my sides, rough and reverent. Sand clings to my skin, but I don't care. I'd burn for this. For him.

His hands find the tie of my wrap dress, fingers deft as they work it loose. The fabric slips from my shoulders in a whisper of silk, falling away entirely as cool air kisses my exposed skin. His gaze sweeps over me—dark, hungry, devouring.

"You're exquisite," he breathes, voice rough and reverent.

Before I can answer, his mouth claims mine again, deep and slow, as if he wants to memorize the taste of me. His lips blaze a path down my neck, along my collarbone, to the swell of my breasts. Each kiss, each graze of his teeth, sends a tremor through me. My hands clutch at him, nails raking his back, claiming him as my own.

And when his hand slides down my thigh, hitching my leg over his hip, I sense the evidence of his desire. Hard and hot, pressing against me. The friction makes me gasp, and my body arches, longing for more.

"Kaisner," I breathe, my voice breaking. "Please…"

His gaze snaps to mine, fierce and demanding. "Say it," he rasps, his lips brushing my skin. "Tell me what you want."

"You," I whisper. "All of you."

A growl rumbles in his chest, dark and dangerous. And then he's there, claiming me, joining our bodies in a rhythm as ancient as the sea.

The world falls away. There is only this. Only him. Every touch, every kiss, every breath is magnified. His hands gripping my hips. My fingers threading through his hair. The taste of him, the feel of him, the sound of his name on my lips. It's fire and shadow, heat and surrender. It's ruin and rapture, all at once.

And as I fall apart beneath him, as pleasure sears through me, I realize it's not just lust burning in my chest. It's something deeper. Something I'm terrified to name.

Later, as we lie tangled beneath the stars, I can't hold back the fear pressing at my throat.

"What if this is the last time?" I whisper. "What if we're discovered, or—"

Kaisner silences me with a kiss, tender and sure. "Then we'll make every moment count," he vows, fierce and unshakable. "Whatever comes, Clarissa, know this—what I feel for you is real. It's more real than anything I've ever known."

And in the quiet that follows, I believe him.

When it's time to board the jet for our return flight, I

hold tight to the memories we've made—the warmth of his skin, the flavor of his kiss, the whispered promises shared beneath the falling sun.

No matter what tomorrow brings, Amalfi will always be ours.

33

KAISNER

*P*ower always comes with a price—the question is whether you pay it in blood or souls. The silver light from my laptop carves shadows across my office like a blade. Outside, Paris hums with life—streetlights flickering like stars, distant traffic threading through the night. But here, in my study, it's quiet. Still. Only the antique clock on the mantel dares to disturb the silence, its ticking a constant reminder of passing time. Of decisions, yet to be made.

I scan the encrypted message on my screen, fingers steepled beneath my chin. The deal is almost complete—a shipment of state-of-the-art weaponry, officially bound for a private security firm in Dubai but destined for less savory hands. The kind of transaction that would make headlines if it ever came to light. The sort of deal that cements the Drachenstein clan's position in the shadows of the supernatural world.

A sharp ping from my secure line breaks my concentration.

"Yes?" I answer. My tone is clipped, cold. Professional.

"Mr. Drachenstein," comes my contact's voice on the

other end, brittle with tension. "We have a complication with the Dubai shipment."

My jaw tightens. "Explain."

As he outlines the problem—a nosy customs official, a bribe that wasn't quite enough—I listen, but my mind drifts. Not to contingencies or threats, but to softer things. Warmer things. Clarissa's laugh, light and golden. The way her eyes shine when she speaks of art, of magic. The feel of her skin beneath my fingers, satin-smooth and burning with need.

I shake my head, forcing myself to focus. "Double the bribe," I instruct quietly. "If that doesn't work, remove the obstacle. Permanently."

"Understood, sir."

The line clicks dead.

I lean back, exhaling slowly, the leather chair creaking beneath me. Once, this life had thrilled me. The power, the danger, the constant dance of shadows—it was intoxicating. Now, all I feel is the burden of it pressing down on me.

My gaze drifts to the photograph on my desk. Amalfi. A shot of the seashore at sunset, silver-framed, nothing that would draw attention. To anyone else, it's a simple vacation memento. But I know the truth that lies behind that captured moment—Clarissa's laughter as we sailed along the coast, the warmth of her skin against mine as we lounged on the yacht's deck, the taste of her lips flavored with limoncello and desire.

The photograph was taken just moments before I pulled her into my arms, unable to resist the sight of her bathed in the golden light of the setting sun. Her hair had been tousled by the sea breeze, her cheeks flushed with excitement and maybe a touch too much wine. She had never looked more beautiful, more alive.

I remember the way she had melted into me, her body fitting perfectly against mine. The soft gasp she let out as I trailed kisses down her neck, the way her fingers had tangled in my hair, pulling me closer.

That evening in Amalfi had been a stolen moment of perfection, a brief escape from the complexities of our lives and the secrets we are forced to keep. For a few precious hours, we weren't Kaisner Drachenstein and Clarissa Draken, heirs to rival supernatural dynasties. We were just a man and a woman, hopelessly, recklessly in love.

The memory of it all—her scent, her touch, the sound of her whispered "I love you" against my skin—is so vivid, so all-consuming, that for a second I forget where I am. I forget the deals waiting to be made, the power waiting to be claimed. I forget everything but her.

A ripple of movement catches my eye. I turn, my gaze landing on the mirror that hangs on the far wall. At first, it's only my reflection. The polished veneer of power—a tailored suit, a keen stare, the mask I wear for the world.

But then the image distorts. And it is no longer me who stares back.

Azrakan grins, its face a twisted shadow of my own. Dark eyes glowing, sharp teeth bared in mockery.

"Ah, the great Kaisner Drachenstein," it sneers. "Mooning over a woman like a lovesick fool. How the mighty have fallen."

Anger flares hot in my chest, but I keep my voice cold, hard. "I don't recall summoning you."

The daemon laughs, and the grating sound makes my skin crawl. "You didn't need to. I'm always here, warlock. Always watching. And what I see... disappoints me."

I stand, fists clenched at my sides. "What I do with my time is none of your concern, daemon."

"Oh, but it is," it purrs, eyes glowing. "Have you forgotten our bargain so soon? Clarissa's blood is the key, warlock. The final ingredient to awaken your dragon. To claim the power that is rightfully yours."

The words strike like iron, cold and sharp. Clarissa's blood. The ritual. The ancient promise of strength beyond imagining.

I stagger back, the ground tilting beneath me. How could I have let myself forget?

"I haven't forgotten," I say, though the statement scrapes my throat raw.

Azrakan's grin widens. "Good. Then you understand what must be done. Take the girl's blood. Complete the ritual. Fulfill your destiny." It tilts its head, mockery in its eyes. "It's what you've always wanted, isn't it? To be the most powerful dragon shifter in existence? To elevate your clan above all others?"

I turn away, unable to bear the sight of it. My gaze lands once more on the photograph. A flash of Clarissa's smile. Her eyes, bright with joy… My heart constricts.

"Yes," I whisper. "It's what I've always wanted."

But even as I say it, the lie coils in my gut. Because once, it was true. Now… now, I'm not so sure.

The daemon's laughter cuts through the silence. "Love is a weakness, Kaisner. A distraction. Do you think she'd love you if she knew the depths of your ambition? If she knew what you've promised in the dark?"

I whirl back to face the mirror, anger burning hot in my veins. "You know *nothing* about her," I snarl. "Nothing about *us*."

Azrakan's cackle rings out again, mocking and cruel. "I know more than you think, warlock. The fear that lurks in her heart, the doubt that plagues her mind. I know that deep down, she wonders if she can truly trust you. And she's right to wonder."

I want to argue, to deny the daemon's words, but they

strike too close to home. How many times have I glimpsed a flicker of uncertainty in Clarissa's eyes? How often have I noticed her withdrawal, just slightly, when conversation shifts to the grimmer realities of our world?

"She loves me." The words seem weak, brittle. "And I love her."

"And what is love," Azrakan hisses, "compared to power? Compared to destiny? You were born for greatness, Kaisner Drachenstein. Will you throw it all away for a fleeting human emotion?"

The question lingers, cold and brutal.

I sink into my chair, my head in my hands. The demon's advice echoes in my mind, warring with memories of Clarissa—her laugh, her touch, the way she looks at me like I'm something precious, something *good*.

"You know the answer, warlock," the daemon murmurs. "You always have."

And that's the truth that terrifies me most.

Because I do know.

With those final words, the mirror shimmers once more, and I'm left staring at my reflection. But the man looking back at me is a stranger—eyes haunted, face drawn with conflict.

I look away, unable to stand the sight of myself. The photograph catches my attention once more, and a powerful surge of emotion nearly brings me to my knees.

Love or power. Clarissa, or my destiny. The choice stands before me, impossible and inevitable.

I reach for my phone, my fingers hovering over Clarissa's number. One call, and I could end this. I could tell her everything, beg for her forgiveness, find a way to be with her that doesn't involve betrayal and blood magic.

But even as I contemplate it, I recognize I won't make

that call. Not yet. The allure of power, the pull of centuries of Drachenstein ambition, is too strong to ignore.

I set the phone down and turn back to my laptop. There's work to be done, deals to be made, a clan to lead. And somewhere, in the back of my mind, a ritual waits to be completed.

Azrakan's words echo in my thoughts as I lose myself in the familiar routine of business and intrigue. But beneath it all, like a steady heartbeat, I hear another voice. Clarissa's voice, soft and sure: "I love you, Kaisner."

And in that moment, caught between love and power, between the man I am and the dragon I could become, I've never felt more lost.

34

CLARISSA

onight is the night—the Lumière Foundation Gala I've spent months planning. The Grand Palais rises before me, its glass dome catching the last blush of twilight, iron latticework gleaming beneath the glow of gilded lanterns. From my perch on the upper balcony of the *Salon d'Honneur*, I watch the steady stream of limousines and luxury cars as they pull up to the red carpet below. The air thrums with excitement, a current of energy that pulses in rhythm with the fevered clicks of paparazzi cameras.

I smooth a hand over the midnight silk of my gown, the fabric cool and fluid beneath my fingertips. The bodice hugs my curves like a lover's embrace, silver beadwork catching the light like scattered stars before spilling into a full skirt that pools at my feet. A daring side slit runs high along one leg, a bold slash of skin that contrasts with the gown's otherwise classic elegance—an unspoken challenge.

Against my collarbone rests not my family's heirloom, but the dragon pendant Kaisner gave me—white gold and diamonds that shimmer like captured starlight. Dangerous.

Beautiful. A secret pressed close to my skin, its cool weight a constant reminder of him. Of what we are. Of what we risk.

It feels like defiance. Like desire. Like temptation.

Below, the masses surge as another car pulls over, the buzz of speculation reaching a crescendo. The mass of people splinters into distinct groups as they press forward. On the left, men and women draped in amber scarves hoist hand-made signs reading "URSA STRENGTH" and "BEAR KING GAVRIIL" above their heads. Several wear imitation claw marks drawn across their cheeks in solidarity with the shifter clan.

Near the center barrier, a sea of black leather and crimson accessories dominates. One pale young woman, her lips painted blood-red, clutches a poster with "IMMORTAL LOVE FOR LOCKHART" emblazoned across a silhouette of fangs. Beside her, a man in a vintage velvet coat holds aloft a Gothic-lettered placard that simply states "BITE ME, IVAN."

The right flank belongs to the witchcraft enthusiasts, their flowing garments adorned with crystals that catch the evening light. "THE GRAND WITCH LIVES" declares one elaborate sign decorated with dried flowers and intricate symbols. A cluster of young practitioners chant Juliette's name in rhythmic unison, their hands raised toward the sky as though drawing down her power.

Among them, although harder to spot, are the true supernatural observers—ancient eyes veiled beneath human guises. Witches cloaked in glamour, shifters in tailored suits with restless gazes, vampires whose beauty is just a shade too perfect to be real. Mortals stand beside them, oblivious to the proximity of creatures who could end their lives with a whisper.

When the car door opens, camera phones rise from all

sections, the air crackling with excitement as each faction strains for a glimpse of their chosen idol, momentarily united only by their shared belief in the unnatural world that exists just beyond mortal understanding.

I grip the ornate balustrade, leaning closer, eager to see the arrival.

And then, she steps out.

Juliette Deveraux, Grand Witch and matriarch of a dynasty that bends kingdoms to its will. Her emerald gown shimmers with a light that seems woven from magic itself, her red hair crowned with a diamond tiara. Timeless beauty cloaks her like armor, and she wears it well. She moves with the easy elegance of one who knows the significance of her power and wields it like a blade.

"Juliette, share your secrets!" a woman cries, thrusting forward a grimoire for signing. "Teach us the old ways!" another shouts, waving a bundle of herbs that releases a pungent aroma into the night air. "We've kept your traditions alive!" calls a silver-haired woman, tears streaming down her weathered face as she presses against the security barrier.

At her side stands Ivan Lockhart. Dark and severe in a tailored tuxedo, his tousled hair lending him a rakish charm that sharpens when set against the cut-glass edge of his jaw. Behind fashionable sunglasses, his gaze burns with the cold hunger of the undead, and though he wears the trappings of civility, it's the predator I see beneath. Watching. Calculating. Waiting.

"Ivan, we've waited centuries!" screams a group of women in Victorian-inspired gowns—*vampires?* A young man collapses in theatrical fashion, hand pressed to his forehead, shouting, "Take my blood, it's type O negative—the *champagne* of hemoglobin!"

A flicker of amusement crosses Lockhart's expression.

Flashing a smirk, he turns to whisper into his girlfriend's ear, a sensual move that earns him a teasing glare from Juliette, a roaring scream from the crowd.

Suddenly, a blur of movement disrupts the red carpet's careful choreography. A young woman with raven-black hair and a velvet choker vaults over the security barrier, evading the grasping hands of guards with unnatural speed. She hurls herself at Ivan, arms outstretched. My breath hitches as security tenses, ready to tackle her. But with preternatural reflexes, Ivan catches her mid-leap.

"My eternal lord," she gasps, somehow managing to plant a crimson-lipped kiss on his pale cheek. But just before she's torn from him by security, I could have sworn she whispered something more into his ear—impossible to catch, but enough to make Ivan's gaze flicker with sharp, predatory interest.

A secret. A message. Or perhaps… a warning.

Whatever it was, Ivan's expression doesn't falter, but something shifts. The barest tension in his jaw, a shadow in his eyes, gone in a blink. He straightens his collar with deliberate elegance, fingers brushing the lipstick mark as though considering whether to preserve it as a trophy or wipe it clean.

The horde hushes as he approaches the crowd again, his stride measured, unhurried. "An admirer with spirit," he drawls, accent thickening with pleasure. "How refreshing."

He gestures subtly to the guards, halting them with the faintest lift of his hand. "Gently with the lady. Passion should be rewarded. Never punished."

The crowd roars its approval, the woman swooning into the arms of her friends, eyes glassy, lips parted as though still caught in the spell of him. Ivan offers a slight bow in her direction before returning his attention to Juliette.

The striking pair pause beneath the red carpet lights,

posing for photographs—a portrait of preternatural royalty. Power has a scent, a feel, and it radiates off them.

But his eyes linger for a moment too long, as if haunted by whatever secret had been pressed into his ear.

And I can't help but wonder—what did she tell him?

Following close behind is Cassandra Deveraux, her dark hair cascading half down her back in soft waves, half over her shoulder. Her gown, a delicate rose gold that complements her fair skin, flows around her like liquid metal. One hand rests protectively over the slight swell of her stomach, barely noticeable to those who don't know to look for it. Her other hand encircles the arm of the Ursa King himself.

Gavriil towers over Cassie, his imposing figure made even more striking by the crisp lines of his charcoal gray suit. His dark chestnut hair is swept back from his forehead, tied into a sleek low bun. His style balances sophistication with a laid-back vibe, complemented by his neatly trimmed beard, enhancing his rugged, masculine look.

The Ursa King's piercing maroon eyes survey the crowd with the vigilance of a born predator. Despite the easy smile on his face, I can see the tension in his jaw, the way his body is angled slightly in front of Cassandra's, as if shielding her from the world.

To the supernatural community watching with keen interest, they present a united front—the formidable Ursa King and his chosen mate. The diamond-encrusted brand on Cassandra's wrist, visible when she raises her hand to wave, is a clear sign of their engagement. But I know the truth that lies beneath their polished facade. Behind closed doors, their relationship is a tempest of disagreements and unspoken tensions.

And then—Samara. Resplendent in navy silk that hugs her curves before flaring out at her knees. Her chestnut hair is styled to one side, revealing the elegant line of her neck and the glittering diamond earrings that dangle from her ears. She stands tall and fierce beside her brother, Vlad.

Vlad is a storm waiting to break. His bespoke black suit cannot tame the wildness in him, the alpha simmering beneath his skin. Fierce silver eyes scan the horde with cool calculation, every inch of him on edge, as though expecting the night to turn from elegance to battle in the blink of an eye.

I watch them all and feel the world tighten around me. The elite of the supernatural realm, gathered under one roof. All their secrets, their alliances, their rivalries, dressed up in luxury and precious gems. And I am here among them, the sole bearer of the Draken legacy, a name heavy with history and darker with expectation.

The burden of it falls over my shoulders like a mantle, a quiet pressure that straightens my spine and sharpens my gaze. I wonder if they see me, the woman beneath the silk and diamonds. Or if they only see the bloodline. The future. A pawn or a queen.

The crowd stirs again, a ripple of excitement sharp enough to cut through the air. I feel it before I see him, a prickle along my skin, a tightening of breath. My pulse quickens, traitorous and eager. I lean further over the balcony, my eyes searching desperately among the faces below.

And then, Kaisner Drachenstein steps out of the car, and the world falls away.

The reaction is immediate. Those with preternatural knowing stiffen, recognition passing through the hidden supernatural elite. They know him—not just for his lineage, but for the shadowed power that coils beneath his skin, the whispered rumors of darkness and blood magic that follow him like a second shadow.

Scattered throughout are humans, blissfully unaware of

the darker truth. To them, Kaisner is the hottest it-boy of the moment—the recently revealed millionaire art collector, enigmatic and generous, who single-handedly funded this grand event. A European aristocrat turned international benefactor. The kind of man whose name fills tabloids and dreams alike.

Women gasp. Men stir, some with admiration, others with envy. Phones rise, capturing his image as though to preserve a relic of the evening. Whispers ripple along the crowd's edge, their voices tinged with fascination and longing.

He steps onto the red carpet, devastating in black. A tuxedo that speaks of precision and power, its lines sharp as a blade, emphasizing the breadth of his shoulders and the lean strength of his body. His dark hair is combed back but subtly tousled, hinting at something untamed beneath the polish. Danger in a beautifully tailored suit.

Even from this distance, I sense the magnetism of his presence. The crowd parts before him, drawn to his aura of power and danger. His eyes, those deep pools of midnight that have haunted my dreams, scan the horde with casual indifference.

Until they glance up and lock with mine.

For a moment, time stills. There is only Kaisner and me, caught in a silent exchange that speaks volumes. I glimpse the heat in his gaze, the barely restrained desire that mirrors my own. My body responds instinctively, a flush creeping up my neck as I remember the touch of his hands on my skin, the taste of his lips against mine.

Then, as quickly as it began, the clock unfreezes. Kaisner turns away, his attention caught by a reporter calling his name. I step back from the balcony, my heart pounding in my chest.

The evening stretches before us, filled with potential and

danger in equal measure. As I turn to make my way downstairs, to take my place among the glittering throng beneath the Grand Palais' soaring glass roof, a single thought echoes in my mind:

This is going to be one hell of a night.

35

CLARISSA

The most dangerous predators wear designer gowns and offer polite conversation. The building hums with anticipation, a living entity of barely contained energy. I stand just offstage, veiled behind heavy velvet curtains, heart thrumming in my chest. Each pulse is a reminder of my lineage, my responsibility, my danger.

I inhale deeply, the air thick with the scent of gardenias and roses, mingling with the cloying sweetness of expensive perfumes and something more primal. The kind of aroma that lingers when too many immortals occupy the same room.

"Mademoiselle Draken?" A soft voice, hesitant, pulls me from my thoughts. I turn to find an event coordinator, clipboard pressed to her chest. She's young, human, blissfully unaware of the politics swirling beneath the glamour of this night. "It's time."

I nod, smoothing my gown. The silver beadwork glimmers like stars. The high slit along my thigh teases with every step. I touch the dragon necklace at my throat—a silent tether to the truth that lies beneath the veneer of this soirée. Him. Kaisner.

I square my shoulders, lifting my chin. I am Clarissa Draken, heir to a legacy older than this city's stones. A woman with fire in her blood and shadows at her heels. I will not falter.

The moment I step onto the stage, the world sharpens. Light floods my vision, momentarily blinding me, but I focus as the crowd materializes. Faces gleam beneath chandeliers, laughter hanging in the air, glasses poised to toast. Supernaturals woven among mortals, masks in place. Vampires shimmer under the lights, their beauty unnatural. Shifters lounge with casual elegance, danger cloaked in tailored suits and velvet gowns. Witches wear power like silk, radiating energy beyond their charms.

And there, at the back of the room, he waits. Kaisner.

Even at a distance, his presence is undeniable. Our eyes meet for a brief moment, and a jolt of electricity courses through me. His gaze is intense, a heat that makes my cheeks flush. I force myself to look away, focusing on the task at hand.

"Good evening, ladies and gentlemen," I begin, voice steady, though my pulse hammers hard. "Welcome to 'Lumière's d'Espoir'—the inaugural Galerie Lumière's Annual Gala and Charity Auction."

The room hushes, high expectations pressing down on me, but I stand firm.

"We gather not just to celebrate art's beauty, but its ability to change lives. Every brushstroke, every sculpture, carries meaning. Tonight, we add a new chapter to those stories."

The words come easier this time, practiced, poised. I sweep my gaze across the crowd, careful not to linger on Kaisner. I will not be distracted.

"We're honored by the generosity of Mr. Kaisner Drachenstein." I pause. Applause erupts, reverberating through the hall. "Not only has he lent us his private collection for this exhibition, but he's also donated a rare Kandinsky sketch for tonight's auction. All proceeds will benefit the Lumière Foundation's outreach programs."

A ripple of excitement. Murmured approval.

I push forward. "This piece, along with others in tonight's main event, supports our 'Art sans Frontières' initiative—providing resources, education, and opportunities for underprivileged artists across Paris and beyond."

I pause, letting the words settle over them. "Because art knows no boundary, no class, no bloodline. It is universal. As it should be."

Another beat. A quiet nod to those who understand the deeper meaning.

"Please, enjoy the exhibition, indulge in our culinary delights, and above all, open your hearts—and your wallets—for a cause that will change lives. Thank you, and have a wonderful evening."

Applause swells, bright and warm, but beneath it, I sense the layers of understanding. Some clap for the art, others for the cause. But there are those—like Kaisner—who hear the message beneath my words. The fight for legacy. The battle against bloodlines and curses. The struggle to claim freedom within a world bound by ancient rules.

As I step off the stage, the orchestra's music begins, soft and lilting, like a dream spun in silver.

I glide through the crowd, fielding compliments and greetings with practiced ease. The Grand Palais has been transformed, exhibition spaces cleared to make room for round tables draped in white linen, lavish centerpieces of orchids and cut crystal.

My smile is gracious, my posture perfect, though my

pulse races with every stolen glance in Kaisner's direction. His gaze lingers, burning beneath the civilized exterior.

A group of art enthusiasts surrounds him. He gestures coolly while discussing pieces from his collection. Even from this distance, I see the passion in his eyes, the effortless command of attention.

Then, Amélie approaches.

"Channel 24 wants an interview," she murmurs, low and urgent. "You're radiant tonight, Clarissa. They'll be eating out of your palm."

I nod, even as my heart tugs toward the shadowed corner where Kaisner leans, half-devoured by light. Watching me. Always watching.

"Of course. Lead the way."

The interview is a blur. Words flow—about art, unity, legacy. About Kaisner's collection being a beacon of generosity. I say all the right things, smile all the right ways, but beneath it all, my skin burns with memory. His hands. His mouth. The dangerous temptation between us.

When the interview ends, I rise, smoothing my gown. The reporter stands, extending her hand.

With a final nod, I turn away, signaling to staff to escort the crew to their dinner table. Weaving through the crowd, I catch sight of Cassandra and Gavriil waiting nearby. They've clearly been watching. Approval and perhaps concern flicker in Cassandra's eyes.

"Clarissa, darling," she greets warmly, pulling me into a gentle hug. The soft glow of pregnancy illuminates her, lending her an almost ethereal beauty. "You were magnificent. Truly, you've outdone yourself."

I return the embrace. "Oh, Cassie. I'm so glad you could make it."

As we part, I find myself face to face with Gavriil. The Ursa King towers over both Cassandra and me, his presence commanding even in this glittering horde. His maroon eyes, sharp and assessing, seem to look right through me.

Gavriil nods, a slight gesture that conveys approval and authority. "You've made quite a mark in your brother's absence."

His words, though complimentary, make me straighten my spine. I'm acutely aware of the eyes on us, the supernatural community watching with keen interest. To them, Cassandra and Gavriil are the perfect couple—the mighty Ursa King and the Deveraux heiress. Strength and beauty. A match made by the gods.

Here, under the glittering lights, they play their parts to perfection. But the reality of it all is less than appealing. I only hope they get through this gala unscathed.

"I'm merely continuing the work my brother started," I reply, voice steady despite the fluttering nerves.

Gavriil's lips quirk in what might be a smile. "Modesty becomes you, Miss Draken," he says, gruff. "But do not underestimate your own accomplishments. This event..." he gestures around the room, "is solid proof of your capabilities."

Any words I might have said die on my tongue. Juliette sweeps in like a force of nature, her emerald gown shimmering under the lights. "Clarissa, my dear!" she exclaims, pulling me into a warm embrace. "Oh, what a triumph! You've truly outdone yourself."

I return her hug, tension melting in her calming presence. "I couldn't have done it without your guidance," I reply, smiling. "Your venue suggestion was wonderful!"

Ivan stands slightly apart, dark green eyes surveying the room, radiating boredom and disdain. He nods at me, a barely perceptible tilt of his head that I return.

Suddenly, Juliette's phone chimes. She glances at it, brow furrowing. "Oh dear, I'm needed elsewhere." Looking up, she adds, "Clarissa, darling, would you mind keeping Ivan company for a moment? I have him on a tight leash, making sure he stays out of trouble tonight." She casts him a playful glance. "He has a talent for finding it."

Before I can protest, she's gone, disappearing into the crowd with a swirl of emerald silk. I'm left there alone.

Alone with Ivan Lockhart.

His gaze is sharp as glass, his smirk lethal in its precision.

I take a deep breath. "I didn't think invitations were your style—you seem to favor slipping in *unannounced*," I say, voice low but firm.

Ivan raises an eyebrow, feigning confusion. "I beg your pardon?"

"The conservatory at Draken Manor," I clarify, meeting his gaze steadily. "You broke into my home?"

For a moment, something flashes in his eyes—surprise? Amusement? But it's gone so quickly, I can't be sure.

"My dearest Miss Draken," he says, voice smooth as silk, "I assure you, I have no idea what you're talking about." The vampire pauses, sharp stare raking my face, analyzing my expression. "I've no reason to call upon *anyone* in Draken Manor. May I remind you, my quarrel with your family goes back centuries. And one never lets go of such... *beef*, as they say these days. Not when it's the kind from which legends are born."

He smiles, a flash of fang. "You see, my vanity—not my pride—would never allow it. One must live up to one's infamy, after all."

I open my mouth to argue, but I'm swept away by another group eager to congratulate me. Ivan watches, dark amusement lighting his green eyes.

As I move through the crowd, I can't shake the unease his words leave behind. I'm sure it was him in the conservatory —*I saw him with my own eyes.* But if indeed it was not the vampire Lockhart who spoke to me in the garden... then who did?

The evening passes in a blur of champagne, delicate hors d'oeuvres, and endless small talk. The din of conversation, clinking glassware, and whispered gossip fill the air. Beneath it all, the electric apprehension of the night's climax thrums.

At precisely 11 PM, I make my way to the center of the room. My heart hammers with excitement and nerves.

"Ladies and gentlemen," I announce, voice cutting through the hum. "The silent auction for the Kandinsky sketch is now closed."

A ripple moves through the crowd, murmurs of excitement swelling. Our event coordinator presents the sealed bid box. I open it, drawing out the winning bid, the silence thickening.

"I'm thrilled to announce the Kandinsky sketch has been sold for an astounding €2.5 million." Gasps ripple through the audience, followed by applause. "The winning bidder is Monsieur Jean-Pierre Beaumont. Monsieur Beaumont, your generosity will make an incredible impact on our 'Art for All' initiative. *Merci beaucoup.*"

The room erupts into an outstanding ovation as Jean-Pierre steps forward, beaming. Triumph surges through me as I shake his hand and pose for photographs. The gala is a success.

With the main event concluded, guests begin to filter out, their conversations bubbling with excitement. The air is lighter now, filled with laughter and satisfaction. I make my rounds, thanking everyone for their attendance, my cheeks aching from the constant smile.

By the time the last guest drifts out and the cleaning crew begins their quiet sweep of the room, I finally allow myself to exhale.

I step onto the balcony, the cool night air brushing

against my flushed skin. The Eiffel Tower glitters in the distance, its iron frame glowing like a constellation brought down to earth. I press my hands to the railing, breathing deeply, allowing the stillness to seep into me.

And then a voice, low and husky, shatters the quiet.

"Quite an event, Miss Draken."

I whirl around, heart stuttering. Kaisner stands in the doorway, tall and shadowed, framed by the soft amber light spilling from the hall. His eyes catch the faint glow of the city, dark and hungry. The kind of gaze that doesn't just see —it *devours.*

"Mr. Drachenstein," I manage, firm despite the thundering of my heart. "I hope you enjoyed the evening."

His lips curl into a slow, predatory smile that sends heat pooling low in my belly. "Oh, I enjoyed it… immensely," he purrs. "Though I must say, the company left something to be desired."

I raise an eyebrow, masking the tremor in my chest. "Oh? I was under the impression you were quite popular tonight. You were surrounded by admirers at all times."

He steps closer, the night wrapping around him like silk. The glow of the Eiffel Tower frames him in gold, turning him into something otherworldly. Dangerous. Untouchable.

"Admirers of art, perhaps," he says, his voice a dark caress. "But there was only one person whose company I truly desired."

His hand lifts, fingers brushing the line of my cheek. His thumb traces my lower lip, the touch so light it feels like fire. I gasp, the sound soft, helpless.

"Kaisner," I breathe, eyes fluttering shut, "we can't. Not here."

"I know," he whispers, the words hot against the shell of my ear. "But soon, my love. Soon, we won't have to hide."

Before I can respond, his lips crash onto mine, stealing

my breath, stealing my reason. The kiss is brief but searing, leaving me stunned and aching for more.

And then he's gone—slipping back inside as if nothing had happened.

I lean against the balcony railing, my pulse throbbing wildly. The metal is cool beneath my fingertips, a harsh contrast to the heat Kaisner left behind. Fire races through my veins, my mind spins.

Suddenly, my phone buzzes. I fumble it from my clutch, my breath catching at the name on the screen.

"Nik?" I answer, fighting to steady myself as Kaisner's kiss still burns on my lips.

"Rissy," he says, and his voice—sharp, clipped—slices through me like a blade. "I'm in Berlin and… I've just received some… interesting news."

My heart stutters. "What is it?"

"Kaisner Drachenstein," Nik spits the name like a curse. "Not only has he officially *refused* to recognize my claim as Dragon King, but in the same breath, he's positioned himself as our foundation's *most influential* benefactor—backing *your* gala tonight and signing a major exhibition contract for his entire collection. Tell me, sister, what game is he playing?"

I grip the phone tighter, fingers aching. "Nik, I—"

"And don't tell me you didn't know," he bites, anger simmering just beneath the surface. "You've been working closely with him on this gala, haven't you? What *else* haven't you told me?"

"Nik, I didn't plan for this—"

"Whose *fucking* side are you on, Clarissa?" he explodes.

My mind reels, fumbling for words. "It's not like that. The gala was a success. His contribution was—"

"Was what? A peace offering? A distraction?" His voice hardens. "Do you know how this looks? The timing is too convenient. He's up to something, and I fear you're being used as a pawn in his game."

The accusation stings. "What would you have me do?"

"*Stay away* from him." The command is iron. "Kaisner Drachenstein is dangerous. His refusal to acknowledge me as Dragon King has set most European clans against me." His voice rises through the phone, fury bleeding through. "They'd rather bow to a fucking mobster—a *criminal*—than a real dragon. Can you believe that shit? They choose his dirty money and shadowy deals over true draconic power." I hear something crash in the background, followed by his sharp intake of breath. "Don't let that bastard use you, Clarissa."

I close my eyes, torn between blood and heart. "I understand, Nik. I'll... I'll be careful."

The call ends, but the words linger, sharp and heavy. The balance I've tried to maintain—between loyalty and desire, family and love—cracks beneath the pressures of this evening.

A low rumble of thunder echoes in the distance. I lift my gaze. Dark clouds gather, swallowing the stars. The wind picks up, sharp and cool, tugging at my gown, stripping away the facade I've maintained.

It feels like a warning.

I close my eyes, leaning into the breeze, wishing it could take the doubt, the fear, the ache left by Kaisner's touch.

But the wind offers no mercy.

The gala is over. The mask is slipping. And the real storm is just beginning.

36

KAISNER

storm rages outside, rain slashing against the mansion's towering windows. Thunder growls, a deep pulse vibrating through stone and glass. I pace from my study, across the foyer, restless, like a caged beast, a crystal tumbler of aged whiskey clutched in my hand. My mind churns with the complexities of supernatural politics and the gala's possible aftermath.

Then, a knock.

It cuts through the storm, sharp and unexpected. I freeze, instincts on edge. No one disturbs me at this hour—not unless it's urgent, or dangerous. The staff retired hours ago, leaving the mansion cloaked in shadow and silence.

I set the tumbler on the marble credenza with deliberate precision, the crystal catching what little light filters through the darkened windows.

I move toward the door, slow and controlled. Ready for anything.

But nothing could prepare me for the sight that awaits.

Clarissa. Drenched, her midnight gown clinging to her body, golden hair plastered to her face. Her eyes—precious

290

sapphires that haunt my every thought—are wide, red-rimmed, glassy with emotion. Vulnerability. Desperation. Fear.

"Baby..." The word escapes me, unbidden, raw. I take her in fully, concern slicing through me. She trembles, fragile beneath the chill.

I reach out, cupping her face, fingers cool against the warmth of her flushed cheeks. She leans into me, a soft sigh escaping her lips. Her skin is ice, but she melts against me all the same.

"Come inside," I murmur, voice low, urgent. Protective.

I draw her in, shutting the door against the howling wind. She stands in my foyer, dripping onto the black marble. Her dampness soaks into my shirt as I gather her close. She doesn't resist. Instead, she folds into me, silent, as though her usual resilience has drained entirely. It stirs something dangerous in me—a dark, primal urge to destroy whoever has made her like this. To raze it to ash.

But first, I will comfort her. First, I will give her my strength.

"I've got you," I whisper into her rain-scented hair. My arms tighten around her. "You're safe now."

She looks up, her gaze a maelstrom of emotions. And then, she rises on tiptoes, and without a word, her lips find mine.

The kiss is desperate, fevered. A plea and a promise. Any thoughts of restraint crumble as I answer with the same urgency. My hands seize her waist, holding her like something precious. Mine.

Her body trembles beneath my touch, wet silk clinging to her skin as I scoop her into my arms. She buries her face in my chest, and I sense the rapid, uneven beat of her heart.

Past marble and glass, I carry her upstairs, shadows chasing us into my sanctuary—my bedroom.

I ease her into the warmth by the hearth, the flames licking the air, wrapping us in their heat. Kneeling beside her, I steady her with my hands at her waist, reluctant to let any distance grow between us. She's trembling, and I pull her closer, my fingers lingering on her soft skin as I study her features for any sign of what's tormenting her.

I brush a damp strand of hair from her cheek, my thumb tracing the delicate curve of her face, soft but possessive. The hurt I see in her eyes slices deep, tugging at something primal. Her presence, usually a balm to the darkness within me, now fuels it. The mere thought of someone causing her pain sets my blood ablaze.

She averts her gaze, a delicate hand covering her lips.

Her vulnerability cuts me open. Whatever brought her here, whatever demons she's fighting, I silently vow to keep them at bay. Tonight, she needs me, and I'll be damned if I let her down.

"What is it, *Liebes*?" I ask, my voice sheer velvet, betraying the rage buried beneath. My fingers trace her jaw, the curve of her neck, cataloging every tension, every flicker of pain. "Tell me."

Her lips part, but her gaze wavers. She shivers, and I drape a throw over her shoulders. She clutches it tight, and I draw her closer, my body instinctively curving around her to shield her from the world itself. The dragon in me stirs, answering her pain with an urge to possess.

Mine, it growls. *Mine to protect. Mine to avenge.*

Clarissa takes a shaky breath. "It's... everything," she whispers, her voice breaking. "The gala, the secrecy... It's all too much." She pauses. "And then, there's Nik."

The mention of Nikolaas sets my teeth on edge. I tamp down the heat of my anger.

"He called and..." she adds, fresh tears brimming.

"What did he say?" I press, crouching before her, reading every flicker of emotion in her expression.

She hesitates. "Nik found out you were involved in the gala. He's... not pleased." Her voice carries careful understatement. "And now he says you've offered your art collection to our foundation?" Her brow furrows, confused.

I nod sternly. "I signed the contract this morning, lending my full art collection for an exhibition later this year."

It seems Nikolaas keeps a close eye on me too.

Clarissa's eyes widen, surprise flashing across her face. For a moment, a flicker of excitement dances on her features, but it quickly fades. Her lips press into a thin line, gaze darkening again.

"Kaisner," she whispers, "Nik also mentioned you've officially refused to support his claim as Dragon King."

I inhale sharply, my shoulders tensing. "I have," I admit, the words heavy on my tongue.

Her breath hitches, fingers twisting the throw. "Why?" she asks, her voice cracking.

"Baby girl, please understand." My fingers brush against her jaw, tilting her chin so she's forced to meet my gaze. "I bear your brother no ill will. But my lineage, and the clans under my protection, will bow to no one's rule..." My touch trails slowly down her arm, reverent, before it falls away, "...except mine."

The words hang in the air, heavy and final. I watch her absorb them, the rise and fall of her chest quickening. Her fingers curl tighter into the fabric as though it could shield her from the inevitable.

She pulls back slightly, a hand rising to her throat in a nervous gesture. Her eyes dart around the room, searching the shadows for answers. When she speaks again, her voice trembles.

"My brother is furious," she says, the phrase tumbling out in a rush. "He's connecting dots I never knew existed."

My jaw clenches. "And what does he think I'm up to?" I ask, my tone rough.

She hesitates, eyes dropping to the rug. Her fingers twist the blanket. "He thinks you're playing a dangerous game. That you're using me to get to him."

I curse under my breath. Of course, he would see it that way. "And you?" I ask, my gaze sharp. "Do you believe that?"

Her eyes meet mine—luminous with uncertainty and pain. "I don't know what to believe."

The quiet admission lands like a knife in my ribs.

I pull her into me, burying my face in her damp hair. "You know me better than that, *mein Herz*." My hands roam over her back, soothing, claiming. "I would set the world ablaze for you, and I'd burn it *twice* if anyone dared to touch you."

She stills in my arms, her breath catching, but she doesn't pull away. Instead, her fingers clutch the blanket, her knuckles pale beneath the fabric. For a moment, her gaze locks with mine—searching, uncertain—but it's gone just as quickly.

Her voice is a whisper, raw and heavy. "He's adamant that I stay away from you." The words settle between us like ashes after a fire, soft but suffocating. "You should've heard him, Kaisner. I've never heard him so angry. So… suspicious."

"As he should be," I confess, my voice low. Then, seeing the worry in her eyes, I quickly add, "But let's not drag politics into this conversation, my love. Not now."

She draws her knees closer, wrapping the blanket tighter, a shield against more than just the cold. Her gaze is distant, fixed on the crackling flames. Shadows flicker across her face, highlighting the tension in her jaw, the fear in her eyes.

"I'm afraid," she breathes, barely audible beneath the storm. "Afraid of what might happen if he finds out about us. Hours ago, I wanted nothing more than to scream to the world that we're together. But now—"

I shift closer, the warmth of the fire against my skin, hardly noticed. I reach out, brushing her damp hair from her face, my fingers lingering longer than I should.

"Come here," I murmur, my breath warm against her cool skin. "I won't bite... not unless you beg." The words rumble through me, teasing, meant to comfort, to pull her back from the edge of despair.

She doesn't move at first. Then, slowly, a reluctant smile flickers across her lips—fleeting, but real. She moves toward me, the blanket slipping as I pull her into my arms. The moment teeters between fear and desire, the storm outside and the storm within.

I hold her tight, sensing the tension in her body, the depth of her worry. But here, in this small pocket of warmth and shadow, I'll shield her from it all. If only for tonight.

Nikolaas' suspicions are dangerously close to the truth, even if he doesn't know the half of it. "Listen to me, Clarissa. Whatever happens, I won't let anyone come between us. Not Nikolaas, not anyone. Do you understand?"

I capture her mouth in a tender kiss, my hands roaming over her back, her hips, relishing the contact of her. "Every moment at that gala was torture," I murmur against her lips. "Seeing you, but not being able to touch you, to hold you..."

She sighs, her hands fisting in my hair, holding me close. "I know," she whispers, a tremor in her voice. "I could feel your eyes on me all night. It took everything I had not to run to you, to hell with appearances."

"What we have..." I begin, warm and reassuring. "It's worth fighting for. I know it's hard now, but I promise you, we'll find a way. Whatever is to come, we'll see it through."

I look into her eyes, seeing the love, the fear, the desperate hope reflected in them. And in that moment, I vow to move heaven and earth to keep her safe, to devise a plan for us to be together openly.

Whatever it takes. Whatever price I have to pay. For her. For us.

I pull back slightly, cupping her face. "You were magnificent tonight, you know. The way you commanded that room, your poise, your grace... I've never been more proud. Or more frustrated that I couldn't show it."

A small smile plays at her lips. "It was harder than I thought it would be, pretending to be just acquaintances. Every time someone mentioned your name, I wanted to shout that you were mine."

"As did I," I growl, pulling her closer. "No more pretending. No more hiding... Soon, my love, we'll show the world what we are to each other."

She nods, eyes shining with unshed tears. "Promise?"

"I swear it," I vow, sealing the promise with another kiss.

I deepen the kiss, my tongue delving into the honeyed recesses of her mouth, tasting her, consuming her. She opens to me like a flower to the sun. Our tongues tangle in a wild, instinctive rhythm, resonating with the passion of those who came before us.

Never breaking contact from the sweetness of her lips, I walk her backward toward the bed, shedding her clothes along the way, leaving a trail of silk behind. By the time she tumbles onto the mattress, she's bare. I can't wait for us to lie skin to skin, heart to heart.

For a moment, I just look at her, drinking in the sight of her laid out before me like a feast for the senses. Every curve, every hollow, every dip and swell, is a work of art that I long to explore with hands, mouth, and body.

"You are so beautiful," I whisper, my voice rough with

emotion. "Sometimes I look at you, and I can't believe you're real. That you're mine."

She reaches up, cupping my face in her palms, her thumb tracing the line of my jaw. "I *am* yours, Kaisner. In every way that matters. Body, heart, and soul."

I turn my head, pressing a kiss to her palm, my eyes never leaving hers. "And I am yours, *Liebes*. From now until the end of time."

And then I'm kissing her again, my taut frame covering hers. She arches beneath me, a moan escaping her lips, and I swallow the sound, drinking it down like the finest of wines.

I worship her with touch and mouth, mapping every inch of her, committing it to memory. I trail kisses down her throat, her breasts, her belly, savoring the taste of her, the scent of her. She writhes against me, hands fisting in the sheets, my name a litany on her lips.

"Please..." she gasps, her hips rolling against mine.

I smile against her skin, a predatory thing full of dark promise. "Please what, baby girl? Tell me what you need."

"You," she breathes, eyes locking with mine, glazed with raw, untamed desire. "I need you."

I trail kisses down her neck, savoring the rainwater on her skin, before pulling back to feast on her beauty. She lies before me, pale and perfect in the dim light. My chest tightens.

"I should worship you from a distance," I breathe, a sin and a promise. "But I'd rather ruin you up close."

The words hang between us, and I trace the contours of her collarbones, marveling at the softness of her skin. Goosebumps rise in the wake of my touch, and I can't help but smile. Even the lightest caress affects her so deeply.

Unable to resist any longer, I strip off my clothes, casting them carelessly aside until I stand before her, bare and ready.

Her gaze devours my sculpted planes of muscle and tanned skin.

My hungry stare roves over her exposed flesh, her skin blushing from head to toe. My hands move to her hips, guiding her closer until there's not an inch of space between us. Heat radiates from my body, my arousal pressing against her stomach, hard and demanding.

She gasps as my fingers slide up her thighs, deliciously torturous as I move closer to the core of her desire. "I've waited long enough for this," I growl against her skin, my teeth grazing her throat. "And now I'll take what's mine—rough, slow, and without mercy."

I pin her wrists above her head with one hand, holding her captive to my desires. With the other, I trace the curves of her body, savoring every shiver and gasp that escapes her lips. She arches into me, a soft moan filling the air. It's the sweetest sound I've ever heard, and I'm determined to hear it again and again.

"You're mine, Clarissa," I murmur, my voice thick with possession. "Every inch of you belongs to me."

I enter her slowly, savoring every sensation. She's tight and hot around me, fitting me perfectly, as if we were made for each other. For a moment, I'm overwhelmed by the intensity of it all—not just the physical pleasure, but the emotional connection that I've never had with anyone else.

But then Clarissa rolls her hips, and coherent thought becomes impossible. I set a relentless pace, driven by a primal need to claim her, to make her mine. Each thrust pushes us both closer to the edge, the tension building to an almost unbearable level.

"Feel how much I want you," I grunt, eyes locked on hers. I must have her understand, to grasp the intensity of my yearning, my... love? The realization should terrify me, but in this moment, it feels right. Inevitable.

With a growl of pure, untamed instinct, I surge forward, claiming her, filling her, making her mine in the most fundamental of ways. I set a rhythm, a give and take, a push and pull that builds and builds until we are both teetering on the edge of oblivion. Our bodies move in perfect synchronicity, our hearts beating as one, our very souls entwined.

"Oh gods, Kaisner… Yes, right there!" she cries out, her nails raking down my back, her legs wrapping around my waist, urging me deeper.

"That's it," I command, my voice a low rumble. "Give yourself to me completely."

I growl, and my grip on her tightens. I slam into her even harder, hips crashing against hers with a force that should be painful but instead ignites a delicious fire within her. The sound of our bodies colliding fills the room, driving us both further into the realm of unyielding lust.

Around us, the world fades away, replaced by a haze of pleasure and the heat between our bodies. The scent of our mingled sweat permeates the air, only adding to the carnal atmosphere that surrounds us. My eyes never leave hers, deep blue irises burning with a hunger that matches my own.

I can feel her getting close, her body tensing beneath me. "Come for me, baby," I command, my voice rough with exertion and emotion. "Come for me now."

And she does. My words are the trigger that sends her hurtling over the edge. Her release washes over her like a tidal wave, stealing her breath as she arches her back and cries out my name. My teeth graze her neck as I follow close behind, emptying myself inside her with a primal growl that echoes the depths of my soul.

And when the end comes, it is with a force that shatters us both, sending us spiraling into the infinite abyss of pleasure. We cling to each other, anchoring each other as the waves of ecstasy crash over us, through us, leaving us spent and trembling in their wake.

Gods, I want more of her. *All of her.*

We lie entangled, our bodies still joined, our heartbeats slowly syncing. My lips find her temple, her cheek, finally capturing her mouth in a tender kiss that speaks volumes, more than words ever could.

"You have no idea what I'd do for you, *Liebes...*" I murmur against her lips. "And I pray you never find out." It feels like a vow, etched into the very air around us.

She gazes up at me, her eyes gleaming in the flickering flash of lightning. A soft smile plays at the corners of her mouth, and I find myself captivated by the subtle curve of her lips.

"I love you, Kai," she whispers, her voice filled with a warmth that seems to radiate through my entire being.

Kai.

It falls from her mouth so naturally, so sweetly, that for an instant, I forget to breathe. My heart stutters in my chest, a sensation both foreign and exhilarating.

I've been called many things in my life—Kaisner, Mr. Drachenstein, even 'sir' by those who fear me. But never this. Never something so simple, so intimate.

I try to maintain my composure, but I sense a telltale heat rising in my neck. My fingers, usually so steady, tremble slightly as they card through her hair. I hope she doesn't notice, but a knowing glint in her eye tells me she has.

"Say it again," I murmur, my voice rougher than I intend, betraying the depth of my emotion.

Her smile widens, surprise and delight dancing in her eyes. "Kai," she repeats, savoring the name, drawing it out as if it were the most precious thing.

The sound sends a shiver down my spine, igniting a warm and unfamiliar sensation in my chest. Not the usual fire of desire or the burning need for power. This is something softer, but no less intense. It leaves me vulnerable, yet complete.

I pull her closer, burying my face in the crook of her neck to hide the raw emotion I'm sure is written across my features. My hold tightens around her lithe frame, as if I could somehow merge us into one being, never to be separated.

In this moment, I know with bone-deep certainty that I'd do anything for her. Move heaven and earth, challenge fate itself. She has become my everything, my reason for existence.

The depth of my emotions for her is fathomless... unexpected. Inconvenient, even. Attachments in my world aren't just liabilities—they're weapons. Weaknesses waiting to be exploited. And Clarissa? She's the sharpest of them all. She is not meant to be mine. She is meant to be a sacrifice.

It should be simple. Her blood is the final price, the key to awakening the dragon that sleeps within me. A ritual promised, a power long craved. I should be preparing her for the offering, laying her at the feet of the daemon as we agreed.

And yet... I hesitate.

The thought of surrendering her, of watching her lifeblood spill in service of my ambition, coils like a serpent in my gut. The daemon's whispers haunt me, reminding me of what waits beyond sacrifice—limitless power, strength to crush my enemies, to shape the world beneath my will. My birthright. A crown forged in blood.

But not just any blood. It must be freely given. Willingly offered. The ultimate surrender, the deepest trust. *Her trust.* Only then will the ritual be sealed. Only then will the dragon wake.

And gods help me... I don't know which would be

worse. For her to refuse me—or to offer herself willingly, unaware of the price.

Either way, I will destroy her. One with my hand. The other with my betrayal.

But surely, there must be a way to have it all—Clarissa, power, respect. In the shadowed halls of my mind, a plan starts to form, intricate and daring. A high-stakes game, with Nikolaas' recognition as the ultimate prize. Dangerous? Certainly. But I've built my empire on far riskier ventures. Risk is nothing new. The question is—what am I willing to wager?

I study Clarissa for a moment, weighing the cost of betrayal against the promise of strength. Her unwavering gaze meets mine, and in those depths, I see not just acceptance, but understanding. Trust. The very thing I myself cannot afford. It's... intoxicating. Damning.

For the first time, I have no need to hide. With Clarissa, I can be my true self—all of me, the light and the dark. And maybe that's the greatest danger of all.

I lean in, my lips brushing the shell of her ear. My voice comes out low, rough, layered with desire and something darker. "Baby girl," I breathe, feeling her shudder against me. "I need something from you."

"Anything," she whispers, curling closer to me.

"I need..." The words burn my tongue, tasting of iron and ruin. "Your blood."

37

KAISNER

"*K*aisner?"

Her voice, laced with confusion and a flicker of trepidation, slices through the haze of my thoughts. She stiffens in my arms, her breath catching—shallow, uncertain. I can feel the shift in her pulse, scent the sudden spike of adrenaline coursing through her veins.

I tighten my hold, my hand gliding down the smooth expanse of her back, a slow, deliberate caress meant to soothe. "Shh, *meine Kleine*," I murmur, pressing my lips to her temple. "It's all right. I would never hurt you. You know that." The words are a vow, a sacred promise infused with the depth of my devotion.

"Don't be afraid, Clarissa," I say, my voice low, urgent. "I need your help. It's the only way."

She swallows hard, her delicate throat working, her wide eyes flickering between apprehension and something else— curiosity, perhaps. A deep, instinctive understanding that what I'm about to ask will change everything.

"What do you mean?" she breathes. "*What* way?"

The tension in her body softens, just barely, and she melts back into my embrace. Her warmth, her trust, is a balm against the chaos within me. "I trust you, Kaisner. With everything that I am." Her words carve into my soul like a blade, but even as she says them, I glimpse the questions forming in her gaze.

I steel myself. There's no turning back now.

Reluctantly, I disentangle from her warmth, the cool air of the room rushing between us as I stand. I reach for my discarded boxer briefs, sliding them on swiftly. "We should get dressed," I murmur, offering my hand.

She takes it, graceful even now, the moonlight catching in her golden strands as she rises. The sight nearly makes me reconsider the need for clothes at all.

I frown at her rain-damp gown, shaking my head. "You can't put this back on." Without waiting for protest, I stride to my wardrobe and pull a soft black cashmere sweater from its hanger, along with a pair of tailored trousers.

When I return, I help her dress, my fingers brushing over her skin in lazy, reverent strokes. I guide the sweater over her head, smoothing the fabric down her arms. It drapes over her beautifully, swallowing her in warmth—swallowing her in *me*. A quiet, possessive satisfaction hums through me at the sight.

Next, the trousers. I kneel before her, holding them open. She steps in without hesitation. My hands glide up her legs as I pull them into place, fingers grazing her hips. Before fastening them, I press a gentle kiss to her bare skin, inhaling deeply, memorizing her scent.

She shivers. Not from the cold.

Standing, I adjust the sweater, my hands lingering at her waist. "Perfect," I murmur, pressing a kiss to her forehead.

Only then do I turn to dress myself, buttoning my shirt

with measured precision. In the mirror, I catch her watching me, eyes filled with unspoken questions.

I shrug on my jacket, the leather settling around my shoulders like armor. Preparing me.

"We need to talk," I say softly, my hands finding hers. She twines our fingers together without hesitation. A perfect fit.

A perfect offering.

"Come," I say. "Let's walk in the gardens."

The night air is thick with the scent of impending rain, the sky above churning, restless. The starlit path winds before us like a ribbon of silver, leading us deeper into the shadows of my estate.

As we near the marble folly, the first drops begin to fall, cool and sharp against our skin. The heavens open as we step beneath the shelter of the domed roof, rain hammering against stone, a relentless, rhythmic pulse.

Clarissa shivers beside me, wrapping her arms around herself. I fight the urge to pull her closer, to keep her warm, to keep her safe.

I lean against the balustrade, staring out at the darkened landscape. *Now or never.*

"Clarissa." My voice is low and rough, heavy with reluctant truth. "The only way we can truly be together is if your brother respects me."

She turns, confusion knitting her brows. "But he already respects you, Kaisner."

A mirthless chuckle escapes me. "No, baby girl. Nikolaas *fears* me." I exhale, shaking my head. "I don't want his fear. I want him to see me as his equal." The admission is bitter on my tongue, a truth I've spent weeks denying. "But as long as he remains the Last Dragon Shifter, that will never happen."

Her fingers lace through mine, an instinctive offer of comfort. "Then what can we do?"

I turn to face her fully, searching her expression. "You know my reputation. What I do. What I work with."

She doesn't flinch. Doesn't recoil. "You work with daemons." A simple statement. No judgment. Just fact.

Pride stirs in my chest.

"Yes. I've mastered the shadows, forged them into my own." My gaze darkens. "And through them, I've found a way to awaken my dragon."

Her lips part, her breath hitching. Excitement. Fascination, even.

"Tell me," she breathes.

My fingers brush over a rain-dampened strand of her hair, lingering against her cheek. She leans into my touch. "I've found a ritual," I murmur. "An ancient spell that could unlock my power. But I can't do it alone."

Realization dawns in her gaze, cutting through the stormy night like lightning.

"You mean to summon a daemon," she whispers.

I nod.

She blinks once, twice. Her jaw tightens. "The spell calls for blood, doesn't it?"

My throat works around a single, solemn nod. "My clan's bloodline has been too diluted over the centuries."

She exhales sharply. Understanding flickers in her gaze. "So you need *my* blood."

Silence.

Clarissa's brow furrows. "But Kaisner, blood daemons... they're insatiable. How can we be sure it won't demand more than you're willing to give?"

A slow, confident smile tugs at my lips. "You're right, *Liebes*. A daemon always hungers for more. But I've planned for this."

I lift the pendant hanging around my neck, the metal

cool against my palm. The ancient runes etched into its surface glow faintly beneath the dim light.

"This amulet is imbued with powerful protective magic. A relic I acquired through... less than conventional means." I smirk. "It can deceive even the most cunning of daemons."

I lower my voice, my tone threading with seduction, with persuasion. "With this, we can control how much blood is given. It will believe it's drinking deeply, but in reality, you'll be safe."

Clarissa turns away, and I can almost see the thoughts racing through her mind. The risks, the consequences—every warning she's ever been told about daemons.

And yet, she doesn't run.

"It's dangerous, I know," I say. "But with your lineage, with our combined strength, we could control it. Harness its power." I pause, letting the words settle. "It's the only way, baby girl. The only way Nikolaas will ever see me as his equal. The only way we can be together without fear."

I reach for her, my hand resting on her shoulder. "Clarissa," I murmur, leaning close. "I wouldn't ask this of you if there were any other way."

A slow breath. A heartbeat of silence. The fate of my future, of our future, hangs in the balance of her decision.

And then—

"Then take it, Kaisner."

I tense.

She turns, her eyes blazing with something fierce. Unwavering. "Take what you need. I told you, I trust you with everything that I am. My heart, my soul... my blood. It's all yours."

Relief slams into me, raw and brutal.

Before I can stop myself, I fall to my knees. And in a moment that feels both unexpected and inevitable, Clarissa mirrors me, sinking before me.

The moment crashes over me. I'm struck senseless with shock. This woman—this beautiful, fearless woman—has just offered me the one thing I never thought I'd ask for. She's willing to risk it all, to stake her trust in me, despite everything.

A tidal wave of devotion surges through me, a fierce, possessive love that shakes me to the core. This isn't just desire. This is something far deeper, something I didn't know I was capable of feeling.

I gather her in my arms, crushing her to me, inhaling the scent of jasmine in her skin, the scent of home.

"You humble me," I breathe against her hair, my voice cracking with the force of it. "Your trust… your love—gods, Clarissa, it's more than I ever dared to ask for. More than I ever believed I deserved."

And in that moment, for the first time in my life, I believe in forever.

I draw back, cupping her face in both hands, my thumbs brushing away the tears she doesn't realize she's crying. My eyes bore into hers, and for once, I don't hold back.

"Know this, *Liebes*: everything that I am—every breath, every sin, every shadow—is yours now. My soul. My blood. My fucking heart."

A low, reverent growl rumbles in my chest. "Some bonds are written in blood, others in starlight. But ours? Ours was forged in dragon fire… *Du bist mein Ein und Alles*," I breathe. You're my everything.

She pulls back just far enough to whisper, voice trembling but unshakable, *"Und du bist meine Welt."*

I still.

"You speak German?" I can't stop the smile tugging at the corners of my lips.

A delicate blush colors her cheeks. "Enough to tell you that you're my world." Her arms tighten around me, her voice a breeze of devotion against the shell of my ear. "No matter what comes, I will stand by you."

The words *ruin* me.

And gods help me, I know then—I will destroy anything that dares take her from me.

Even myself.

38

KAISNER

The ancient stone walls of my private chamber seem to close in around us, their weathered surfaces carved with arcane symbols and forgotten incantations. Flickering candlelight casts dancing shadows, illuminating shelves stacked with grimoires, jars of exotic ingredients, and artifacts brimming with untold power. The air is thick with the heady scent of burning incense—a potent blend of myrrh and dragon's blood.

At the far end of the room stands the altar, black as midnight. Its polished surface gleams with an unnatural sheen, absorbing the light rather than reflecting it. Resting atop it is my Book of Shadows, bound in nightshade-tanned leather, its silver runes shifting in the dim glow.

In the center of the room, the summoning circle dominates the floor. Chalk lines form intricate sigils, their edges pulsing faintly with otherworldly energy—power just on the verge of eruption. I stand at the edge, my pulse a steady war drum, each beat a countdown to what comes next.

Beside me, Clarissa is a vision in sapphire silk. Her gown, chosen for this ritual, shimmers like the night sky, making her appear like a goddess caught between mortal and divine. Yet, her beauty is marred by the uncertainty in her gaze, the tremor in her fingers as she clutches the pendant I placed in her hands.

A necessary precaution.

With practiced movements, I hold the amulet between her palms, closing my eyes as I murmur the activation spell. The words are dark, guttural, resonating from somewhere deep within me. As I speak, the runes etched into the metal begin to glow with an eerie pulse.

"This will keep you safe from any unexpected mischief," I murmur, each word bitter on my tongue. I despise that I've dragged her into this ritual—forced her into a game where the stakes are far beyond her understanding. Yet, I cling to the certainty that my plan will hold. That my magic—*my will*—is strong enough to deceive even a daemon. Ordinary warlocks may falter, but I am not ordinary. I never have been.

Clarissa tilts her chin, allowing me to fasten the pendant. The metal warms against her skin, recognizing its new bearer.

"For protection," I say, brushing my lips to her forehead. "And this…" I kiss her briefly, lingering for just a moment longer than necessary. "…for luck."

She nods, trust shining in her eyes. My chest tightens, the weight of what I'm about to do pressing down like an iron vise. Azrakan's whispers slither through my mind. Perhaps no charm can shield her from the cost of this ritual.

The blood must be freely given.

I push the doubt away, lock it deep inside. It's too late for second thoughts now.

I step away, crossing to the altar. My Book of Shadows hums with latent energy as I flip it open, the pages fluttering eagerly as though alive. They settle on the incantation, the words already burning against my tongue before I even speak them.

A deep breath. A steadying exhale.

Then, I begin.

The first syllable rumbles through the chamber, thick with power. The air shifts—denser, heavier—charged like the space before a lightning strike. The candle flames stretch unnaturally, their golden glow turning an eerie blue. Shadows creep at the edges of the room, twisting and writhing like sentient beings waiting to be unleashed.

Clarissa shivers beside me. I don't look at her. I can't afford to.

The book grows hot in my hands, unbearably so, but I don't falter. I return it to the altar, the pages still shifting of their own accord. The silver runes on the cover blaze with a cold fire, searing against my fingertips.

The ritual circle pulses. Tendrils of dark smoke rise from the chalk lines, twisting into the air like hungry serpents.

A heartbeat of silence.

Then—

The ground trembles beneath us. A low, guttural sound begins to vibrate through the walls, through my bones, through the very foundation of the mansion. It starts deep in my stomach and spreads outward, curling like a living thing within me.

The shadows congeal, thickening into a humanoid form. It towers over us, a being of pure darkness. Claws of shadow flex and curl, leaving trails of inky blackness in the air. Two slivers of burning red pierce the darkness—eyes, ancient and cruel.

A voice, like shattered glass scraping against stone, echoes through the chamber.

"Who dares summon me?"

I step forward, my stance strong. "I, Kaisner Drachenstein, have called you forth."

The daemon shifts, its amorphous form undulating. Its

jagged mouth stretches into something resembling a grin. "Ah," it purrs, its voice slithering through us. "And you've brought me a gift."

Clarissa stiffens beside me. Her hand finds mine, fingers tightening. I feel the tremor in her grip, the pulse of her uncertainty.

"She is not an offering," I say firmly, though doubt claws at me. "She is here to assist in the ritual."

The daemon laughs, a sound like ice splintering. "Is that what you told her, warlock? What pretty lies you weave." It leans forward, pressing against the invisible barrier of the circle. "Did you tell her the true price of awakening your dragon? Of the blood that must be spilled?"

I don't look at Clarissa, but I feel her gaze burning into me.

"What is it talking about?" she asks, her voice barely above a whisper.

I remain silent, too afraid of what might slip out if I speak.

Azrakan widens its grin. "Ah, I see," it muses. "He hasn't told you everything, has he? Poor, trusting little dragoness."

"Enough," I growl, forcing my voice to be steady. "I didn't summon you for riddles. You know why you're here. Fulfill your part of the bargain, and you'll have what was promised."

The daemon's form swells, shadows stretching and thickening. "Very well, warlock. Let us begin."

It raises its clawed hands, the atmosphere crackling with dark energy. The circle flares, the symbols burning white-hot, and the temperature in the room plummets. The stench of sulfur and brimstone fills the air.

Then, something shifts.

The pendant around Clarissa's neck blazes—bright red,

incandescent. The runes carved into its surface twist and writhe as if trying to escape.

Before I can react, the glow intensifies. A crack rips through the air. The amulet—the safeguard I crafted so carefully—disintegrates.

Ash. Dust. Nothing.

The daemon laughs again, louder this time.

"You fool!" it hisses. "Did you truly believe you could trick me? That I wouldn't see through your pathetic deceptions?"

Panic claws at my throat. I miscalculated. The ritual is spiraling beyond my control. I never *had* any control.

How could I have been so blind? How could I have ever thought that any power, any glory, was worth the risk of losing her?

"Embrace your dragon, warlock!" Azrakan roars, its shadows surging forward. "I will claim what is owed!"

Heat erupts from my core. Power, fire, searing through my veins. My skin prickles, then *burns* as obsidian scales ripple across my forearms, spreading upward.

My dragon, so long dormant, roars to life within me. I can feel its hunger, its desire, its overwhelming need to be unleashed. The *need* to complete the ritual is overwhelming. I'm so close to seizing my destiny—

But then, through eyes rapidly changing, pupils stetching into slits, I *see* her.

Clarissa.

Her sapphire eyes are wide with fear. *Fear of me.*

The realization hits like a death blow.

If I take this power, if I let this ritual complete—Clarissa will die.

I won't let that happen.

I clench my fists, forcing the fire down, forcing my dragon back. "No!" I growl.

The daemon snarls, sensing my resistance. "You cannot back out now, warlock!" It lunges toward her, claws extending—

I move.

A blur of instinct and desperation, I throw myself between Clarissa and the daemon. My hand rises, fingers drawing on the depths of my power. Shadows coil around me, gathering like a storm. I call on them, shaping them into a solid, unyielding barrier.

The air thickens, the shadows expanding into a shield that flickers and pulses with dark energy. The daemon snarls, claws scraping against the wall of darkness. Its shadowed form presses against the shield, and I can feel the strain in the magic. It will not hold much longer.

Pain sears through me, white-hot agony, as the daemon's wrath begins to burn through the thinning shield. The shadows quiver under its pressure, and I stagger back slightly, teeth gritted.

"Run!" I roar at Clarissa.

She doesn't.

Instead—

I hear her footsteps racing, not toward the door, but to the altar. My heart lurches in my chest, dread and admiration warring within me as I realize what she's doing.

Through the haze of pain, I see her seize the Book of Shadows, its worn leather cover gleaming in the infernal light. Her voice rises, strong and clear, as she begins to chant an ancient banishing spell.

Pride and terror rush through me. She shouldn't know these words. She shouldn't be involved in this magic. But her voice—her strength—ignites something within me. A spark of hope, a surge of strength.

I force myself to stand, pain be damned, and join her, our voices intertwining, rising.

A piercing howl rips through the air, Azrakan's form writhing as the ritual circle burns even brighter, its runes flaring in defiance. The air crackles with energy, the scent of scorched sulfur thick in the room.

The ground trembles violently, books flying from shelves, their pages flipping open midair before slamming to the floor. Artifacts topple from pedestals, their ancient magic sparking and hissing in protest.

"You will pay for this, warlock!" Azrakan growls.

Its form begins to unravel, its edges fraying like smoke caught in a storm. The summoning circle flares, a final act of defiance, sealing the daemon's banishment.

I stagger back, breath ragged, muscles coiled in anticipation of retaliation. But nothing comes.

For a fleeting second, relief floods through me. We've survived. Clarissa is still standing, her chest rising and falling rapidly. Alive.

The barrier held. The spell worked.

We won.

And then—agony.

The air splits with a sickening *shlkt* as shadowy talons spear through my flesh. A sharp, searing torment ignites across my shoulder, a sensation so sudden and raw that my vision flashes white. I barely have time to register the metallic scent of my own blood before my knees buckle.

A ragged breath escapes me, my body instinctively locking against the pain—then, with a brutal inevitability, I collapse.

Azrakan may be gone, but its parting gift is carved deep into me.

The last thing I see is Clarissa kneeling beside me, her face a portrait of horror and angst.

Then—

Oblivion.

39

KAISNER

*C*onsciousness returns to me in waves, deliberate and disorienting, like surfacing from a fathomless abyss. At first, there's only warmth—real, grounding, unmistakable. A delicate, trembling hand laced with mine.

Then the pain. A slow, dull throb beneath my skin, radiating from my shoulder, coiling like a fiery ember in my bones. It's a phantom sensation at first, distant, almost forgettable—until I inhale. The scent of sandalwood, old parchment fills my lungs, and something sweet—a familiar trace.

Clarissa.

My eyes flicker open. Dim candlelight stabs into my pupils, sharp as a blade. The world slowly sharpens—ornate black wooden beams overhead, shelves lined with grimoires and arcane artifacts, velvet drapes shrouding the windows. My room. Safe. Yet the acrid stench of brimstone lingers in my memory, a cruel reminder that not all dangers can be locked away.

I shift, only to be met with a jolt of pain that burns through my shoulder like molten steel. A sharp breath hisses between my teeth, and immediately, her grip on my hand tightens.

"Kaisner?" Her voice, barely a whisper, is frayed, as though she's been sitting beside me for hours. Waiting, hoping.

I force my gaze toward her. And for a moment, I forget to breathe.

She's utterly undone. Golden hair, once pristine, spills over her shoulders in damp waves. Her sapphire eyes are luminous with unshed tears, rimmed with exhaustion, but there's something else—relief. A quiet, aching solace that settles in my chest, twisting painfully.

"You're…" My voice is raw, barely more than a rasp. "You're here."

A tremulous smile ghosts over her lips. "Of course I am." Her fingers tighten around mine. "I'm not going anywhere."

For a long moment, I simply watch her, memorizing the way candlelight glows against her skin, the way the shadows play against the elegant line of her throat. I've seen her in the throes of passion, in the heat of battle, but like this—worn, but steadfast—she has never looked more divine.

And then, like a sickness crawling through my veins, reality creeps in.

Images slam into my mind in ruthless succession—Azrakan's wretched form coiling in the summoning circle, the flickering runes scorching into the stone, my reckless ambition tearing through my being like wildfire. The way her body tensed when she realized what I was prepared to do. The moment my carefully woven plan unraveled.

The moment I nearly lost her.

A tremor grips my limbs, sharp and involuntary. I make an attempt to sit up, to confirm that the damage Azrakan inflicted is real, but before I can move, her hands are on my chest, pressing me back against the pillows with surprising force.

"Easy," she murmurs, voice thick with quiet command. "You're okay. You're safe now."

I search her face, thoughts sluggish, tangled. "But… how?" My gaze flickers downward, half-expecting to see my shoulder torn open, but instead, I find only smooth, unmarred skin. "The daemon… it—"

"I healed you," she says simply, but the words land heavily between us. "I'm a witch, remember?" A hint of mischief, barely there, veils the raw emotion simmering beneath.

My breath hitches.

She saved my life.

The notion should seem foreign, impossible. Kaisner Drachenstein does not need saving. Yet as I look at her, reality hits me like lightning.

Clarissa—my Clarissa—stood between me and the daemon's wrath. She risked everything for me, when it should have been the other way around. And gods help me, I nearly…

"Clarissa," I choke out, gripping her hand like a lifeline. My pride is a splintered ruin, but none of it matters. "I—"

She silences me with a single touch, pressing her fingers lightly to my lips.

"Shh," she whispers, shaking her head. "It's okay. We're okay."

The words are meant to comfort, but I see the fracture in her gaze, the burden of everything unsaid. We are not okay. Not after this. The daemon may be gone, but its shadow lingers, a chasm between us, filled with broken trust and buried fears.

The bed dips as she shifts beside me, her hands still

cradling mine, her expression turning uncertain. "After everything… I didn't know what else to do. So I called Janik."

I exhale slowly. Janik—trustworthy, competent Janik. Of course, she'd turn to him.

"He brought us here. Made sure we were safe," she continues, but there's an undertone beneath her words, something unspoken.

She doesn't say it, but I already know—*you weren't safe before.*

The shame I've buried for so long claws its way up my chest. My hunger for power, my arrogance, blinded me. I thought I could control Azrakan. That I could outmaneuver a creature born of darkness. Instead, I nearly damned us both.

I take a sharp breath, steadying my voice. "Clarissa… what I did—what I was willing to do—" I pause, jaw tightening. "I don't expect you to forgive me."

A shadow flickers across her face, but she says nothing.

My throat constricts. "But you have to know… I never meant to put you in danger." I close my eyes, swallowing hard. "I thought I could outplay Azrakan. I thought I could have it all. My pride, my conceit—" A humorless laugh escapes me. "I was the fool. And you… you're the only thing that truly matters."

Tears slip down her cheeks, silent but burning.

"Oh, Kai…" she whispers, and my name on her lips nearly undoes me.

She collapses against me, and I wrap my arms around her, burying my face in her hair. She is warmth, life, salvation, and I clutch her to me as if she might disappear between my fingers.

"I love you," she murmurs into my chest, her words fragile yet fierce. "And I would do anything for you."

A shudder racks through me as I grasp this foreign sensation, this terrifying feeling.

Devotion.

A gift I don't deserve.

I pull back slightly, enough to tilt her chin, forcing her to meet my gaze. "I'll find another way," I vow, my voice hoarse, gravelly. "I'll win Nik's respect without risking you, *Liebes*. I swear it."

Her eyes search mine, finding the truth there. Slowly, she nods. "I know you will."

Her faith in me is overwhelming. In that moment, it dawns on me—I will move heaven and earth to be the man she deserves.

I shift, intent on rising, but my body rebels, a fresh wave of exhaustion crashing over me. The mattress creaks as she gently presses me back down.

"Not yet," she says, her fingers brushing against my temple, her touch tender. "Stay with me. Just a little longer."

I exhale, surrendering to the moment.

I am Kaisner Drachenstein—warlock, kingmaker, a man who has walked through the abyss and returned.

And right now, I am simply hers.

As we cling to each other in the flickering candlelight, I know the road ahead will be far from easy. There are consequences, trust to rebuild. But with Clarissa in my arms, I'm ready to face whatever comes next. Because now, I understand what true power is, and it has nothing to do with dragons or demons.

It's this. Us. Love.

And it's worth fighting for.

Her gaze locks with mine, and I pull her closer, urging her to glide beside me on the bed. Her body molds against me like it was always meant to. I lean in, my lips brushing against hers softly at first, savoring the moment, the warmth of her breath mingling with mine.

Then, with a growl of need, I deepen the kiss, pulling her in, the fire of her desire igniting against me. My hands thread into her hair, tilting her head as I want more, my tongue sweeping into her mouth, claiming her with a hunger I can no longer control, demanding everything she has.

She gives it willingly.

Her sweetness is addictive. I drink from her like a dying man, our tongues entwining in a delirious rhythm. Candlelight flickers over our bodies, casting our passion in gold and shadow, painting it sacred.

But it's not enough.

I need more—more of her skin, more of her sounds, more of her soul.

My hands fumble at the buttons of her gown, impatience setting in. I tear the fabric, exposing her ivory flesh until she stands before me in nothing but lace and vulnerability.

"Kai…" she breathes, her voice trembling on the edge of need, cheeks flushed with heat. "Can we… Can you…?"

I take in every inch of her exposed form—every curve, every line. My blood roars in my veins. She doesn't need to finish the question.

"Oh, I can," I growl, seizing her with the kind of grip that says *mine*. "And I will—until your body knows nothing but me."

She shivers, anticipation crackling in the air, and I sweep aside the final barrier. My hands glide over her thighs, hips, as I lay her back on the bed. And she straddles me, skin flushed against my touch.

I take my time, memorizing her with mouth and tongue, but the fire within me burns too hot. With one last, forceful heave, I pin her beneath me with deliberate, possessive intent. The movement sparks a sharp, burning pain searing through my shoulder—Azrakan's wound might no longer mar my skin, but dark magic always leaves a trace.

I grit my teeth, refusing to let weakness dictate my actions. No. I take the pain, seize it, and twist it into something else. Fuel. Hunger. A fire that burns hotter than before.

"You smell so fucking good right now." My breath is ragged against her skin, every word edged in lust. "I can almost taste your need—thick and heady, like the sweetest perfume."

She shivers, a pulse fluttering at her neck. "Take it…" she moans. "Take everything."

A satisfied rumble vibrates in my chest as she clutches my shoulders, instinctively yielding to me. "Mm… I will," I rasp, rough and possessive. "I'm going to devour you, Clarissa— ruin you so beautifully you'll beg me to do it again."

Her breath comes fast, lips parted, eyes dark with need— but it's the way she looks at me, as though I'm the only force in the world that matters, that nearly breaks me.

I lower myself over her, caging her in, my fingers tracing down her body, staking my claim. "You're mine," I murmur, my voice raw with hunger. "Say it."

Her breathing catches. "I'm yours, Kai."

And that's all I need to hear before I take what belongs to me.

Her hands tremble as she reaches for the fastenings of my trousers, and I suck in a sharp breath as they hit the floor. Kicking them away, I stand before her, naked in her lust-filled gaze. She drinks me in greedily, and the hunger I see there sends a torrent of need straight to my core.

As our bodies press together, a primal urgency overtakes me—raw, consuming. I tear my mouth from hers, trailing heated kisses along her jawline, down the supple curve of her neck. She moans, tilting her head, offering herself without hesitation. My teeth graze the spot where her nape meets her shoulder, and she shivers beneath me, her breath catching.

The scent of her arousal floods my senses, drowning out everything else, stoking the inferno already raging inside me. I want to worship her, to linger on every inch of satin-smooth skin, to savor this moment I've hungered for. But that patience has long since burned away.

With a groan dragged from the depths of my soul, I thrust into her, sliding in to the hilt. Her inner walls clench around me like a velvet vice, and we both cry out—one sound, one breath—as our bodies finally, irrevocably, become one.

Her nails dig into my back, sharp crescents branding me as hers. I drive into her with reckless abandon, our hips colliding in a rhythm both frenzied and fated. The room dissolves into shadows and flame, the scent of sweat, sex, and something more filling the air. Something ancient awakens with us.

"You're trembling," I rasp, dragging my mouth up the column of her neck. "D'you feel that, baby girl? That's your body begging me to claim you."

She nods, breathless. "Yes…"

The climax builds like a storm on the horizon, but with it comes another hunger—deeper, darker. A hunger that stirs from the marrow of my bones. My fangs extend, unbidden, aching for the offering so close, so willing.

Compelled by sheer instinct, I lower my mouth to her throat. Her gasps fan the fire inside me. And with a final growl, I plunge my fangs into her pulse.

Her blood pours into me—hot, sweet, sacred. Ambrosia. I drink like a man starved, like a dragon unleashed, and the world fractures around us into color and sensation. Clarissa arches into me, her body shuddering, pleasure crashing over her in waves that pull me deeper.

I feel it all. Her cries, her ecstasy, the raw truth of our union. I'm not just claiming her—I'm being *remade* by her.

Her exquisite form clenches around me, convulsing in time with each pulse of blood against my tongue. The taste of her, the feel of her, the bond sealing between us—it's too much. I lose myself completely, breaking apart as I come, roaring her name into her skin.

In this moment, we are one. Bound by heat, by blood, by a love that reshapes everything I thought I was. And within my very being, I know—

I will never let her go.

"Mine," I roar as the ecstasy of her blood and climax courses through my being. "You're mine."

The pleasure is so intense that I fear it might shatter my very soul, yet I welcome the oblivion. With one last, primal thrust, I stiffen inside her, our releases crashing like a stormy sea against the shore.

"Yes," she cries out, grazing the edge of delirium. "Yours."

As the ecstasy subsides, I retract my fangs, leaving behind a crimson trail on her porcelain skin. Tenderly, my tongue sweeps away the blood, sealing the wound with a soft kiss. The crimson liquid vanishes as soon as it touches my lips, and her skin knits itself together before my baffled eyes.

I sigh in relief. "My beautiful love," I whisper, stroking her cheek.

Her voice is breathless as she says, "I've never known such pleasure... such... belonging."

My body answers immediately, hunger rising anew—but I master it, just barely. Not now. There will be time for that. Endless nights to claim her, to explore every hidden corner of her body and soul.

A shiver runs down my spine—not from her touch, but from her words. The bare truth in them. I glance at her, and my breath catches.

There, on the smooth column of her neck, something begins to emerge—an intricate mark blooming against her skin as if inked by invisible flame. A coil of fire, elegant and unmistakable. Within its curling design, our initials are entwined—K and C, bound together inside the brand of a dragon.

I stare, stunned. It isn't just a mark—it's a seal. A claiming. A bond.

"Gods, at last," I rumble, and tug her back into my arms, unable to keep the possessive edge from my voice. "You are mine. Completely mine."

Clarissa melts against me with a soft, contented sigh, her breath warm against my throat. "Yours," she moans, the corners of her lips curving in the faintest smile. "All yours. Forever."

I roll to my side, pulling her with me, our naked bodies molding together beneath the satin sheets. Her head rests against my chest, and I can feel her heartbeat syncing with mine—steady, sure, familiar.

And yet... something has changed.

As I lie there, basking in the warmth of her body, I cannot ignore it. A sensation rising inside me, slow and undeniable. A stirring at the center of everything I am. Not pain. Not power. Something deeper. Older. Wilder.

I try to dismiss it. Tell myself it's residual adrenaline. Aftershocks of ecstasy. But it grows—persistent, electric.

I close my eyes, concentrating, trying to trace the pulse of this strange new rhythm. It's subtle at first, a murmur beneath my pulse. But as I sink into it, it strengthens, grows louder, more insistent.

And then, with a clarity that sends a shiver down my spine, I realize what it is. A heartbeat other than my own. An ancient power that has lain dormant within me for so long, finally awakening.

My dragon.

4 0

CLARISSA

Kaisner's eyes fly open with a sudden gasp, his body jerking with the force of it. It's not pain —it's awe. Shock. A raw, living energy pulses through him like fire through frost.

I rise slowly. "Kai?" I whisper. The word dies on my lips as I watch his chest heave, ribs expanding and contracting like bellows feeding a forge. Heat radiates from his skin—not the warm glow of passion, but something that makes the air shimmer above him like a mirage.

And then, his tattoos writhe in the candlelight.

I blink hard, certain I'm seeing things, but no—the dark ink beneath his skin moves with a life of its own. Serpentine patterns flow and shift, as if something is trying to claw its way out from within.

"What—" I start to reach for him, then snatch my hand back as his flesh burns my fingertips.

Speechless, his eyes find mine. My heart stops.

Gold bleeds through the maroon like molten metal poured into wine. His pupils stretch into vertical slits, predatory and foreign, yet somehow still achingly familiar.

328

A low rumble builds in his chest—not a groan of pain, but something deeper, more primal. The sound vibrates through the floorboards, rattling the crystal on his nightstand.

"Oh gods." The words tumble out as understanding crashes over me. "Oh gods, Kai."

He frowns. "What's happening?" he rasps, dazed and breathless.

"You're shifting," I manage, the words grazing against the rising panic in my throat.

Obsidian scales ripple across his shoulder blade, each one catching the candlelight like black glass. I can almost hear them, like stone scraping stone. Beautiful. Terrifying.

He looks down. Freezes. Then curses low under his breath.

I scramble backward, my bare feet tangling in the sheets. "You need to get out of the house," I gasp, pointing toward the balcony. "Now! Before you—"

He's already moving, rolling from the bed with inhuman grace despite the tremors wracking his frame. His movements are jerky, uncontrolled, as if fighting against his own body. He drags on his boxers, muscles bulging beneath skin that grows too tight.

The air around him begins to warp, heat waves distorting his silhouette. Every candle flame in the room gutters and dances, casting wild shadows on the walls. The crystal decanter on his dresser develops a hairline crack.

I yank my dress over my head, fingers fumbling with the fabric as I watch him stagger toward the balcony doors. Each step leaves scorch marks on the Persian rug.

"Clarissa." My name is barely recognizable, distorted by vocal cords that are changing, lengthening. "Get back."

By the time he throws open the doors, he's no longer just

a man. He's becoming something vast. Ancient. Myth made flesh.

The night wind rushes in, carrying the scent of rain and something else—sulfur, smoke, the electric taste of lightning.

I follow despite his warning, one hand pressed to the doorframe for support. The wind whips my hair across my face, but I can't look away as he steps to the edge of the balcony.

The stone railing crumbles under his grip.

For a heartbeat, he pauses, silhouetted against the star-drunk sky. Then he looks back at me one last time, and I see the man I love trapped behind those shifter eyes—afraid, awed, apologetic.

And then, meeting no hesitation, he leaps.

A concussive blast of energy knocks the breath from my lungs. The force of his takeoff cracks the stone beneath his feet, fractures racing across the balcony like spiderwebs. Stone fragments pepper my arms as I throw them up to shield my face. The very air splits with a sound like the world tearing in half. Light erupts from where he fell—not the warm gold of candleflame, but something fierce and incandescent that sears my retinas even through my closed eyelids.

When I lower my hands and I dare to look below... he's gone.

No—not gone.

Transformed.

A dragon crouches where a man once stood.

Black scales shimmer like oil on water, each one the size of my palm. Wings stretch wide enough to shadow half the courtyard, membrane stretched between bones that could snap a tree in half. Talons gouge trenches in the ancient cobblestones as he shifts his weight.

But it's the eyes that steal my breath.

Still gold. Still his. Still looking at me with an expression

I recognize, despite the foreign features—wonder, terror, and desperate love all warring in that draconian gaze.

Shouts erupt from the guards' quarters. Boots thunder across stone. I hear the distinctive slide of weapons being drawn.

"Stop!" The scream tears from my throat, raw and commanding. "Don't shoot!"

The dragon's massive head swivels toward the sound of approaching footsteps, smoke curling from his nostrils. A warning growl rumbles through the courtyard, felt as much as heard.

"It's Kaisner!" I lean over the ruined balcony railing, voice cracking with desperation. "Stand down!"

The footsteps falter. Confused murmurs replace the battle cries.

I force my legs to move, to carry me down the winding stairs despite how they shake with each step. The cold stone bites at my bare feet, but I barely notice. All my focus narrows to the creature waiting in the courtyard—beautiful and terrible and mine.

He watches my approach with the stillness of a predator, but there's nothing threatening in his posture. If anything, he seems... uncertain. Vulnerable, despite his size.

"Kai," I whisper when I reach the bottom step.

His great head tilts at the sound of his name, ears swiveling forward like a cat's. The gesture is so achingly familiar that tears blur my vision.

I take one more step. Another.

He lowers his massive head until we're nearly eye to eye, close enough that I can see my reflection in those molten pools. Close enough to feel the heat of his breath on my skin.

My hand rises without conscious thought, trembling as it hovers inches from his snout. This close, I can see the scales, each one perfect and deadly sharp. One wrong move could slice me open.

I don't care.

My palm settles against the warm obsidian of his muzzle, and the world shifts.

Power floods through the connection—ancient, vast, barely contained. It's like touching a live wire, electricity singing through every nerve ending. But beneath the raw strength, I feel something else: the steady pulse of his heartbeat, the familiar rhythm that lulled me to sleep countless times.

He's still there. Still mine.

A sound escapes him—part purr, part sigh, wholly content. The vibration travels through my bones, settling into the hollow spaces of my chest like coming home.

"There you are," I breathe, pressing my forehead to his scales.

Without warning, he moves. One massive claw curls around my waist with impossible gentleness, lifting me as easily as picking up a flower. I don't have time to protest before I'm settled onto the broad expanse of his back, hands scrambling for purchase on the ridge of scales along his spine.

"Kai, what are you—"

His wings snap open with a sound like thunder. The courtyard falls away. My stomach lurches as we rocket upward, the ground shrinking to toy-soldier size below us. Wind tears at my dress, my hair, stealing the scream from my lungs.

And then, impossibly, his voice fills my mind.

"Trust me."

The words don't come through my ears but resonate directly in my thoughts, warm and familiar despite the strange method of delivery.

"I can hear you," I think back, not sure if it will work.

His answering pleasure floods our link, rich as honey, sweet as wine. "*Hold on, my love. Let me show you the world as I see it.*"

We soar higher, until the air grows thin and cold. The city spreads below us like a carpet of stars, and above, the real stars shine with crystalline clarity. Wind rushes past us, but somehow I'm warm, protected by his heat and the curve of his wing.

Through our bond, I sense what he feels—the intoxicating freedom of flight, the power thrumming through his massive frame, the joy of finally being complete after years of carrying half a soul.

"*This is who I am,*" he tells me, vulnerability threading through the mental contact. "*Can you love this too?*"

I lean forward, pressing my cheek to the warm scales of his neck. "All of you," I whisper aloud, knowing he'll feel the truth of it through our connection. "Always all of you."

His pleasure floods through me, warm and fathomless, a spiritual embrace of such depth I almost cry.

The sky lightens around us as we chase the dawn, painting the clouds in shades of rose and gold. We're flying toward the sun itself, and for the first time since this began, I'm not afraid.

This is where I belong.

With him.

Forever.

41

KAISNER

The sky bruises with the first hints of morning, violet bleeding into gray as Paris exhales its last breath of darkness. I stand motionless on the balcony, the marble balustrade cool beneath my palms, watching as night surrenders to day. A crisp, biting air slides across my bare chest, but I barely register the chill. How could I, when Clarissa's warmth presses against my back, her arms encircling my waist, her cheek resting between my shoulder blades?

Her presence anchors me to this moment, this reality, when I might otherwise drift into the surreal euphoria of what transpired last night. The memory of flight ripples through my muscles—the stretch and power of wings, the sting of wind against scales, the intoxicating freedom of true form after years of dormancy.

Clarissa shifts, sliding beneath my arm until she faces me. Dawn light catches in her golden hair, turning it into threads of fire. Her sapphire eyes search mine with reverence that makes my chest ache.

"I still can't believe it," she whispers, her voice carrying both wonder and fragility, like a prayer. "You're a dragon, Kai. A real, honest-to-gods dragon."

The childlike awe in her expression transforms something that should feel monstrous into something holy. I've spent my life surrounded by those who feared or coveted what slumbered in my blood. Never has anyone looked at me as she does now—as if I were a miracle made flesh.

My lips curl into a genuine smile. "And it's all because of you, *Liebes*."

Confusion clouds her gaze, her brow furrowing delicately. "I don't... understand."

The truth coalesces in my mind with sudden, devastating clarity. I draw in a deep breath, lungs expanding with air that tastes of revelation. Below us, Paris awakens—the distant rumble of delivery trucks, the scent of fresh bread rising from boulangeries. These ordinary sounds frame the most extraordinary realization of my existence.

"All this time, I believed I needed rituals. Blood. Bargains." My voice drops lower, edged with the shadow of what might have been. "I spent years chasing forbidden magic, convinced that awakening the dragon required sacrifice. The daemon demanded your blood, willingly given."

Her gaze darkens, the memory of my near-fatal miscalculation hanging in the air like smoke. "Kai..."

I silence her gently, pressing my forehead to hers in a gesture more intimate than any kiss. Our breath mingles, warm and alive. "But it was you, Clarissa. Your love. Your trust." Each word falls like a stone breaking the surface of still water, ripples expanding outward. "You were the key. When we claimed each other, when that bond took root..." My fingers tighten imperceptibly at her waist. "It unlocked everything. The dragon stirred not because of sorcery—but because of you."

Tears gather at the corners of her eyes, sunlight fracturing through them into miniature rainbows. One slips free, tracing a silvery path down her cheek. "But how?" she whispers. "How could that be enough?"

I catch the tear with my thumb, its warmth seeping into my skin. "Because you're my mate," I say simply, the word inadequate for the cosmic phenomenon it attempts to name. "My soul recognized yours, and the dragon recognized the bond." I cradle her face between my palms, memorizing every curve, every line, every freckle across her nose. "Everything that's ever been dormant in me—woken by you."

Her lips part, trembling slightly with raw emotion. The space between us vibrates with unspoken intensity. "I'm glad I could help," she says, voice catching. "But don't forget—your strength made it possible. You held back. You chose me. That matters."

A notion tugs at the edges of my consciousness—a strange, ephemeral sensation, like trying to recall a word just out of reach. I narrow my focus, probing this peculiar awareness.

"Wait," I murmur, brow furrowing. "There's something else."

Clarissa tilts her head, curiosity brightening her gaze. "What?"

I close my eyes, turning my attention inward. The connection that had flowed between us during flight—effortless, natural—feels muted now, almost nonexistent. I reach for her mentally, forming the thought with deliberate precision.

"Can you hear me?"

When I open my eyes, I find only puzzlement written across her features.

"What do you mean?" she asks, confusion knitting her brow.

"You... don't hear me now?" I ask aloud, surprised by the hollow absence where her presence had been so vibrant.

"No, should I?" She smiles, but the expression doesn't quite reach her eyes. "You're right here."

I rub my jaw, the scratch of stubble rough beneath my fingers. "Only when I'm shifted," I murmur. "It was so clear when we were in the air, like our thoughts were interwoven."

She nods slowly, comprehension dawning. "I felt it, too. Like I was in your head... and you were in mine."

"It must be the bond," I say, fascination coloring my tone. "Tied to the dragon. When I shift again, we'll test it."

The shrill ring of her phone cuts through the moment. Clarissa stiffens, fumbles for the device, her movements uncharacteristically clumsy.

"Sam?" Her voice wavers, uncertainty flooding through. Then her body goes rigid, as if electricity has coursed through her. "What? When?" Her fingers grip mine with desperate strength. "No, I'm... I'm not at home. I'm with Kaisner."

I watch the emotions flicker across her face—guilt, apprehension, determination. Her throat works as she swallows hard.

"Sam, listen," she says after a beat, her voice steadier now. "There's something I need to tell you. About Kaisner and me. We're... we're mated. He claimed me. And there's more. He shifted into his dragon last night."

She falls silent, listening. Her knuckles whiten where they grip the phone. "I know, I know it's a lot to take in. But please, can you break the news to Nik gently? It'll be so much better coming from you."

When she finally ends the call, her face has drained of color, leaving her almost translucent in the morning light.

"Nik's back," she says, the words falling like stones. "He just landed at the private airstrip."

I tug her near, pressing my lips to her temple, sensing her pulse beneath my touch. Her scent—jasmine and rain and something uniquely her—fills my senses. "How do you want us to handle this?"

She exhales slowly, the air shuddering from her lungs. "I think... we should give him a day to process. Meet with him tomorrow. Is that okay?"

Every instinct screams for immediate action—to claim, to mark territory, to establish dominance. But years of hard-won control assert themselves. This is not about me. This is about her, about what *she* needs.

"Of course, my love," I murmur against her hair. "Whatever you think is best."

Sunlight stretches across the room, brightening the silence between us. It feels like the world dares not intrude on what we've become.

I guide her inside, our steps slow as we make our way to the bed. Clarissa lies beside me, the light gilding her skin, casting amber tones over the curves I've come to memorize. I don't move. I simply watch her, committing every breath, every rise and fall of her chest, to memory. She is still. Peaceful. Mine.

I should get up, prepare for what's coming—but I don't. Not yet.

Instead, I shift closer, my fingers brushing the slope of her shoulder. She stirs, murmuring my name in that sleepy, honey-drenched voice that undoes me every time. "Kai..."

"Ich bin hier, mein Leben," I whisper, lips trailing against her temple. "Always."

The morning unfolds slowly. I feed her grapes from a silver tray, her laughter soft as I kiss her ankle, knee, and thigh. Each touch is a prayer, every caress a pledge.

We bathe together in the cedarwood-scented water, her fragrance mingling with mine as I wash her hair, untangling it with newfound patience. She calls me ridiculous, and I smirk.

By midday, we share Drachenstein wine, aged in fire-touched oak. She smiles at the first sip, leans in for more, tasting it from my lips. We toast nothing and everything. Her bravery, my survival, the flame between us.

Evening finds her barefoot in the solarium, wrapped in one of my robes, her silhouette glowing in twilight. I watch her, a pang in my chest. She is the reason I'm whole, powerful… and terrified, because now I have something to lose.

A low thrum hums beneath my skin, the burden of duty and the coming confrontation with Nikolaas. Our bond, my shift—it will be seen as a threat.

And isn't it, really?

Clarissa turns, sensing the restlessness in my silence. "Kai," she says, crossing to me. Her hand rests over my heart. "Please don't shut me out."

I pull her into my arms, burying my face in her neck. "I'm trying to hold onto this moment," I murmur. "After tonight, everything changes."

She looks up at me, eyes steady. "Then let's make it count."

And we do. I take her, not in haste, but with ceremony. I mark her with my body, my vow. She is mine. My mate. My queen.

Later, as she sleeps curled against me, I watch the stars. The pulse of the dragon still burns beneath my skin.

Tomorrow, I'll face Nikolaas Draken, the so-called *Last Dragon Shifter.* The golden boy whose claim to supremacy I've just shattered by simply existing. But tonight… tonight belongs to us.

Hours drift as Clarissa sleeps beside me. I stare at the ornate ceiling, shadows dancing on intricate plasterwork. Her peaceful face undoes me—this woman who not only accepted the beast within me but embraced it. Loved it as part of herself.

I won't let her suffer for loving me.

The decision crystallizes with brutal clarity. Rising silently from our bed, I dress methodically—selecting a slate-gray suit that feels like armor against what's to come. Each button, each fold, each adjustment serves as ritual preparation for battle.

When I step into the hallway, Janik materializes from the shadows like a specter, his expression unreadable in the half-light. He stands at parade rest, hands clasped behind his back, awaiting instruction.

"Congratulations are due, *mein König*," he says, his voice pitched low.

I pause, momentarily thrown. "I've not proposed yet." Then, suspicion flickers. "Janik, how did you—"

My enforcer harrumphs. "I meant your dragon's awakening," he clarifies. "Though the news of a queen is equally welcome."

A soft laugh escapes me, tension briefly broken. "*More* than welcome," I admit, with an unfamiliar warmth spreading through my chest. "I owe her everything."

"You are fortunate indeed," he remarks, but something in his tone shifts, hardening. His posture stiffens imperceptibly.

"What is it?" I ask, instantly alert to the change.

His voice clips each word with military precision. "The Last Dragon Shifter has returned to Paris."

I straighten my jacket, a predatory gleam in my eyes. "He can say goodbye to that title," I murmur. "I'm on my way to see him."

I stop mid-step. "Janik."

"Yes, sir?"

"When Miss Draken wakes, escort her to Draken Manor." I don't ask, I command. "I'll wait for you there."

He inclines his head. "Understood, *mein König*."

Before I descend, I glance at the bedroom door—the threshold where everything I never knew I needed sleeps peacefully.

I'll face Nikolaas alone. She need not witness the clash of dragons that's coming.

42

CLARISSA

*M*orning light spills through the curtains, gilding the edges of the room in warm gold. It paints lazy strokes across the duvet, the velvet chaise, the edge of the clawfoot tub in the corner. Everything feels unreal, like I've woken in a dream spun from silk and smoke.

And maybe I have.

I blink against the glow, slowly coming into awareness. The scent of him clings to the sheets—amber, spice, something darker that I now know belongs to no cologne. It's his essence. Kaisner. My dragon.

A quiet ache pulses low in my hips, a tender reminder of everything we shared last night. I stretch beneath the blankets, languid, sated, and yet already missing the weight of his body next to mine. My hand reaches for the space where he was, finding only residual warmth. I sigh.

It was real. All of it.

The bond. The shift. The kiss that felt like worship. The flight that tasted like freedom.

And now, the quiet after the storm.

A knock draws me from the haze. Gentle. Discreet.

"Miss Draken?" a soft voice calls from the entrance.

I sit up quickly, the sheets falling from my bare shoulders. The door opens a fraction, revealing a familiar face—one of the household staff, a young woman with dark hair pinned in a neat twist and warm brown eyes.

She steps inside, balancing a silver tray with the kind of effortless grace that comes only from years of service. "Good morning, Miss Draken," she says, offering a polite smile. "Mr. Drachenstein requested that you be served breakfast here."

"Oh," I manage, caught between surprise and gratitude. "Thank you."

She glides toward the bed, sets the tray gently on the low table beside me, and lifts the cover to reveal a spread fit for royalty—flaky croissants still warm from the oven, fresh strawberries glistening with dew, a small dish of whipped butter infused with honey and thyme. A porcelain cup steams with dark roast coffee, touched with vanilla.

My stomach tightens—not with hunger, but something else. The realization that I'm not merely a guest here anymore.

"Shall I draw a bath, Miss?" the maid offers.

"That would be lovely," I reply.

She nods and leaves. I'm alone again—with countless questions building in my mind, but one rises above the rest.

Where is Kai?

I reach for the coffee. It warms my palms, and as I take the first sip, the bitterness cuts through the remnants of sleep and nerves. I stare out the window for a moment, watching the breeze toy with the gauzy curtains.

Then another knock—this one firmer, familiar in its precision.

I don't need to ask who it is.

"Miss Draken," comes Janik's voice. Even muffled, it

carries his usual clipped composure. He opens the door slightly. "Forgive the intrusion. Mr. Drachenstein has requested that I escort you to Draken Manor. He awaits us there."

My pulse quickens. Draken Manor. Nikolaas.

I swallow hard and set the cup back on the tray. "I'll be ready shortly," I reply.

He gives a swift nod through the gap before closing the door. His silence says everything I need to hear—he's giving me space. But the clock is ticking.

I slip out of bed, gathering the satin robe draped at the foot. The room is still scented with Kai—cedarwood, spice, and something distinctly his. It lingers on my skin as I cross to the bathroom, where a fresh bath waits, steam curling like whispers into the morning air.

I let myself sink into it slowly, the heat loosening every last knot of tension in my body. Beneath the surface, I touch the new truth in me—that I am not the same woman who stepped foot in this manor two nights ago.

Claimed. Chosen. Changed.

When I emerge, the chill air kisses my damp skin. I wrap myself in a towel and step back into the bedroom, where sunlight now fills the space. On the chaise, an array of clothing has been arranged with deliberate care—half a dozen ensembles, each more elegant than the last. Blouses of silk and lace. Trousers with sharp tailoring. A fitted coat of fine wool. Leather gloves. Scarves. Kai's hand in every detail.

I run my fingers across the options, lingering on a blouse the color of bone, sheer at the sleeves with delicate lace at the cuffs. I pair it with black trousers that hug my waist perfectly, and a charcoal coat I remember him wearing once with dark gloves and a knife at his hip.

His world. My world now, too.

I knot a burgundy scarf loosely around my neck—his

family's color—and smooth my palms down the length of my coat.

In the mirror, I catch my reflection.

My hair, still damp, curls at the ends. My lips are fuller than usual. My skin glows faintly. But it's the eyes that stop me. There's a quiet stillness in them, the calm before impact. Not fear—resolve.

I don't know what awaits me at Draken Manor. But I know who I am when I arrive.

Descending the stairs, I find Janik waiting by the door in his usual crisp black. He regards me with a brief, almost imperceptible smile.

"Morning, Miss Draken. I trust you slept well."

I nod, offering a smirk in return. "I did."

He opens the car door for me without another word. I slide into the passenger seat of a sleek black sedan, leather soft beneath my fingertips. Janik settles behind the wheel, and we pull away from the manor, slipping into the quiet streets of Paris.

It's beautiful, this hour. The sky painted in hues of lilac and silver, the world still holding its breath.

After a long silence, Janik speaks—his voice softer than usual. "Miss Draken… If I may. I wished to say that your presence has brought something back to this house. To *him*. There's a light in His Majesty I haven't seen in many years."

I turn to him, startled. Janik rarely mentions anything beyond logistics.

"That means more than you know," I reply, the words catching in my throat.

He nods once, eyes never leaving the road.

His hands tighten on the steering wheel. "The night his father was murdered," he continues, "we were ambushed at Schloss Drachenstein, the family's castle in Bavaria. Arrived for what we thought was a routine meeting. Fifteen men, maybe more, waiting for us."

Janik's jaw tightens. "I took a blade to the leg, went down hard. Couldn't stand, couldn't crawl. Young Master Drachenstein was eighteen. He could have run—everyone was screaming at him to escape. Instead, he picked up a knife and threw himself between me and my executioner. Took the man's throat out with a single cut."

He glances at me briefly. "Then he grabbed a gun from the ground and shot the remaining three. An eighteen-year-old boy chose to stay and bleed with his father's enforcer rather than save his own skin."

My breath catches. I try to imagine Kaisner back then—barely older than I am now—walking into that trap and reacting so fiercely.

Janik's voice carries absolute conviction as he adds, "That's when I knew I wasn't just serving the Drachenstein heir anymore. I was serving a *true* king."

That's who he's always been, I realize, my chest tightening with sudden understanding. Not the cold king others see, but the boy who would rather die than leave someone behind. The man who still makes that same choice, again and again.

The silence stretches between us, broken only by the hum of the engine and the whisper of tires on pavement.

A quiet breath escapes me as I gaze out the passenger window, watching the Parisian cityscape blur past in a hush of gray stone and gold morning light. The knowledge that Kaisner went ahead, alone, settles over me like a balm—unexpected and strangely tender. He didn't wait for me to shield him. He went ahead to shield *me.*

Not from my brother's anger—Kaisner isn't afraid of that. But from the strain of divided loyalties. From the first explosive impact of Nik's disapproval. From the sting of old wounds being torn open in my presence.

He's granting me time. Space. Grace.

Whatever else today brings, I'll remember this: that on this day, Kaisner Drachenstein, the man feared across Europe, chose diplomacy over dominance—for me.

For us.

We turn onto a familiar avenue lined with towering trees, their branches forming a canopy overhead. The sight elicits a sense of nostalgia, memories of my childhood at Draken Manor flooding back.

Suddenly, tires screech nearby. Janik hits the breaks. A black SUV swerves in front of us, blocking our path. He curses under his breath.

"Stay here," he commands, then exits the vehicle.

I stare through the windshield as Janik approaches the SUV, shoulders squared, his gait taut with restrained aggression. Before I can make sense of it, the vehicle's doors explode open—metal groaning, boots hitting pavement. A swarm of black-clad men spills out in coordinated formation, tactical gear gleaming under the morning light. They fan out like predators, cutting off Janik's escape in a matter of seconds.

Terror grips me. I lunge for my phone, fingers scrabbling across the screen, but they won't obey—shaking too violently to type the passcode. A shout yanks my gaze upward just in time to see one of the men drive his fist into Janik's jaw. He staggers, then drops like a felled tree.

"No!" I scream, throwing open my door.

Before I can react, two men surge toward me like wolves breaking from the pack. I lash out, my heel slamming into one of their knees. He snarls, staggering with a grunt—but doesn't go down. The second lunges in, grabbing my arm and wrenching it behind my back. Pain sparks up my shoulder.

"Let me go!" I cry, twisting violently in his grip, heart pounding like war drums in my chest.

"Easy, Miss Draken," one of them says with a sneer. "We wouldn't want to damage the merchandise."

Rage flares through me. I whip my head around and sink my teeth into his hand—hard. Blood floods my mouth, metallic and warm. He howls and recoils, and in that heartbeat, I tear free. I bolt.

But I don't make it two steps. A third man slides into my path like he's been waiting. He doesn't speak—just lifts a cloth, already soaked with something acrid.

"Sweet dreams, beautiful," he murmurs, closing the distance in a single, fluid motion.

His arm snakes around my waist, yanking me tight against his chest as he presses the cloth to my face. I buck and thrash in his hold, clawing at his forearm, kicking wildly, but it's like fighting quicksand.

No. No no no—

My muscles betray me. Everything slows. The pavement rushes up as my knees buckle, the world tilting like a sinking ship.

Janik's body comes into view—crumpled, unmoving. Too still.

The man holding me whispers something else, but his voice distorts, swallowed by the roaring hush that fills my ears.

Then everything disappears into darkness.

And I am gone.

43

KAISNER

orning mist clings to the cobblestones like breath from the underworld, curling around my boots as I ascend the drive toward Draken Manor. Paris is only beginning to stir behind me, the city unaware of the storm gathering at its heart. Above, the sky is a wash of pewter, neither night nor day—just the hush before something breaks.

Draken Manor rises ahead as a mausoleum of power—stoic, ancestral, and unwelcome.

I slow as I reach the massive doors, my hand hovering over the dragon-shaped knocker. The cold brass bites into my palm when I finally rap against it, a deliberate echo sounding through the house like a warning shot. My breath fogs faintly in the frosty air, but I barely feel it. I think only of her.

Clarissa. Safe. Warm. Still asleep, if the gods are kind. If awake, she already knows I've come here. She knows why.

After what feels like an eternity, the door creaks open, revealing a stern-faced butler. His gaze widens slightly as he recognizes me, but he quickly schools his features into a mask of polite indifference.

"Mr. Drachenstein," he says, his voice clipped and formal. "I'm afraid Mr. Draken is not expecting any visitors, sir. You'll need to make an appointment."

I resist the urge to roll my eyes. Bureaucracy, even in a place like this. "I'm not *the type* to make appointments," I murmur, brushing past him and into the grand foyer.

The butler sputters indignantly behind me, but I pay him no mind. My senses are on high alert, scanning for any sign of Nikolaas. A low hum of voices draws my attention to a door at the far end of the hall. Without hesitation, I stride toward it, my footsteps echoing in the cavernous space.

As I approach, the sounds become clearer—Nikolaas' deep timbre, tinged with frustration, and the Ursa princess' softer tone, attempting to soothe him. My hand closes around the doorknob, and for a split second, I consider turning back. But the image of Clarissa, vulnerable and alone, steels my nerves.

I twist the handle and push the door open.

The study radiates the grandeur and elegance of old-world opulence. Rich mahogany bookshelves line the walls, filled with ancient tomes and priceless artifacts. A massive desk dominates the center of the room, behind which stands Nikolaas Draken, his posture rigid with tension. His mate Samara is perched on the edge of a nearby armchair, her expression a clash of concern and surprise as she sees me enter.

For a moment, silence reigns. Then, Nikolaas' gaze stumbles upon me in the doorway. Recognition ignites like a spark to gunpowder.

"Where is she, you power-hungry bastard?" Nikolaas roars, eyes flashing with barely contained fury. He jabs an accusing finger at me. "You crossed a line, Drachenstein. There's no going back from this."

A confident smirk pulls at my lips. "Bold words for someone who just lost his crown."

He storms around the desk, fists clenched at his sides, ready to strike. "You brand her, and now you want to play king? I'll see you dead first, Kaisner!"

I stand my ground, my voice cutting with silk-wrapped steel. "Say my name again, Draken, and I'll give you a reason to fear it."

"Both of you, please!" Samara jumps to her feet, positioning herself between us. Her gaze darts between Nikolaas and me, pleading for calm. "This is not the way."

I breathe deeply, forcing my tone to remain controlled. "Listen to your mate. Let's do this the civilized way—for Clarissa's sake."

But my words only fuel Nikolaas further. His face contorts with rage, a vein pulsing at his temple.

"If you truly cared about her, you'd walk away now. Leave her the hell out of your twisted games." His fist slams down on the desk, crystal rattling in its tray.

His remarks slice through my pride, anger flaring in my chest. "You mistake my restraint for weakness, Nikolaas," I say, my tone cold. "The only reason you're still breathing is because she loves you." I want to lash out, but for once in my life, I swallow the fury. This isn't about my ego. It's about Clarissa.

"She should be home—where she's safe," Nikolaas murmurs.

"Your sister *is* safe," I bite back. My voice turns to ice, but only just. "Safer than she ever was under your watch."

That hits its mark. Nikolaas reels back as if I've physically struck him. "Excuse me?" he scoffs, but there's a tremor in it—disbelief already giving way to outrage.

"You heard me." The leash on my temper snaps. "You were too busy chasing glory—vanishing from Paris without so much as a backward glance, while Clarissa stayed behind, exposed. Unguarded." I step closer, voice rising. "She faced threats you never saw coming, and you weren't there. *I was.*"

His face drains of color, then flushes with heat. "What kind of threats? Predators like you?" he growls, venom lacing his words.

I bare my teeth in a dangerous grin. "Every alpha in this city, sniffing at her heels while her 'fearless' brother played hero abroad." My claws threaten to breach the skin of my fingers, and I fight to keep the dragon contained. "You want to talk about danger? Try walking in late with a target on your back and no backup. That was her reality. You think that crown you chase makes you a king? You're not even a shield."

Nikolaas sneers, but the tremor in his jaw betrays him. "You expect me to thank you? For crawling into her life like a parasite and feeding on her weakness?"

I don't flinch. I've heard worse from men who now lie in unmarked graves. "She's not weak," I say dangerously. "But *you* are if you believe love makes someone fragile."

"She doesn't *love* you," he spits. "She doesn't even know who you are."

I meet his glare, unblinking, and close the distance between us until our breaths mingle. "She knows *exactly* who I am. And she chose me. That's what keeps you up at night, isn't it, Draken? That she saw everything I am—and still opened the door."

He bristles, hands clutching the desk's edge. "You manip-ulated her," he accuses, eyes filled with fury. "You've used her—"

"I've bled for her!" My roar shakes the air. "I've gone to war in her name, risked everything for her safety. I'd set the world on fire if it meant keeping her warm. Can you say the same?"

A muscle twitches along his jaw. "You don't get to talk about sacrifice."

"Don't I?" I tilt my head, my cruel smile returning. "Tell me, Nikolaas, where were you when she woke up screaming? Who held her when the cruelty of our world came crashing in?" I lean in, venom lacing my voice. "Not you."

"Enough!" Samara gasps, her hand gently brushing Nikolaas's arm, trying to keep the beast at bay.

But it's too late.

"You're poison," Nikolaas hisses. "Everything you touch turns to ash." A fine shimmer of golden scales flashes at his jawline before vanishing.

"I warned her," I say, the words soft now—lethal. "I told her I would ruin her. She looked me in the eye… and asked me to do it anyway."

With a fierce growl, Nikolaas lunges at me. But Samara steps in, arms stretched wide. "Don't!"

I don't flinch. Let him see the monster he's always feared I'd become.

Because I am.

But I'm also the one Clarissa chose.

The tension hangs in the air like smoke from a smoldering battlefield—thick, bitter, and undeniable.

Nikolaas doesn't reply. His jaw ticks. His glare is a loaded gun with no safe. But he doesn't pull the trigger—he's smarter than that.

I lower my voice, rough and steady. "You don't have to like it. You just have to accept it."

Before he can fire back, my phone rings, sharp and insistent. I ignore it, eyes locked on him.

Samara's stare flicks between us—one a storm, the other a wildfire—and settles in the uneasy middle. "Let's keep this civil, remember? For Clarissa." Her voice comes tight. "Where is Clarissa, anyway?"

I exhale slowly. "She's safe."

"That wasn't the question," Nikolaas growls from behind her.

"She's at my estate," I say evenly. "Under guard. No one touches her unless they go through me first."

"She shouldn't *have* to be guarded," he snaps.

I look him in the eye, hard. "Whatever you think of me, Nikolaas, understand this—Clarissa made her choice. You can hate me all you want, but you *will* respect her."

Silence stretches between us like a drawn blade, humming with the promise of blood.

Nikolaas watches me, still simmering. Samara says nothing, but her demeanor is calculating, wary.

Then, with a controlled breath, I pull back. I straighten to my full height, spine taut with resolve. "She's not a pawn," I say, my voice low and firm. "She's the queen. And I'm the only one playing this game who knows how to keep her from falling."

The words hang in the air, thick with truth and conviction.

Before I can speak again, my phone vibrates, cutting through the silence. Persistent. Urgent.

I pull it from my pocket, irritation burning—until I see the name on the screen.

Janik.

My chest tightens. He never calls twice unless it's blood.

I answer. "What is it?"

There's a beat of static. Then Janik's voice filters through, grave and clipped.

"*Mein König...* It's Miss Draken." A breath. "She's been taken."

Everything inside me comes to a screeching halt. My heart. My thoughts. The air in my lungs.

"What the hell happened?" I manage.

"Ambush on the highway," he replies, voice sharp and efficient. "Black SUV. Tactical gear. Military precision. It was clean, fast. But one of them…" He exhales. "One of them had a tattoo. A tiger. I'd know it anywhere."

The name drops into my mind like a guillotine.

Mahindra.

I don't say it aloud. I breathe it. A curse. A vow.

"Confirmed," Janik growls. "It was them."

A frigid calm seeps into my bones, replacing the burning anger with something far more lethal. My dragon stills inside me—no longer raging. Waiting.

Nikolaas sees the change in my expression. He steps forward, his gaze sharp.

"What is it?" he demands.

I lower the phone, my hand still clutching it. My voice is ice. "She's been taken. By the Mahindra clan."

Samara gasps. Nikolaas goes rigid, his face draining of color before rage surges in to replace it. His fists curl, his nostrils flare.

"What the hell do they want with her?" he growls.

"They want *me*," I say darkly. "She's leverage. A message." My jaw clenches. "And a mistake."

Nikolaas looks ready to shatter something, fury barely restrained. "You should have brought her straight here!"

"And you should never have left her alone in the first place," I snap, my words biting. "But here we are."

Nikolas bristles, but he stays silent, knowing I'm right.

Samara steps forward, her voice tight with anxiety. "Do you know where they're holding her?"

My response is immediate. "I absolutely do."

The silence that follows trembles, suspended on the brink of war. And I? I'm already walking into it.

I turn to them slowly. "The Mahindras will pay dearly for their sin," I growl, my voice a low tremor that rattles the air.

Fire licks my spine. My wings itch to burst free. My dragon is no longer patient—it wants blood.

"Don't you dare meddle in this family's affairs!" Nikolaas roars. "You have no right—"

"I have every—fucking—right!" I explode, the last thread of restraint snapping like bone. "Clarissa is my mate!"

My fists clench, claws threatening to tear through my skin as my dragon surges forward, obsidian scales prickling beneath the surface of my arms, my neck. Rage coils hot in my chest, and I can barely keep it contained.

His features harden. "You fucking monster," he snarls.

"Call me monster, if you want," I inch closer, voice dropping to a growl. "She calls me hers."

Nikolaas curls his fists tight, knuckles whitening. "This is your fault!" he lashes out. "The Mahindras are your enemies. You brought this on her!"

His words cut deep, carving truth from bone. Guilt rises like poison in my throat, but I swallow it down. Self-recrimination won't bring her back—rage will.

"Will you *please* stop this?!" Samara's voice cracks like a whip between us, sharp enough to draw blood. "She doesn't care whose fault it is. She just needs both of you to stop posturing and go save her!"

Her words snap us both to attention. She's right. Our squabbles mean nothing in the face of Clarissa's danger.

Nikolaas looks away first, jaw clenched, hand dragging down his face. "We can't just storm into their territory," he says. "There are rules. Protocols."

"To hell with politics," I mutter, moving toward the door. "Every second we waste talking is another second she spends in their hands."

Samara turns to face us both, shoulders squared. "I see *two* dragons standing in this room. That's more than enough fire to melt through a fucking clan."

Her words stop me. I turn to Nikolaas, and to my surprise, he's looking at me the same way.

Not as an enemy. Not as a rival. But as a weapon he needs.

"She's right," I say, voice steady. "I'm going in."

Nikolaas's lips curl into a humorless smirk. "On your own? Not a chance."

I study him for a moment. That jaw of his is set like stone.

And for the first time… I don't hate him for it.

We won't be friends. We won't trust each other. But for Clarissa? We'll raze hell.

Without another word, we move.

Two dragons. One bond. One enemy.

And the world has no idea what's about to be unleashed.

44

KAISNER

"*Hold on, Clarissa,*" I think, clenching my fists in my lap as the dark blur of trees rushes past the windows. "*Just hold on a little longer. I'm coming for you.*"

I don't know if she can hear me. Not in this form. But the bond still hums—faint, erratic, like a heartbeat beneath ice. And I pour everything I have into it. Rage. Love. My promise. She will feel it. She *has* to.

The silence inside Nikolaas' SUV is unbearable. The leather seats groan beneath us, the tires humming over black asphalt as we speed through the countryside outside Paris. The scenery is a blur of moonlit forest and distant fog—but all I see is red. All I feel is her absence.

Clarissa.

Every breath I take is laced with the ache of it. The need to get to her. To *burn through all obstacles* between us.

Nikolaas hasn't spoken since we left Draken Manor. He's gripping the wheel so tightly the leather creaks, his jaw clenched like iron. We're not allies. Not friends. But the storm in his eyes matches mine—and for now, that's enough.

I don't care that we travel in silence. I don't need his words. All I need is a target. All I need is *her.*

The compound comes into view like a wound in the forest. Hidden deep within the Forêt Domaniale de Rambouillet, the Mahindra base sprawls out beneath the trees—camouflaged with glamours and illusion, encircled in layers of magical wards and reinforced steel. From above, it's nothing more than shadows and brush. From the ground, it's a fortress.

Nikolaas kills the headlights as we roll to a stop in the shade of old pines. The air is crisp, quiet—but wrong. It smells like old metal, burned incense, dried blood. I open the door, stepping out into the night, and every muscle in my body coils with anticipation.

The dragon beneath my skin is already stirring, hungry and poised. He can *smell* her. The fear. The blood. The chains.

I draw a deep breath, steadying myself against the tremor of fury. The trees whisper around us. Magic pulses faintly through the underbrush.

Nikolaas shuts his door softly and circles around the SUV, his voice low and razor-edged. "Remember what matters. We get in, we get Clarissa, and we get out."

My gaze flicks to him. His face is hard, expression unreadable—but his eyes betray him. Gleaming gold. He's on the edge.

"Understood," I growl. "Nothing else matters."

But we both know that's a lie. Because if they've hurt her —if she bears even *one* mark from them—I won't leave anything standing.

We move through the trees like shadows, fast and silent. Every branch we pass hums with latent magic. Wards—sloppily disguised, hastily triggered. They knew someone might come. But they never prepared for us.

Not for *two dragons*.

Nikolaas raises a hand, signaling a stop. I freeze, crouched beneath a thicket of brambles, the static buzz of protective spells prickling over my skin like needles. Ahead, a tall iron gate glimmers with spellwork—veins of light pulsing up and down its frame. Behind it, the compound stretches inward like a beast's maw.

"We need to hit them fast and hard," Nikolaas mutters. "Their wards are tuned for stealth threats—not shifters. If we breach with force, it'll confuse them long enough to break through."

He turns to look at me.

"On my count, we shift. Straight through the front. Let panic be our cover."

I nod, my muscles already tensing in anticipation. As much as it galls me to follow his lead, I know this isn't the time for power struggles. We need to work together if we're going to save Clarissa.

Nik starts the count—three fingers raised.

Three…

Two…

One.

I let the change rise like a tide.

Strength surges through my limbs—searing, electric, ancient. My spine arches as bones stretch and reforge, scales racing across my skin in black ribbons of obsidian and ember. My hands become talons. Wings explode from my back, massive and midnight-hued. Fire rises in my throat, caged and ready.

Nikolaas shifts beside me, golden and radiant, his form larger than mine but barely contained, heat rolling off him in waves. His eyes glow like twin suns.

Together, we erupt through the trees, claws tearing through undergrowth and ward lines alike. Alarm spells burst in showers of sparks as we tear through the compound's perimeter. The wards scream—but we bellow louder.

The gates break in half beneath the might of our maws.

Our combined roar shakes the forest.

Mahindra guards spill from buildings, wide-eyed and shouting, casting frantic incantations that bounce harmlessly off our scales. One of them raises a gleaming hand—Nikolaas incinerates him with a single breath. Another tries to run. I snap my jaws and crush the earth at his heels, sending him sprawling.

Steel towers rise ahead. Tunnels snake beneath them.

Clarissa's scent burns in my nostrils—faint, but unbroken. *She's alive.*

I tilt my wings and launch skyward, leaving Nikolaas to wreck their perimeter. He charges toward a weapons depot with a roar, gold fire trailing from his maw. The compound erupts in chaos. Sirens wail. Stone cracks. Screams rise like a chorus… A reign of chaos.

There's no subtlety here. No mercy.

Only war.

And she's the reason. She's worth it.

I'm coming, Clarissa.

45

CLARISSA

*P*ain rips me from the darkness.

It starts as a slow pulse, a throb deep in my head, expanding outward in waves of nausea. It sinks into every bone, every muscle, and every breath, an angry heartbeat thrumming through my limbs. My skin feels too tight, my mouth dry as dust.

Where am I?

What happened?

Memory floods back in razor-sharp fragments. The ambush. Janik's blood on pavement. The chemical-sweet cloth pressed to my face. But also—the tactical gear, the coordinated movements, the tiger tattoo I glimpsed on one attacker's wrist before the world went dark.

Mahindra clan. This isn't random—it's calculated. They want something from Kaisner, and I'm the leverage.

Which means I'm valuable. Alive.

Through barely cracked eyelids, I catalogue my surroundings—three walls of stone, rough and ancient. One side barred with iron rods thick as my wrist, rusted with age.

I'm in a cell.

A literal cell. The air reeks of damp mold, burnt wood, and something sharper... the unmistakable stench of scorched magic.

No window. No light but the dim, fading glow of a rune-inscribed sconce flickering weakly outside the bars. Its enchantment pulses faintly, sputtering out like a dying breath.

My eyelids flutter closed, and I slip into oblivion again.

A deafening explosion tears through the silence, dragging me back into awareness. The sound slashes through the space like a violent storm cracking apart the sky. The ground shakes, a ruthless rumble. My eyes snap open, but I immediately regret it. Dust and smoke fill the air, choking me as I cough violently, my throat raw. The world spins, and I fight to stay conscious.

The ceiling groans above me, and my spine presses painfully against a cold, unyielding surface—stone, jagged and unforgiving. I blink rapidly, struggling to focus through the haze, fighting the dizziness.

Another tremor shakes the floor, more violent this time. The walls groan under the strain, and dust sifts down from the ceiling, coating my skin. My heart hammers as screams echo in the distance—sharp, desperate. The scent of burning metal, of smoldering steel, seeps into the chamber, filling my nostrils.

They're under attack.

Panic grips me. I try to sit up, but my limbs feel like they've been weighed down with stone. My stomach lurches, the drug still clouding my thoughts. I claw at the wall beside me, fingers slipping on the damp rock, pulling myself up inch by inch.

You have to move. Get up. You can't stay here.

With a grunt, I manage to get to my knees, gasping for breath. My body fights against me, but I push through, fighting the fog still lingering in my mind. My pulse races now, not just with fear, but with something sharper. A deeper urgency.

Survival.

I can't stay in this cell. I need to know what's happening. I need to escape.

Another tremor rocks the floor, but this one is different. It's not an explosion. It's lower, deeper, like the world itself is shifting beneath me. A vibration that rattles my chest, my bones.

And then I hear it.

A roar.

Not human. Not even close.

It shakes the air around me, primal and unrestrained, a thunderous force of fury and power. The sound rips through the stillness, filling the room with ancient terror. My heart skips a beat, my breath catching in my throat.

Because I recognize it. I know it in my soul.

"Kai?" The name slips from my lips, barely a whisper.

Could it be him?

Has he come for me?

The thought strikes me like lightning—sharp, bright, painful—and it sends a jolt of hope through my chest, fierce and terrifying.

46

KAISNER

haos erupts as Nikolaas and I tear through the defenses, magic and gunfire alike ricocheting off our scales. My eyes scan the buildings, frantic, searching for any sign of Clarissa.

Then, as though answering an unspoken prayer, I hear her voice in my mind.

"Kai? Is that you?"

Relief floods me, so overwhelming it's almost painful. *"I'm here, baby girl,"* I project, hoping she can grasp the depth of my love, my determination. *"Nikolaas is with me. We're getting you out."*

Through our bond, I sense her—her location. A windowless room at the heart of the compound. With a roar, I change direction, plowing through walls and guards in my desperation to reach her.

Nikolaas provides cover, his bursts of flame keeping the bulk of the Mahindra forces at bay. But I can't focus on anything but her.

Smoke billows in the distance—sharp, acrid, tinged with the scent of burning metal and something more sinister—

scorched magic. I can smell blood beneath it. I can hear the crackle of wards being shattered under brute force.

The Mahindra compound looms ahead like a festering wound in the middle of the forest, hidden beneath layers of illusion and glamour. But those spells are useless now.

I slice through the sky with my wings stretched wide, each beat sending shockwaves that ripple down through the trees. Below, Mahindra's guards scatter as roaches, their magic useless against the fury I bring. They weren't expecting a dragon. Certainly not two.

Nikolaas flies ahead, his golden scales gleaming. He dives with deadly precision, strafing the perimeter in calculated bursts of fire—targeting weapon caches, guard towers, anything that could slow us down. This was supposed to be a strike-and-rescue. Distraction, not destruction.

But then I see it—how his fire lingers, how he doubles back to obliterate a watchtower that was already crumbling. Power surges from him, relentless, uncontrollable, growing hotter by the minute.

Nik's not just destroying. He's incinerating.

He's off plan.

I snarl low in my throat.

He lands with a roar and launches himself through the eastern wall of the compound, tearing through an entire barracks with the force of his impact. Stone, steel, bodies— all of it erupts into a blaze of fire. His dragon is free. Unbound.

So, this is it. The Draken Curse. The whispered flaw that could lead to his fall.

I can't worry about that now. Clarissa's heartbeat pulses through our bond—weak but steady. Still here. Still alive. And close.

I zero in, cutting through the smoke like a blade. The

compound is a maze of hidden rooms and corridors, but I've studied the plans. I know exactly where they'd keep her.

I find the building. The last one still standing.

With a snarl, I beat my wings and dive.

The roof rips apart beneath my talons. Reinforced beams snap like twigs under the force of my attack. Rubble and dust rain down into the room below—and through it all, I see her.

Clarissa.

Disheveled. Pale. Eyes wide in shock.

But alive.

Her arms lift weakly, reaching for me through the falling ash. "Kai!"

Her voice spears straight through me—raw, hoarse. My name on her lips is a prayer and a lifeline.

I land in the debris and shift instantly—my dragon form folding into my human shape in a burst of searing heat. Flesh replaces scales, but my obsidian wings remain, sheltering her from the world as I fall to my knees beside her.

She's crumpled in the corner, bruises blooming along her jaw, hair tangled. I pull her into my arms, holding her close. She's warm. Real. Breathing. The feel of her against my chest nearly brings me to tears.

"I've got you," I whisper, my voice breaking, "You're safe now. I'm taking you home."

Looking at her, limp but alive, I understand the truth that remade me: *I was born in darkness, raised in shadow, forged in fire—but she, she taught me how to fly.*

I kiss her forehead, her hair, her temple—over and over, desperately soaking in the essence of her. The bond thrums between us, faint but unbroken.

Outside, the compound quakes again—an explosion echoes nearby. Nikolaas roars in the distance, shaking the earth. I sense the heat of his rampage climbing like a fever. We're not out of danger yet.

We need to move.

I cradle her face, gently, forcing her to meet my eyes. "Clarissa, do you trust me?"

She nods without hesitation, her voice rough but clear. "Always."

With that, I shift again, careful to keep her close, holding her against me as I take flight.

We burst from the building, Clarissa secure in my grasp. She curls against me instinctively, her heartbeat steady against my chest. Nikolaas soars ahead, a golden inferno against the dark sky that turns the treeline into molten ruin. His wings slice through the smoke, fire spilling from his jaws in blinding arcs. He's not targeting strategic positions anymore. He's cleansing the entire forest of Mahindra taint.

Below, the compound is nothing but a charred ruin.

I grit my teeth, flaring my wings as we rise higher. *"Enough,"* I snap, projecting my thoughts to Nikolaas. *"They're gone. Pull back."*

But he doesn't answer. Or won't. His dragon is in full berserker mode now, leaving a path of devastation in its wake —charred earth, shattered towers, smoke coiling skyward in mourning spirals. The gold in his scales still glows with anger.

I let out a sharp cry—a burst of draconic sound only he can hear. Nikolaas finally notices. He jerks in mid-air, wheeling to my side, eyes burning with residual fury.

"Enough," I growl again, my voice a thunderclap in the wind as I lock eyes with Nikolaas across the rising thermal. *"She's safe. It's done."*

For a breathless instant, his wings falter mid-beat. Then, slowly, reluctantly, he begins to ascend beside me—his fire dimming, though not extinguished. He's not ready to stand down. Not fully.

And neither am I when I see him.

Viktor Mahindra.

Amid the smoldering wreckage of his stronghold, he stands—blood streaking his temple, flanked by two wounded men. They're cloaked in enchantments, flickering like torn veils in the smoke. His stance is defiant.

He's daring us to finish what we started.

My dragon stirs inside me, wings snapping wider. Fire builds in my chest, a vow. *One blast,* it whispers. *One well-placed strike and we could end him. End this. Burn the rot from its root.*

But then I feel her.

Clarissa stirs faintly in my hold, her fingers curling against my scales like a whisper. Her heartbeat flutters—unsteady but strong.

I look back at Viktor, his defiant silhouette standing among ash and ruin, taunting me.

Not today, I tell the beast inside. *He's not worth risking her.*

With a growl, I wrench my gaze from him, fire still thrumming in my chest. *Later,* I promise. *Later, when she's safe and whole, I will come back. I will finish this.*

Nikolaas catches the direction of my stare. His fury flares anew, and for a moment, I think he'll turn and descend—to deliver the killing blow I'm resisting. But I snap my wings wide in warning and bare my fangs. *"No."*

His jaw flexes, but he doesn't argue. He knows the risk. She comes first.

Together, we rise.

The canopy shrinks beneath us, nothing but fractured treetops and smoking ruin. The compound is gone—just a scar on the forest floor. The wind bites cold at this altitude, but I feel only the warmth of her pressed to my chest.

Clarissa stirs again, her cheek brushing the curve of my scales. Her voice doesn't form words, but I hear her spirit reaching out to me through the bond, even if dim. Even broken, she's *with* me.

And that's what matters.

What remains now is awe—sharp-edged and humbling. We came for rescue.

Nikolaas brought retribution. But I… I chose restraint. I chose her.

We burst above the clouds, veiled by mist and sky and enchantment. I cloak us with old magic—stealth and silence woven into the air. Below us, the world still burns, but we rise untouched.

Clarissa is safe.

She's in my arms, where she belongs.

And though Viktor Mahindra may walk away today, he will not forget the day two dragons blackened his sanctuary and stole back what was never his to take.

I swear it—on fang, on flame, on the bond I share with her—I will never let her go again.

Not while I breathe.

Not while I burn.

47

CLARISSA

*R*eality has sharp edges that cut when you've been living in a dream of scales and flame. The world feels distant, as if I'm drifting between realms. The last thing I remember is chaos—the searing heat, the deafening roars, the sensation of being lifted into the sky. Now, I return slowly to myself, bringing with it the dull ache of my body and the weight of memories pressing down.

I'm aware of softness beneath me, the familiar scent of cedarwood, and something uniquely him. The realization hits me like a wave—I'm home. Drachenstein Manor. Safe.

A gentle pressure encircles my hand, grounding me. The fog in my mind begins to clear, like mist burning off in the morning sun. I summon what little strength I have and blink, eyes fluttering open against the muted glow of lamplight.

At first, everything is a blur—the flickering shadows dancing across high ceilings, the familiar drape of curtains pulled low. And then, him.

Kaisner.

He sits beside the bed, head bowed, one hand wrapped

373

around mine as if it's the only thing keeping him tethered. His other hand rests on his knee, tapping rhythmically, a barely-contained storm beneath his stillness.

Something about him looks different.

His black dress shirt is neatly pressed, collar open to reveal the line of his throat. The sleeves are fitted, cuffed neatly at his wrists, revealing the powerful lines of his fore-arms, a hint of the tattoos that cover his arms.

His charcoal trousers are tailored to perfection, the fabric smooth and untouched by the chaos of battle—as if he changed just to sit by my side, as if this moment mattered more than anything that came before.

His hair is combed back, every strand controlled. His jaw is dusted with a deliberate, neatly trimmed stubble that only sharpens the contrast of his features. A shallow cut curls along his cheekbone, half-healed, but even that doesn't take away from his beauty.

The gold in his eyes catches the lamplight when he lifts his gaze, and the sheer reverence in his demeanor almost knocks the breath from me. He looks at me then—really *looks*—and his expression shifts. His shoulders drop. His hand tightens around mine. And for a heartbeat, he seems as though he might shatter. Not from fear, but from the relief of seeing me awake.

"Clarissa," he breathes, his voice thick, wrecked. My name on his lips is a prayer, one he's whispered a thousand times.

Then, I see it. This isn't the man who carried me out of fire and ruin. This is the man who would've *burned the world* if he hadn't found me alive. And right now, he's trying to believe I'm real.

"Hey," I whisper, voice ragged.

He leans over me instantly, brushing a stray lock of hair

from my face. The intensity in his stare is overwhelming, a storm barely held in check.

"You're awake," he breathes, as if it's a miracle.

I attempt a weak smile. "Thanks to you." I shift under the sheets, muscles protesting. "What happened? After we flew away?"

Kaisner's jaw tightens, his gaze darkening. "We brought you home. The compound… It's gone. Mostly destroyed in the fire."

His words drop heavy in my chest. A small, pained gasp leaves my lips. "Nik?"

"Alive. Pissed. Bloodied." Kaisner leans back just enough to read my reaction. "He tore through the building like a wildfire. The plan was distraction. He chose annihilation."

"I felt it," I murmur, my voice trembling. "The ground shook like the world was ending."

"It nearly was," Kaisner replies, his jaw tight. "That wasn't a battle tactic—it was a dragon untethered. Your brother didn't just attack the compound—he *obliterated* it. Every building, every escape route, every living thing within a mile radius."

The words hit me like ice water. Suddenly, fragments click into place with sickening clarity—Samara's careful positioning between Nik and others at gatherings, the way she'd touch his arm when his eyes began to glow, those faint bruises I'd glimpsed on her wrists that she'd explained away as mere accidents.

"The Draken Curse," I breathe, the pieces finally forming a picture I've been too blind to see. "It's not just a legend."

Kaisner's expression darkens. "It's real. And it's getting worse. The more powerful the dragon, the stronger its hold." His fingers tighten around mine. "Samara's been fighting to keep him anchored, but she can't do it forever."

My stomach drops as I remember Nik's sudden rages, the

way he'd disappear for hours after arguments. And Samara—brave, fierce Samara—standing guard over a secret that could destroy everything she loves.

"She's been protecting us all," I whisper, horror and admiration warring in my chest. "Protecting *him* from what he might become."

"The Last *Draken* Shifter," Kaisner says grimly. "Heir to all that power, and all that madness. What we witnessed today... that was just a taste of what's brewing inside him."

I close my eyes, finally understanding the true weight of the crown my brother wears—and the woman who refuses to let him bear it alone.

A tense silence fills the room, and I ask the question that's been clawing at my chest.

"And us?" My voice is fragile, raw. "Did you tell him...?"

He doesn't flinch. "He knows."

"And?"

"He's furious." Kaisner's thumb brushes over mine. "But also shaken. What we did to save you cracked something open. He may not like me, but... he's listening now."

I study his face, tracing the tension in his jaw, the weariness in his eyes. "Maybe it's not about him liking you," I murmur. "Maybe it's enough that he sees what you are to me."

A shadow crosses his features, and he shakes his head. "I almost lost you." His voice cracks, the anguish unmistakable. "I should have been there sooner."

I squeeze his hand, summoning every ounce of strength I have. "But you were there. You saved me."

He leans down, pressing a tender kiss to my forehead, lingering as if to reassure himself that I'm real. The warmth of his lips sends a shiver down my spine.

We sit in silence for a moment, countless unspoken

words hanging between us. His eyes betray the turmoil raging within him, and I reach up, cupping his cheek with a trembling hand.

"Kai," I murmur, drawing his gaze back to mine. "I'm here. We're together. That's all that matters."

He closes his eyes, leaning into my touch, his breath warm against my palm. "I can't imagine a world without you," he whispers. "The thought of losing you... terrifies me."

My vision blurs with forthcoming tears. "You won't lose me," I vow. "I'm yours, Kai. Always."

He looks at me with a flash of determination, then shifts abruptly, like he's wrestling with an intention. Concern tightens my brow.

"There's something I need to do," he says, his voice steady but intense. He meets my gaze with a quiet resolve. "Can you stand?" His tone is unsure, but before I can respond, he mutters, "Hell—you don't have to."

Then he rises.

In one smooth motion, Kaisner drops to one knee next to the bed.

The sight of him—this powerful, scarred man, who tore the sky open to bring me home—kneeling beside me steals my breath away.

He slips off one of his rings—a heavy band of blackened gold etched with dragon wings and flames. He doesn't speak grand words; his eyes tell me everything. Raw. Wild. Deep.

And then he speaks, not as a question, but as a vow.

"I should've waited. For moonlight. For peace. For a moment not soaked in blood and smoke," his voice breaks as he continues, "But I can't wait another second, Clarissa. Not after what we've been through. Not after almost losing you."

My heart stutters. My fingers tremble.

He lifts the ring slightly, like it's not just metal—but a

sacred promise. "This isn't the one you'll keep. You'll choose yours. But I need you to know what I want. What I've always wanted."

His voice softens, trembling with fire and urgency. "You." He leans forward, gaze searing. "Marry me."

My breath catches in my throat.

"I want to wake up with you every morning. Fight for you. Burn for you. Live and die for you. Be yours in name, in blood, in bond."

His hand remains steady, though the significance of the moment seems almost too much to bear.

"I cannot offer you peace," he says softly. "I'm offering you a kingdom made of fire and devotion. I'm offering you... *me*."

Tears prick my eyes. My chest tightens with emotion I can barely contain. Slowly, painfully, I sit up and reach for him, my fingers weaving into his hair as I draw him near, until our brows touch.

Kneeling before me is not just the man I love—it's the echo of every cautionary tale, every whispered warning. The dangerous Willem rises in my memory, Juliette's voice haunting: *"A Dragon King... a man whose touch brought only ash and ruin."*

I know what he might become. I've seen his salvation and damnation written in starfire and shadow.

And I choose him anyway.

"Kaisner Drachenstein," I sigh, my voice shaking. "There's no other future I want. Yes. Yes, I'll marry you."

His eyes close, jaw tightening as my words cut through him. He slips the ring onto my finger—his ring—and pulls me gently into his arms.

He kisses me then. And gods, it hurts—in the best way. It's not soft. It's not gentle. It's teeth and tongue and grief and gratitude all twisted together. I clutch at his shoulders, fingers trembling as I pull him closer.

Bound by fire, united in love, we have chosen our destiny.

48

CLARISSA

*D*everaux Manor's grand hall stretches before me, opulent and timeless, embodying centuries of influence and unspoken power. Gilded mirrors glint in the golden spill of chandelier light. The marble underfoot is immaculate, too pristine for the kind of conversations that might unfold tonight. The air smells of old books, polished cedarwood, and faint perfume—expensive, elusive, and hauntingly familiar.

My hand rests on the cool brass of the door handle, reluctant to push forward. My heartbeat thrums like a war drum in my chest, betraying nerves I'd hoped to conceal. Though weeks have passed since the Mahindra compound, the shadows of that place still cling to the edges of my thoughts, smoke that refuses to lift.

Kaisner stands at my side, his presence a silent comfort, his warmth radiating through the thin fabric of my dress where his hand rests against my lower back. He leans in, his voice brushing the curve of my ear like velvet.

"Are you sure you're up for this, baby?"

I glance at him. He's crouched slightly to catch my gaze,

380

his hands gentle as they settle on my shoulders, steady and strong—always steady when I'm unraveling.

I force a smile. "I'm fine." I hope I sound more confident than I feel. "It's been two weeks. You need to stop coddling me, Kai."

His eyes flicker as he searches my expression for cracks. I see the storm behind his calm—the tug of instinct urging him to shield me, tempered by respect for the woman who's choosing to stand on her own.

Finally, he nods and presses a kiss to my forehead. "All right," he murmurs. "But if it gets to be too much, say the word. We walk. Screw politics and alliances."

That brings out a real smile from me. "My hero," I whisper, brushing his jaw with my thumb.

Before he can answer, the sharp click of heels draws our attention.

Cassandra glides across the marble, regal and composed. Her dark hair flows over her shoulders, stormy gaze bright with thoughtful scrutiny.

"Clarissa." She embraces me softly. "I'm so glad you're here." She turns to Kaisner with a knowing smile. "Kaisner, darling. Congratulations on your engagement."

Heat rises to my cheeks. Our mating may be no longer secret, but hearing it spoken aloud still feels… new. Real.

"Thank you," Kai replies coolly. I sense the slight tension in his spine, the way he carries himself like a blade waiting to be drawn. Tonight, words are weapons—and every gathered clan is a different kind of battlefield.

Cassandra's gaze lingers on us both, sharp with insight. "Samara will need you more than ever," she says gently, directing her remark to me. "Your presence will be a great comfort to us all."

Just as I'm about to ask what she means, the double doors at the far end of the hall sweep open.

My breath catches in my throat when I see.

Nikolaas strides in, flanked by Samara. My heart stumbles. It's the first time I've seen him since he and Kaisner pulled me from the ruins of the Mahindra stronghold. My brother's expression is unreadable—hardened by duty, shadowed by guilt. I discover love in his eyes, yes, but I also recognize fear. Not for me. For what I've become. A threat to his rule.

Behind them, Vladimir and Gavriil Alexeev make their entrance. The Ursa brothers are tall and commanding, their tailored suits doing little to conceal the quiet menace they carry.

Nikolaas locks stares with Kaisner, and the air all but crackles.

A silent storm brews between them, heavy with resentment, spite, and unspoken truths.

Kaisner's revelation as a dragon has sent shockwaves through the supernatural world. Nikolaas' carefully laid plans to proclaim himself Dragon King have crumbled in its wake. Most of Europe had quietly supported Kaisner before, offering whispered pledges behind closed doors. Now, those hushed promises have become open declarations of loyalty.

Nikolaas's discomfort is clear. I brace, half-expecting them to clash right here in the middle of the hall.

But then, Nik finally breaks eye contact and stalks toward the study. Kaisner guides me to our seats on the opposite side of the room, his hand lightly at my back. Across the space, Samara meets my gaze, offering a faint smile—a lifeline.

Gavriil settles into his chair with the quiet confidence of someone who believes they know exactly why they've been summoned.

"So, Cassandra," he says, voice smooth with presumption, "I assume we're finally setting a date for the wedding? Perhaps a summer ceremony at the Alexeev estate?" His smile holds an air of entitlement—he's accustomed to things falling into line with his plans.

Cassandra's expression shifts slightly—resignation flickers before she steeps herself in composure behind the imposing desk. She places her hands on the polished surface, steady despite the gravity of the moment.

"Actually, Gavriil," she says, her voice gentle but firm, "we have more pressing matters to discuss today."

His smile falters, confusion creasing his brow.

"Gentlemen," she continues, her tone commanding, "shall we begin?"

The room falls silent, all eyes on her.

"We face a threat greater than any blood feud or political game," she begins, and her voice carries effortlessly through the space, every word weighted with authority. "Darkness is coming."

Nikolaas leans forward, brow furrowed in deep scrutiny. "What kind of darkness?"

Cassandra's gaze turns grave. "One that tears through the veil between realms."

Ice skitters down my spine. I've seen this darkness in my visions, felt it in the pages of the Book of Vaelmir.

Kaisner shifts beside me, his hand tightening around mine—a silent reminder of his vow.

"Some of you may have doubts," Cassandra continues, her voice soft but unwavering. "I understand. But this is no longer theory or myth. The signs are clear."

"Signs?" Vladimir interrupts, his voice edged with skepticism, his fingers steepled as he watches Cassandra closely. "Forgive me, Cassandra, but talk of prophecies and veil-tearing sounds like something out of a grim fairytale. We need more than poetry."

"There is more," I interject before Cassandra can reply. "Visions. Glimpses of terror and destruction threatening us all." I pause, gathering the strength to meet their eyes. "They began weeks ago. At first, I thought it was just noise in my head. But they've grown stronger. Clearer."

A beat of silence hangs in the air.

"It's true," Nik adds, his voice steady. "She told me about them even before Paris. Before Kaisner shifted."

"Clarissa's visions are the first ripple in a much deeper current," Cassandra says, full of certainty. Her stormy eyes take in every face in the room, steady, unflinching. "The Book of Vaelmir has awakened." She looks directly at me, her gaze piercing, before carrying on. "Pages once veiled to even our strongest seers now spill ink like tears."

A long silence follows, thick with anticipation.

"And something ancient has risen in Spain," she adds, her voice low, almost a whisper.

That draws several raised brows.

"In the Pyrenees," Cassandra continues. "A temple, long believed to have collapsed during the Shadow Wars, has reemerged. León, alpha of the Regalis pride, tells me the mountains trembled beneath his territory. He believes the structure didn't just rise—it was *pulled forward*. Or backward. He sensed the twist in time itself."

Unease grips the room. The air thickens, the significance of her words pressing down on us all.

"But the most disturbing sign is this," Cassandra says, her voice barely audible now. "Juliette has experienced it firsthand. Not once, but twice." She looks at me before speaking again. "Last Yule, in Draken Manor, she stepped through a corridor and came face to face with Willem Von Draken."

I gasp involuntarily, shock and wonder clashing inside me.

Nikolaas goes rigid beside Samara, his eyes narrowing. "My… ancestor?" His voice is hoarse.

"And Juliette's late husband," Cassandra adds solemnly.

"Three centuries gone, and yet... she spoke with him. *Touched* him."

Before I can fully process this revelation, the great doors of the study creak open.

All eyes turn.

Juliette Deveraux enters, tall and poised in an emerald silk gown. Her red hair falls like a fiery cascade down her back. Her companion is striking—lean, elegant, and pale, with dark green eyes. Ivan Lockhart. His presence is commanding, though he remains silent.

Kaisner straightens beside me. Even Gavriil stops mid-sentence his murmured words to Vladimir, his attention caught by Juliette's entrance.

Juliette's gaze sweeps across the room, cold yet calculating. "I'm sorry we're late," she says, her voice carrying an almost imperceptible tension.

Cassandra steps aside. She nods, gesturing to the chair behind the imposing desk. "Juliette, please."

The Grand Witch dismisses the offer with a subtle headshake. Ivan releases her arm with a soft kiss to her knuckles, standing behind her like a sentinel.

When she turns to face the room, there's something rare in her—vulnerability.

"Last week," she begins, her tone soft but clear, "a ripple passed through the manor's east wing. A distortion—felt more than seen. The air thickened. The clocks stopped. The chandeliers flickered blue, though there was no wind."

The room falls into absolute silence.

"The disruption lasted the longest minutes of my life," she continues, her eyes distant, haunted. "But as it happened... I could swear I smelled Willem's cologne. Heard his voice."

I hold my breath, waiting for the impact of her words to settle.

Her fingers tremble ever so slightly as she raises them to her lips. "The fireplace in the Gold Room was burning," she murmurs, almost to herself. "Though no one had lit it for days."

Nikolaas's posture stiffens beside Samara. A question tugs at the back of my mind—why is Willem Draken's grimoire in my brother's possession? Is the Draken Curse connected to these disturbances in time?

Nikolaas chooses silence on the matter. I do the same. There will be a moment to confront him, but this isn't it.

"Then—I saw him," Juliette continues, her voice soft but tremulous as her gaze settles on Nikolaas. "We... *talked.*"

Her eyes hold him a moment longer than necessary, as if caught by the striking resemblance he shares with Willem. It's in the sharpness of his features, the intensity of his clear-blue gaze—something unmistakably familiar.

Nikolaas shifts, his expression unreadable, but there's a flicker of discomfort in the tension of his jaw.

"Reality is folding," she concludes, her voice barely audible. "Not just weakening at the edges—but warping. And if this continues, we won't face darkness alone. We'll face a collapse of time, memory, and meaning itself."

"How do you propose we fight this darkness?" Gavriil rumbles, his voice skeptical, filled with tension.

Cassandra's lips curve into a faint, sad smile. "By remembering what truly matters," she says. "By finding strength in the bonds of family—both old and new."

Her glance takes in the room, settling on each of us in turn. "The Drakens have long been our allies," she adds, nodding to Nikolaas and me. "And now, an opportunity rises to forge new alliances with the Ursa clan and the Drachensteins."

Kaisner stiffens beside me, his grip on my hand tightening imperceptibly. I can feel his discomfort with the thought of aligning with those he once saw as enemies.

"Pretty words," Gavriil scoffs, crossing his arms. "But words alone won't be enough to face this threat you speak of. What assurances can you provide that this isn't just another political ploy?"

Cassandra's expression softens. "You're right, Gavriil," she says. "Words alone won't be enough. That is why I have something to offer you—a token of my sincerity and commitment to this alliance."

She rises and moves to a side door. My curiosity piqued, I lean forward, straining to see what she's doing.

Cassandra pauses with her hand on the doorknob, turning back to face us all. "What I'm about to show you may come as a shock," she says, voice tinged with apprehension. "But I ask that you keep an open mind and remember why we're here—to find unity in the face of great danger."

With that, she opens the door.

For a moment, nothing happens. Then, a figure steps into the room, and the world seems to grind to a halt.

She's beautiful—petite and willowy, with long blonde hair cascading in soft waves. Her violet eyes scan the room, landing on Gavriil. In an instant, her entire demeanor shifts. Her shoulders straighten, chin lifting, a glimmer of love and trepidation flickering in her gaze.

"Gavriil?" she breathes.

The Ursa King goes rigid in his seat. His massive frame trembles as though struck by an invisible force. His eyes widen in disbelief, and tears fill them, softening his usually impenetrable gaze. The color drains from his face, leaving him ashen and shaken.

"What trickery is this?" he chokes out, his voice rough with emotion.

Cassandra steps forward, hand extended in a placating

gesture. "It is no trick, Gavriil," she says, her tone gentle. "I promise you."

The Ursa King remains frozen, eyes locked on the woman in the doorway. Slowly, as though moving through molasses, he rises from his chair. By the time he reaches the center of the room, his legs give out beneath him, and he falls to his knees, his expression a mix of devastation and wonder.

"Luciana!" Samara cries out.

"This isn't real," Gavriil whispers, broken and raw. "It can't be."

The woman moves toward him, her steps hesitant at first, but soon gaining strength. She kneels before him, a quivering hand coming up to cup his face with infinite tenderness.

"It's real, my love," she says, her voice thick with unshed tears. *"Io sono qui."* I'm here.

The room erupts in gasps and murmurs of shock, but I barely register them. My attention is fixed on Gavriil, watching his stern composure crumble in the face of this unexpected reunion.

Tears stream down Gavriil's cheeks as he cradles her face in his hands. "Oh, my darling…" he whispers. "My beautiful love." His massive frame shakes with silent sobs as he gathers Luciana into his arms, burying his face in her hair.

Beside me, Kaisner's grip tightens around my hand. I tear my gaze from the heartbreaking scene to meet his eyes. There's wonder in them, and something deeper—longing, aching, raw—that makes my heart clench in return.

In that moment, I understand. This is what we're fighting for—not just survival, but for moments like this. For love that transcends time and space, that can bring even the mightiest of alphas to their knees.

"We should... leave them," Vladimir suggests gently, rising from his seat. His fierce eyes glimmer with hushed awe.

A collective exhale moves through the room. One by one,

we rise. Samara wipes at her cheek with a quiet sniff, then links her arm through Vladimir's. "I need a drink," she murmurs.

"You're still recovering from last night," he says softly, gently pulling her hand away from the whiskey decanter Nikolaas is already reaching for.

Nikolaas pours himself two fingers of Glen Ord, drinking it down like water, his expression unreadable.

No one utters a sound.

Cassandra motions toward the adjacent parlor, and we drift that way—some of us quietly, others exchanging soft murmurs. The study doors remain open behind us, and I catch one last glance of Gavriil and Luciana—foreheads pressed together, arms wrapped around each other as though holding the very world in place.

Kaisner places a hand on the small of my back, guiding me forward. I lean into him, the warmth of his palm grounding me.

As we settle into the candlelit parlor, I realize how much I needed this moment of calm. But even here, in the quiet, with thick velvet drapes muffling the world outside, I can feel something stirring beyond the manor's walls—a sense of anticipation, a whisper of danger.

And deep in my soul, I know this is only the beginning.

49

CLARISSA

The initial shock of Luciana's appearance begins to fade, and the room slowly comes back to life. Whispers ripple through the air, hushed conversations filled with awe, confusion, and a lingering suspicion. I catch snippets here and there—questions about how this is possible, what it means for the balance of power among the clans.

I spot Sam near the fireplace, her posture stiff, arms crossed tightly as though holding herself together by sheer will. Her gaze is locked on the shadows in the room.

For a moment, she looks impossibly frail—Samara, usually all biting wit and fire. Tonight, she burns quieter. Sadder.

I approach her slowly. She doesn't look at me as I draw near, simply says, "I never found her body."

Her voice is soft, yet heavy with pain, as if the words have been trapped inside her for so long they've become inescapable truth.

"Gavriil blamed me for not trying hard enough, with my scrying." Tears shimmer in her eyes. "Hell—I blamed myself." The confession escapes her throat, strangled.

I stand beside her, watching the flames flicker in the window's dark glass. "He was grieving his lost mate," I assure her gently. "You all were."

"She was more than that," Samara murmurs. "She was his soul. I used to listen to the way he spoke about her—quietly, like a prayer he didn't want the world to hear. Luciana was everything to him, Clarissa. Before life taught him to bury his heart deep."

She sniffs, blinking fast. "I just wonder if it's too late... if my brother can come back to life, just as she did."

I glance at her, but she's staring at the door, her throat working.

"I'm happy she's alive," she adds, her voice trembling. "I'm so happy. But it breaks me, too, in ways I didn't expect."

"Because of Cassandra?" I whisper.

Sam's gaze cuts to mine, sharp and lethal. In that instant, I catch a glimpse of the predator beneath her polished exterior—the Ursa princess who could tear out a throat without remorse.

"Careful," she warns, voice dropping to a dangerous edge. "Whatever you're thinking, whatever you're about to say—be very careful, Clarissa."

I meet her stare, unwilling to back down. "I'm simply acknowledging what we're both thinking. Gavriil's true mate has returned, but he's publicly bound to another. A witch carrying a vampire's child."

Sam glances toward the doorway, then grabs my arm with unexpected force, guiding me deeper into the shadows. Her touch—both controlled and strong—sends a chill down my spine.

"Listen to me," she says, each word precise and measured. "That child is under the protection of the Alexeev clan. *All of us.*"

The emphasis in her tone carries weight. I search her face, finding no hesitation, only fierce conviction.

"I know what you're doing," she continues. "What you've always done, Clarissa. Looking for cracks in the foundation, places where loyalties might split." Her eyes narrow. "There are none to be found here."

For a second, I flinch in disbelief. "It's not like that at all… Surely, you realize every supernatural faction will be watching," I point out. "Waiting to see how your brother handles this… complication."

Sam's smirk is sharp as broken glass. "Let them watch. The fools who mistake this for weakness don't understand what's truly at stake." She releases my arm, her expression softening fractionally. "What happened at your brother's dinner was just the beginning. The child Cassandra carries will change everything—the old rules, the boundaries between our kinds."

"And Luciana?" I ask, keeping my voice neutral. "Where does *she* fit in this new world order?"

A flicker of something crosses Sam's face—grief, uncertainty, determination—before settling into fierce resolve.

"Luciana is family," she says simply. "As is Cassandra. As is the child. My brother…" She pauses, glancing toward Gavriil, his posture rigid as he watches Luciana speak with Vladimir. "My brother will find a way forward that honors all he has promised. The Ursa King does not break his word."

I follow her gaze, studying the tableau before us: Luciana, returned from death's embrace; Cassandra, power and secrets growing within her; Gavriil, caught between past love and present duty.

"And if he can't?" I ask quietly.

Sam turns back to me, and there's something ancient in her stare—a knowledge that makes her seem suddenly older than her years.

"Then we will all bear the cost," she whispers. "But the child remains protected. That is non-negotiable." She straightens, the momentary vulnerability vanishing beneath her usual poise. "Now, if you'll excuse me, I believe my mate is looking for me."

As she turns to leave, I catch her wrist. It's a bold move—perhaps foolish, given her lineage. But I do it anyway.

"Sam," I say softly, ensuring no one else can hear. "Are you all right?"

Her composure falters, just for a heartbeat. Something raw flashes across her face before she rebuilds her walls.

"Of course," she replies, but her pulse jumps beneath my fingers—a tell no witch would miss.

"Nikolaas seems..." I search for the right word, "*intense* tonight."

Her eyes dart to where her dragon mate stands, his knuckles white around his glass, ocean eyes tracking her every movement with predatory focus. Even from here, I sense the barely contained storm within him, threatening to spill beyond his control.

"He's under considerable strain," she says carefully. "Learning your sister is mated to Kaisner Drachenstein would unsettle anyone."

The name hangs in the air like a blade. Kaisner—the man who shattered centuries of dragon hierarchy with a single transformation.

"This isn't just about Kaisner," I risk saying. "This is about Nikolaas. About what's happening to him."

Sam's expression freezes, fear and protectiveness warring across her features. "*Nothing* is happening to him," she states, but the tremor in her voice betrays her.

"Sam," I whisper, letting genuine concern color my words. "Whatever it is—whatever's wrong—you don't have to face it alone."

For a moment, I think she might confide in me. Her shoulders drop slightly, the burden of secrets clearly taking their toll. But then, Nikolaas appears beside us, materializing with dragon swiftness that makes us both start.

"There you are," he says to Samara, his tone deceptively light, but his eyes burning with something primal and possessive. His hand settles on her waist, fingers splayed wide —not just a lover's touch, but a claim.

"Nikolaas," I greet him, keeping my voice neutral despite the tension crackling in the air. "We were just discussing the unexpected nature of tonight's reunion."

"Were you?" His gaze shifts between us, suspicion darkening his features. The temperature around us drops several degrees as his control slips. Frost patterns form at his feet, spreading outward in jagged lines.

"I was checking on Clarissa," Samara says quickly, offering me a look that's both apology and warning. "The evening has been overwhelming for everyone."

"Of course," Nikolaas agrees, but his arm remains firmly around her waist. "Though I'm certain Clarissa is perfectly capable of managing her... complicated loyalties."

The barb hits its mark. My connection to Kaisner— unwanted though it may have been—has transformed me from trusted ally to potential threat in his eyes.

"We all have *complicated loyalties* these days," I reply evenly. "The wise among us know better than to judge what we don't fully understand."

His eyes narrow, dragon fire flickering in their depths. For a terrible moment, I fear his control might snap entirely.

Sam places her hand on his chest, drawing his attention. "Nik," she murmurs, her voice carrying that particular inflection I recognize from my own experiences with Kaisner—the tone that soothes the dragon, that reminds the beast of its humanity.

Something shifts in Nikolaas' expression—a momentary softening, a flicker of shame—before he nods tersely. "We should rejoin the others," he says, already guiding Samara away.

She glances back at me over her shoulder, and in that unguarded moment, I see everything she hasn't said: fear, love, determination, and something that might be a plea for understanding.

I watch them move through the crowd, noting how she subtly positions herself between Nikolaas and other guests, how she whispers to him when his eyes begin to glow too brightly, how her hand never leaves his as if she's physically anchoring him to this world.

The Draken Curse. I've known its effects now in two dragons—Willem's madness in family lore, and now, my brother. But Nik's manifestation seems somehow worse, as if the power of the Last Draken Shifter amplifies the curse's grip.

My gaze drifts to Samara, trapped in an impossible situation, protecting everyone from the truth of what her mate is becoming. Then, my attention shifts to Gavriil and Luciana. They've risen to their feet, but remain locked in each other's embrace, as if afraid the other might disappear if they let go. Luciana is engulfed by Gavriil's massive frame —a man suspended between past and present, love and duty.

I look at Cassandra, taking on the monumental effort of concealing the chaos reigning inside her.

So many secrets in this room. So many fault lines waiting to fracture.

The sound of a throat clearing interrupts my thoughts. I turn to see Nikolaas, his expression a complicated mix of emotions. "As touching as this reunion is," he says, voice carefully controlled, "I think we all deserve some answers.

Cassandra, how is this possible? Gavriil's mate was dead. And suddenly, she's back? Why now?"

All eyes turn to Cassandra, who stands at the room's entrance, her posture regal and composed. She meets each of our gazes in turn, her eyes filled with wisdom.

"The *how* is... complicated," she begins. "Suffice it to say that Luciana's return to us is the result of forces beyond our full understanding. As for the *why*..." She pauses, her gaze softening as it lands on Gavriil and Luciana. "Because we need hope. We need reminders of what we're fighting for. In the face of the darkness that's coming, we need every bit of light we can find."

I shudder at her words, leaning closer to Kaisner, seeking his warmth and strength. He wraps an arm around my shoulders, pulling me to his side. Through our bond, I sense his own clash of emotions—wonder at the miracle we've witnessed, wariness at what it might mean for the future, and a fierce determination to protect what's his.

"You speak in riddles, Cassandra," Vladimir snaps, his voice sharp with suspicion. "We need facts, not vague warnings."

Cassandra nods. "You're right, of course. You all deserve to know what we're facing." She takes a deep breath, her eyes closing briefly as if steeling herself for what's to come. When she opens them again, they're filled with a gravity that sends chills down my spine.

"There is an ancient prophecy," she begins. "One that speaks of a time when the veil between worlds will thin, when shadows will seek to devour the light. It speaks of a great battle, one that will determine the fate of not just our kind, but of all reality."

The room falls silent, hanging on her every word.

"For centuries, this prophecy was thought to be nothing more than a myth, a cautionary tale told to frighten young witches and warlocks," Juliette adds. "But recent events have made it clear that the time spoken of in the prophecy is upon us. The signs are all around us, for those who know how to look."

She pauses, her gaze sweeping across the room once more. "The sudden resurgence of long-dormant powers. The blurring of lines between different supernatural races. The return of those thought lost to us." Her eyes linger on Luciana for a moment before moving on. "These are not isolated incidents. They are the first tremors of a coming earthquake that will shake the very foundations of our world."

As Juliette speaks, a strange pressure coils at the base of my skull—faint initially, resembling the beginnings of a headache. Then it deepens. Sharpens. A buzzing energy pulses through me, syncing with every syllable she utters. My breath hitches.

The room tilts.

I sway on my feet, a hand reaching blindly for the edge of the table—but I miss. The chandeliers above blur, warping into threads of gold. Shadow and light streak across my vision like a shuttered film reel tearing loose.

Kaisner is there instantly.

"Clarissa—" His arms wrap around me with swift precision, his voice rough with panic. "*Liebes*, what's happening?"

"I... I don't—" I gasp, blinking hard, but it's no use. The visions surge like a tidal wave.

Shadows devour my surroundings. Not the kind born of night, but something older, hungry—coiling like haze around skeletal frames, fangs bared, wings unfurling.

"*It begins with fire,*" the words echo in my skull, slipping from my lips before I even realize I've spoken them.

The vision seizes me without warning—cities I recognize flashing before my eyes. Paris. Venice. London. Dreary columns of dark smoke rise toward indifferent skies, each plume a marker where something—someone—has been erased from existence.

Screams. Fire. A sky cracked open.

And then light. Brilliant. Blinding.

Swords of starlight clash against beasts carved from void. At the center of it all—Kaisner and me. Our forms tangled in radiant flame, standing back to back, holding the line as the world crumbles around us...

A strangled cry escapes me.

"Clarissa—sit," Kaisner commands, already guiding me to the velvet couch near the window. I collapse into it, my body trembling, eyes wide but unfocused.

He kneels in front of me, both hands cupping my face now. Through our bond, I feel it—his terror, his rage at whatever is hurting me, his need to *fix it*.

"Tell me what you see," he pleads.

I struggle to speak through the shuddering breath caught in my throat. "I... I see it all. The darkness. The flames. Us. Kaisner, we're—" My voice breaks. "We're at the heart of it."

His eyes flash, but he says nothing. Only draws me closer, wrapping himself around me like a living shield.

"I don't know how I'm seeing this," I whisper, gripping the lapel of his coat. "But it's real. It's not a dream or a warning—it's a truth waiting to happen."

And in the deep well of his dark stare, I see it mirrored back.

He believes me

Juliette moves toward me, her eyes wide, concern etched in her brow even as excitement brightens her gaze. "Clarissa, breathe," she says gently, kneeling beside my chair. "Let the visions pass through you. Do not fight them."

"Juliette, what does this mean?" he demands, his voice tight with barely contained apprehension. "Is she in danger?"

She shakes her head, her expression thoughtful. "No. At least, not immediate danger. The prophecy is resonating with her gift, showing her glimpses of what's to come."

Her words send a ripple of murmurs through the room. I feel everyone's gaze on me, their expressions oscillating between awe and wariness.

Nikolaas rushes to my side and leans closer, his brow furrowed with concern. "Rissy?" he speaks softly, as if otherwise I might break. "Rissy, are you all right? Do you need anything?"

His tenderness, so at odds with the tension that exists between us, brings a sudden sting to my eyes. I manage a small smile, shaking my head. "I'm okay," I assure him, holding his hand. "I'm just... overwhelmed."

As the visions begin to fade, leaving behind a dull ache in my temples, I become aware of a change in the room's atmosphere. The initial shock and skepticism that greeted Cassandra's warnings have given way to a grim sort of acceptance. The reality of the threat we face is sinking in, made all the more real by my unexpected vision.

Gavriil now stands by the room's entrance, an arm wrapped around Luciana's narrow frame. When he speaks, his voice is rough with emotion, but there's a steel in it that wasn't there before. "So what do we do?" he asks, his massive hand gliding down Luciana's arm until their hands entwine. "How do we fight this darkness?"

Cassandra turns to face him, a small smile playing at the corners of her lips. "We do what we should have done long ago," she says. "We put aside our differences, our old grudges and power struggles. We stand united, as one force against the coming storm."

Her words hang in the air, heavy with implication. I look around the parlor, taking in the faces of those gathered here. Nikolaas, torn between worry for me and the burden of his rivalry with Kaisner. Samara, her expression laden with concern and unwavering loyalty. Vladimir and Gavriil, the Ursa brothers, their usual stoicism softened by the miracle of Luciana's return.

And Kaisner. My mate, my partner, my anchor in the storm. His steady gaze meets mine, and in it, I find a reflection of my own emotions—fear, yes, but also hope. A fierce resolve to face any challenge.

"She's right," I say, stronger now as the last echoes of the vision fade away. "We can't afford to be divided anymore. Not with what's coming."

Kaisner nods, his hand squeezing mine gently. "I agree," he says, his voice carrying easily through the room. "Whatever differences we may have had in the past, they pale in comparison to the threat we now face."

"Easier said than done." Nikolaas stiffens at Kaisner's words, a flicker of the old resentment passing across his face. But then he looks at me, *really* looks at me, and his expression shifts. He nods, almost imperceptibly, before turning to address the room.

"But… as much as it pains me to admit it," he begins, a wry smile tugging at the corners of his mouth, "Kaisner is right. We've spent too long fighting amongst ourselves, jockeying for power and influence. If we're going to survive what's coming, we need to stand united."

Relief washes over me at my brother's words. I hadn't realized how much I needed to hear him say that, to see him take this first step toward reconciliation.

A quiet resolve roots in my bones. The darkness may be rising, but so are we—and we won't go quietly into the night, not while there's light left to defend.

50

CLARISSA

I should have left a while ago with the others, but Juliette wouldn't hear of it. "Absolutely not," she'd declared after my visions had left me trembling and hollow-eyed. "You're staying until you're properly recovered." Cassandra had nodded her agreement, that quiet authority of hers brooking no argument.

So here I remain, curled in the velvet armchair while the dying fire paints amber shadows across the walls. Kaisner hovers at my side, one hand resting on the chair's arm, the other tracking every movement I make with predatory focus.

The porcelain teacup in my hands steams faintly—Juliette's special blend, she'd called it. Chamomile and valerian, yes, but threaded with something older, more potent. Magic that tastes like moonlight and peace.

"Drink," Kaisner murmurs, his fingers brushing mine as he steadies the cup when my hands still. "All of it, *Liebes*."

His thumb traces the back of my hand, a gentle command wrapped in silk. I take another sip, letting the warmth spread through my chest. Already, the edges of my sight feel softer, the electric buzz that usually precedes my visions mercifully absent.

"Better?" He crouches beside my chair, bringing himself to my eye level, studying my face with fierce intensity. His free hand comes up to cup my cheek, thumb stroking across my skin. "The tremors are stopping."

I hadn't even realized I was still shaking until his touch soothed me. "The tea is helping," I admit, leaning into his palm. "I feel... quiet."

Relief and satisfaction flicker in his gaze. "Good. No more visions tonight. No more pain." His voice carries the weight of a vow, as if he could command the universe itself to obey.

Through the crack in the study doors, I glimpse them—Gavriil and Luciana, lost in their impossible reunion. His massive frame trembles as he cups her face, thumbs catching tears that slip down her cheeks like liquid starlight. I watch as Gavriil falters forward, the once-imposing Ursa King now undone.

They kiss like a myth being written—tears falling, their brows pressed together in reverent reunion. Like lovers who've defied death, each breath a borrowed miracle.

My throat tightens. Kaisner's hand finds my back, his thumb brushing a steady line between my shoulder blades.

"Love like that never fades," I whisper, my voice catching.

"It doesn't," he agrees softly, taking my hand and pressing it against his lips. "And neither will ours."

The silence stretches taut as a bowstring when footsteps ring against marble—measured, deliberate, each one echoing like a death knell through the corridors.

Cassandra appears in the doorway like an apparition conjured from moonlight and sorrow. Her gown catches the dying firelight, silver-rose fabric that should shimmer but seems to absorb the glow instead, as if even light dare not touch her tonight. She moves with the careful precision of someone walking across breaking ice.

Her face is porcelain perfection—every line controlled, every breath measured. But her eyes... her eyes hold the hollow exhaustion of someone who has just bargained with death itself and won. The kind of fragility one wears only after performing a great act of sacrifice.

She doesn't enter. Doesn't speak. Simply stands sentinel in the threshold, watching the reunion she orchestrated with the quiet intensity of a goddess surveying her handiwork.

Gavriil lifts his head from Luciana's golden hair. When his gaze finds Cassandra's, the world stills—magic hanging in the air like motes of dust caught in the hazy beams of dawn, each particle shimmering with unspoken truths that linger between them, waiting to settle into reality.

Understanding sails through the silence, delicate as the first light filtering through ancient windows, and as profound as destinies being rewritten in real time.

He knows. The cost. The price. What she sacrificed to tear his love from death's embrace.

Cassandra's hands clasp before her, knuckles white against rose silk. She turns, ready to leave the room—

"Cassandra."

Her name falls from his lips like a prayer, like a plea, like an absolution.

She freezes mid-step, spine rigid as iron.

The silence that follows could shatter glass.

Slowly—so slowly the movement feels carved from eternity—she pivots. Her chin lifts, meeting his gaze with the unflinching courage of someone prepared to face judgment.

"My loyalty," Gavriil says, his voice breaking on the words, "my friendship, my debt—they are forever yours."

The words don't just land—they detonate. The very air seems to crack with the force of an oath sworn in blood and starlight. Luciana's breath catches, her fingers tightening in Gavriil's as she adds her own silent pledge with a bow of her golden head.

Cassandra's composure fractures for a single heartbeat. Her lashes flutter like butterfly wings against her cheeks, and when she nods, the gesture carries the might of destinies shifting.

Gavriil's arm tightens protectively around Luciana's waist, drawing her close. "However you managed this..." His voice drops to a rumble. "There *will* be consequences." He pauses, letting the truth settle between them like ash. "But whatever they may be—you won't face them alone."

Something swells in my chest, vast and wordless. Having witnessed so much anger between them, so many battles fought with words sharp as blades, this moment of profound gratitude feels like watching winter finally surrender to spring.

"After countless nights walking in shadow," Cassandra says, her voice heavy with shared grief. Her gaze shifts to Luciana, taking in the impossibility of her presence. "You have found your moon again." A faint smile tugs at the corner of her lips. "At last, happiness has returned to you."

"And may you find yours," he replies, voice gentled now, "with the one fate has chosen."

"Dristan." The name escapes her lips like a confession, like a promise she's afraid to speak too loudly lest the universe hear and snatch it away. "There can be no one else."

The admission costs her. I see it in the tremor that runs through her frame, the way her breath stutters.

Gavriil's expression softens with something achingly close to tenderness. "Then may the gods smile upon your union, Cassandra. And know this—" His voice grows grave with meaning. "My intentions were never meant to bind you. Only to protect what I couldn't bear to lose."

A silent exchange flickers between them—forgiveness offered and accepted in the space of a heartbeat.

Then Gavriil lifts his hand.

The air itself holds its breath.

Ancient magic unfurls from his palm like smoke, like starlight, like the very essence of creation itself. It spirals through the space between them, visible as silver threads that sing with power older than memory.

Along Cassandra's throat, just above her collarbone, a sigil blazes to life—a brand forged in desperation and grief. The magical bond burns against her skin for one eternal moment, marking her as his in ways that transcend flesh and blood.

And then—with a sound like the universe exhaling—it vanishes, dissolving like mist come dawn.

The light dies. The magic fades.

Cassandra's gasp is sharp enough to cut—surprise, relief, and something that might be grief all tangled together. Her hand flies to her throat, fingers pressing against skin that bears no mark, no scar, no evidence of the chains that bound her for so long.

She's free.

The word *sings* through the air, a note of pure liberation that makes the crystal chandeliers chime in harmony.

Free to choose. Free to love. Free to walk into whatever future she dares to claim.

When she turns from the doorway, her face is a mask of composure rebuilt from shattered pieces. But I catch it—the tremor in her fingers as she smooths nonexistent wrinkles from her gown, the way her breath comes just a little too quick, the hope that blazes in her eyes like a beacon in the dark.

The doors close behind her with a whisper—an ending, a beginning, all held in that single breath of sound.

Tears slip down my cheeks before I realize I'm crying. Silent, unstoppable, they fall for Gavriil's joy, for Cassandra's sacrifice, for the impossible beauty of love conquering death itself. I press my fingers to my lips, trying to contain the sob that wants to escape, but it's useless.

Beside me, Kaisner's arm tightens around my waist, his thumb brushing away the tears that continue to fall. "This might be the first time I've ever seen her shaken," he murmurs against my temple, his voice a low rumble meant to soothe. "Whatever it took to bring Luciana back... it surely was no small thing."

"She never does anything small." I sniff, the edge of a smile lifting one side of my mouth.

Kaisner leans in, his breath warm against the shell of my ear. "Neither do you."

The corners of my lips curve, but the smile doesn't quite reach my eyes. Not tonight. Not after everything we've seen.

"Whatever is coming..." he begins, and his voice a vow. "I'll annihilate it before it reaches you." His hand finds mine, fingers interlacing with desperate precision. *"I don't care if it's fate, fire, or the fucking gods themselves—nothing touches you, Clarissa. Not unless it goes through me first."*

Kaisner's thumb traces my pulse point, feeling the steady, calm rhythm—so different from the frantic flutter it's been for weeks.

"The visions will come back," I whisper.

"But not tonight." He rises smoothly, lifting me from the chair and settling into it himself, arranging me across his lap like I'm something precious that might break. "Tonight, you rest. Tonight, you're safe."

His arms wrap around me, a living fortress of heat and devotion. When he kisses my temple, it feels like a benediction.

CLARISSA

The diamond fractures twilight into a thousand burning stars across my palm. Through the boutique's windows, Paris bleeds rose gold and indigo, the city's pulse slowing to that intimate rhythm that belongs only to dusk.

"It's too much," I breathe, watching light dance through the stone like captured fire. "Kai, I can't—"

"Nothing is too much for you." His voice cuts through my protest, silk over steel. He leans against the glass display case, all sharp angles and contained power, lamplight turning his hair to burnished gold. When he reaches for my hand, his thumb traces the ring's edge with reverent precision. "It's not about the stone, *Liebes*. It's about the promise."

The words settle into my bones, warm and certain. I step closer, fingertips finding the steady rhythm of his heartbeat through fine cotton. "When you put it like that..."

He lifts my hand to his mouth, lips brushing my knuckles in a kiss that tastes like forever. The world narrows to this—rose-scented air, polished wood gleaming amber, time suspended like honey in sunlight.

I glance up at him, about to tease, when something catches my eye in the mirror behind him.

A shadow. Watching.

My breath catches, spine straightening as recognition slams into me. Across the street, framed by dying light, stands a figure I'd know anywhere. Motionless as carved marble, hazel eyes fixed on us with the patience of eternity itself.

Kaisner feels the shift in my body before I speak. His head turns slowly, following my gaze to the reflection. The moment he sees, something predatory ripples beneath his skin—not fear, but recognition of a different kind.

"I didn't know he was back," I murmur, already moving toward the door.

The bells chime our exit into twilight's embrace. Paris flows around us in streams of gold and shadow, but this being stands apart from it all, untouched by the mortal world's hurried rhythm.

"Dristan," I call out gently.

His smile blooms, slow and genuine. "Clarissa," he replies, his voice like smoke and dusk. "Radiant as always."

I stop just within arm's reach, close enough to see the ancient kindness in his eyes. "You're back."

"*Called back*, more like." His gaze drops to my hand, taking in the diamond's fire. "Congratulations are in order, I see."

Heat spreads through my chest. "This is Kaisner. My—"

"*Schattenkönig.*"

Shadow King. The word falls from Dristan's lips like a stone cast into still water, sending ripples through the very air between us.

Kaisner says nothing. His silence *is* an answer.

"What does that mean?" The question slips out before I can stop it.

Dristan's attention shifts to me, weighted with memory and sorrow. "Heir of the Hollow Flame. Last blood of the Forgotten Court." His voice lowers, barely above a whisper. "I watched his lineage burn once, torn from the Unnatural Brethren. Never thought I'd see it rise from the ashes."

The twilight seems to deepen around us, shadows gathering at Kaisner's feet like loyal hounds. In this light, he looks less man than myth—something carved from darkness and dreams.

"I stood vigil the night they fell," Dristan continues, addressing Kaisner now. "Swore to keep the secret buried." A pause, heavy with implication. "But old blood calls to old blood. Your mate's fire was always going to wake what slept."

My skin prickles with goosebumps that have nothing to do with the evening chill.

Dristan's expression shifts, ancient recognition flickering in his amber eyes.

"The old blood remembers," he says, voice heavy with witnessed history. A pause, thick with unspoken implications. "Will you take on the role fate has entrusted to your hands, I wonder?"

"What are you doing here?" Kaisner's voice carries ancient authority, though his tone remains conversational.

"Watching. Waiting. Following the threads as they weave themselves back together." Dristan's smile turns sharp. "The world knows more than it pretends to forget."

He steps back, inclining his head with old-fashioned courtesy. "May fortune smile upon your union," he says, the formal blessing rolling off his tongue like ritual. Then his expression turns cryptic. "Shadows have a way of finding their way home, don't they? *Especially* royal ones."

The words hang between us like a challenge, a prophecy... a warning.

Then he's gone, melting into the crowd as if he'd never been there at all.

I turn to Kaisner, questions burning on my tongue. "Shadow King? Forgotten Court? What—"

"The past," he says simply, pulling me against his side with possessive certainty. "Nothing more."

But I catch the lie in his eyes, see the way his jaw tightens as he scans the street where Dristan disappeared.

"*Liebes.*" His voice drops to that careful tone that means he's thinking too hard about something. "Luciana's eyes— they were violet, weren't they?"

The question hits like ice water. "Yes. Why?"

"I thought Samara said they were blue."

My pulse stutters. "She did."

Something flickers across his features—too quick to name, too dark to ignore.

"Kai, what is it?"

"Probably nothing." But his fingers tighten around mine, and I know it's everything. "Come. Janik's threatening mutiny. He survived the Mahindra ambush just fine, but apparently, he *won't* survive us being late for dinner at Lake Starnberg."

My mouth quirks upward in what I hope looks like contentment, but my mind races with new questions, new fears.

"Just dinner, then?" I ask, needing the shelter of his heat, his certainty.

He pulls me to him, with an urgency that leaves no space between us, my palms pressed flat against his racing heart.

Then he growls—low, rough, entirely unholy. "Dinner… and *everything* that happens after I tear this dress off you with my bare teeth."

A shiver licks down my spine. And this time, my smile is true, slow, and indulgent.

"Sounds perfect."

And gods, it is.

Arm in arm, we move through the twilight haze. Behind us, Paris glows like a dying star—smoldering, beautiful, veiled in secrets.

The world is changing. The storm is gathering.

But I am not afraid. Not with him at my side.

My mate.

My king.

The one who shields me beneath wings of shadow.

ACKNOWLEDGMENTS

As I close the chapter on Kaisner and Clarissa's journey, my heart overflows with gratitude for the incredible people who helped bring *Wings of Shadow* to life.

To my family—my foundation and my heart. *Eric*, my husband, my fierce protector and defender, and the one who keeps me grounded when I get lost in worlds of dragons and magic. Your unwavering belief in me gives me the courage to write the next sentence, the next chapter, the next book. Our story is written in *chaos* and *calm* (my ADHD, your AS1), and I wouldn't have it any other way. *David*, my son, your creativity and spirit inspire me every day. You both are my greatest treasures, and I love you beyond words.

To my dear friend *Julie Cocaigne*—where do I even begin? Thank you for being my anchor through every meltdown, for hyping me up and reminding me that my creative chaos is actually brilliance in disguise. Our endless conversations and passionate debates about these characters' destinies have shaped every story in ways you might not even realize. You don't just critique my work—you *live* in these worlds with me, and that kind of friendship is beyond precious. Thank you for being my creative soulmate and the keeper of all my fictional secrets.

To my loyal Darklings—my readers who have followed me through blood and shadows, who champion my characters and share their love for these stories with infectious enthusiasm. You make this writing journey feel like coming home to family. Thank you for embracing the darkness and finding the light within it.

To my wonderful ARC Team and beta readers—the brave souls who venture into my rough drafts and help me polish them into something worthy of publication. Your honest feedback, your eagle eyes, and your patience with my endless revisions make every book better than I could achieve alone.

Special thanks to my dear friend *Kristin Childs,* who has been my number one fan from the very start. Kristin, your support means the world to me. Through every doubt, every celebration, every moment of creative uncertainty, you've been there cheering me on. Your friendship is a gift I treasure more than you'll ever know.

To everyone who has shared this journey with me—thank you for believing in love stories that bloom in darkness, for embracing morally gray heroes who fight for redemption, and for understanding that some flames truly are worth the burn.

With endless love and gratitude,
Silvana.

ABOUT THE AUTHOR

 Silvana G. Sánchez is the USA TODAY bestselling author of sinfully addictive dark fantasy new adult novels *Ash and Snow, Steel and Stone, Written in Blood,* and more paranormal and fantasy romance stories, including the *Vesely Academy* series. She lives in Mexico with her husband, son, and two adorable Shih-Tzus she calls her dragons. When not plotting away in her writing den, she's known to poke eyes in her practice as an ophthalmologist.

For more information:
silvanagsanchez.com
sgs.author@gmail.com

www.ingramcontent.com/pod-product-compliance
Lightning Source LLC
Chambersburg PA
CBHW050605170726
48283CB00001B/116